# STARLIGHT

# Starlight

 PATRICIA HAGAN

HarperPaperbacks
*A Division of* HarperCollins*Publishers*

This is a work of fiction. The characters, incidents, and
dialogues are products of the author's imagination and are not
to be construed as real. Any resemblance to actual events or
persons, living or dead, is entirely coincidental.

HarperPaperbacks  *A Division of* HarperCollins*Publishers*
                  10 East 53rd Street, New York, N.Y. 10022

ISBN 0-06-108058-6

Cover illustrations by Roger Castel

First printing: July 1994

Printed in the United States of America

HarperPaperbacks, HarperMonogram, and colophon are
trademarks of HarperCollins*Publishers*

# Prologue

Paris
1867

*The small bedraggled figure* attracted no particular attention from those entering the Abbaye du Vale-de-Grace for morning
mass. Just another street waif, they thought, if they paid him any
mind at all. Only a beggar, hoping those worshiping with the Benedic-
tine nuns would kindly toss a few coins his way.

They did not notice when the youngster walking with head down,
shoulders slumped, suddenly disappeared into the thick shrubs lining
the narrow pathway.

Neither did they suspect that what they thought was a beggar boy
was actually a girl.

And Samara Labonte, who had adopted the sobriquet of Sam at
the same time she had assumed the identity of a boy, quickly settled
into her hiding place.

The church was a perfect spot for snatching ladies' reticules, small
bags of silk or network. The elderly living in the Montparnasse district

liked to attend mass at the convent chapel, rather than make their way to a larger church elsewhere. All Sam had to do was lurk in the shrubbery outside to await a late arrival after services began. Then, with no one else around, she could make her move to grab the bag, then dart away to the entrance to the catacombs on the Place Denfert-Rochereau just around the corner. No one could find her then, unless they, too, knew the secrets of the twisting, winding tunnels.

Sam felt a sudden twinge of guilt.

She did not like being a thief, especially in the shadows of the church, which seemed to make it an even bigger sin.

But in the same instant, her stomach gave a painful, hungry lurch, reminding her that she had not eaten lately. So perhaps God would understand that she resorted to stealing only when she was desperate and would somehow forgive her.

Moments passed, and then she heard music coming from inside the chapel and knew mass had finally begun. Peering through the foliage, she was disappointed to see that the street beyond was now clear. Perhaps there would be no late arrivals, which meant she would have to wait till tomorrow and try again.

But what to do in the meantime? She had to have food.

She could try to steal from some of the people who also lived in the catacombs, but that was risky. They were not old women. Able to run, they might catch her, and if they did, they would discover she was not a boy, and heaven help her if that happened.

The sound of horses on the cobblestones made Sam tense with both apprehension and hope, as she watched a carriage pull to a stop.

The coachman hurried to help his passenger alight, and Sam felt momentary disappointment to realize it was not an elderly woman, but a girl who looked to be about her own age. But, seeing how elegantly she was dressed and noting the fine carriage, Sam knew she would probably steal enough that day to last quite a while.

The girl, with golden curls trailing from beneath a blue satin bonnet, hurried toward the chapel as the carriage quickly pulled away from the curb.

Sam waited for exactly the right moment, then lunged from hiding to grab the silk reticule from her unsuspecting victim and took off running. But, instead of hearing the usual outraged screams fading in the distance, she heard footsteps pounding right behind her and the shrill cries of, "Stop! Stop, I say! You can't take my money. That's for my Mimette's rosary. Give it back."

Sam could not believe what was happening. Was the girl out of her mind? Most thieves carried weapons and would not bat an eye at hurting, even killing, a victim who dared fight back. This girl obviously wasn't thinking about that, and she was also a fast runner, because Sam was barely able to keep ahead of her.

Rounding a corner, she had a fleeting glimpse of two men sitting on the curb, sharing a bottle of wine. They cheered Sam on as she passed, realizing what was taking place.

She was almost at the entrance to the catacombs when she heard the scream and, looking back, saw that the men had grabbed her pursuer and were wrestling her into a nearby alley.

Sam slowed as horrible memories came flooding back.

Another alley.

Another time.

Another girl kicking and screaming as her clothes were torn from her.

Recalling what she had witnessed from where she was hidden behind a trash barrel, Sam felt a wave of sickness. It was one of the reasons she had disguised herself as a boy all these years, so that the same fate would not befall her. And she knew beyond doubt that she could not, would not, allow it to happen. Stealing money to keep from starving was one thing, but she'd not carry the guilt for having caused someone to be savagely raped.

Sam turned and ran back, charging into the alley, screaming, "Let her go, damn you! Let her go!"

Stunned at the intrusion, the men did just that, and the girl ran back into the street, yelling for help at the top of her lungs.

The men turned angrily on Sam then, but she was ready for them. Rushing toward one, she bent double to ram him in the stomach, knocking his breath from him, and he slumped to the ground, gasping. Then, with fists clasped together, she slammed into the other with a blow to his crotch that sent him to his knees.

Still hanging onto the bag, Sam retreated, only to dart right into the waiting arms of a gendarme who had heard the commotion and responded. Meanwhile, the men managed to escape out the other end of the alley.

"That's him." The golden-haired girl was pointing, blue eyes shining excitedly. "He's the one who saved me."

"He's also the one who stole your reticule," the officer declared, taking it from Sam as he held her by her neck. "Now it's off to prison for this scalawag."

Sam twisted and struggled, but to no avail. Suddenly the girl took a step forward and protested, "No. Wait."

The gendarme paused.

"Release him."

"But, mademoiselle, he is a thief." He was astonished. "I cannot allow it. I must take him to jail."

The girl was not to be dissuaded. "You will let him go."

He shook his head. "You do not realize what you are saying."

"And you do not realize who I am—Mademoiselle Celeste de Manca. My father is the Marquis Antoine Vallois Bruis de Manca, and if you do not obey my wishes, you will answer to him."

With a shrug, the gendarme let his prisoner go. Why should he care if nobility wanted to magnanimously free one criminal? There were plenty of other gutter snipes to be caught, and the jails were already crowded. "As you wish, mademoiselle." He turned on his heel and left them.

Sam was tempted to run but instead yielded to her curiosity to ask, "Why did you do that?"

"Because you probably saved my life. There's no telling what those men would have done to me. Besides"—she grinned saucily—"I need a new companion and friend. My Mimette died recently. I was on my way to attend a rosary being given for her after today's mass. Will you go with me? Then I'll take you to my house. You don't have a home, do you." It was more an accusation than a question as her eyes swept over Sam in scrutiny.

Sam remembered her ruse and gave a sharp laugh. "But I'm a boy."

"No, you're not."

Sam, caught off guard, stammered, "What . . . what makes you say that?"

"I'm not sure. Something in your eyes, I think. Maybe your voice. But you *are* a girl, aren't you?"

Reluctantly, Sam nodded. "Nobody ever noticed before."

"Nobody probably ever caught up with you before. Now will you accept my offer to go home with me? If you don't, you'll eventually wind up in prison. You know that."

Sam figured she would have time for a decent meal, at least, before the crazy girl's parents threw her out. "I will go for a little while, but I can't stay long."

"You have nowhere else to go." Celeste clamped a possessive hand on Sam's arm and led her toward the chapel.

"How do you know?" Sam was stunned by the way the girl had assumed she would get her way.

"I just do, as I knew somehow you weren't a boy. Now come along or mass will be over by the time we get there. We'll have time to talk later."

And, indeed, they did.

That night, by the time Sam had gorged herself with the most delicious food she had eaten in years, the two had become instant friends.

As it turned out, Celeste was as lonely as Sam. Her mother was dead, and her father, she admitted with bitterness, spent all his time with his many mistresses. That was why she missed Mimette so terribly. Mimette had been more than just her maid; she had been the sister Celeste now wanted Sam to be.

Sam agreed to stay the night and, after borrowing a nightgown from Celeste, wound up revealing her own past. As they lay side by side in the big bed with its lace canopy, she told how her life had not always been one of crime and desperation.

Her father, Franchot Labonte, Sam explained, had once been a rich and prominent man. "If it hadn't been for the Civil War in America, my family and I would probably still be living in the cool green hills of Virginia that I remember so well."

Her parents had gone to America before she was born. Backed by a huge inheritance from his father, Franchot had transported fine stallions from France and a few brood mares to become a successful breeder in only a short time. "But when war broke out, the Confederate government seized all his stock for consignment to its army. My parents didn't have any interest in the war, but it made them lose everything they had."

Celeste's eyes grew wide with wonder and pity. "So what did they do?"

"There was barely enough money to pay their way, but they had no choice except to come back to France. I was only eight years old." Sam blinked away the tears that always came when she thought back to that awful time. "Once, they had been among the wealthiest people in Paris, but when they returned stripped of everything they had, my mother couldn't bear the humiliation and shame. She died of a broken heart. My father gave up then and didn't care what happened to him or to me."

They had wound up living with the derelicts in the catacombs, a labyrinth of tunnels beneath Paris streets. The diggings, begun back in the Roman days, were presently used to store bones from excavated cemeteries, and Franchot and Sam, like their neighbors, had taken shelter in the deeper recesses, away from the macabre storage chambers.

With her father constantly in a drunken stupor, begging on the streets for money to buy his cheap wine, Sam was left alone to fend for herself. After secretly witnessing the brutal rape of her friend when they were both not quite eleven years old, Sam had cut off her long, thick, silver-colored hair and had disguised herself as a boy. Thus, she was passed over when men came looking for young girls to abduct for work in the brothels or for their own lust. And to survive, she became expert at picking pockets, as well as adept at snatching ladies' reticules.

Then one night her father went to sleep and, like her mother, just didn't wake up. After that, Sam was truly on her own.

"So here I am," she concluded. "I've managed to take care of myself, and I'll keep on doing it, as long as I stick to robbing little old ladies instead of girls who can run as fast as I can," she added with a forced smile intended to lighten the moment.

But Celeste did not return her smile. Instead, she stared at her with solemn, thoughtful eyes for long moments, so long, in fact, that Sam began to feel uncomfortable and started thinking maybe she had said too much. Maybe Celeste would even prefer that she just get up and leave and not stay the night. And she was about to suggest that maybe it would be best if she did, when Celeste surprised her by declaring in her confident way, "You are not going to continue as you have been, Sam. You are going to stay with me."

Sam laughed nervously. Surely Celeste could not be serious. "But your father—"

"My father"—Celeste paused to give an unladylike snort—"is so busy with his women he doesn't even know I'm around. And soon I won't be. Next week I leave for school in Switzerland. Mimette was going with me, but she died suddenly. The doctor said she was probably born with a weak heart. But now you will go instead."

Sam tried to protest. "No, I can't—"

"You *can*. And you will. Why would you refuse?" Celeste cocked her head and looked at her in wonder. "I am offering you a life of wealth and luxury over struggling to survive in the gutters, and if you won't agree, I think I shall have to send for the gendarme to return, but this time to take you to an asylum, because you have to be insane to refuse me."

Sam saw the play of a smile on Celeste's lips and knew she was teasing about the gendarme, but not about her offer. And Sam knew she would, indeed, be truly out of her mind to refuse.

After all, what else was there for her?

# 1

*Sam knew she should be* having a wonderful time, but actually she was miserable.

For two years she had enjoyed a life of near royalty. Exposed to all the finest in culture and refinement, surrounded by luxury, she had lacked for nothing. Magnificent gowns had been created especially for her. She had been tutored in music, language, the arts, manners, charm, and grace.

And now she and Celeste had returned to Paris from school in Switzerland, and a sumptuous dinner had been prepared in celebration. No expense had been spared. There were candles in cut-glass holders, fine china and silver, and a large crystal bowl of fragrant fresh roses had been placed in the center of the lace-covered table.

Servants hovered nearby, ready to accommodate her every wish, and certainly the food was delicious—*bisque d'ecrevisses,* a crayfish bisque, followed by *bouribout aux raisins,* a ragout of duck and grapes.

And she had glimpsed the dessert tray to see her favorite, *crème renversée caramelisée,* a caramelized cream custard.

So the evening should have been pleasant, only it was not, because Celeste's father, the Marquis Antoine Vallois Bruis de Manca, was making Sam terribly uncomfortable.

At first she told herself it was an accident when his hand had brushed her bosom as he'd seated her next to him. And when his fingers touched her knee under the table, that, too, had meant nothing.

She was being silly, she chided herself, to think he was looking at her as if he could see right through her clothes to naked flesh beneath. She did not know him well enough to decipher his thoughts. After all, she had met him only once, briefly, right before she and Celeste had left for Switzerland. He had viewed her dismissively, without interest.

But now everything was different, for in the past two years the metamorphosis to womanhood had taken place.

And something told Sam that the marquis was well aware of that fact.

Celeste was recounting her experiences from school, telling about learning to jump her horse. "*I* jumped, but *he* didn't, and I couldn't sit down for a week. Could I, Sam?" She turned to Sam for confirmation.

Sam managed a nod and a little smile, relieved that Celeste was having a good time. She was well aware her treasured friend had problems of her own, for as soon as they had returned, Celeste had renewed her secret and very forbidden romance with Jacques Onfroi, son of the estate gardener.

To complicate things, Celeste lived in fear that her father was going to honor a long-ago pact made between her maternal grandfather and his best friend. The two men had pledged their firstborn grandson and granddaughter to wed each other, and if her father made her go through with it, Celeste would have to marry a man she had never met.

So as Celeste chattered incessantly to hide her inner turmoil, Sam was struggling to conceal her own distress over her present situation, imagined or not.

"I don't like you calling her that, Celeste."

The girls exchanged puzzled glances.

"*Sam*"—Antoine wrinkled his nose in distaste—"is not a fitting name for such a beautiful young woman. *Samara.* That is her name. And that is what she shall be called."

He lifted his wineglass in salute, and Sam shuddered inwardly.

"So what do you girls have planned now that you are home?" he went on pleasantly.

"We plan to go riding a lot." Celeste winked at Sam. The estate was huge, with many secluded trails where she could have a rendezvous with Jacques.

"Well, don't do any jumping. That doesn't appear to be your forte. Now if you girls will excuse me, I have plans for the evening."

He got up to leave, and Sam felt a cold chill as she glanced up to see him run his tongue across his lips like an animal licking its chops before devouring prey.

Celeste was unaware of Sam's discomfort, for as soon as they were alone, she urged, "Forget dessert. I managed to see Jacques earlier and told him I would meet him at nine o'clock, and it's half-past. We have to look as though we're retiring for the night so I can slip out. Now you go to your room, and—"

"You're going to get in terrible trouble," Sam felt the need to caution. "There's no telling what your father will do if he finds out."

Tears suddenly welled in Celeste's blue eyes. "You don't understand. Jacques and I love each other, and we haven't seen each other in such a long time. We have to be together."

"It can never be, and you know it."

"We'll find a way. We have to. Now please. Just go to your room and stay there."

Sam had no intention of rambling around the vast château, and she did not like being alone, either. Though they had shared quarters at school, Celeste was so preoccupied with thoughts of Jacques, she hadn't said a word when Sam was given her own room on their return.

As they made their way out of the dining room and on upstairs, Celeste again expressed hope the marriage pact had been forgotten. "Papa hasn't said anything about it since I got home, and the last time we heard from the Ballard family was four years ago, when Mrs. Ballard wrote to let us know that her husband had passed away. And even though it's terribly wicked of me, I'm hoping by now she's dead, too, and that Jarman has married someone else."

"And you've heard nothing since?"

"Not a thing. I might be worried if they lived in Europe, but Mr. Ballard migrated with his family to America before Jarman was even born. That gives me even more hope that it's all been forgotten. The idea is absurd, anyway."

"Celeste, prearranged marriages are not unusual, and you know it. You only think so because this one affects you."

"Maybe. I'm just praying we'll never hear from the Ballard family again, and that I'll find a way to marry Jacques."

Sam did not share her optimism. Even if the pact were forgotten, she was sure the marquis would never consent to his daughter marrying into a lower class. But Celeste was stubborn, and she was also in love, and from what Sam had witnessed among other girls at the school, being in love did not encourage rational thinking. But she wouldn't know personally, for she had never been even close to caring about a boy in that way.

At the top of the stairs, Celeste turned toward her room and called softly, "I'll see you in the morning."

Sam went to her own quarters and forced herself to put the marquis out of her mind. She had other things to worry about, such as what was to become of her now that schooling was over. She had no money of her own and no place to go, and she could only hope that whatever fate held in store for Celeste, she would be included.

At last she drifted into a restless sleep, but she was jolted awake sometime later, terrified to feel a hand pressed over her mouth.

"Don't scream," came the whispered command. "I'm not going to hurt you."

Sam's fear dissolved to rage when she realized it was the marquis. He moved his hand, and before she could unleash her anger, he hastened to explain, "I apologize for frightening you, but your door was locked, and I didn't want to wake up everyone by knocking, so I came in through the terrace. I was afraid you'd scream, so that's why I put my hand over your mouth. I have to speak with you."

"Couldn't it wait until morning?" she asked warily, sitting up and moving back against the headboard, making sure to pull the satin sheets all the way up to her chin. "It is not proper for you to be in my boudoir," she added.

"Again, I apologize, but I wanted to know what this says before I let Celeste see it." He reached to light the bedside lantern, then took an envelope from the pocket of his coat and handed it to her. "It's in English, which I can't read, but you can."

Given her apprehension over what was contained in the letter, Sam's fears as to his intentions eased a bit. She asked, "Is it from that man she is promised to marry?"

He nodded. "It arrived only a few days ago."

She began to read, and with each word, her heart constricted with sympathy for the friend she loved so dearly.

Jarman Ballard had written from a place called Fort Leavenworth, in the state of Kansas, where he was a captain in the United States Army. He would be discharged soon and had decided it was time that he and Celeste be married. He calculated she was nearly seventeen and should have been properly groomed by this time to be a wife.

"Dear Lord, she doesn't want this," Sam thought out loud.

"I'm afraid it doesn't matter," Antoine commented absently, then, with a slow smile, urged, "Read it again, the part about her dowry."

Sam reread the lines:

*I am confident that you will see fit to provide Celeste with a proper dowry. It is my intent to insure a secure future for her, of course, but when my father died, he left many debts, and being a man of honor, I assumed responsibility, which has been a great burden. However, I anticipate being able to turn her dowry into great wealth for us in the future, for it is my plan, upon my discharge, to move to Abilene, a boomtown created by virtue of being the destination of cattle drives from the West, as well as the center of railyards for transporting the cattle east. I intend to build a hotel, and—*

"That's quite enough." So, Antoine thought with amusement, it was the expectation of a large dowry that brought Jarman Ballard to claim his bride. Well, he was in for a surprise, because the amount would be quite modest. Let his daughter be treasure enough. What did he care, anyway? Once she left France, he would never see her again.

Sam scanned the letter once more to read the part about how Jarman would be in touch soon as to the exact date he would like for Celeste to arrive in America. That meant a month or more, at least. But would it be time enough for Celeste to persuade her father not to make her go?

Sam ventured to attempt to set the stage for Celeste's plea by pointing out, "Surely you don't want your only daughter to go so far away to live. Can't you write to this man and tell him you've decided not to honor the pact? After all, you had nothing to do with it, and—"

"Nonsense. The family honor is at stake. I would never dream of it, and she knows that. Besides . . ." He leered at Sam. "I will still have a daughter, only I find it harder and harder to think of you as a daughter, Samara." His fingers began to dance across the sheet in her direction.

"Don't." She moved farther away, repulsed and frightened. Now she knew it had not been her imagination or her mind playing tricks. He did have dishonorable intentions, and dear Lord, what was she going to do?

A confident smile was frozen on his lips. "Perhaps you should consider being nicer to me, my dear. After all, what's to become of you when Celeste leaves for America? You can't go back to your life in the streets and pretend to be a boy, and a beautiful woman like you would not survive very long on her own, I'm afraid."

Taken by surprise, Sam blurted out, "Why, I'll go with her, of course."

"Oh, I can't allow that."

Sam's heart slammed into her chest. "You have to. She has to have a traveling companion, and—"

"She will, but it won't be you. That would be a terrible waste. You see, I have plans for you, Samara, now that you have grown into a beautiful young woman. When I have finished grooming you, the world's wealthiest men will envy me, be willing to pay any price for your favors, but you will belong to me, and—"

"No." The sound was raspy, hoarse, spoken from the pained recesses of her very soul. "I won't—"

He chuckled softly, mockingly. "But, my dear, you have no choice." His fingers wrapped around her throat to caress softly, yet with a firm touch to warn that she should not attempt to scream. "And please do not even think about saying anything to Celeste. I would be forced then to tell her how I caught you stealing from me, and oh, how hurt she will be to find out you haven't changed at all, and how disappointed and sad it will make her to see you sent to the prison at St. Lazare.

"Do you have any idea what it is like there?" he went on as she stared at him in disbelief and horror. "It's where the whores are sent when they have syphilis. So unless you want to spend the rest of your life there, you had best think about my offer to care for you once Celeste is out of the way."

He removed his hand from her throat to pat her cheek as he whispered, "Now, go to sleep, Samara, and don't worry about a thing. You will continue to live like the princess you are."

Sam cringed as his face came closer, knowing he was about to kiss her, knowing if he did, she was going to scream and fight with all her strength no matter what, and—

Suddenly there was the sound of the doorknob jiggling, followed by rapid, soft knocks as Celeste called, "Sam, let me in."

Antoine sprang back, releasing her.

"Are you awake? Let me in. I want to talk to you."

Antoine grabbed Sam's shoulders to give her a quick shake. "Remember, not a word. Celeste will be leaving soon, and then we'll talk about this again." And then he was gone, moving soundlessly to the open doors to disappear into the shadowed night.

Washed with dread and fear of what the future now held unless she could think of a way to escape, Sam hurried to open the door.

Celeste was too excited to notice that Sam was upset. She ran across the room and jumped in bed. "I was dying to tell you how wonderful it was with Jacques tonight." She hugged her knees against her chest and gave a squeal of delight. "I just love him so much, Sam, and he says he thinks we can start breathing easier since Papa hasn't said anything about Jarman. So now we're going to concentrate on figuring out a way to get Papa to accept how we feel about each other. It will take a while, but we've got lots of time, and . . ."

Celeste talked on dreamily. She did not notice how Sam was biting back tears of pity as she prayed silently that somehow they would both be able to find a way to escape the madness that was descending so rapidly upon them.

**2**

Sam dreaded going to breakfast the next morning. She deliberately took her time dressing, wanting to prolong the inevitable moment when she would have to face the marquis. How could she behave as though nothing had happened, as though he had not brazenly told her of his intent to make her his whore? But she had to pretend, for in no way could she hurt Celeste by letting her know the kind of monster her father really was.

Besides, Sam thought sadly, Celeste was about to have problems of her own. Learning of Jarman Ballard's letter would bring her dreams crashing down around her. So she did not need additional misery heaped upon her.

Seated at the skirted dressing table, Sam glanced about at the opulence surrounding her—the huge bed with its hand-crocheted canopy, the Regency love seat of pink tufted velvet, the bombe commode of kingwood, and the enormous armoire that ran nearly the entire length of one wall and was filled with exquisite gowns of every color designed especially for her.

She was well aware that she had been given every luxury imaginable and had been undyingly grateful till slapped with the cold reality that she was expected to repay it all with her very soul.

She got up and went to stand at the terrace doors. Locked and bolted now, they would stay that way no matter how warm the room became. It was a gorgeous spring day, but it might as well have been cold and wintry for all the zest she felt for life at that moment.

A fool, she told herself. That was what she had been. In school they had studied Milton, and lines from his *Paradise Lost* suddenly seemed terribly apropos as they danced across her mind—*the paradise of fools, to few unknown* . . . How arrogant and stupid she had been to think the fairy tale could last, that there would not come a day of retribution. Blithely, she had not thought of the future, content to enjoy the good fortune that had rescued her from the streets. But now it was ending. She would remain at the château and somehow find a way to avoid being alone with the marquis until Celeste was gone. Then she would run away and lose herself in the catacombs until she figured out what to do with the rest of her life.

Finally, doggedly, she forced herself to go downstairs.

Celeste and her father were already seated when she entered the breakfast room. Through the big window, the view of the tulip garden in full bloom was breathtaking, but in her miserable state, Sam could not appreciate the splendor.

Lost in anticipation of her planned rendezvous with Jacques later in the morning, Celeste did not notice Sam's depression.

Antoine, however, was not about to ignore her. "Are you feeling bad, my dear? You don't look as though you slept well."

"I'm fine." She did not look at him.

Celeste giggled. "It's my fault she's sleepy. I kept her up late last night talking, I'm afraid."

Antoine's lips twitched. He was trying not to smile as he feigned surprise. "Really? But I thought you retired separately last night. Did Samara go to your room?"

Sam gritted her teeth. How glibly he could lie.

Celeste shook her head, oblivious of the tension that hung like an invisible shroud. "No. I went to hers. I guess I'm just not used to being alone at night."

"Well, you won't have to worry about that much longer."

Sam held her breath and concentrated on the bowl of strawberries that had been placed before her. Through lowered lashes, she could see how Celeste was staring at her father with wide, curious eyes as she asked thinly, warily, "What do you mean?"

He lifted his cup of tea in salute. "I have splendid news. Jarman is ready to marry you. In another month or so, you will join him in America and be married there."

The fork Celeste was holding slipped from her trembling fingers, striking her plate with a loud clatter.

Antoine, ignoring her obvious distress, continued, "Naturally, I would have preferred that he come for you, so the wedding could be here, but he'd rather you go there, and I suppose I can understand that . . ."

He droned on, and Sam watched with pity rising as Celeste listened in horror, swinging her head slowly from side to side. Finally Celeste exploded, "No. You don't mean it. You won't make me do it." She looked to Sam in disbelief, but Sam continued to keep her eyes down.

Antoine tapped his soft-boiled egg with the back of his spoon, responding almost distractedly. "Why are you so surprised? My goodness, you've had your whole life to prepare for this. You've always known you would one day marry him. Good heavens, child, it was arranged before you were even born."

"I know, I know." The words began to tumble out of her. "But, Papa, you remember how Mama even said she didn't think it fair that my grandfather should decide who my husband would be. And it's been so long since we heard from the Ballards that I naturally assumed the silly old pact was forgotten. Surely you can't be planning to honor it. I mean, I should have the right to choose my own husband, someone I love, and—"

"Celeste."

She fell silent, dropping her chin as she fought back tears.

Antoine put aside his spoon and reached to cover her trembling hand. "I won't have you behaving this way. Now I want you to start getting ready to leave."

"But don't you care at all?" she beseeched him, face suddenly gone pale. "I've been gone two years, and now you're sending me away. What if we never see each other again?"

"Don't be absurd. Of course, I care about you, dear child, and it will break my heart for you to leave me, but I have no choice. To dishonor the family name by refusing to honor the pact is unthinkable. It simply cannot be done."

"Papa, don't make me do it, please. I don't even know this man, and I'll never be able to love him."

"It is not important that you do. What matters is that you maintain the dignity of this family by fulfilling your duty and obligation."

Sam was about to start crying herself as Celeste once more looked to her in misery. Her heart went out to her, but there was nothing she could do.

"At least," Celeste whispered wretchedly, "Sam will be going with me."

"Yes, it appears I will lose both my daughters."

Sam whipped her head about to stare at him, daring to hope that by some miracle he spoke the truth, but she knew by the gleam in his eyes that he was only trifling with them both. He had no intention of allowing her to go but would not let Celeste know that until the last moment. *Another victim of a fool's paradise,* Sam mused bitterly.

Later, after her father had gone, Celeste fell into Sam's arms. "I can't do it. I love Jacques. I can't marry anybody else, and I won't. You have to help me think of a way out of this."

Sam tried to find words of comfort, but there were none. She had no answer, and even while she ached for Celeste, she was also worried over how she could get through the next weeks herself. Her first impulse was to run, then and there, but she could not desert her friend at such a devastating time. With heavy heart, Sam knew she had no one to turn to in her desperation.

Once again, she found herself all alone.

**3**

*In the weeks that followed,* as Celeste sneaked about to be with Jacques whenever she could, Sam was determined the marquis would not find her alone and vulnerable again.

Often, Celeste and Sam would pretend to spend the day riding, but as soon as they got out of sight, Celeste would join Jacques, and Sam would continue on, staying away until it was time for them to meet and return home. Sam spent the evenings with Celeste or locked in her room.

It was a miserable, nerve-racking time, and each day Sam wondered how much more she could take. The marquis was obviously enjoying his cat-and-mouse game, continuing to stare lasciviously at Sam when Celeste was not looking, sending the secret message he was anxious to have her all to himself.

Almost two months had passed, and then came the night when Sam and Celeste went in to dinner, only to freeze at the sight of the letter, placed so ominously, beside Celeste's plate. With an anguished gasp, Celeste snatched it up.

"I have no idea what Jarman has written," Antoine said quietly.

"There was no one about who can read English. I could not find Samara." He shot an annoyed glance at Sam.

Sam watched Celeste's eyes fill with tears as she hastily read the letter.

"Well?" Antoine prodded. "What does he say?"

"He . . . he says I should come right away," she said miserably. "As soon as arrangements can be made."

"I thought that might be the case, so I went ahead and contacted the Compagnie Générale Transatlantique line so I would know their crossing schedule. A paddle steamer, the *Napoleon Troisième,* leaves next week for New York from Le Havre. I will make the necessary arrangements in the morning."

"Papa, please don't make me do this."

"Stop it. I will not listen to any more of your whining. It is settled."

With a shadow of hope, Celeste looked to Sam and murmured, "At least you will be going with me."

"No, she won't."

"What are you talking about?" Celeste cried.

He feigned surprise that she could even suggest such a thing. "Why, surely you don't expect me to give up both my daughters."

Sam clamped her teeth together so hard that her jaws began to ache. It was all she could do to keep from exploding with rage.

Celeste was staring at him in wonder. "Whatever are you talking about?"

He lifted his shoulders in a careless shrug. "Why, my dear, Samara has become like a daughter to me, and I suddenly realized that if she goes with you, I won't have any family at all, so I can't allow it. You can take Francine instead."

"Francine?" Celeste echoed, stunned. "She's my maid."

He raised an eyebrow. "So? Every proper young lady has a maid. Jarman will expect you to bring one with you, and Francine is a perfect choice. She has no family, and when I spoke with her about going with you, she was most willing."

Sam watched helplessly as Celeste seemed to crumple before her eyes. Her desperate words were barely audible: "Dear Lord, Papa, why are you doing this to me?"

Antoine got up and went to put his arms about her as he chided gently, "We simply cannot have you behaving like this, my dear. It's a matter of family honor, and you have to realize and accept that fact."

"Honor is more important than my happiness?"

"Honor *is* happiness, my dear. Remember that. Now I want you to go wash your face and compose yourself. We have guests arriving in a little while, and I don't want them to see you like this. We will talk again in the morning, and I will try to make you understand this is all for the best."

Sam was astonished. She had never known the marquis to entertain anyone. Surely he hadn't planned some sort of gathering to celebrate Celeste leaving. That would be too cruel.

Celeste dabbed at her nose with her napkin, swaying in her misery. As though echoing Sam's thoughts, she murmured, "Tell me you haven't planned a party for me."

"Oh, nothing like that." He returned to his chair. "It's just the Marchioness Eglantine."

Celeste blew her nose, then scoffed, "Another séance. Just what I need. A crazy old lady trying to call up the dead, when right at this moment, I think I'd like to be in my own grave."

"Enough." He slammed his hand on the table. Celeste jumped. Sam did not. She had been watching from the corner of her eye and had seen the angry gesture coming. "Now do as I say." He dismissed them both with an irritated wave.

Celeste bolted from her chair. Sam scurried after her, anxious to comfort and certainly not wanting to remain behind to dine alone with the marquis. Besides, she had formulated a plan and was anxious to share it with Celeste. She had only been waiting for the marquis to admit he had no intention of allowing her to accompany Celeste. Now she could tell her friend that she was going anyway, because instead of running away, she intended to sneak on board the ship and stow away.

But Celeste was in no mood to listen to anything Sam had to say. She ran to her room and locked the door, refusing to let Sam in. "Please," Sam begged. "We've got to talk."

"Leave me alone, and tell Papa I refuse to go to that silly séance."

Sam tried a few more minutes, then gave up. In her own room, she found Francine turning back her bed, as was her custom before retiring to the servants' quarters for the night.

"What is a séance?" she asked, plopping down on a chair, wanting to take her mind off Celeste's problems as well as her own.

Francine was only too glad to tell her. "It's a gathering to try to communicate with the dead. Those who believe in it say the dead speak to a medium. That's someone with a special gift," she added.

"Do *you* believe in it?"

Francine's round face spread in a wide grin. "Not hardly. The medium Marchioness Eglantine uses was a friend of my mother's, so I know her well. She's a fake, but a good one. She gives people their money's worth and makes them happy for a little while.

"Except for the Marchioness Eglantine," she went on to explain, sounding apologetic. "Actually, I feel sorry for her. She's been trying to communicate with her dead husband for nearly fifteen years. Madame Felice does enough to ensure she believes contact has been made, but there's never any vocal communication."

"Why not?"

"Madame doesn't know how to answer. You see . . ." Francine instinctively lowered her voice, even though they were alone, for to have the wrong person overhear her sharing such secrets could have dire consequences. "Marchioness Eglantine's husband, the Marquis Dominique, built this house. He was murdered in the library twenty years ago tonight."

"Was the killer caught?"

"No. Some say it was the jealous lover of one of his courtesans. Some believe the killer was the father of a young girl Dominique is thought to have deflowered. There is even a tale that he reneged on a gambling debt, but all of Paris knows the marchioness refuses to accept any of those theories. She believes, or *wants* to believe, that it was merely a thief, caught in the act, who never intended to kill her husband in the first place."

Francine went on to explain that when the marchioness heard about the spread of spiritualism in Britain, she'd become interested, convinced that if she could communicate with her dead husband, she would learn the truth and end the ugly gossip once and for all.

"She always has the séances in the library, because she thinks his spirit might be trapped there, caught between the here and hereafter, tormented because the truth isn't known."

Sam was fascinated but, like Francine, felt sorry for the poor widow. "I'm surprised the marquis allows it."

"Actually, he has no choice. It was part of the agreement when she sold him the house. But listen." She leaned closer, eyes glittering. "This is the best part. I spoke to Madame Felice when she was here yesterday to discuss the arrangements for tonight, and she confided to me that the marquis has told her he doesn't care what she does, but he wants this to be the last séance. That means she's going to pretend to have Dominique give his wife the motive for his murder, so she will be satisfied. I can't wait to hear what it will be. You and Celeste have to tell me about it the minute it's over."

"Celeste isn't going."

Francine clapped her hands in delight. "Wonderful. That means *I* can go. Since the other servants don't know it's all fake, they're too scared to go. That only leaves me to take her place."

"Well, I wish you could fill in for me, too."

"Why? Because you can't stand the thought of holding hands with the marquis?"

Sam stared at her, agape.

"That's right." Francine's eyes were grim. "I know what's been going on. So do the other servants. They aren't blind, and we all see how you've been avoiding him. And I also know it's really you Mademoiselle Celeste wants to go with her to America, but he won't allow it, because, no doubt, he plans to have you all to himself after she's gone. I'm sorry for you. I truly am."

Sounding more confident than she felt, Sam responded, "Well, there has to be a way out of all this. There just has to be."

Antoine was annoyed that Celeste refused to attend the séance but allowed Francine to take her place. All he wanted was to have the evening over with as quickly as possible.

They gathered in the library. A round table covered with a white cloth had been placed in the center, and a single candle provided the only light in the room. There were six chairs. Sam cringed when she felt the marquis's hand clamp down possessively on her shoulder as he steered her to the one next to him.

As he went to greet the guests, Francine explained, "The one dressed in white is Madame Felice. The old lady next to her is Marchioness Eglantine, and the other woman is just a companion."

Sam noted that the marchioness was dressed in black. "She's still in mourning? After all these years?"

"Yes, and she's vowed to continue mourning till she finds out why her husband was murdered."

Wryly Sam pointed out, "If she waits a little longer, she can ask him in person."

Francine giggled. "I doubt she thinks they'll wind up in the same place."

Despite her worries, Sam could not help giggling, too. And, in response, the others glared at them coldly. The marquis did not bother to introduce the girls, but Sam did not care. She was fast becoming interested in what was going on and grateful when Madame Felice

asked them to join hands. Even though she hated the clammy feel of
the marquis's fingers, it was better than having him grope at her under the table, which she figured he would do.

Sam jumped, startled by the sudden eerie sound of a violin coming
from somewhere outside the room.

"Celestial music from heaven," the marchioness murmured, smiling.

Francine leaned over to whisper, "Don't be frightened. It's just part
of the act."

Sam whispered back that she had already figured that out.

Madame Felice commanded, "Silence. All eyes closed."

When she was satisfied everyone had obeyed, she began speaking
and, for the next several minutes, uttered a strange incantation. Sam,
growing bored, sneaked a look at the marchioness. Her head was
lolled back, as though she had slipped into some sort of trance.

The marquis gave Sam's hand a painful squeeze to chastise her for
not keeping her eyes closed. She made a quick face at him. If he had
been obeying the rules himself, he would not have known they were
open. She heard a cracking noise that seemed to be coming from
under the table, and she tensed. Francine dared lean over to whisper,
"She's popping her toes. It's an old trick."

"Can you hear us?" Madame Felice asked suddenly, sharply.

Sam felt a sudden gust of wind. The candle went out, and the room
was plunged into darkness.

Madame Felice asked sharply, "Is that you, Marquis Dominique?
Let your presence be known to us, please."

Sam was trying not to giggle. Next to her, Francine was also struggling for composure. They could hear the marchioness's breathing
coming in excited little gasps, but what had them on the verge of
hysteria was the sound of snoring, because the marchioness's companion had fallen sound asleep. Then a voice spoke from directly behind,
jolting them from their humor:

"I am here."

The marchioness gave a soft little scream, and Madame Felice at
once snapped at her to be quiet, lest she frighten him away.

"This night, I will not leave until I tell the truth."

The marchioness ignored the medium's orders and cried, "*Mon
Dieu!* Oh, my beloved, how I have waited for this moment."

Madame Felice spoke in an annoyed hiss. "You must be quiet. He
will respond to me and no one else."

Sam was fascinated. Leaning back in her chair, she became accustomed to the darkness, and she could actually see the ghostly form as it began to move slowly about the table. It seemed to be floating, a mere whisper of white amid the shadows.

The music grew louder, and Francine, also watching and again anxious to share her knowledge, leaned over to whisper, "There's a man under the sheet, and he's using a stick to raise it up and down and give the illusion he's floating."

"Tell us," Madame Felice urged, her voice sounding strained, desperate. She had not become one of the most sought-after mediums in all of Paris by being a poor actress. "Why were you murdered? Who took your life and why?"

The marchioness made a whimpering sound, then begged, "Say it is not so, my beloved. Say it was not a jealous husband or angry father. For years I have walked with my head down, for your memory was shamed. Tell us—"

"He will answer only to me," Madame Felice repeated with icy annoyance. It was extremely important that she maintain complete control over the séance. Otherwise, the overwrought woman might leap from her chair and grab at the sheet and ruin everything. She had to get things over quickly. "Tell me, Marquis Dominique. Tell me the reason your life was taken."

"So simple," came the reply. "A thief. I surprised him. I do not think he meant to kill me. He was afraid. So you see, there is no shame, only regret you were not strong enough to reach me before now so my beloved widow's suffering would end. . . ."

As quickly as it had come, the ghost disappeared. With a gasp of relief, the marchioness fainted.

As soon as possible, Sam and Francine scurried from the library and ran all the way to Sam's room to collapse in gales of laughter.

"She was good," Sam admitted. "If you hadn't told me it was all a fake, I might have believed it."

"Oh, that was nothing. Let me tell you about some of the tricks Madame uses."

Sam was enthralled to hear of the various devices used to dupe people into believing they were communicating with the dead. Francine also told her how societies were springing up all over, called "home circles," named by the American medium Mrs. Hayden, who started the spiritualist movement in Britain in 1852.

"But *she's* not a fake," Francine said in awe. "She has never been caught in one fraudulent act. So in fairness we can't accuse all mediums of being fakes just because Madame Felice admits to being one.

But you have to look at it in another way, too—she's made the marchioness happy, and . . ." She fell silent at the sound of someone knocking on the door, and they both tensed.

"Don't let it be the marquis," Sam prayed out loud.

"Sam. Let me in."

"Celeste." Sam shared a relieved sigh with Francine.

Francine hurried to open the door, and Celeste rushed in. "Leave us," she said to her brusquely, then crossed the room to drop to her knees before Sam.

Sam saw the stricken look on her face. "My God, what's wrong?"

Celeste grabbed her hands and squeezed tightly, waiting until they were alone. "You must help me. There is no other way."

Sam's heart went out to her. "I will do whatever I can. You know that."

"I'm begging you, Sam. If you refuse, my life is over."

Sam was bewildered. "Just tell me what it is you want me to do. You know I'll do my best."

Celeste drew a deep breath, held it, then said raggedly, "I want you to take my place."

Sam shook her head, confused. Surely she did not mean . . .

But she did. "I want you to go to America in my place, pretend to be me. Jarman will never know the difference. We're the same age. Marry him, Sam. He will give you a good life, I'm sure, and—"

"This is crazy." Sam laughed nervously and drew her hands from Celeste's almost painful grasp. "I mean, I know how disappointed you are, how you love Jacques, but maybe you will fall in love with Jarman. It happens, you know." Sam attempted a confident grin, which quickly faded at Celeste's next words.

"Will he love me when he discovers I married him carrying another man's child?"

Sam felt her eyes go wide. She realized Celeste had been hoping that by some miracle that she and Jacques would find a way to be married before another letter came. "Oh, dear God," was all Sam could say.

"It's true." Tears streamed down Celeste's stricken face. "I am going to have Jacques's baby. We didn't mean for it to happen, but it did, because we love each other so much. And if you won't help me, Sam, I will kill myself. I swear it."

And somehow, Sam knew she meant it.

# 4

**Leavenworth,
Kansas**

*Cade Ramsey's head was* throbbing like a drum cadence
leading infantry into battle. He squeezed his eyes shut against the
pounding and cursed.

Beside him, the woman stirred. He did not recall her name, and
memories of last night's passion were as stagnant as the taste of whiskey in his mouth. He reached beneath the pillow to make sure his gun
was still there, then watched as she pulled on a robe and padded to
the door. Upon opening it, she gave a gasp of terror and leaped back.

Cade was on his feet, forgetting he was naked. Whipping out the
gun was instinctive, and at the same time the hammer clicked back,
he recognized Bold Eagle. "Damn it, that's a good way to get shot."
He put the weapon aside.

The Indian laughed and spoke in his native Kansa tongue. "Because I knock on a door at noon? And please tell your woman I did
not mean to frighten her."

Cade replied in the same language, for he knew it as well as his own. "Who wouldn't be scared?"

Bold Eagle's appearance was ominous. Tall and broad-shouldered, he had a hawkish face and dark, almost black, piercing eyes. His head had been plucked bald, except for a scalp lock running along the top and back. Bare-chested, he wore breechclouts over deerskin trousers. In the Kansa tradition, he had also plucked the hairs from his face and chest.

Cade reached for his trousers. "How did you know where to find me?"

"I have ways."

Cade knew that was so. Bold Eagle was like a shadow. "Well, thanks for waking me up. I'm supposed to be at the fort at one." He buckled on his holster.

"I know. This is the day you learn whether you will be the new agent to the Indians."

"Maybe."

The woman, staring from one to the other as they conversed in the choppy, guttural language she could not understand, finally demanded of Cade, "Look, are you a half-breed, or what? I mean, we had a fine time last night, and you paid me good, but I can't be honeying up with no breeds, you understand?"

Cade did not bother to respond. As she had said, he had paid her well. He didn't figure he owed her an explanation. He hurried out and knew he would not be back.

Outside, Bold Eagle had his horse waiting. Cade knew by the look in his eye that the warrior had not come merely to remind him of his appointment, and he did not have to wait long to find out that his suspicion was correct.

"I think I have found a way we can have some vengeance for Little Fawn."

Cade was struck by the painful memory of how Bold Eagle's sister had been raped by drunken soldiers and, unable to live with the shame, had later taken her own life. Captain Ballard had whitewashed everything by quickly transferring the soldiers responsible out of the territory. They had gone unpunished, and Little Fawn's people had been itching for revenge ever since.

"Let me hear it," Cade said grimly, for he, too, longed for retribution.

Bold Eagle proceeded to tell him. As Cade knew, no one at Fort Leavenworth was aware that Bold Eagle was Little Fawn's brother.

He was just another Indian scout, believed to speak scant English and understand even less. The soldiers talked about him freely, and he pretended not to hear, and that morning, he had been able to find out that Captain Ballard's fiancée would be arriving soon from France.

"But we will take her before she arrives at the fort," Bold Eagle said fiercely, black eyes flashing.

"And make her suffer as Little Fawn did? No, my friend. It is not our way."

"That is not exactly what I had in mind."

Cade raised an eyebrow. "Then what?"

"If Indians take his woman, Ballard will be tormented to think of what must be happening to her. Remember. He is proud and arrogant, and he will not like it said that his woman has been defiled, especially by the Indians he loathes and despises. Later, when we let her go, she can tell him she was not touched, but it won't matter by then. He will have suffered."

Suddenly, Cade realized he liked the idea. Bold Eagle went on to say he was sure he would be able to find out exactly when she would arrive, and, locking forearms in a symbol of unity, they agreed the abduction would take place.

Cade dug his heels into his horse's flanks, urging him into a gallop as they reached the outskirts of town. His long black hair whipped about his face in the wind, and the sun felt good on his bare back. He had no Indian blood, but his skin was tanned to a golden bronze. Hard-muscled and lean, he was as fit and strong as the mightiest of warriors.

He felt good that morning, riding with his blood brother beside him. Something told him maybe the gods were smiling at last. By some stroke of luck, perhaps the position of Indian agent was going to be his, and he could finish the job his father had started.

But now there was even more to be elated about, because he dared hope there might be some revenge for Little Fawn at last.

Then he thought about Ballard's bride, how she was going to be a victim of undeserved scorn. But a woman involved with scum like Ballard, Cade figured, was not worth his concern.

So be it.


Cade arrived on time, only to be kept waiting. Leaning back, he propped his boots on the edge of the desk and thought again about how Ballard had probably tried everything to sabotage the appointment; but Cade wasn't worried. After all, he had the personal endorsements of Generals Grant, Sherman, and Sheridan, and even if his exploits in the war as a cavalry officer were not legend, he had his own experience with the Indians. That by itself was enough to persuade anyone doubting his ability to become a federal agent.

His father, Stewart Ramsey, had been agent to the Kansa tribe on their reservation at Council Grove back in 1850. Only nine when his mother died, Cade had plenty of relatives back then who had offered to adopt him, claiming his father had to be crazy to take him to live among what they considered bloodthirsty savages. But his father was determined they stay together, and he went on to become one of the most respected agents in the territory.

Cade took to the life, making friends with the Indian boys. He became especially close to one his own age, then called Tinook, as well as Tinook's younger sister, Little Fawn. It was Cade's devotion to Little Fawn that led to his being invited by the tribal council to join in the ancient puberty rites that led to his being named a brave.

One day, when Cade was nearly twelve, a deadly rattlesnake was about to strike Little Fawn, but Cade pushed her aside and took the bite himself. It was spring, and the snake's venom was plentiful and strong, and he hovered near death for several days.

The council, impressed by his courage, issued the challenge for him to join the vision quest with Tinook. Cade, with his father's blessing, accepted.

For ten days the two boys endured a period of isolation and self-denial in the wilderness. They ate special mushrooms and dreamed of conversations with mysterious spirits known as *wakans*. Then, on the last night, the two slashed their forearms and allowed their blood to flow in a symbol of eternal brotherhood.

When they had returned to the reservation, Stewart Ramsey had stood proudly beside the chieftains for the ceremony of manhood. Tinook was given the name Bold Eagle, for he had envisioned the mighty raptor repeatedly during his hallucinations. When Tinook described how Cade had danced about while in his own trance, long black hair flying about him in the wind, the chieftains decided Cade would be called Wild Spirit, and thus he had become a member of the Kansa tribe.

The years on the reservation had passed all too quickly. Life was good, except when Cade fell in love with Little Fawn. As beautiful as a rainbow after a fresh summer rain, she had only to look at him with her soft brown eyes and his heart was hers to command. But she had been promised to another, and Cade was not about to challenge the ways of his adopted people. He could only suffer in silence, although Bold Eagle sensed how he felt.

When the War between the States exploded, Cade, along with many of his Kansa friends, joined the Union army. Assigned to the cavalry, Cade was separated from Bold Eagle, but the two reunited briefly at the funeral of Cade's father during the last year of the war.

When the fighting was done, Cade felt he had no home to return to and volunteered to join the troops chasing after Confederate General Joseph Shelby and his force of about a thousand soldiers, all of whom fled to Mexico in the waning days of the war. The Rebels had hopes of forming a foreign legion, but Emperor Maximilian had turned them down, instead providing a large tract of land near Vera Cruz and an invitation to settle there. Many did, and Cade joined them, but when word finally reached him about Little Fawn's death, he hurried back with heavy heart to find out what had happened.

It was a tragic story. And when Bold Eagle finished telling it, Cade had been so enraged he'd driven his fist into a nearby tree so hard that bones had cracked.

Little Fawn, recently married, had been gathering wildflowers when a band of drunken soldiers came along. There was no one around to hear her screams, as she had wandered too far from the reservation. When she was found, after being brutally raped over and over, the tribal council angrily went to the army and demanded justice.

But there was none to be had, for the investigating officer had said there was no proof, no witnesses, and no way to identify those responsible. The case had been treated like dirt swept under a rug and forgotten.

Feeling herself shamed and disgraced before her people, as well as her new husband, Little Fawn killed herself with a knife to her heart. And a few days later, her husband, Running Deer, did the same.

Cade would never forget her, nor would he forget that the investigating officer had been none other than Jarman Ballard. In the war, though they had fought on the same side, there had been some unpleasant encounters between them, and Cade considered Jarman his archenemy.

The door opened, and before Cade had time to spin around, a familiar voice barked, "Get your feet off the desk, Ramsey."

Jarman Ballard crossed the room to stand behind the desk. Plucking one finger at a time, he removed his white gloves, grinning cockily all the while.

Cade moved his feet but did not stand as he would have respectfully done for another officer. "I was told the post commander wanted to see me," he said dryly. "Surely the army hasn't become so desperate they would give you the job."

Jarman informed him snappishly, "I won't tolerate your insubordination, Ramsey, and for your information I am in charge here for the time being. General Schofield is the new department commander, but headquarters has been moved temporarily to St. Louis to make room here for the Seventh Cavalry coming in from the plains to winter. Meanwhile, I am doing the routine paperwork, which includes your request for a federal appointment as Indian agent."

Cade watched, silent and expressionless, as Jarman sat down and began to leaf through a file. If the conniving bastard had found a way to sabotage the appointment, he would just take his request to a higher authority, but he'd be damned if he would grovel.

As he waited, Cade thought how Jarman was actually too pretty to be a man, with blond, curly hair, brown eyes fringed with long, thick lashes, and delicate lines to his face. Cade figured God had been working on a woman when he'd made Ballard, then changed his mind but was too lazy to do as good a job on a man as he should have.

"So you want to live among the savages. How fitting. I remember seeing you in battle, screaming like a banshee, charging right in to kill the enemy bare-handed. Some called you courageous, but I knew what you were—a savage, like the redskins. I heard how you were raised by them, which makes you no better, so I suppose it's natural you want to be with them."

"It's better than living among cowards."

Jarman gritted his teeth. "I am not going to debate the need for officers to remain behind the lines, how a dead officer can cause the deaths of an entire regiment by virtue of there being no one to command them."

"Remaining behind the lines to direct a battle is different from turning tail and running when you're caught in the middle of one, Ballard. And those who would challenge your leadership abilities are dead, unfortunately. Now get to the point of why I'm here," he concluded with a sharp nod.

Jarman wanted to hit him but instead declared, "You got the appointment, but I want you to know I tried to stop it."

"I'm sure you did."

"I don't like you, Ramsey. I wish I'd had you hanged when I had the chance."

Cade's lips twitched in a humorless smile. "You didn't have the chance, and you know it. Now are you going to give me the details, or do I have to go to St. Louis and talk to Schofield in person?"

Jarman was not about to let that happen and proceeded to taunt, "Oh, I'm glad to inform you it's not the assignment you planned on getting, because you won't be lazing about a reservation. You're going to be out in the wilderness, trying to run down those who break the law where the Indian is concerned. Maybe you'll get killed doing it. I'd certainly be pleased to hear you did."

Cade allowed him to enjoy his gloating, not about to tell him he didn't care where he was sent, just so he could do some good for the Indians. And he was also thinking how glad he was Bold Eagle had come up with a scheme to make Ballard squirm for a while.

"Tell me, Ramsey," Jarman prodded with a sneer. "Why does anyone want a job that only pays fifteen hundred a year? That's certainly small compensation for having to deal with people who live like animals, or trying to track down the traders out to cheat them or sell them whiskey. Maybe there are secret benefits to the job. Maybe you're thinking about how much money there is to be made by selling government goods that rightfully belong to the Indians. I've heard there are lots of crooked agents, and maybe that's why your father liked his job—"

In a movement so quick that Jarman never saw it coming, Cade leaned across the desk to grab him by his throat with one hand and lift him up and out of the chair. "My father was one of the most respected agents in Nebraska territory, and you know it. You're only trying to get my dander up, and doing a damn good job of it, so if you want to keep that scalp and those pretty golden curls of yours, back off. Understand?"

Jarman's eyes had grown so wide, he could feel the skin begin to tear at the corners. Struggling to swallow, he nodded vigorously. Cade released him. Jarman, gasping, clutched his throat and doubled over coughing.

Cade walked out and did not look back.

Bold Eagle was waiting a short distance outside the fort. They had agreed when Bold Eagle became an army scout that it would be best if no one knew of their friendship. By pretending to speak only a few words of English, Bold Eagle was looked upon as just a stupid, harmless Indian. He was then able to listen for news concerning his people, and that was how he had learned how carelessly the investigation of Little Fawn's brutal attack had been handled. The army had not been aware that he was her brother.

Cade and Bold Eagle were even gladder they had decided upon the ruse after learning that Ballard had been assigned to Fort Leavenworth. It would not do for him to know they were in cahoots.

"Did you get the assignment?" Bold Eagle wanted to know at once.

Cade shared the news, adding, "I think I'll like running down the bastards who prey on Indians. I remember my father saying he'd like to get his hands on a few of them. I'll get the opportunity."

"So it is settled, and now we can make our plans to give Little Fawn's spirit some peace, even if we cannot avenge her death in the way we would like."

"But we can't let anything happen to the woman," Cade reminded him.

Bold Eagle nodded grimly. "You think the younger braves will be tempted."

"Exactly. Unless she's ugly enough to scare the horns off a billy goat."

"You will have to be the one to guard her, then. I cannot be absent from the fort for very long, especially when I'll be asked to lead patrols into Indian country to search for her. But what if she remembers what you look like and later describes you?" Bold Eagle frowned at such a dangerous possibility. "Indians do not have blue eyes. When Ballard realizes it was done for revenge, as he will eventually, he will remember Little Fawn was a Kansa and that you are a friend of her people."

"I'll put on war paint. As for my eyes, let her think me a half-breed."

"And *your* hair?" Bold Eagle looked at Cade's shoulder-length tresses, black as the crow's wing.

"I'll braid it. With my face painted, she'll never identify me if we happen to meet one day, which I doubt will ever happen. Do you think you will have any trouble finding out exactly when she'll be arriving?"

"No. All I have to do is keep my eyes and ears open, as well as sneak into Ballard's room to read his mail. Her name is Celeste de Manca, by the way."

"Well, I don't relish the thought of spending all that time with any woman who'd fancy herself in love with a rat like Ballard, but it will be worth it to see him squirm."

Bold Eagle teased, "Well, maybe she won't be so ugly as to scare the horns off a billy goat, and your task won't be as unpleasant as you think."

"Maybe not off a billy goat," Cade said, laughing, "but a long-horned steer, for sure. And believe me," he added, "it's going to be a miserable experience."

# 5

*Sam knew there was no other way.*

Taking Celeste's place was the only solution for both their problems. Otherwise, without money, family, or friends, Sam would be forced to run away and live as best she could. By agreeing to help Celeste, however, there was a chance for a new life, and Celeste could marry the father of her baby.

But there were many questions to be answered. First of all, Sam was concerned as to what would happen once Celeste and Jacques eloped. If the marquis found out about the ruse, he might write Jarman and tell him, which meant big trouble for Sam.

"No chance of that," Celeste had been quick to say. "We've decided we'll go to England to live. Jacques has relatives there. I don't intend to ever return to France. And my father won't care if he never hears from me again," she added bitterly. "I've only been fooling myself to think he might love me."

Sam was also uneasy to think how she would be marrying a total stranger and said as much.

But Celeste had brushed aside her anxiety. "He comes from a nice family, and no doubt he'll provide for you and take care of you. And who knows? You might even learn to love him."

Sam doubted there was even a remote possibility that would happen. "It just seems strange, that's all."

"Women do it all the time. Mail-order brides, they're called. I've read about it. Don't worry. You're going to be marvelously happy, Sam. But I will miss you terribly," she had added with a touch of sadness—but only a touch. Sam knew Celeste was so ecstatic over finding a way to marry Jacques that nothing else mattered.

The night before the scheduled departure, Celeste told Sam the details of the plan, how she was to plead sickness come morning and say she was not up to going to the pier to say good-bye. After Celeste, her father, and Francine had left, Jacques would rush Sam to the pier, where she would board the boat under the pretense of wishing a friend bon voyage and make herself scarce until after the sailing. Then she would assume Celeste's identity and take over her cabin.

Celeste, meanwhile, would have the task of saying good-bye to her father and getting him to leave in time for her to sneak ashore to run away with Jacques. Then, when the marquis returned to the house, he would find a note from Sam, explaining she could not bear to remain there without Celeste and had gone to live with a distant relative in Grenoble. He would have no reason to suspect a switch had been made.

Sam nodded in agreement, not confiding that she had no intention of leaving a note. The marquis would know why she had disappeared and think she had gone into hiding. Secretly, she was delighted to think how he would hire people to search for her and how infuriated he would be when she could not be found.

"Oh, he will be upset for a while," Celeste had said. "But so what? He'll have his women to keep him company."

They seemed to have thought of everything, but at the last moment, two things happened to disrupt the carefully thought-out plan.

The first surprise came when the marquis changed his mind about going to the pier. He walked with Celeste to the carriage, where Francine was already waiting inside, then helped her up. After a perfunctory kiss to each cheek, he had stepped back to announce, "I've decided I won't go with you to the boat after all. I'd rather say farewell here. So bon voyage, my darling, and have a happy life. I promise to try to visit you one day, and perhaps Jarman will bring you here before too long."

Celeste was not upset over the change and hid her delight as she thought how things would go much smoother. "But, Papa . . ." She pretended disappointment. "Now there's no one to see me off." She glanced about, anxious to find Sam and a way to let her know. "And where is Sam? I know she isn't feeling well, but she promised to come outside and say good-bye."

Then the second surprise came, but this one was not met with glee. Instead his words caused her to go pale. Even Francine was stunned, because, of course, she was aware of the scheme for Sam to switch places with Celeste.

"Actually, she's not really sick. That was just an excuse, because she hates farewells as much as I do. She's getting dressed. I told her I would take her shopping to lift her spirits. Now be off." He waved at the driver. "The boat leaves in an hour, and by morning you will be in Le Havre."

He blew her a kiss. The driver popped the reins and started the carriage rolling. Celeste was frantic but could do nothing except pray Jacques could do something about the mix-up and get Sam to the pier in time.

Sam, meanwhile, was straining to see out the locked terrace doors, but only the top of the carriage was visible. "Damn him," she cursed, clenching her fists as she began to storm about the room. "Damn him to hell."

She was sure the marquis had not suspected what was going on but, instead, thought she would try to run away as soon as Celeste left and had locked her in her room to prevent it. Fear and dread washed over her. Sam knew he would soon come to forcefully take what he wanted. In the past, he'd been concerned Celeste might find out, but now it did not matter who heard her screams. No one would help her, and never had she felt so helpless.

Jacques was watching from just inside the stable doors. He had saddled horses for him and Sam. The plan was for her to say a tearful good-bye to Celeste, then pretend to go back inside the château, and the moment the carriage left, she was to rush to meet him at the stables so they could follow at a safe distance.

But something was wrong. Terribly wrong.

The marquis was obviously not going to the pier, and Sam was nowhere around. He chewed his lower lip, staring thoughtfully after the carriage as it turned out of the drive and into the main road that led to the Seine River and on to the waiting boat. There was no time to waste. He and Sam had to leave right away.

He hurried to the rear of the house, where his mother worked in the laundry. She was pressing table linens and looked up, surprised to see him, especially when she noted his distress. He said he had to find Mademoiselle Samara.

Aveline Onfroi had suspected for some time that her son was taken with the marquis's daughter but, in hopes she was wrong, had kept silent. Still, it had been a relief to learn Mademoiselle Celeste was betrothed and leaving. Now she knew true solace to realize it was actually Samara who had stolen her son's heart. Still, there could be trouble if the marquis found out, and she was quick to tell him he had to remember his place.

"Mama, you have to tell me where she is," he pleaded. "Or else go spill tea or something on the marquis to keep him occupied till I can get her out of here. You'll understand everything later, but just do it, and don't argue, please."

Aveline knew he was truly desperate. "All right," she said finally, "but I hope you know what you're doing." She went to the cupboard to take down a cup and saucer. "Heaven help us if you cost us our jobs here, because we will also lose our home, and—" She turned and saw he was already on his way up the back stairs.

At the top, Jacques saw one of the maids and quickly demanded, "Lavergne, which room is Samara's?"

Lavergne frowned. Jacques had no business being there, and she opened her mouth to tell him so.

He held up his hand and cried, "Please. No lectures. Just tell me where I can find her."

"The marquis has told all of us to stay out of that wing today. You are asking for trouble to go there."

"Damn the marquis. Now where is she?"

From the wild look in his eyes, Lavergne decided it was best not to cross him. Later, if there was trouble, she'd deny having seen him at all. She pointed. "That way. The last door on the left in the far wing."

Jacques hurried there and knocked softly but urgently, but he was instantly taken aback to hear Sam's furious response: "Go away, you devil. Leave me be. I'm warning you."

Something smashed against the door, and he jumped back. "Samara, it's me—Jacques. What's going on? We've got to leave right away or you'll miss the boat and ruin everything."

"The bastard locked me in," she was quick to tell him. "He's been after me for weeks, and he was afraid I'd run away once Celeste was gone. But never let her know. It would kill her."

"Don't worry. Besides, I'd heard the rumors about your staying away from him. Now I've got to get you out of here."

He quickly examined the door, found the outer bolt up near the top, and slid it open. She promptly fell into his arms. Then he rebolted the door to give the marquis something to ponder when he discovered she was gone. He grabbed her hand and pulled her toward the back stairs. "We have to hurry, and we have to be careful he doesn't see us from a window. We'll cut through the garden."

Lavergne pretended not to see them as they passed, telling herself the less she knew, the better.

Aveline, however, blocked their path to ask, "What are you two doing? I spilled tea on the marquis, as you asked me to, and now he's changing clothes, and he's furious with me."

Jacques kissed her cheek, again promised she would understand everything later, then stepped around her, pulling Sam behind him.

At the pier, Celeste was beside herself with worry and refused to board.

"We have to," Francine urged. "I know it's not what you want, but there's no other way now."

"Oh, just shut up. You're only thinking of yourself, because you want to go, so leave without me."

Francine wished that were possible but did not dare abandon her.

"There they are!" Celeste screamed and began jumping up and down at the sight of Sam and Jacques, their horses at full gallop, thundering toward the pier.

When he reached her, Jacques swung down from his saddle to take her in his arms. As she asked what had happened, his eyes met Sam's in silent agreement not to tell her. "It doesn't matter," he replied brusquely. "Just confusion in plans. Now let's get Sam on the boat so we can get out of here."

Celeste turned and hugged Sam, then thrust the satchel into her hands. "Take this. Tickets and money for train fare from New York, along with my dowry. Papa just gave it to me this morning. I've no idea how much it is, but I'm sure it's huge. I'm surprised he gave it to me, instead of sending it by mail, but I'm glad he did."

Celeste, of course, had no way of knowing that her father had chosen not to send her dowry ahead for fear that when Jarman realized it was much less than he had expected, he would refuse to marry her. And Antoine did not want that, for Celeste was in the way of his plans for Sam.

Sam had not thought about the dowry and asked, "But don't you need to take some of it for you and Jacques? You have nothing to start out on, do you?"

"I've a little saved," Jacques assured her.

Celeste told her, "You must take it all. Jarman will be expecting it. A custom, you know."

With Francine tugging at her, Sam started away, but Celeste reached out once more to hold her back. "Thank you. For what you're doing for me, for Jacques, and for our baby. We'll never forget you."

Sam kissed her and hurried on, lest she burst into tears. Dear Lord, she prayed fervently as she and Francine pushed their way into the crowd on deck, let this crazy scheme work to the good of everyone.

Together they moved to the railing to wave to Celeste and Jacques, but the happy couple had already disappeared from sight.

After an uneventful cruise up the Seine, Sam and Francine reached Le Havre and boarded the impressive paddle steamer *Napoleon III*. The marquis had booked a deluxe cabin, consisting of a parlor and bedroom with adjoining bathroom and toilet room, but the two young women did not spend much time in their quarters. On the first day of the voyage, Francine met a young man named Pernel Higgins, who was just as fat as she was. He was on his way to America and traveling alone, and the two quickly became inseparable, which left Sam to entertain herself. She did not mind, glad Francine was having a good time.

Brooding about her own situation, Sam dared hope the future might not be so bad after all. As Celeste had said, mail-order brides married strangers. Well, she would just set her mind to make the best of the situation. There was no need for Jarman Ballard to ever discover she was not Celeste, and Francine was already addressing her as such so they could both get used to Sam's new identity before reaching their destination.

Celeste had packed only a small bag to take with her, leaving the rest of her clothes for Sam. The gowns were exquisite, though tight across the bosom, since Sam was larger than Celeste. Some were provocative, but Sam wore them with a lace shawl. So, in the evenings, while Francine and Pernel partied in the second-class saloons, Sam explored social life among the wealthier passengers.

In the beginning, young men seeking romance looked about eagerly, wanting dances or moonlight walks on deck. But when she let it be known that she was engaged, they turned their attentions to other young women who were available. Consequently, Sam became lonely.

One night several days into the voyage, she ventured into a saloon she particularly liked. It had paneled walls of dark mahogany, and hog-skin-covered settees were positioned before round tables set in recesses of the wall. There was a long, curving bar with a mirror behind. It was early in the evening. Most first-class passengers were lingering over dessert and coffee, but Sam had left before them, wanting time to explore before all the parlors became crowded.

She slid onto a seat near the door, watching as a group of men gathered about a table in the distance to play cards. From where she sat, she was visible from the door leading to the promenade deck. A woman passed by, glanced in, froze momentarily, then marched inside and right up to her.

"Young lady, what do you think you are doing?" she admonished Sam. "Get yourself out of here right now. It is not proper."

Sam got up and followed her outside; the woman seemed quite upset, but Sam was bewildered as to what she had done wrong.

"Don't you know better than to go into the men's smoking saloon?" the woman asked at once.

Sam stiffened. "I wasn't doing anything but watching."

"They are gambling. And that is nothing for a lady to be around. You have no business being in there. Now if you haven't anything to keep you busy, you can come with me to my spiritual study group. We meet every night after dinner to pray while the heathens drink and sin and forget about God and salvation."

Innocently, Sam asked, "Do you have séances?"

The woman's chin lifted imperiously. "I beg your pardon?"

"Séances," Sam repeated. "You said it was a spiritual study group, and séances are part of spiritualism, and—"

Indignantly, the woman retorted, "Absolutely not. We study the Bible and pray. We do not resort to demonology by trying to communicate with the dead. I think you should come with me. It's obvious you have much to learn, young lady."

Sam looked at the woman's narrowed, condemning eyes, pointed nose, and pinched, disapproving lips and decided her friends were probably equally as unpleasant. She declined and hurried back to the saloon to find a place in a shadowed corner where she could watch what was going on.

She found the atmosphere exciting and would have liked to get closer to observe the card games, but she did not dare. Then, a short while later, one of the waiters noticed her and reported her presence, and an officer was dispatched to politely suggest she join the women's activities elsewhere. She did not think it was fair but knew she had no choice.

As the voyage continued, Sam felt out of place around families and couples and subsequently spent most of her time in her stateroom. She knew once the ship docked in New York, Francine and her boyfriend would part and she would have someone to talk to again. There was, however, much time before then to ponder the fate awaiting her. She was determined to be a good wife and never give Jarman Ballard cause to be sorry he had married her. Still, she could not help observing couples who seemed very much in love and wondered what it would be like to really care about someone, to have someone truly care about her. Sadly, wistfully, she doubted she would ever know.

At last the ship reached New York. Francine waited until they had disembarked before making the stunning announcement that she would not be going on to Kansas. She was clinging to Pernel's hand, her plump face aglow, eyes dancing. "We're getting married. Pernel has an uncle in New York who owns a bakery. That's why he came, to work for him. He says I can work there, too, and there's a room upstairs where we can live."

Sam was jolted. She had known the two had grown extremely close but had not stopped to consider that Francine might abandon her. "But you can't do this to me," she protested. "I don't want to travel by myself. Continue the rest of the way with me and then you can come back. I don't know a soul where I'm going."

But Francine was not to be dissuaded and suggested, "Stay here. I've told Pernel everything, how you don't really want to marry that man, and he says now that you're here, you should just forget the charade and settle down in New York. What's to stop you? You've got Celeste's dowry, so you'll have plenty of money to live on, and what difference does it make if Jarman Ballard writes the marquis and tells him Celeste never showed up? She can't ever go home again anyway, not married to Jacques and having his baby."

Sam was not about to consider it. "I gave my word, and I will keep it, even if I do have to go the rest of the way by myself."

Francine shrugged and continued to cling to Pernel, who remained silent. "Well, do as you please. That's what I'm doing."

"That's obvious," Sam said sarcastically.

"Oh, don't be that way. I've got a right to my own happiness, and just because you're crazy enough to give up yours for someone else's doesn't mean I have to do the same. Change your mind and stay. As pretty as you are, you'll meet someone and get married, and then we can all be a big happy family."

"Big" was the right word. Sam figured Pernel and Francine working in a bakery was like turning a fox loose in a henhouse. A year from now they'd be twice as fat.

"I wish you well," Sam said, meaning it, despite feeling betrayed.

"Same to you," Francine responded tonelessly.

Maybe Francine was right, Sam thought miserably as she walked away. Maybe she was crazy, but she had made a promise and would do her best to keep it.

**6**

*After spending one night* in a hotel, Sam left New York on the Union Pacific, bound for St. Louis.

So excited to be boarding a train, she was oblivious of those who glanced admiringly at her but was well aware of those who stared disapprovingly at the young woman traveling alone.

She was wearing a traveling ensemble in a new Paris fabric, tussore foulard. The tight-fitting jacket was yoked. The skirt was in the pannier style, and she wore a crinolette underneath instead of bulkier crinoline petticoats. Because it was a day dress, the hem was shorter, revealing attractive brown leather shoes trimmed with jet beads and black tassels.

The color was also new, a stunning garnet that complemented her silver hair. Her Tyrolese hat was adorned with a velvet band and cockade and a bright gold feather, which added a saucy touch.

"My own car?" she gasped as the conductor opened the door and stood back for her to enter.

"Yes, ma'am," he confirmed. "That's what your ticket calls for. It's one of our new Silver Palace cars. Big for just one person, but you'll enjoy it."

Sam made no comment. She still had Francine's tickets in her purse but saw no reason to divulge that she'd been abandoned.

He went on to say, "No doubt you'll meet some nice ladies you'll want to invite to take tea with you. It's a long way to St. Louis, and passengers will be out socializing in the saloon cars. You're traveling first class, so you can go anywhere you like."

She wondered if that included where men gathered but was not about to ask.

Sam was entranced with her quarters. No stranger to opulence, she still found it interesting to experience such luxury while traveling on rails. There were several chairs in gold-and-white brocade and a blue velvet-tufted couch. All were positioned for splendid views out the windows, which were adorned with white lace curtains. Rich hangings adorned the walls, while the ceiling was covered in hand-carved inlaid paneling. The carpet was thick and soft, a blending of gold-and-blue patterns.

"I'll have your trunk brought in," said the conductor, and he went to the opposite end of the car to pull a gold-braided cord. White velvet drapes parted to reveal two beds, with a mirrored wall behind and a skirted dressing table opposite. "Once you get settled, you should walk about and get familiar with the train. Besides the different saloons there's a library, a hairdressing salon, and a music room with an organ. And I'm sure you'll like the food in the dining car. It's equal to any gourmet restaurant in New York. Some passengers complain they gain five to ten pounds during a round trip in a month to California. Blue-winged teal, antelope steaks, roast beef, boiled ham and tongue, fresh fruit, hot rolls, we have it all."

Sam laughed and patted her stomach. "I don't think my groom-to-be would be happy if I came on board as a passenger and left as big as my trunk."

"As pretty as you are, miss, I don't think he'd mind one bit if there was more of you. Now you have a good trip, and if there's anything you need, pull that bell cord over there. My name is George, by the way."

Though tired, Sam was also hungry, and once she had unpacked her toiletries, she decided to find the dining car.

The train chugged and rattled, lurching from side to side, and she had to make her way slowly and carefully, lest she fall. In high spirits and feeling adventuresome, she took it all in stride, laughing as she stumbled along.

Dinner was enjoyable, and she did not mind at all being seated at a table with strangers, two men and one woman. They all chatted amiably. When the couple finished eating and left, Sam found herself alone with a man who looked at her with the familiar light of interest in his eyes.

"So you're on your way to be married," remarked the man, who had introduced himself as Clayton Downing.

"Yes, my husband-to-be is an officer at Fort Leavenworth."

"And you're traveling alone?" He raised an eyebrow. "I find that surprising. Most young ladies, particularly going such a long way, have companions."

Sam had not said she was alone. She had merely introduced herself and said she was going to meet her fiancé. Now, feeling uncomfortable, she decided to lie. "No. I have a companion. She wasn't hungry and went to bed early."

"I see. Well, it's a pity you won't be going all the way to California. We need more beautiful women like you out there. And I would be delighted to show you around. You would love San Francisco."

Sam could not help thinking how she would probably also enjoy having him escort her, because he was not an unattractive man.

"Frankly, I wouldn't want to settle in Kansas."

Sam felt a little stab of apprehension. "Why not?"

"It's rough country. Indians. Outlaws. Cowboys raising Cain after pushing cattle to railheads. It's a wild and woolly place."

Sam was concerned only about the danger of Indians, for she'd heard terrible things about them. She asked whether he thought there might be an attack on the train as they traveled farther west.

"Oh, the railroad had its problems a few years ago, when the Indians got angry about tracks being built across their land, but most of that has been resolved by the government putting them on reservations. There are random attacks on settlers from time to time, but I don't think we have cause to worry. And *I* will protect you." He suddenly leaned forward to cover her hand with his. His touch made her uncomfortable.

Drawing away, she dabbed her lips with her napkin, then stood. "I must go now. Others are waiting to be seated."

Politely he rose also. "I do hope we'll have time to talk more later. I really would like to tell you about Kansas."

She responded with vague consent and hurried on her way. If he could keep his hands to himself and remember his place, perhaps they could spend time together, but now she was too tired to cope with any kind of situation. All she wanted was to curl up in bed and let the steady rocking of the train lull her to sleep. She made her way back to her car, opened the door—and promptly froze at the sight that greeted her.

Sitting on the sofa was a woman dressed in black bombazine. A veil of mourning was tossed back from her face. She was idly shuffling a deck of cards, which she promptly put away at the sight of Sam. Sam judged her to be near her own age. "Who are you and what are you doing here?" she asked at once.

"My name is Belle Cooley." The woman gave a helpless little shrug and offered an embarrassed smile. "There must be a mistake. Evidently we were given the same car, but I'm willing to make the best of it, since everything else is taken."

Somehow Sam knew she was lying. "Let me see your tickets."

"Oh, they're around here somewhere. Take my word for it. Ticket printers make mistakes sometimes. It's nothing to worry about. It won't be so bad. These fancy cars are too big for one person, anyway."

Sam went to the bell cord and gave it a yank. "We'll let the conductor straighten it out. If I'm not supposed to be here, I want to know it."

"I wish you hadn't done that." Belle sank back against the sofa in defeat. "I really think we could work something out."

"You don't have tickets, do you?" Sam sat down opposite Belle, pity starting to well. After all, the woman was in mourning, unless that, too, was a lie.

"No. Actually, I don't have any money to buy any, either. My husband died, but before he did, he made me promise to take him back east and bury him in his family's plot. So I did, but I had to spend what money he left me to do it. Now I'm broke, and I'm trying to get back home.

"I saw you get on the train in New York," she went on. "You stood out because you were by yourself. Then I saw when you got out your tickets, you had another set. So I followed alongside the train while the conductor showed you back here. I figured somebody was supposed to be with you, or I don't think you'd have had this big a place."

"And you thought you could just move in here and trick me into letting you stay?"

Belle smiled in surrender. "Well, it was worth a try. I'll just go find a bench somewhere and hope they don't kick me off at a water stop. I was hoping to at least make it to St. Louis."

"Why didn't you do that in the first place? Seems to me it would be easier to stow away in second class than trick somebody into sharing a car with you."

"People stare at me, because I'm in mourning. Besides, I thought if I had some privacy, I could make some money."

Sam was bewildered and hated to ask, but she wanted to know. "You mean you're a . . ."

"Prostitute?" Belle laughed at the notion. "No. And I don't think I'd make a very good one, either, because going to bed with a man is something I don't enjoy unless I'm in love with him, or fancy myself to be, anyway. No, dearie, I'm not a whore. I'm a gambler. And a damn good one, too."

Sam thought she was pretty. Dark, curly hair framed a heart-shaped face, but her eyes drew the most attention. Keen. Intent. Sam felt Belle could see into her mind and tell exactly what she was thinking. "So that's why you had those cards?"

Belle brought the deck out from where she had tucked it in the folds of her skirt. "That's right. You see, I play poker, and the railroads discourage it. That's why I need a private car, so I can invite people to play without the conductors finding out."

"But what if you get caught?"

"Oh, I wouldn't have large games. Two or three people, that's all. Nobody would have to know."

Sam nodded thoughtfully and recalled how fascinated she had been to watch the men playing on the ship, what little time she had managed to do so.

"Poker. Vingt-et-un," Belle went on. "Like I said, I'm good, but I'm only one of maybe three hundred cardsharps operating on the Union Pacific system alone. People like to play cards. It's a diversion on a long trip. When I save up enough money, I'm going to open up my own casino somewhere.

"And if you'll let me stay here," she rushed on to plead, "I promise not to be a bother. And you do have an extra bed." She nodded to the beds sitting side by side.

Sam bit down on her lip thoughtfully, then said, "I don't know. There could be trouble. You just said you need a private car to play in, because the railroads discourage it. I don't think I want to be involved."

"There won't be any trouble," Belle assured her, "because they won't find out about it, and if they did, they'd just ask me to stop. Besides, I'll share my winnings with you."

Sam neither needed nor wanted the money. Once she reached Leavenworth, she would have a husband to look after her, so she didn't care about the offer to share winnings. Yet another idea was taking hold. It was going to be a long trip, and she would soon become bored with whiling away the hours making idle conversation with fellow passengers. What better way to pass the time than learning to play a game she found utterly fascinating? "I don't care about the money, but we might be able to work out something else."

Belle sat up straight. "Let's hear it."

"Would you teach me to play?"

"If you want to learn, sure. Why not?" Belle studied her for a moment, then asked, "But first, tell me something about yourself, where you're headed, and why somebody as highbrow as you is traveling alone. You're obviously rich, or you wouldn't be riding in a Silver Palace car. And you'd also take me up on my offer to share my winnings. So what's going on here?"

Sam introduced herself as Celeste and repeated her story. And, without quite knowing why she did so, she admitted her coming marriage had been prearranged.

Belle listened with interest and was delighted. "So you're going all the way to Kansas City. That's perfect. I'd planned to stay there a while before heading on to Abilene, where there's lots of gambling 'cause of the cowboys coming into town after a long cattle drive, all of 'em ready to raise hell and spend money. But tell me, how come you want to learn to play poker? It doesn't make sense, not with the kind of life you're going to have."

"I don't know," Sam admitted. "I guess it's just a way to pass the time."

"Well, who knows? Sometimes prearranged marriages don't work out. Your husband might kick you out, and you'd have no way to take care of yourself. This way, you can put yourself in business like me." She held out her hand. "It's a deal. I'll teach you everything I know."

Just then, George arrived, and when Sam opened the door, he looked from her to Belle in question. Sam went to her bag and took out Francine's tickets.

"It seems my companion made a mistake and entered the wrong car. I was afraid she'd got lost and missed the train."

"And you're in mourning." He took off his hat and bowed to Belle. "My sympathies, madam."

"It's all right." She winked over his head to Sam. "I'm sure I'll find something to do on the train to take my mind off my sorrow."

Sam pressed her fingertips to her mouth to hold back a giggle. She liked this vivacious, spirited girl and suddenly knew the trip was going to be an experience she would never forget. Yet she was sadly aware that this might well be the last carefree time in her whole life.

She intended to enjoy it to the fullest.

Jarman Ballard folded the letter and returned it to the envelope. A satisfied smile touched the corners of his mouth. The marquis had, by way of an interpreter, written to inform him that Celeste was on her way. Everything was falling into place. Soon, he could thumb his nose at army life and move to Abilene to make his fortune—which was the only reason he had decided to honor the stupid pact.

He had warned his parents he would never go through with it, and his father had been angry about it when he died. Even his mother's last words were a plea for him to change his mind. Marry some girl he'd never met? The thought was absurd. Not only was she probably as ugly as spitting in church, but he didn't want to be tied down to one woman for a long, long time.

"Aren't you coming back?" the naked woman purred lazily, patting the pillow next to her. "We've got time for more. Nate is on duty till noon. You made sure of that," she added with a wicked giggle.

True, he had given her husband extra duty so she could slip into his quarters during the night, but he'd had his fill of her. Actually, he had been glad for the interruption of mail being slipped under his door. She had not been all that wonderful, and he had not wanted seconds.

"I have work to do, Selma. How about getting out of here?"

She bounded from the bed to pad across the floor and twine her arms about his neck. He could feel her breasts pressing against his skin, arousing disgust rather than desire. "I said get out of here. For heaven's sake, woman, what does it take to get rid of you?"

With a broken sob, she jumped away from him, then whirled about and began to snatch up her clothes. Tears streamed down her cheeks, but she fought to keep from breaking down completely. That would come later, when she was alone and thinking how she had foolishly thrown herself at him. Captain Ballard was known as a ladies' man, but Selma hadn't cared about that. She only knew he was gorgeous and charming, and—

"Hurry up, will you?" He placed the letter on the dresser and reached for his shirt and trousers. "That lazy husband of yours might bribe someone to take the rest of his duty and get home in time to ask questions about where you are. And the last thing I need is to get caught with somebody's wife."

Selma did not pause to button the front of her dress. Right then she didn't care how she looked. All she wanted was to get out of there as fast as possible. After snatching up her shawl, she ran from the room.

Jarman finished dressing, whistling all the while. He took one last look in the mirror, running his fingers through his golden curls. Careless. Reckless. The women liked the look.

He smiled. So what if he did have to marry in order to get his hands on the money he needed? He would make sure the barmaids he hired in his establishment were the most beautiful to be found anywhere, and part of their job—he winked at himself in the mirror—would be to keep their boss happy.

Jarman noticed one of the Indian scouts standing outside the building, near the window to his room. Had he heard anything? Probably not. Most of them knew only enough English to get by. Still, he didn't want him around.

"Get out of here, damn you!" he yelled. "You've no business loitering. Go to the stables and let them put you to work shoveling dung if you've nothing else to do."

Bold Eagle shuffled away to disappear around the corner of the building. When he was sure Jarman was gone, and that no one else was watching, he crept about to enter the building. As he did every morning after Ballard left, he sneaked into his room and examined his mail to find out whether he had received a letter from France.

And Bold Eagle could not only understand English—he knew how to *read* it as well.

**7**

Any doubts Sam might have had about taking in a stranger quickly faded. Belle proved to be amiable and enjoyable company.

A talkative sort, Belle confided her escapades during the war as a spy for the Confederacy. Sam was a rapt listener but had to bite her tongue to keep from exploding with personal bitterness over the dreadful war. After all, the confiscation had led to her family's ruination. But she dared not say anything for fear of giving herself away, for why would a French girl traveling to America for the first time be so opinionated about a war that had ended four years ago?

Belle told her about how, when the guns had finally been silenced, she had married an army surgeon, who had taken her to a post in Texas to live. "But now he's dead," she said, "and I've got to find a way to support myself, which isn't easy for a woman. So I'm going to try to do it playing poker. I played a lot with the soldiers during the war and got pretty good."

Sam could sit for hours and listen to her talk, enthralled as she shuffled and dealt cards, sharing her secrets for becoming an expert player.

"Tricky shuffling and dealing is an important part of the game, but you've got to do more than be good yourself if you want to win. You've got to be able to spot other cardsharps, like the man who pretends he's just casually touching the cards while he's dealing, when all the while he's feeling for the hidden punctures he made earlier to tell him which is the high card. Then there's the one who'll sort of thumb the edge of the deck while he's shuffling, but what he's really doing is finding the aces that he's carefully trimmed to a wedge shape so he can find them and slip them on the bottom of the deck.

"Then there's what's known as a cold deck," Belle went on. "I stack a pack of cards just so, then hide them, usually under my handkerchief, then switch decks without anybody noticing. I've got it fixed, you see, to deal good enough hands to keep everyone betting and raising the stakes, but I make sure I deal myself an even better hand."

"What you're doing is cheating."

Belle smiled. "Exactly. And anybody who wins big at poker usually does. I don't believe in luck. I believe in these." She spread her hands. "You've got to have good hands, like a surgeon. My husband would've made a hell of a poker player, but he didn't think much of gambling. So I never played and got kind of rusty. But I've been practicing, and it won't take me long to get the feel back."

Sam started practicing with her, learning the false shuffle, when the cards appeared to be thoroughly mixed but really weren't. Then she perfected the false cut by neatly putting each half of the deck back in its original position. She became quite good at dealing seconds, keeping the top card in position until needed, all the while dealing from underneath the deck.

"Anybody can learn to deal from the bottom," Belle told her, "but the trick is to be able to do it while everybody is staring at your fingers. It takes a lot of nerve to do that while they're watching, believe me."

Belle described the only two hands in poker that were unbeatable —four aces, or four aces and one king. "But sometimes players want to use a fifty-three-card deck, and that gives you a joker, which is also known as a *cuter,* or an 'imperial trump.' Then that makes it possible to have five of a kind, which would beat anything anybody had."

Belle finally said she was ready for a game but said she didn't want to waste her time with penny-ante players. "I want high stakes. Of course, I'll start off with the usual one- or two-dollar limit. It takes time to build up a big pot, as it's called."

Sam gestured to her mourning garb. "It might be hard for you to get any kind of game going at all. I can't imagine anybody wanting to gamble with a grieving widow."

Belle was undaunted. "I'm hoping it will have the opposite effect by making people feel sorry for me. My story will be that it was my husband who taught me to play, and although I'm not very good at it, I'd like to try it to get my mind off my grief. It's worth a try. After all," she reminded Sam with a mischievous twinkle in her eyes, "I'm the one who always tries to draw for an inside straight, so I guess that means I'm bold enough to try anything."

And bold she was. That very night, Sam marveled at Belle's performance.

Appearing quite vulnerable and innocent, Belle had managed to gather three men to join her and proceeded to lose nearly fifty dollars on purpose. Afterward she elicited the promise from two of them to play again and give her a chance to win her money back. The third was getting off at a stop along the way.

The next night, as they entered the dining car, Belle declined to be led to a table for two. Instead, with Sam in tow, she marched right over to where a man was sitting by himself. When he politely rose as they took their seats, Sam recognized Clayton Downing. Beaming with pleasure, he greeted Sam.

"Mademoiselle de Manca, isn't it? Or may I just address you as 'Miss,' since we aren't in France?"

Belle stared from one to the other in surprise. "You two know each other?"

"And you must be the companion who retired early the first night." He raised her hand to his lips. "Clayton Downing at your service, madame. And, yes, I had the pleasure of previously sharing a table with Mademoiselle de Manca and making her acquaintance."

Belle flashed a knowing look at Sam that communicated she understood. But, quickly assessing Clayton, she decided he was not only charming, polished, and wealthy, but was also the sort who would not turn down a game. Cheerily she suggested, "Well, I think we should dispense with formalities since the trip isn't that long. You may call me Francine, and she's Celeste, and I'm pleased to meet you, Clayton." She sat down and picked up a menu.

Clayton was surprised to have propriety so easily cast aside, especially by a widow in mourning, but nonetheless he was eager to move into familiarity with Celeste. He found her devastatingly lovely and wanted nothing more than a chance to get to know her during the trip. After all, he was well aware of his own appeal to women and had the ego necessary to hope she might abort her wedding plans and continue with him to California.

"So tell me . . . *Celeste*." He spoke the name like a caress. "Are you keeping an eye out for Indians?"

"Indians?" Belle hooted.

"Yes, I was telling her she's on her way to a rather primitive country."

"And where are you going that's any better?" Belle sniffed airily. "The last time I noticed, this train was heading west, and I can't think of a single place in that direction that can be called totally civilized."

Sam was relieved that Belle was making conversation but noticed how Clayton's brow furrowed in observation and was not surprised when he inquired of Belle, "From your accent, or I should say lack of, I assume you are not French."

"Uh, no." Belle fidgeted, aware she had forgotten the ruse. "Actually, I'm Celeste's cousin. The family came over years ago, and—"

"You don't owe me an explanation. I didn't mean to be nosy. I was just wondering why you felt you knew the country, but you're mistaken. San Francisco is my destination, and I find it to be a very modern city in every sense."

"Fascinating." Belle put her elbows on the table, propped her chin on her hands. "And do you play poker out there, Clayton? My husband taught me, and I find since his death it takes my mind off my grief. We have a private car, and I had some gentlemen in for a game last night, but one of them got off the train, so we need a fourth to play tonight. Are you interested?"

Sam turned her head to look out the window, lest her amusement show. In the reflection, she could see that Clayton was also having trouble keeping a straight face. Belle might be a wonderful bluff at cards, but in everyday encounters with people, she was an open book. Clayton pretended to take the bait.

"I'd be delighted. Perhaps having men around will keep Celeste from worrying about an Indian attack."

Belle gave an unladylike snort. "If they do attack, we'll just ask them to join us. Some of them are quite good. And not just at poker. They've got a game they call *pedro*, and I heard that in Nevada, on the new transcontinental railroad, when passengers get off the train, they find Indians waiting with a deck of cards."

Belle babbled on, Clayton pretended to listen politely, and Sam allowed her mind to drift away. She was, however, very aware of how Clayton looked at her from time to time. Though she did find him attractive, she did not feel drawn to him and wondered whether it was possible to experience that kind of feeling for any man.

Reluctantly, Clayton allowed Belle to persuade him to go with her so they could find the others and start the game.

"You'll be along later to bring me luck?" he asked Sam with a dimpled smile that would have set most women's hearts to fluttering.

"I just want to have dessert," she hedged, deciding to prolong the time before being forced to endure his adoring gazes for the rest of the evening—and probably on into the wee hours of the morning, if last night's game was any indication of how long this one would last.

She was enjoying a bowl of rice pudding when a waiter led a couple and a small boy to her table. The man was much older than the woman, and Sam decided he had to be her father. Introductions proved her right.

Judge Newton Quigby, his widowed daughter, Miriam Appleby, and her five-year-old son, Tommy, were on their way from Rochester, New York, to Kansas.

Sam explained cordially that she was traveling from Europe to be married, but the judge was obviously not interested and expounded loudly enough for everyone around to hear, "Yes, we're going to make a new life for ourselves. That's why I accepted the appointment as district judge. Wide-open spaces. Yes, ma'am. That's where I want my grandson to grow up. Of course, sooner or later Miriam will find another husband, and then the boy will have a daddy."

Miriam was not in mourning. "It's been a while. My Thomas was killed in the war," she explained.

Sam's heart went out to her, for in one sweeping instant, the situation became painfully clear. Judge Quigby was out to get a husband for his daughter, which was not going to be an easy task. Though she seemed sweet and gentle, and was obviously a good mother as evidenced by how she doted on her son, Miriam Appleby was, without a doubt, the plainest woman Sam had ever seen. There was absolutely no expression in her face at all. When she smiled, which was not often, her lips merely twitched. No twinkle appeared in her lackluster eyes.

Everything about her was drab. The gray muslin dress did nothing to disguise her shapelessness, and her brown hair was pulled back from her face in a severe bun at the nape of her neck.

Sam liked her, though, and thought how if a man took time to know her, maybe he wouldn't mind how she looked. Her father, however, provoked instant dislike. He was loud and arrogant. Sam pitied those who were destined to appear before him for sentencing, for she could tell he was a man of little compassion.

"Yes, I'm looking forward to being a part of the shaping of that wild and uncivilized country," Judge Quigby said around mouthfuls of roast beef. "I plan to make my name so feared by outlaws that they'll think twice before committing a crime in my district.

"Murder, rape, robbery," he went on, stabbing at his food with the same vengeance with which he spoke. "Those should be tried by state courts, but in a wide territory, the district judge has to try them. But I'll be handling federal crimes as well, like obstruction of the mail, counterfeiting, selling whiskey to Indians." He waved his fork in the air, raising his voice even higher. "Why, if this train is robbed, I'll be the one to see the culprits hang."

Sam decided she would rather put up with Clayton's flirting. She started to rise. "Well, I wish you both a pleasant journey."

"You there." Judge Quigby turned from her to address a man sitting by himself. "Where are you headed? Maybe you'll be in my territory. Are you traveling with your wife?"

Suddenly noticing how Miriam was blinking away tears, Sam hesitated to leave. Tommy, meanwhile, was devouring mashed potatoes swimming in gravy, oblivious of anything the grownups were doing.

"I hope you'll be happy in your new home," Sam offered, not knowing exactly what to say but feeling as if she had to keep a conversation going or the pitiful girl was going to burst into tears.

Judge Quigby had moved to sit opposite the man, eager for an audience other than female. Miriam watched him for a few seconds, then turned to Sam. "You're very kind. Most people find an excuse to get away from my father much earlier."

"Oh, but I don't mind—"

Miriam's mouth twitched in another attempt to smile. She held up her hand in gentle protest. "Please. It's all right. I know how he is. I also know, as does everyone who meets him, how desperate he is to see me married again so Tommy will have a real family. It's embarrassing, but that's the way he is."

"Well, he loves you and wants to see you happy," Sam said awkwardly, attempting to lift the woman's spirits.

"I'm not going to be happy till I see my Thomas again. And I will. Soon."

Sam was startled to wonder if she were contemplating suicide but relaxed at her next words.

"I need to talk to him, so he can guide me and help me. I've been trying, but so far there's been no contact. My father says I'm crazy, and that's another reason he accepted the appointment to come way out here. He wanted to get me away from my friends, who believe in spiritualism as I do."

"I know about that," Sam began. She intended to make her see she was wasting her time, that it was all faked, but Miriam suddenly seemed to come alive.

"Tell me about it," she urged, leaning across the table and keeping her voice low so her father would not overhear. "Have you been to a séance?"

"Yes, I—"

Miriam prodded excitedly, "Were you trying to contact a loved one?"

Sam wriggled uncomfortably, wishing she'd never gotten involved in the conversation. "No, I was helping, and—"

"Oh, dear Lord." Miriam's hand flew to her throat. "*You* were the medium. Oh, I should have known. There's something about you. A kind of aura, I think. You must tell me everything. Are you a follower of Mrs. Hayden? I'm sure you've heard of her. She's the medium from this country who went to Europe to help establish the spiritualist societies there. I understand she's done a wonderful job."

Tommy, taking on a worried look to hear his mother discuss the subject that his grandfather disapproved of so vehemently, nervously took his plate and moved to sit next to Judge Quigby. Sam's heart went out to the boy. It was as though an inner switch had been thrown and Miriam Appleby had changed from docile and plain to lively and exhilarating as she launched into a diatribe in defense of her newfound religion.

"Spiritualism is spreading all over. Everyone is talking about it. I've tried to learn as much about it as I can, and after I met the Fox family, I really got involved in the movement. No doubt you've heard of them."

"No, I—"

"Well, it's been a while, but people still talk about how the Foxes moved into a house in Hydesville and discovered they could communicate with a spirit who was murdered there. Of course, curiosity seekers drove them crazy, and they had to leave, but they're in Rochester now, and Mrs. Fox gives séances. She had two for me, and although Thomas didn't actually appear to us, she said the feeling was so strong she knew he was trying to. It just may take some time, but I won't stop trying.

"But what about you?" she rushed on. "Have you been able to get through to the other side many times?"

Sam felt trapped. Obviously spiritualism was the only thing in Miriam Appleby's life, besides her son, that meant anything to her. And, Sam reasoned, if it gave her any joy in an otherwise bleak existence, she had no right to take it away from her.

Sam knew she would admonish herself later, but what difference did it make? She would probably never see Miriam again, and what was the harm in lying if it made the poor woman happy for a little while? So she recounted the story of the séance given for the Marchioness Eglantine that she had witnessed, making it sound as though she herself had been the medium.

When she had finished, Sam wondered if maybe she had done the wrong thing. Miriam was looking at her with narrowed eyes and pursed lips, and she feared any second she was going to start screaming and call her an imposter. Perhaps she had seen right through her.

Sam reached for her reticule and murmured, "Well, I'd best be getting back to my car." Maybe, she thought, she just wasn't the type to pretend to be someone she wasn't, because it was too easy to get caught up in a world of fantasy and make-believe.

Miriam had been holding her breath and suddenly let it out in a rush as she begged, "Do it for me. We have a private car. I'll make my father let me do it, and—"

"Miriam."

Sam whipped about at the same time as Miriam to see that the man Judge Quigby had been talking to had managed to get away, and now Quigby had turned his attention to their table and realized what they had been discussing. With glowering, accusing eyes, he focused upon Sam.

"Don't think you're going to get any of my daughter's money, you fake. I know all about your kind, how you prey on the bereaved like maggots on a corpse. If you ever come before my bench, I'll try to find a law that will let me hang you."

"Father, no—"

He whirled on Miriam, face red with fury and nostrils flaring. And from the way his chest was heaving, Sam wondered if he was about to have an attack.

"When are you going to give up this nonsense? Don't you know it scares men away from you? How do you expect to find a husband? A father for Tommy? Think of someone besides yourself, Miriam. Thomas is dead and buried, and nothing is ever going to change that.

Now come along. I'll not have you make a fool of yourself this way." With one last withering stare at Sam, he grabbed his daughter's arm and whisked her from the dining car, Tommy trudging along behind, head down. Even at the tender age of five, he was embarrassed that people were staring at his family.

Sam, realizing she was now the center of attention, also hurried out. Making her way through the lurching train, remembering to brace herself every few steps to keep from falling, she decided she would be glad when the trip was over, before she got in real trouble. She was allowing gambling in her room, was on the way to becoming a cardsharp herself, and now she had brought down the wrath of a federal judge by lying to make his daughter happy.

And although Sam was dreading the fate awaiting her in Fort Leavenworth, she decided she'd had enough excitement in the past few months to last a lifetime. Even if she had to pretend forevermore to be Celeste, at least there would be some normality to her existence.

Dear Lord, surely nothing else would happen before she reached her destination.

Bold Eagle wasted no time in finding Cade to tell him what he had learned from the letter he had read in Ballard's quarters.

"So now we know when his woman is to arrive. All we have to do is decide the best place to stop the train and take her off."

Cade knew that once Celeste de Manca reached Kansas City she would then take a route that ran alongside Two Mile Creek to a point known as Normoyle Junction. No doubt Ballard would be there to meet her, but he wouldn't chance going out alone—not with reports coming in that the Cheyenne had been raiding settlements along the Solomon up in the northern plains. Any time word came that there was Indian trouble anywhere, everybody got jumpy, so the abduction had to take place before the train got too close to the waiting soldiers.

After explaining his reasoning to Bold Eagle, he then made the decision. "We'll attack when the train is slowed by that slight grade that's about five miles from Normoyle Junction. There are never many cars hooked up on that route, and not many passengers, either, so we won't have any trouble finding her. And by waiting till the train is that close, we'll be assured that everyone will still be in hysterics when they arrive and pile off screaming about how a white woman was carried off by Indians."

"And when Ballard thinks of what is probably happening to his woman, he will go insane with rage." Bold Eagle nodded to himself in satisfaction. Though the plan would not avenge his sister's death, it would surely bring some appeasement to her spirit. He asked to make sure, "Can you be away for as long as it takes?"

"I don't have to start for six weeks. No one will miss me that long."

"I do not envy you your task. The woman will not like being held captive."

**8**

Sam *told Belle about the* encounter with Miriam Appleby
and how terrible she felt about it. "I shouldn't have let her think I was
actually the medium at that séance. Now she's going to be more determined than ever to communicate with her husband, and that
means swindlers are going to take her money, and that's not right."

"It's not entirely wrong, either."

Belle was sitting cross-legged on the bed, wearing only a corset and
silk stockings as she counted her latest winnings. With hair stringing
down, eyes bloodshot from too much whiskey and not enough sleep,
and a cheroot clamped between her lips, she looked nothing like a
woman in mourning.

"How can you say that?" Sam asked.

"Simple. If it gives her pleasure to spend her money trying to talk
to her dead husband, it's her business. Like the men I play poker
with. Maybe they think I'm cheating. Maybe they think I'm good.
Either way they lose money, but they keep coming back. Why? Because they think sooner or later their luck is going to change, and that
makes them feel good. It's the same with Miriam Appleby spending

her money on séances. She knows the odds are against it, but maybe, just maybe, it'll happen. She's happy, and when you look at it that way, like I said before, how can it be wrong?"

"You don't see anything wrong with cheating?"

Belle shrugged. "I think of it as skill. But that's not the point. Poker players know there's a chance they're going to lose, whether it's because somebody cheats or because fate is against them. But there's also a chance they're going to win, because maybe they're cheating, too, or luck is on their side. Whatever their reasoning, they keep on trying. That's how it is with life, dear Celeste." She grinned around the cheroot. "You lose sometimes, but you keep on trying to win, because that's how the game is played. Then one day, when you least expect it, you're dealt that final hand that nothing can beat—death. Then it's over, and all that ever really matters is how much you enjoyed playing the game. Understand?"

"Yes, but it's different with poker, because it *is* possible to win. It is *not* possible, however, to communicate with the dead, but I let Miriam Appleby think otherwise. That's wrong, and I've got to right that wrong by telling her the truth."

Sam had been dressing as they talked. It was nearly noon, and the dining car would be open. "I'm going to find her and tell her that I was just an observer at that séance and that I know for a fact it was rigged anyway."

"I think you should forget it. From what you said, she's got enough problems with that ogre of a father of hers letting the whole world know he's got an ugly duckling on his hands." Belle tucked her money next to her bosom and boasted, "I'm starting to get real big up here, but I can't think of a safer place for a widow to hide her money.

"Hey, don't forget," she added as Sam started to leave. "Part of this is yours if you want it. That was our agreement."

Sam told her again that she didn't want it. "You're going to need it more than I will. I'll have a husband to look after me, remember? And you're going to be on your own. For a while, anyway."

"Forever." Belle scowled. "I'm starting to like my freedom. Oh, I loved my husband while we were married, but, frankly, there were times I hated pretending to be something I wasn't—a dutiful wife who did nothing but clean house, cook, and be at a man's beck and call. Many a night I lay awake thinking about how much fun it was to deal cards, smoke a good cheroot, and drink liquor."

Sam did not lie awake pining to gamble and drink, but she was plagued with thoughts of how the rest of her life she would be living a lie. Not only would she pretend to be something she wasn't—she was going to have to pretend to be *someone* she wasn't.

Reaching the dining car, Sam saw that Judge Quigby and his grandson were there, but not Miriam. And since he was sitting at a table with another couple, Sam knew he was not expecting his daughter to join him.

Clayton Downing was also there, eating with one of the men who had been gambling in her car earlier, so Sam left, even though she was hungry. She did not want to join them and feared they would ask her to, since there was an empty chair at their table.

She had not really expected to find Miriam, thinking she had just decided not to have lunch, so it came as a surprise to see her in the ladies' sewing lounge, talking to an elderly woman. They were sitting in a corner by themselves, partially concealed by potted plants.

"It's true," Sam heard Miriam proclaim excitedly. "A real medium is on this train. She's from Europe, and she told me how she communicated with a man who had been murdered, and how he put his poor wife's mind at ease over the motive for his death. Oh, how wonderful it must be to have a gift that brings so much joy to people's lives."

"Well, maybe," came the woman's skeptical response. "If you believe in that sort of thing."

"And you don't?"

"Oh, I believe it's possible, but there are so many fakes, my dear. One has to be careful, or they're throwing money away."

"Well, I don't care about that," Miriam replied defensively. "As long as I believe in my heart Thomas speaks to me, let it be a fake. Just don't let me know it."

Sam saw the expression on the woman's face as she looked at Miriam first with shock that she could say such a thing, then with compassion as she realized Miriam was quite sincere.

"You loved him a great deal, didn't you, dear?" she asked almost reverently.

Miriam's voice cracked as she shared her feelings. "Yes, I did. He was my life. My best friend, really. And if it weren't for my little boy, I don't know what I would do. Thomas was the only man who ever made me feel pretty. And I'm glad I met that medium. She's given me hope one day I can reach him on the other side."

Sam felt her resolve waning. How could she admit she had lied after hearing all this? But it was not over yet, for Miriam was not through pouring out her heart to a total stranger.

"I know I shouldn't be telling you all this. You don't even know me, but it's nice to have someone to talk to besides my father. All he cares about is finding a husband for me, to take me off his hands," she confided bitterly.

"Oh, I'm sure he has your best interests at heart, my dear," the woman interjected politely.

"It doesn't matter. All I want to do is talk to Thomas and find out what he'd have me do with my life. If I see that medium again, I'll find a way, somehow, to get her to do a séance for me."

The woman clapped her hands in anticipation. "You must find me so I can be there, too. I've always wondered about that sort of thing."

*And you can keep on wondering,* Sam vowed silently, *because neither one of you is going to see me before this train reaches Kansas City if I can help it.*

She hurried out, silencing her guilty conscience with the knowledge that she'd brought a little happiness to Miriam Appleby's life, and no harm was done. But that was it. She was not about to conduct a séance. After all, there was enough pretense in her life as it was.

So for the remainder of the trip, Sam managed to avoid Miriam. She took her meals late, when the dining car was nearly empty, and she stayed away from the public accommodations, spending her time in her own car, practicing dealing and shuffling cards.

Finally the conductor announced they would be arriving in Kansas City soon. The journey was almost over.

Bags packed and ready, Sam and Belle sat at the window, watching the last few miles speed by.

"Are you sure you won't take some of my winnings?" Belle asked. "Like I said, I'll be glad to share."

Sam shook her head.

Belle sighed. "Well, have it your way. I offered. And I want you to know I appreciate your taking me in like you did. If you ever get to Abilene, look me up. Just ask for Belle Cooley." She winked. "I'm planning on getting my name known in that town real fast."

With an indulgent smile, Sam agreed, "I'm sure you will."

"And if you ever need a job, you've got one."

"Dealing?" Sam laughed. "You can't be serious."

"I sure as hell am. You're a natural if I ever saw one. You've got real good hands. Keep practicing, and one day you'll be as good as I am."

Sam was flattered but did not share Belle's enthusiasm. Besides, she thought dolefully, what difference did it make? She had no say in her future.

They said good-byes, with Belle heading into town to find a place to stay for a few days. Sam decided to take a walk around during the time between trains. It was early morning, and there was not much activity on the streets, but she enjoyed looking in the windows of the stores near the terminal.

Finally, upon her return to the depot, Sam was startled to see Miriam and her father boarding the train for Normoyle Junction. There were not many cars hooked up behind the engine, only two for passengers and a caboose, and Sam knew she had to think of something fast or chance an encounter she did not want.

"What's wrong, miss?" The conductor had noticed her reluctance to get on board. He glanced at the ticket she was holding and said, "Oh, I see. You've had a Silver Palace car since you left New York, and now it's disappointing to ride a bench car. Well, the ride isn't so long. We'll be there by late afternoon.

"Wait a minute," he said sharply, suddenly. "Are you Miss de Manca?"

Sam nodded uneasily. She was still uncomfortable with the deceit.

"We got a telegram asking about you. I'm supposed to tell the station agent you're on board, so he can send confirmation to Normoyle Junction that you're on your way."

Sam allowed him to help her step up to the car, but she did not continue on inside. Instead she waited until he headed for the terminal to see the agent, then got off and hurried back to the caboose.

She was not about to be in such close quarters with Miriam, not even for a short time, knowing the woman would seize the opportunity to ask more questions. Probably she would not even care how angry it made her father, with time so short for talking. And obviously they were going to the same place. What if Miriam tried to get her to do a séance at the fort? That would never do and would, no doubt, get her off to a bad start with Jarman. He probably scoffed at spiritualism like so many others and would not approve of his bride being involved.

Hoisting herself up, she met the surprised face of a man seated at a desk just inside.

"You can't come in here, ma'am," he protested. "Employees only. You have to go to the next car."

Sam sat down on a nearby bench. "I'll be fine here. You just go on with what you were doing."

"But . . . but you can't," he protested. "It's not . . ."

His voice was drowned out by the train's sharp whistle, signaling the train was leaving. Sam felt the first lurch forward. Now all she had to worry about was getting off without Miriam seeing her, which might prove difficult. But surely Jarman would whisk her away, wanting a private moment between them.

"Miss, you gotta get off now."

The train began to move. "Too late," she said with a saucy smile, wrinkling her nose at him coquettishly.

He looked her up and down. Obviously she had money and class, because the frosty blue linen duster she was wearing was about as stylish and expensive as any he'd ever seen. And he'd seen them all. That was one of the things Purdue Jamison liked about his job, seeing all the fine-looking women who got on and off the trains. This one had pretty hair, too. The color of a shiny bar of silver he'd seen once. And strange eyes, too. Like a cat's. Gold one minute. Green the next.

"You got a funny accent," he said. "You a foreigner?"

"Actually, I was born . . ." She fell silent, chiding herself for nearly falling out of her role. She had been about to explain how she was an American by virtue of having been born in Virginia but had lived in France for the past ten years. How stupid of her. She had to forget that Samara Labonte had ever existed. She was Celeste de Manca now and explained in a confident voice, "Yes. I am French. I was born in Paris."

"Well, you speak good English," he said begrudgingly, "except for the funny accent."

She made no comment but turned her back and pretended to focus on the passing scenery, hoping he would take the hint that she did not want to talk. And he did, finally returning to his paperwork; but he still glanced at her every so often.

Sam was exhausted, because she had not been to bed. Belle had had one last game going till near dawn, then the two of them had talked until it was time to leave the train. Now the steady rocking was making her sleepy, and soon her head nodded to her chest and she drifted off.

The clerk wondered how anybody could sleep, the way the caboose bumped and careened around curves; but eventually he forgot about her presence as he became more and more absorbed in his work.

The afternoon wore on. Sam slid farther down, until her head was resting on the arm of the bench. She tucked her feet beneath her and slept on.

Finally the train began to slow. The clerk pulled his watch from his pocket. An hour late starting up the grade. Not bad, he thought absently. The last time he had been on this run, they were almost two hours behind schedule. He stood up and stretched, work completed. Now he could enjoy the rest of the ride, which would not take much longer.

Walking to the rear of the car, he braced himself against tipping forward as the engine chugged upward. The incline was a rare diversion from the flatland and would be the last seen for a while. The track was laid in the bottom of a culvert, with steep banks on each side. There was nothing to see but brush and scrub and rocks, but he always enjoyed the view from the top, and—

With a blood-chilling shriek and a loud thud, the first Indian landed on top of the car. The clerk stared up at the ceiling in wonder and muttered, "What the hell . . ."

Another thud. Purdue managed to come out of his bewildered stupor, and he started for the gun rack on the wall toward the front of the caboose.

From the top of the other two cars, as well as the engine, the Indians were scrambling on board. Screams from passengers competed with cries from the attackers as bedlam exploded all around.

Sam awoke with a start, groggily fighting to grasp what was happening. She saw the clerk lunging for a weapon at the same instant someone came swinging feet first through the window and was jolted to realize it could only be an Indian. He was big and bare-chested, his skin a blending of red and brown. She was terrified of his face, macabre with garish streaks of paint.

Holding up her hands to fend him off as he approached, she cried, "Don't touch me. Get away from me."

The clerk had retreated to cower beneath his desk, hoping that since the savage had focused his attention on the woman, he would be forgotten. So what if some people called him a coward for not making an attempt to grab a gun and try to save her? He had not lived thirty-three years to get himself killed for a stranger, by thunder.

As Sam sat frozen in horror, wondering what was going to happen next, another Indian entered from the rear platform. He spoke in strange guttural tones, and the other responded in the weird language. One of them pointed to her bag, then snatched it up to rummage through it. She didn't care and actually felt a small flutter of hope that maybe all they had in mind was stealing.

Just then, with a squeal of protest, the train came to an abrupt halt as a knife was held to the engineer's throat.

Bold Eagle wore more war paint than the others. He could not take a chance on the woman perhaps one day recognizing him should she see him at the fort. With his face a mask of white, he swept through the first car. After seeing the only occupants were men, he hurried to the next and cursed to discover the women were all too old to be Ballard's, except for one with a small boy clinging to her, and he knew she couldn't be the one, either.

He leaped angrily to the ground to whirl about in frustration. One of the braves had fought in the war and knew how to listen to the singing on the wires, so they knew Captain Ballard had sent a message asking to be notified that his bride was on board and had heard the reply of confirmation. But where was she? he fumed.

Then he saw that something was going on in the last car, the one where passengers never rode. Two of his people were struggling with someone, and as he hurried to investigate, he was both stunned and amused to realize it was a woman, and she was giving them a good fight.

"Take your dirty hands off me, you bastards!" Sam shrieked, fear having quickly turned to rage when they jerked her from the bench, intending to drag her out. "So help me, I'll kill you both."

One of them, called Red Wolf, grimaced as Sam hammered away at his shin with the sharp toe of her shoe. He was holding one of her arms, while his comrade, Dog Eyes, was trying to stay out of the way of her slashing nails. They had been told not to hurt her, but when she finally succeeded in clawing his cheek, Dog Eyes raised his hand to slap her. He would not tolerate being hit by a woman, and a *white* woman at that.

"Do not hit her," Bold Eagle commanded in their language as he swung up into the caboose. With one quick movement he grabbed Sam and spun her about, pinning her arms behind her. She continued to struggle, kicking out, swinging her head from side to side. But she was held fast. Bold Eagle sneered, "Some warriors you are, when you cannot even restrain a woman."

Dog Eyes defended them. "She surprised us. We have never known a woman to fight."

"Or curse," Red Wolf added.

Sam was unleashing every profanity she had ever heard in the catacombs and gutters of Paris. She was not about to cower before them and would fight to her last breath. Her purse had fallen to the floor, and the envelope containing her ticket stubs had fallen out.

Red Wolf bent to retrieve them. Bold Eagle took them from him and nodded when he saw the name on the envelope. "She is the one we want," he said triumphantly. "Now we must hurry. Grab her legs and help me get her out of here. And take her bag."

Dog Eyes and Red Wolf exchanged uneasy glances. They did not want to touch the she-demon, not when they were not allowed to do what they wanted, which was to give her a few hard blows to teach her a lesson. But, knowing Bold Eagle would tell the others they had behaved like women themselves, they moved together, each grabbing one of Sam's ankles.

And that was how they left the train—three Indians carrying one furiously shrieking woman, who bucked and fought with all her might.

The other passengers had crowded to the windows to watch in fascinated horror as Sam was taken away. The nightmare, at least for them, appeared to be over.

Seven Indians had managed to stop the train and abduct a woman without a single shot being fired, and while they felt obligatory sympathy for the unknown woman, the other passengers exchanged loud sighs of relief that they had been spared.

"Is anybody hurt?" The clerk in the caboose had finally crawled out from under the desk, armed himself, and entered the car to assess the damage.

Judge Quigby, recovering to assume an authoritative air, spoke for them all. "No. The ones who came through here didn't touch anyone. Evidently they were looking specifically for the woman they took."

The clerk hurried on through to check the passengers in the next car.

"Who was she?" someone asked.

Quigby replied that he did not know her name. "But I remember seeing her on the train to Kansas City."

Miriam, still clutching her frightened son to her bosom, knew it was the young woman she had spoken with, the medium. She had wanted so desperately to get to know her better, to try to persuade her to conduct a séance and bring Thomas to speak from the other side, but she had not seen her again after that one encounter.

Now it was too late. No one would probably ever see the poor soul again, and Miriam bowed her head and wept for her.

# 9

*Once out of sight of the* train, the other Indians rode away. Bold Eagle felt the fewer involved from then on, the better. He told Dog Eyes and Red Wolf where to take the woman, reminding them sternly, "She is not to be harmed."

They looked at their captive. She had been placed, facedown, over the back of a horse. Her ankles and feet were securely tied. Part of the fancy coat she wore had been torn off to make a gag to stifle the white man's curses that poured from her mouth.

"Wild Spirit will be there by nightfall. I have to get back to the fort before I am missed." Bold Eagle rode away, leaving them to their task.

Terror was a snake, slithering and choking as it wrapped about Sam from head to toe. Dear God, what were they going to do to her? She would prefer that they go ahead and kill her then and there, rather than force her to suffer the horror of the brutal images dancing before her fear-crazed mind. She struggled and screamed against the gag in a frantic attempt to plead for mercy, but her captives ignored her.

The horse started forward, adding nausea to her misery as she was jostled and bounced about. The late afternoon sun beat down relentlessly. Sooner or later they would have to stop. She was trying desperately to stay alert, to be able to seize any chance to catch them off guard.

The Indians were riding side by side, pulling her horse along by a rope one of them held. They talked among themselves, and she wished she knew what they were saying. In terror she wondered why she was the only one they had taken off the train.

Turning her face toward the ground, Sam stared numbly at the thick buffalo grass. The upward grade where the train had been stopped was a rare part of the terrain, for the land was part of the Central Plains, with little elevation. But even though they were traveling on mostly flat surfaces, the horse's jolting was making her terribly sore. She was also thirsty and felt as though she would choke from dryness, made worse by the gag and the dust whenever they passed over barren stretches.

Finally, as dusk began to cloak the earth in a pale shroud of blue and lavender, they reached a steeply banked river. Starting downward, Sam felt herself pitching forward, but just as she was about to roll off the horse, one of her captors thought to drop back and hold her in place.

At last they reached the bottom. The same Indian who had kept her from falling lifted her off the horse and to the ground. With a knife that seemed to come from out of nowhere, he sliced through the ropes binding her, then gestured first to the river, then to his lips, indicating she should drink.

Sam did not have to be told twice. Although wobbly, she got to her feet and quickly yanked off the duster. At the water's edge, she dropped to her knees and dipped her face. She had taken only a few gulps when rough fingers dug into her hair to yank her back.

The Indian, with a frown, rubbed his stomach and pointed to the water to indicate she would get sick from drinking so much. He was the smaller of her two captors, maybe half a head taller than she was. The other one was busy tending the horses, not looking in their direction.

Courage was returning, for Sam had always been a fighter and a survivor, and she welcomed the diminishment of fear as her spirit began to come back. Confident the Indian could not understand her, she said, "You don't know it, but I'm a damn good swimmer, and if I get half a chance, I'm going to dive in that river, and once I hit that current, I'm gone. Come after me, and so help me, I'll drown you."

Red Wolf heard her voice and looked about. Dog Eyes returned his curious glance with a shrug. By silent consent they agreed to let her talk. They might not understand her, but at least she was not screaming, so there was no harm. Thinking she might be asking for food, Dog Eyes went to his horse and returned with a bag. Inside was pemmican, dried meat that had been pounded up with wild cherries, marrow, and suet. He turned to hold it out in offering at the same instant that Sam sprang toward the river.

"Get her!" Red Wolf yelled. He started after her himself, although he was a good distance away and could not reach her in time to keep her from plunging into the water.

Dropping the bag, Dog Eyes began to run; he was right behind her, but she was quick. She leaped in before he could stop her. The water was deep and had a bold current. Sam disappeared below the surface, then came up several feet away. As Dog Eyes jumped in behind her, Red Wolf realized she was being swept away and began to run along the bank. He positioned himself in front of her, then, as Sam was helplessly carried toward him, he leaped in to wait for her to be swept right into his waiting arms.

Sam thrashed and fought and tried to pull him under, but Dog Eyes arrived in time to help subdue her before they all drowned. After dragging her back to the muddied bank, he slung her down roughly while Red Wolf rushed to make sure the horses did not run away.

"She-wolf bitch," he cried hoarsely, bare chest heaving as he stood over her. "You think you, a stupid woman, can escape from strong Kansa warriors?"

Sam had no idea what he was saying but knew he was not complimenting her swimming skills.

"You haven't seen anything yet, mister," she fired back, not caring that he didn't understand her, either. It felt good to scream. "You're going to find out I'd rather die than have you touch me, and I'll fight you to the death, damn you."

Despite her raging, Dog Eyes felt a warmth spread over him as he allowed his gaze to travel up and down her writhing body. He liked the shape of her, especially the way her wet clothes were clinging to her body, outlining her every curve. Licking his lips, he longed to take his pleasure and also make her suffer as Little Fawn had when she was raped by the white soldiers. But Bold Eagle and Wild Spirit had given orders that could not be disobeyed, for they were mighty warriors, next in authority to the supreme council of the tribe. So he dared not take her as he longed to do.

His gaze went to her hair. He had never seen a woman with hair that color before. It would make a nice trophy, to be sure, but it would be a shame to scalp someone so lovely, even if he had the liberty to do so. But what was the harm, he reasoned, in taking a lock for a souvenir?

Dog Eyes whipped out his knife and dropped to straddle her between his knees. Sam thought he was getting ready to cut her throat and shrieked at the top of her lungs as she tried to claw at his eyes, but he quickly wrestled her hands behind her back to render her helpless. Pinning her with his weight as he pressed against her chest, Dog Eyes held up a long silver tress and cut it close to her scalp.

Sam continued to cry out, cursing him and all his ancestors, unleashing foul words she had not realized she even remembered as she lay powerless beneath him. Dear God, he was scalping her. She'd heard about that horror and was terrified, quaking from head to toe as a great dark hand seemed to reach out to carry her away to merciful oblivion. But she held on. She would not faint. She would remain conscious somehow, in hopes of getting her hands on that knife to turn it on him.

Red Wolf heard the commotion and came running. "Are you mad?" he yelled at Dog Eyes. "What are you doing to her? You know the orders. She is not to be harmed."

"I am not hurting her." Dog Eyes laughed and waved the lock of hair at him. "See? I have a token of her silver hair. Do you want one, too? She has plenty." He grabbed up another handful.

"You are crazy. You will get both of us in trouble with the elders, and—" Red Wolf swallowed the rest of his words as he was grabbed about his neck and flung several feet away. Dog Eyes quickly went sprawling after him. Eyes wide with fear, the two Indians sat side by side, staring up at the livid face of their warrior-brother, Wild Spirit.

Sam stopped screaming to stare up at the huge stranger who had appeared without warning. She noted at once that he was different from the other two. His head was not shaved, and he had no scalp lock. This one's hair was thick and black and hung down to his broad shoulders. In the fast-gathering twilight, Sam could not tell much about his face, especially since it was painted in stripes of different colors. But she could see that he was marvelously built, with powerful arms and chest. Though his costume was the same as the others'— breeches made of some kind of animal skin—his were tight, molded to rock-hard thighs. They were low slung on his hips, and by the dark shadow Sam could see a thin line of hair trailing downward. He was not, however, wearing the apronlike covering over his loins.

A thin, beaded band about his forehead kept his hair from falling forward as he reached down to pull her up and into his arms. Without a word or sound, he lifted her over his shoulder and turned and walked away from Dog Eyes and Red Wolf, who continued to stare mutely.

Sam came out of her stupor, silently cursing herself for being so docile. Just because he was so big and powerful and there was something about him that emanated strength and authority, she was not about to yield. Kicking her legs wildly and beating on his back with her fists, she began to yell, "Damn you for the pig you are, put me down! I'll cut your heart out, you crazy savage. Damn you, damn the whore who birthed you . . ."

Cade blinked and shook his head ever so slightly. He had known plenty of women in his life, and some of them had been from the rougher walks and could curse as well as any man. But he had assumed Ballard's fiancée would be of a cultured, refined class, a lady of dignity, and he was astonished to hear the vulgarities she was unleashing.

He felt like dumping her smack on her bottom and telling her what a little foul-mouthed bitch she was, but he knew it was best she not hear his voice any more than necessary. Preferably not at all. Even though she was a foreigner and had probably never seen an Indian before today, it would not take her long to figure out he wasn't full-blooded. So let her think him a half-breed, some kind of renegade. But he did not intend to converse with her in English, because he did not want her to go back and have too good a description to give to Ballard.

He kept on walking but became incensed when she began to claw at his back. After setting her on her feet, he swiftly twisted her arms behind her, then jerked her back against him so he could push her along in front of him.

Sam continued her raging torrent of curses. Exploding verbally was her only means of self-preservation, as she feared she was being taken away to be brutally tortured, raped, and probably murdered or left to die. By ranting and raving, she could swallow the fear.

When she began to scream in French, Cade was glad. One thing was for sure—he'd take no chances with her, and he gleefully knew Jarman Ballard was going to have his hands full when his wife got mad. What he couldn't understand, though, was why Ballard had ever picked her. Surely he had realized she had a foul vocabulary. But she wasn't ugly, and as best Cade could tell, steers and billy goats didn't have to worry about losing their horns.

He found the cave, but only because he knew exactly where it was. Hidden behind tree roots, exposed where the river had eroded during a past flood, the way was not noticeable to anyone passing by. Cade, however, knew how to wind his way through the webbed mass of growth.

Sam, her clothes snagging, hair catching on thinner appendages of roots, raged on. "What are you doing? Why are you bringing me here? I should think you'd want your friends for an audience, to witness how brave you are against a defenseless woman." She had begun to speak in English again, daring to think he might understand a few words.

He had been to the cave to take buffalo skins for them to sleep on and a few cooking utensils, and he'd left a torch burning. Finally they reached the small opening, a cavity created when another, larger tree had been uprooted and swept away, and he could do what he'd been itching to do—drop the arrogant little snit right on her butt.

Sam landed with a painful bounce and was about to spring to her feet and fight him with every shred of strength she could muster, but he had anticipated she would try something and had already snatched up the rope he'd left. He was on top of her in a flash to bind her securely once more. As he wrapped her ankles, Sam fumed.

"Good. Tie me up. That means you aren't going to take me yet. Oh, God, if I only had my hands on a gun, I'd blow that smirk off your face."

Cade kept his face turned lest she see the amusement mirrored there and realize he could understand her every word. He decided not to gag her again. Perhaps she would rage on until she got hoarse and lost her voice. No harm, anyway, for she couldn't be heard outside, and no one ever came here anyway. That was why he had chosen this location. It was branched slightly from the river, away from passing boats, eventually ending in a swampy area. Only Indians happened by from time to time, hunting or fishing.

He left her and returned to where Dog Eyes and Red Wolf waited. Cade did not mince words. "If you had hurt her, I might have killed you, Dog Eyes."

Dog Eyes was quick to tell him, "I only wanted some of her hair."

"Well, you've got it." Cade snatched up the duster Sam had abandoned. "Now get out of here, before I take *yours*." He gave the Indian's scalp lock a vicious yank, and Dog Eyes took off running, Red Wolf right behind him.

Cade did not immediately return to the cave. He wanted to give the woman time to calm down. The waxing moon had risen to cast hallowed ripples across the shadowed waters. Leaves rustled in the slight breeze. The stars seemed smaller than usual amid the celestial luminance, and myriad fireflies danced about tangled vines clinging to the trees.

Cade only minded being alone at night, for it was a special time, a time when the splendor and beauty should be shared. Perhaps that was why he had become so fond of Little Fawn, even fancied himself in love with her: because she was the only person he'd ever shared the magic with. So many nights they had lain beneath the stars to stare up into the universe and confide intimate hopes and joys and sorrows. And young though they were, Cade had dared to think of a lifetime with Little Fawn as his wife. Then, to his sadness, it had been on one of those special nights when Little Fawn had crushed his heart by opening her own to confide her love for another.

Yet even though his heart had been broken in the mystical wonder of night, Cade still drank of its sanctity and peace and, deep within, dared wonder if there would ever be another in his life with whom he would want to share his special time.

He got up and made his way back to the cave. The woman was asleep. He took the torch from its hanging place and moved closer to take a better look at her.

Long hair that reminded him of moonlight fanned out about her. She was lying on her back, and he could see her face now. Long, thick lashes that seemed to be dusted with flecks of gold brushed skin as smooth as lilies. A saucy, upturned nose. Lips full, as though kiss swollen.

Cade was spellbound. He was also surprised to admit to a stab of jealousy to think this delightful creature was promised to a despicable character like Jarman Ballard. Maybe she liked pretty men with tousled curls and petulant dispositions. And maybe Jarman, disgusting bastard that he was, liked women who were obscene in their language.

Disgusted, Cade decided the two deserved each other. He retreated to the far side of the cave to make his bed on another skin. And, after a time, he slept.

Sam opened her eyes. She had only been pretending to sleep. She had heard him returning and feared what he might have in mind. It had come as a shock, but also a relief, when all he did was stare at her, then go away.

She managed to sit up. He had tied her hands in front, thank goodness, so she was not too uncomfortable. She could make him out in the shadows, lying on his side, back to her. He had returned the torch to hang above, and in its glow she confirmed she had been right—he did have a magnificent body and was much larger than the other Indians she had seen. Again, she was puzzled as to why he seemed so different.

With knees drawn up, she began to rock slightly from side to side, scooting from the buffalo skin and moving toward him. At first all she had in mind was a closer look, wanting to know more about her enemy, but then, heart slamming into her chest, she saw the knife tucked at his waist.

Holding her breath, trying not to make a sound, she continued her approach. If she could slip the knife out without waking him, she could cut her ropes and escape. She had no idea where she was, but surely she could find help. Hide out by day, creep along at night, she knew it would be dangerous with Indians and wild animals roaming, but it was a chance. And any risk was better than merely surrendering to her fate.

Her fingers reached out. He stirred slightly, and she drew back at once. She waited. His breathing was even, and Sam chanced making another move. This time she went all the way, fingers easily grasping the knife to bring it toward her. Then she began to reverse her scooting movements, returning to her side of the den.

Feverishly, frantically, she tried to saw at the ropes, but it was awkward, so she bent to take the knife's handle in her teeth and clamped down firmly, then lifted her wrists to the blade and began to draw them back and forth.

Soon the rope was cut and Sam's hands were free. Then she went to work on her ankles. At last the bonds were severed, and she scrambled to her feet. She recalled looking out the train window the night before and seeing a full moon. If there were no clouds, she would have enough light to find a hiding place.

Hesitating and not knowing why, Sam suddenly felt the need to take one last look at the Indian to assure herself he was sound asleep. She turned—and choked on a scream. He was sitting up, his arms wrapped casually about his knees as he watched her quietly, silently, his mouth curved in amusement.

As she stared at him in panic, nerves raw and screaming, Sam suddenly recalled how she had always wondered, during the sometimes violent days and nights of her street life, whether, if occasion demanded, she could actually take a human life in defense of her own. Now she knew the answer.

Gripping the knife, Sam lunged.

**10**

*Cade rolled backward,* catching Sam's arms as she came at him. He squeezed hard, making her drop the knife and at the same time lifting his knee to her stomach to easily throw her up and over him. She landed with a grunt of pain and outraged fury. He was amazed when she did not hesitate to bounce up and come at him again. Was she crazy? As far as she knew, he was an authentic warring Indian, vicious and brutal. And no matter how angry and desperate she might be, she was no match for his strength.

With hot tears of rage blinding her, Sam cried, "You'll have to kill me, you spawn of the devil."

He wrestled her back to her bed, laid her facedown, then pressed firmly to indicate she was to stay there. When she kept on struggling, he put his foot on her back to hold her still.

"Damn you, damn you, damn you," she muttered between clenched teeth, banging her chin up and down and beating the ground with her fists. "Damn you straight to hell, you son of a whore."

Cade's lips quirked slightly. How he would love to be a fly on the wall when the newlyweds had their first fight. Jarman Ballard would probably drop dead of a heart attack when he heard how his supposedly genteel, well-bred bride could unleash profanity to make some men blush.

He found another rope and trussed her again, this time making sure she could not wander about. He had to get some sleep but knew if she weren't properly tethered, she'd come after him again.

She spat another oath, and he clamped his hand over her lips and motioned he would gag her if she didn't shut up. She understood and fell silent, not wanting the rag stuffed in her mouth again. He sat and watched her for a while, thought about offering her something to eat but knew she was too mad to care about food. Eventually, when she came to realize that no one was going to harm her, maybe she would calm down. If not, he knew the next weeks were going to be miserable.

Finally he slept, but Sam was awake much longer, emotions torn between fear and anger.

The next morning she awoke with a start, and the nightmare came flooding back as she saw the Indian. He was sitting with his back against the wall, his hands folded casually on his knees, which were drawn up to his chest. Was he smiling? She could not be sure, for it was difficult to tell because of the way his face was painted. But she did notice something odd—his eyes were *blue*.

Sam didn't know much about Indians, actually knew nothing except what she'd heard, and most of that had been on the train, but somehow she knew they didn't normally have blue eyes. She'd noticed the others had dark eyes, almost black.

And there was more to bewilder her, such as the way he didn't really appear to be hostile. This morning she could see, feel, a warmth in his piercing gaze. She noticed something else, something she'd not seen in the dim light last night. There was a scar on his chest, perhaps six inches long. No doubt he had been seriously wounded in the past.

"I wish you spoke English," she said dolefully. "Maybe I could talk you into letting me go."

His expression did not change.

"The entire army will be out looking for you, because my fiancé is a commander there. By now he knows what you've done, and they have hundreds of soldiers out searching for me."

He did not even crook a brow, which told her he wasn't trying to understand. She might as well be talking to someone unable to hear. But even the deaf tried to read lips; this brute just kept on staring, which was maddening. She decided to try again. After all, what did she have to lose? He might know a word or two.

"Let me go, and we'll forget it ever happened. I'll persuade the soldiers not to go after you."

Cade was fascinated. Not only did he find her lovely, despite being potentially dangerous if he dared turn his back, but he also admired her spirit. Most women would never have fought as she did, much less sit before their enemy and try to reason despite a language barrier.

He looked at her mesmerizing eyes and realized she strangely reminded him of a bobcat with which he'd once come face to face. It was during the war, while on a raid into Alabama. He had made his bed away from everyone else in his regiment that night, wanting to be alone. The moon was full, the night bathed in an eerie, silver glow. He was just about to fall asleep when the cat had suddenly dropped from the tree above to land only inches from his face.

At first Cade had been too stunned to move; then, as shock subsided, he'd realized it would probably be a fatal mistake to go for his gun. The creature was close enough to leap right for his throat and would no doubt do so if threatened. So he had lain there, fascinated, looking at the cat and realizing that as the beast's emotions seemed to change, so did the sheen and color of its eyes. At first the animal had been angry to encounter a human, an intruder into its world. Its lips curled back in a snarl, fangs gleaming ominously, and its eyes had seemed to glow with dark red embers. Then, evidently deciding there was no danger, a golden hue appeared, wary but not so menacing. The bobcat took a few steps back in retreat, then hesitated as their gazes continued locked for long, tense moments. Gold. Green. A wary flash of red, an eventual blending to hazel.

Cade had watched each transition of feeling, and now he found himself intrigued once again with the mirror of intense emotion—only this time he had an idea there would be no peaceful retreat.

"Why are you staring at me like that?" Sam asked, suddenly annoyed. "And why can't you untie me? If you keep me trussed like this, I'll be so stiff I can't move. And the ropes hurt, too. They're too tight, see?" She held up her hands.

Cade knew she was lying, because he had made sure the ropes did not cut into her flesh. Still, he knew he had to free her long enough to take her to tend to her personal needs. He got up and untied the end of the rope from where he'd looped it about protruding roots, then led her through the tangled passageway and into the morning sunshine. After unbinding her, he pointed to a clump of bushes about twenty feet away, then to the narrow branch before them that fingered off from the main channel of the river.

Sam took a hesitant step, afraid he would follow. Realizing he was apparently headed for his own privacy in the opposite direction, she quickly appraised the situation, heart pounding, and realized there might be a chance to escape. She rushed into the shrubs, relieved herself, then kept on going.

There was a spot just up ahead, narrow enough that she could wade across and reach a junglelike islet on the other side. Then she would be at the river and could hide among the brush until a boat passed. The current was strong, but she was sure she could stay afloat long enough to be spotted. It was risky, but she knew she had to try.

Cade had anticipated what she would do and had circled about. As she came out of the bushes, he was standing to block her path, arms folded across his chest, legs apart.

"Oh, damn you!" she exploded at the sight, and without pause turned sharply and plunged right into the water.

Cade was right behind her, lunging to catch her as she threw herself out into the stream and began to swim. They both went down, but Sam did not stop struggling. The water was not deep there, and they rolled and scraped against the rocks on the bottom. Surfacing, she gasped for air, at the same time kicking out at him, her foot slamming into his stomach to stun him momentarily. Again she started swimming, but he caught her, and she continued to thrash wildly as he managed to stand and hoist her up over his shoulder as he'd done the night before.

Hearing laughter, she lifted her head to see two Indians, a man and a woman, standing on the bank. But it was only the man who was amused, because the woman, who appeared to be near her age, was not smiling. Her expression was grim and severe as she watched them approaching.

"You were the one who said there would be no problems." Bold Eagle spoke in his own language. "And what do I find? You fighting with her in the middle of the stream. Dog Eyes told me she was a shewolf to be reckoned with, but I never thought the great warrior Wild Spirit would find himself doing battle with a mere woman."

Unsmiling, Cade walked on by to take her inside the cave and drop her unceremoniously onto the buffalo skin. With a flashing glare of warning to let her know she'd better stay right where she was, he left her.

Sam was too worried over the sudden change of events to rail after him. What did the arrival of the others mean? Dear Lord, when was she going to find out what they planned to do with her? The anger was worsened by not being able to communicate with them.

Then she thought of her purse. Obviously robbery was not among their motives, or they would have already taken it from her. Still, she grabbed it and hid it in a crevice in the dirt wall.

Back outside, Cade greeted Bold Eagle in exasperation. "I'm glad you're here. Maybe Sun Bird can make her see she's not going to be harmed."

He nodded to the girl and was not surprised to see that she was defiant as well as reluctant to bring any kind of comfort to this white woman, who was pledged to marry the man who had denied justice for those responsible for raping Little Fawn. It had been Sun Bird's brother who was married to Little Fawn, and well she knew how he had anguished over the tragedy.

Bold Eagle was also aware of Sun Bird's resentment, but he assured Wild Spirit, "She has agreed to do what she can."

"Anything to make the white demon suffer," Sun Bird said with vehemence.

Cade saw that she was carrying a bundle of clothes. He had ordered the Indians just to grab Celeste de Manca and get off the train. There was no time to get her luggage. He doubted she would like buckskin but had no choice unless she could stand wearing what she had on, without change, in the coming weeks, which he doubted. Despite her ability to hurl oaths and obscenities like a guttersnipe, it was obvious she took pride in her appearance. "Just let her know she's not going to be harmed, Sun Bird. That's very important."

Sun Bird picked her way through the maze of roots. Reaching the hollowed-out cave, she saw that the girl appeared more angry than anything else. She dropped the clothes at her feet and stood back.

"What's this?" Sam unrolled the bundle. There was a dress, which appeared to be made of some kind of animal skin. Nonetheless, it was soft and looked as though it would be comfortable. There were beads sewn across the bodice, and the artistry of the hand work was exquisite. And there were shoes, also decorated prettily with beads and fringe.

Sam raised questioning eyes. "You want me to put these on?" Then, assuming the girl was equally as uncommunicative as the others, she said defiantly, "Well, I won't. I've no intention of looking like you people." She tossed everything aside and lay back, folding her arms behind her head. She was starting to feel a bit more confident since the big Indian hadn't punished her for trying to escape, so she wasn't worried about this puny female harming her. No doubt she carried a knife, but Sam would give her a good fight if she attacked and watched her out of the corner of her eye for any sign of threat.

"You can glare at me all you want to, I'm not scared of you. Now why don't you get out of here and leave me alone? The soldiers are going to come soon, and then you'll all be sorry you ever did such a stupid thing."

Sun Bird stooped to pick up the clothes, then threw them in Sam's face.

Sam bolted upright. "I told you, dammit, I'm not wearing your clothes. I'd rather wear what I've got on, even if it is dirty. Now get out of here."

"Perhaps you like dirty clothes to go with your dirty mouth."

Sam gasped. "You speak English."

"I went to a settlement school, not that it is any of your concern. Where did *you* go to school to learn such ugly words?"

Despite her situation, Sam could not help feeling embarrassed. Normally she did not curse, and the times she had were during her street days, when it was sometimes necessary to show that she had no fear and could match anything others threw at her. She lifted her chin imperiously, not about to be chastised or intimidated by the current enemy. "I demand to know why I was abducted and why I am being held prisoner."

Sun Bird matched her arrogance and declared frostily, "It is not for you to know. But you need not be afraid. No harm will come to you if you do not make trouble. Now I have brought this for you to wear. It is clean. But if you want to wear that dirty rag"—she paused to grimace in distaste—"then so be it."

Sam looked down at her dress. Twice she had been in the river, and now it was muddy, filthy. One sleeve was nearly ripped off after the scraping on the bottom of the stream, and the skirt was torn in several places. She had to look a sight but wondered dismally what difference it made. Still, pride dictated cleanliness. "All right. I'll put it on. But why can't you at least tell me the reason I am here?"

Sun Bird merely stared at her.

"Well, what about last night?" Sam said, exasperated. "You tell me not to be scared, but one of your friends was about to scalp me."

"He was only after a piece of your hair. But do not worry. The one who guards you now will not touch you. He finds you are disgusting."

Sun Bird had been in love with Wild Spirit for as long as she could remember and knew him to have great resolve. He had said the white woman would not be touched, and she knew he would keep his word.

"That one?" Sam yelped to think of the blue-eyed Indian. Dear Lord, he was the last person she wanted around her, especially when he seemed to be able to read her mind and anticipated her every move. "I don't want to be near him. Send someone else."

Sun Bird sneered. "You have no say. Just do as you're told, and when the time is right, you will go free. On this, you have my word."

Now Sam was truly baffled. "Do as I'm told? You are the first person who has spoken to me in a language I understand, so how am I to know what's expected of me when everyone else speaks in gibberish?"

"It does not matter, because I will be coming every day to talk with you and find out if there is anything you need. I will go now and bring you food while you change."

Food. Sam's stomach growled. "I haven't eaten since yesterday."

"You were not offered anything last night?" Sun Bird saw the food bag and looked inside. The pemmican and buffalo meat Wild Spirit had taken from camp was still there. "Why did you not eat this?" She took it out.

Sam's nose wrinkled at the sight of the brown, stringy things the girl pulled out of the bag. The gooey seed concoction balled in her hand was even less appetizing.

Sun Bird threw the sack at her feet. "You will eat if you get hungry enough. And you will not be catered to. Understand." She took a step forward to point a finger in warning. "I do not like your people. I do not like you. And you would be wise to give me no trouble as you have given Wild Spirit. He is reluctant to thrash a woman. I have no such hesitation." Head high, Sun Bird walked out.

Sam made a face at her back. True, she had lived a life of gentility and luxury the past few years and no longer considered herself a street scrapper. And she had come to enjoy the good life and behaving, and being treated, like a lady. But if that girl tried anything, Sam vowed she would quickly discover she had a fight on her hands.

And so would Wild Spirit, as she had learned he was called. But at least she felt a bit better after hearing the promise of no mistreatment and eventual freedom. All she had to worry about was whether or not the girl kept her word and whether Wild Spirit went along with it.

*  *  *

Jarman paced up and down his office in angry frustration. Outside, the people who had been on the train from Kansas City when the Indians attacked were waiting to be interrogated one more time to make sure they had not overlooked some detail of the incident. But what could they say that would help the situation? Indians had attacked the train as it slowed for the grade, putting a knife to the engineer's throat to make him stop. They had harmed no one, stolen nothing—except his fiancée, damn the red-skinned devils!

And what about Celeste's traveling companion? The marquis had written that Celeste was being accompanied by her maid, but she had boarded the train in Kansas City by herself. So what had happened to the maid?

Sergeant Meese was watching him from where he stood near the door. "Sir, that man waiting out there is a judge, and he's getting real irritated. Says he's tired, and so's his daughter and his grandson. They didn't get much sleep last night, and you had them come in real early this morning."

"I know, I know." Jarman waved away his protest. "I'm just trying to figure out why Mademoiselle de Manca would be the only woman they would take off that train. It's as if she were all they were after."

"Yes, sir. It does seem that way."

Meese was uncomfortable. He had heard the talk going around and hoped it wasn't true, that the captain's fiancée had been seized as a form of revenge for the attack on that Kansa maiden and for the captain transferring the soldiers responsible out of the area to protect them and for them to avoid punishment. The Indians had been plenty mad over that, but Meese was not about to tell the captain about the gossip. Instead he related, "The judge says if you don't hurry up and see him soon, he's leaving, and there's nothing you can do about it."

Jarman went on as though he had not spoken. "They were Kansa Indians," he murmured to himself.

Meese thought he was talking to him. "Well, they had scalp locks."

"Kansa," Jarman repeated with contempt. "The scalp lock means Kansa."

"The Osage and Quapaw pluck and shave their heads, too." Meese dared hope it was coincidence. Besides, how would the Indians have known Ballard's fiancée was even on board the train? How would they have known he had one, anyway, and that she was on her way here? Rumors. Speculation. That's all it could be. "I don't think it means anything, sir."

Suddenly Jarman swung around to face him. "You know damn well it means something, Meese. I'm not a fool. I saw how my men reacted the minute they heard Indians with scalp locks had snatched my fiancée off that train. They're thinking the same thing as you—that it was the Kansa, out for revenge. They blame me for not hanging the men responsible for raping that Indian girl, but she wasn't worth the lives of good soldiers. And if they think I'll let them get away with this, they're crazy."

"Yes, sir." Meese did not know what else to say.

Jarman poked his chest. "Now spread the word that I want to question all the Indian scouts at this fort. They're bound to know something, by God, and I'll get it out of them one way or another."

# 11

"*Why won't you speak* to her, let her know you have a tongue?" Sun Bird demanded of Cade. "It has been over a week, and each time I come, she talks my ears off. She is hungry for someone to talk to."

Cade was lying on his stomach at the water's edge. Spear ready, he waited for a trout to swim by. "You know the reason. We want her to have as little as possible to tell the soldiers when we let her go."

"And when will that be?" She was irritated, because she was finding it harder and harder to resent the white girl now that she had stopped cursing and throwing her tantrums. Actually she was quite likable, and Sun Bird was starting to enjoy their daily talks, when the girl would tell her what it was like to live across the great water. But that was not how it was supposed to be. Sun Bird did not want to like any woman who could love the man who had refused to punish the devils responsible for the attack on Little Fawn.

Cade tensed. A large fish was coming toward him. He lunged and missed, water splashing his face. Crossly he replied, "I told you—

when Ballard has been torn up long enough. Bold Eagle will let us know how he's reacting when he gets back from the fort."

He wasn't about to say so, but the time to release Celeste de Manca couldn't come soon enough for him, and he had his own reasons. Being around her was making him uncomfortable. It had been a lot easier when she was acting like a shrew, but she had changed, and now he realized he found her intriguing. There were times he took her outside for fresh air when Sun Bird was busy with her chores back at the reservation. She would describe the scenery to him as though his facade of being unable to understand her language also affected his ability to see.

As he had sat and listened, he had realized he was actually seeing the world before him in a different way. He had never thought of the color of the river as a blending of different shades of sherry, from rich brown to pale amber. Nor had the sight of a hawk soaring overhead brought to mind the sweetness of the music of a violin. And never had he contemplated that each tree stood by itself, be it oak or elm or beech or chestnut—that each was an individual, living its own life. Listening to her was like reading a book of poetry, something he hadn't done since he was a boy, when his mother was alive and together they had enjoyed and savored the magic only words can create.

He heard Sun Bird's disgruntled snort at the same time he lunged for another fish and missed. "Aren't you supposed to be keeping an eye on her?" he asked irritably.

"She's walking about. She won't try to run away. She knows that except for her privacy bush the braves are everywhere watching. She says she is sick of being stared at, especially by you."

"I'm watching her, Sun Bird. Not staring."

"It would not be so bad if you would just talk to her."

"Are you starting to feel sorry for her?" he asked incredulously. "She's not being harmed, just inconvenienced. Think of Little Fawn and how she suffered."

Sun Bird flared, "I will never forget, nor will the memory of my brother's anguish leave me. And the sooner she is out of my sight, the better. Each day she asks when that will be, and I, too, would like to know the answer."

"I'm more interested in knowing why Bold Eagle hasn't been able to come back. Things must be really stirring at the fort."

"Yes. There are many patrols. We have seen them. And they came and looked around our reservation. They know Indians with scalp locks were responsible, so they blame our people."

"As we planned," Cade affirmed. "After all, it wouldn't be much revenge for Little Fawn if Ballard's woman had been taken by the Pawnees or the Caddo, now would it? And the Osage and Quapaw have no reason to want vengeance." He lunged again, this time successfully, and held up a properly speared fish to announce, "You can go tell our guest I just caught her dinner."

"Of course." Sun Bird smirked. "And no doubt you will cook it and serve it to her. The women laugh when I tell them how the great warrior Wild Spirit has become slave to the white soldier's woman."

"That doesn't bother me. They're always jealous of white women."

Sun Bird was not about to admit it, but she thought the girl was pretty. She had also noticed how Wild Spirit looked at her. His eyes would shine in a special way, and the corners of his mouth would twitch as if he were trying to keep from smiling with joy just at the nearness of her. "I am going now," she said tightly, turning away.

Cade knew he'd hurt her feelings, and he hadn't meant to. He was just having problems dealing with his own lately and didn't need her nagging. "Stay and eat with us," he offered. "You've nothing to do back at the village, have you?"

"Hmmph," Sun Bird grunted, lifting her chin, hands on her hips. "You only want me to clean the fish and cook it for you. Then I will have to do all the talking, as I have done all day. Maybe I will stay away tomorrow and leave her to you."

"At least help her gather wood." He started upstream to gut the fish.

Sam could see them talking and wondered, as always, what they were saying. The Indian girl was not as hostile as when they first met. Though still reserved, she had begun to warm a bit but still could not be persuaded to divulge further information as to why Sam was there or how much longer they planned to keep her. But Sam was daring to believe maybe she was being told the truth about no harm coming to her. Except for that first night, when the Indian had cut off a piece of her hair and she'd had the tussle with Wild Spirit, she had felt no real threat. Still, she was alert for any chance to escape. Docility and abatement of her anger was only an act meant to fool her captors into believing she had bowed to her fate.

She saw Wild Spirit stab the fish and walk upstream and thought how, despite the camouflaging paint, he was attractive in a feral sort of way. And he had to be half-white, so surely he knew a few words of English. But why didn't he ever talk to her? She found that terribly frustrating and annoying, but thank goodness Sun Bird had been dispatched to communicate with her.

Sam did not like the funny little rush she experienced as she watched Wild Spirit walk away and thought what a new emotion it was for her, this awareness of a man.

She had never behaved as the other girls, giggling and sharing fantasies over boys. Neither had she been obsessed with the idea of one day marrying a rich man. She'd been an avid reader and feasted on the school's library, devouring books by all the great writers. Accordingly, her instructors had been impressed by her intellect, especially when they were aware that she was apparently bourgeoise, merely sent to school as a companion to the daughter of a marquis. But Sam did not mind raised eyebrows and ignored the way some of the girls snubbed her as she pored over her studies. She made the most of the opportunity, knowing it was the chance of a lifetime.

So there had not been time, or reason, for her to seek romance. And, as she allowed her gaze to move over Wild Spirit's body, she told herself it was only because she had nothing else to occupy her mind for the moment, and that was why she found herself drawn to him.

His back, broad and strong, gleamed bronze in the sun. Her gaze dropped to his buttocks, firm and well shaped in the tautly stretched deerskin. His hair, though reaching almost below his shoulders, was clean and shining, and never had she seen it tangled. She found herself thinking how glad she was he didn't pluck or shave his head like the others in order to have the strange lock of hair protruding. He was much better looking this way, and—

Oh! She cursed herself for thinking such thoughts. What difference did it make what he looked like? He was still a savage.

Sun Bird came to tell her, "Wild Spirit says I am to help you gather wood to cook the fish, but you can do it yourself. I must go."

Sam could tell she was angry but had no idea why. They'd had a good day together, and Sun Bird had actually cracked a smile at a few of her stories about escapades at school. Curious as to her change in mood, she prodded, "Why can't you stay? It would be nice for you to eat with us."

Sun Bird looked from her to Wild Spirit, who was busily cleaning the fish farther upstream. No doubt he did not want the girl to see the blood, and Sun Bird was annoyed by his consideration. He certainly did not offer the same to her. "*Nice.*" Sun Bird spat the word in scornful echo. "It is not supposed to be nice. You are a prisoner. I wish you were not here. I will be glad when you are gone. So why do I care if things are nice for you? I am going. I may not come back. You have Wild Spirit. I waste enough time with you. Let him tend you like the child you are."

Bewildered, Sam watched her go. Lately she had dared think they were becoming friends, which could mean a better chance of catching her off guard, maybe stealing her horse and escaping. But something had certainly upset her.

Sam picked up wood and dumped it where Wild Spirit usually made the fire. She had given up hope that the smoke would bring the soldiers. Obviously this location had been chosen because the army would never think to search here. None of it made any sense, and as she gathered more wood, she started getting mad all over again. Why should she be kept in the wilderness, forced to dress and behave and work like a squaw? What did the Indians really want with her? And were they really going to let her go, or was she just being told that so she'd not try to escape? Maybe they were saving her for some great warrior as a kind of reward. Maybe they were even fattening her up to become a sacrifice in an ancient blood ritual.

By the time Cade came with the fish, Sam had worked herself into a foul disposition.

Cade, likewise irritated by Sun Bird's parting barbs, was in no mood for Sam's petulance. After getting the fire started, he took a stick, sharpened the end into a skewer, and speared the fish. He handed it to her with a gesture indicating she was to cook it. Then he sat down to wait. She could serve him, by God, like the great warrior she was supposed to regard him as being.

Sam stood there for a moment, holding the skewer and looking from the raw flesh to him. Bad enough to be held captive, but she'd be switched if she'd be his slave, she decided. She threw the fish at his feet. "I don't want it, so you can eat it, and you can cook it."

She turned away haughtily but had not taken even one step before he was upon her, grabbing her arms. He spun her around, then stooped to pick up the fish. Pointing to the water, indicating she should wash off the dirt, he thrust it at her. She knocked it out of his hand and stamped her foot, not caring that he stood nearly a head taller than she or that his blue eyes had turned to ice, muscles in his jaw twitching with his fury.

"I don't want your old fish, and I'm not cooking it." She threw it down again.

He stooped again to retrieve the fish, then clamped a hand on the back of her neck and half dragged her to the water. Pushing her down on her knees, he thrust it toward her.

All the emotions Sam had been suffering exploded—the terror of abduction and the horror of attack that first night, how she'd had to endure sleeping on the ground in a cave, guarded by a mute savage and hating herself for feeling even the least bit attracted to him. Suddenly, it was all too much. She caught him off guard, yanking free of his hold. After slamming her fist into his stomach, she landed a painful kick to his shin, then leaped into the water. Quickly she waded out to where it was deeper and lunged to start swimming.

Cade was right behind her, tossing the skewered fish to the bank. In only a few strokes he was right on top of her, but she continued to fight him.

"Damn you," she cried.

Holding her by her shoulders, he pushed her under to silence her cursing, then lifted her up. The water was deep enough that he was forced to tread water with his legs while keeping a firm grip on her.

Sputtering, spitting, choking, Sam took a deep breath and again yelled, "Let me go, spawn of the devil—"

He ducked her again, lifted her up.

"Filthy savage—"

Down she went.

"Damn—

Again. This time he held her a bit longer, and when she came up, she was seized with spasms of coughing. With one hand still on the back of her neck, he moved his other to her waist. Their bodies were pressed tightly together, and amid the wheezing and choking, Sam could feel his powerful thighs thrashing gently as he kept them afloat.

But she could also feel something else, something large and hard pushing against her belly. With a start, she realized what it was. Staring into his amused eyes, she knew he could sense her awareness, as well as her fear. She was still gasping, spluttering, and after the balmy warmth of the evening air, the water felt cold against her trembling skin.

Abruptly he released her, and she pushed clinging strands of hair back from her forehead with one hand as she stared at him in the fast-descending twilight.

He turned and swam back and, when he could stand, waded the rest of the way in. Sam could only follow after him. There was no escape this way. If she kept on going and tried to make it to the little island, he would come after her. Or maybe other Indians, who had witnessed what had just happened, were waiting there already and when she got there would attack her, and Wild Spirit, angry, would ignore her screams for mercy.

He was standing by the fire. His hair hung long and heavy over his face, and he caught it with one hand and pushed it back roughly.

"You could have drowned me," she accused, wanting to fight to ease the building tension.

He stared down at her in the gentle glow of the flames. She could sense his desire, kindling with her own, and felt uneasiness mounting. Never before had she experienced such strange stirrings. A tingling, low in her belly, was inching its way down to her loins. A tautness had come into her nipples, which rubbed against the wet, clinging buckskin. Dear God, what was happening to her?

Cade had no dry clothes to change into. He had bathed that morning and put on fresh breeches brought by Sun Bird, and she'd taken his others to wash and bring back later. He could only stand there, soaking wet, knowing he was hard with his desire. But what the hell? he asked himself. Let her know, see, that he wanted her. He had never apologized for being a man.

But he found himself wishing she would go and change, because the sight of her standing there with her clothes wet and clinging to her body was driving him crazy. He could make out every detail, every curve, and—

He gave his head a brisk shake, trying to dispel the maelstrom of emotions assailing him. Much more and he would lose control and take her then and there. Hell, a man could only hold back so long, and it had been a while since he'd had a woman. He wished the girl would go somewhere, anywhere out of his sight. Right then he didn't care if she escaped. He only knew she was driving him mad.

Sam raged on, taking out her frustration on him. "Even if you don't know what I'm saying, you know I'm mad enough to break your neck, damn you."

He kneaded his fingers together as though fighting to keep from wrapping them around her throat. He welcomed the anger he was starting to feel. Far better to spar with her than endure this new awareness that had sprung between them.

"What would you do for a hostage if you had drowned me? Isn't that what you're really after? Ransom money? No doubt you've sent a message to my fiancé that he will have to pay to get me back, but if you'd killed me, you'd have nothing to bargain with. How stupid you are, because I still have my dowry."

Cade did not blink an eye. He didn't give a damn how much money she was carrying. He was not a thief and would not allow any of the others to steal from her, either. She would be freed when he felt Ballard had suffered enough and not before. Only now *he* was suffering, too, in a way he'd never figured on, because he never dreamed he would desire this woman like no other.

She was standing on the other side of the ring of fire. In a stance of defiance, her hands were on her hips, her legs apart. The cat's eyes glowed with her ire, but he saw something else within the golden bronze depths. A heat, emanating from smoldering embers that caused her nostrils to flare ever so slightly and her full, sensuous lips to part the least little bit.

He could stand no more. He stepped across the fire to pull her roughly to him, and her head lolled back as she surrendered to the astonishment of the unexpected assault. His mouth crushed against hers, his tongue parting her lips to swirl inside with delicious languor, exploring, devouring.

Sam had never known such sweet ecstasy and gave an involuntary moan of delight as she found herself clinging to him. The wonder of him. The male aroma of his nearness.

With their bodies pressed tightly together, the wetness of their clothing was like a sensual skin, nerves and feelings melding from one to the other. Sam could feel the swelling once more, this time undulating slightly as he began to grind his hips against her. Unashamedly her pelvis thrust in answer, and more moans and smothered sighs escaped her.

Cade knew he'd gone too far to turn back now. Like a wild animal uncaged, he could be satiated only by the feeding of his desire, the ultimate consumption of his prey. Without taking his mouth from hers, he scooped her up and into his arms. He would take her to the cave, and there he would have his fill.

For the moment, Sam was stunned into submission, but he would stand for no resistance. Not this night. He knew ways of making a woman weak with desire, making her beg for fulfillment. And he would stop at nothing to force her hunger and, ultimately, her pleasure to match his own.

Then, like an animal scenting danger, his head came up.

Someone was coming. He set her on her feet, and she came out of her stupor, immediately ashamed for having allowed her body to betray her so easily. About to demand how he dared touch her, she froze at the sound of horses approaching.

Cade knew Kansa ponies when he heard them, just as he knew there were Indians not too far away, keeping watch should any surprise patrols happen by; so he did not fear attack.

All desire cast aside, he grabbed Sam's hand and pulled her quickly into the cave. After indicating she should stay there, he hurried back out.

Three braves were approaching, but he recognized only two of them: Red Wolf and Dog Eyes. The Indian on the horse between them rode doubled over. Cade, knowing whoever it was had to be badly hurt, ran to meet them.

Then, with white-hot rage rushing through him like a river run wild, Cade saw it was Bold Eagle.

And he had been mercilessly beaten.

# 12

*Seeing the shape Bold Eagle* was in, Cade's first reaction had been to go charging to the fort, find Ballard, and put him in the same condition. But that would only land him in the stockade and, no doubt, cost him his appointment.

Red Wolf and Dog Eyes had spotted Bold Eagle and wanted to take him to their medicine man, but he had insisted on reporting to Cade first. "Ballard is a madman," he told him. "He's having all the Indian scouts brought in to question, and he screams and rages."

"And whips them, too?" Cade bit back his rage to see the flesh on Bold Eagle's neck, bloodied and torn by the lash.

Stoically, Bold Eagle fought the pain to tell him, "I do not know. He had this done to me during the night, away from the fort, so others would not see. He knows I am Kansa and says if he can prove our people are responsible, he will kill us every one. He said he would kill me if I told anyone he did this to me."

"Do you know where they're focusing their search?"

"South. The territory."

That was where Cade had wanted them to head, which was another reason he felt secure in the hiding place he had chosen. The declared Indian territory was an immense wilderness of prairies and mountains, and though cattle drives had been cutting through since the war, and a few white squatters were pushing in from the borders, it was still a place of refuge for renegades and outlaws.

Dog Eyes suggested warily, "We should let her go. Before there is more trouble."

Red Wolf nodded in agreement. But Bold Eagle was quick to protest, "No. Not till Wild Spirit reports for his post. Ballard is angry now but has not suffered enough. By then he will be crazy with grief to think she is dead."

Dog Eyes and Red Wolf looked to Cade to take their side, knowing he could persuade Bold Eagle to change his mind. But he would not do that, even though he, too, would like to see it all end. Things just weren't going the way he had planned, damn it, because the last thing he had expected was to feel wild, gnawing desire for Jarman Ballard's fiancée.

But Cade was starting to feel something besides raw lust, and that was what really needled him and made him want to hasten the time for her to be turned over to the army. He said they should get Bold Eagle to the medicine man. "And tell Sun Bird I want her here at first light. I think it's in the line of my duty as an Indian agent to pay Ballard a visit and complain about him badgering the Indian scouts. I'll be away a few days, and I want her to stay with the woman while I'm gone."

Dog Eyes told him, "She does not have time. The women are busy making ready for winter. Many deer were killed today. A few buffalo. She must help with the tanning. And there is meat to dry."

"Then Sun Bird can just take the woman to the reservation to help out. The soldiers already searched there long ago. It's not likely they'll return, and if they do, they'll be spotted in time to get her out of sight."

"She will be able to tell them where she was."

"She won't know where she is. Besides, I like the idea of further irritating Ballard by returning his bride with her dainty little hands blistered from hard work. Now go."

He watched as they rode into the twilight, thinking how he'd never wanted Bold Eagle to get involved with the army in the first place. The army liked to capitalize on long-standing animosities between tribes by using Indians as scouts to find their enemies, and Bold Eagle had seized the chance to avenge his people. He had to formally enlist in the army but told Cade scouts never got involved in the actual fighting, though they would help cripple the enemy by stampeding their horses. The pay for a scout was thirteen dollars a month.

Cade did not go back into the cave. Instead he made a bed on the ground. And as he lay there, restlessly staring up at the velvet sky, he could not help remembering how good it had felt to hold Celeste and kiss her. If Bold Eagle's arrival had not interrupted them, nothing would have stopped him from possessing her. Hell-bent, he would have taken her, no matter how hard she fought. But one question burned: Would she have resisted? Had it been his imagination or had he actually felt her surrender? He told himself it didn't matter. It was over. He was grateful he'd been stopped in time and would make damn sure it didn't happen again.

Sleep would not come. Sam tossed and turned on the buffalo skin, cursing herself for what she was feeling. It was not supposed to be this way. She was not supposed to enjoy it when that villainous savage attacked her. She was supposed to fight and kick and scream, defending her honor to death, if need be—not melt in his arms, every nerve in her body screaming for something she had never experienced but desperately wanted.

Last night, hearing someone approaching, he had rushed her into the cave, then left and not returned since. She thought about sneaking out to see what was going on but decided she was better off where she was for the time being, because what if there had been a fight of some sort and he had been killed? The attackers might not know of her presence, and if she went out to look around, they might kill her, too. She wouldn't let herself hope it might have been soldiers who rode in, for no doubt there were Indians posted about who would have sounded an alarm. So she stayed where she was, haunted by twinges of guilt and shame to know she had yielded to him. And if he had not gone away, there would have been no turning back.

She gave herself a fierce shake. What was wrong with her, for God's sake? Being held prisoner was taking its toll. The man was uncivilized, barbarous, and no doubt she was losing her mind to let him touch her without a fight. The situation was making her crazy. How long had it been now? She had lost all sense of time and wondered miserably how long the madness would continue.

Finally she slept and was puzzled to awaken the following morning and find herself still alone. She braced herself for Wild Spirit's eventual return, for now she was sure last night's visitors had been other Indians, who probably had whiskey and had drunk themselves into a stupor. Sooner or later he would come to her, feeling heavy-headed, sick, and even though he did not understand a word she said, somehow she'd find a way to let him know she would not allow him to touch her again.

At last, she heard someone coming and was surprised to see it was Sun Bird. Sam quickly told her what had happened and asked if anything was wrong.

"You ask too many questions." Sun Bird irritably beckoned her to follow. "Come along and say nothing. I am in no mood this morning for a lot of talk."

Doggedly Sam obeyed and, once they were outside, glanced about quickly in search of Wild Spirit. But he was nowhere in sight. There were, however, two ponies waiting, and Sun Bird pointed to one and told her to mount. Sam had learned riding in school, of course, but with saddles and bridles. The pony's back was bare, and he wore only a braided harness. Hesitating, she asked, "How far is it to where we're going? I don't know how well I can ride without a saddle."

"I told you not to ask questions. Now mount or I will tie you and drag you behind me, which I will also do if you try to run away."

Sam was stunned. "Why are you being so mean to me this morning? I thought we were friends."

"You do not say what will be. *I* say. Now come." Sun Bird dug in her heels, sending her horse into full gallop.

Sam had no choice but to try to keep up. This she did, but only by leaning against the pony's neck and holding on for dear life. Her bottom bounced up and down uncomfortably, and she feared any second she would fall.

It was a ride that took over an hour, and when they finally arrived at the village, Sam found herself surrounded by a small group of women who stared at her in a blend of both interest and hostility. Sun Bird told her not to waste her time trying to talk to them. "They do not speak your language, and they do not like you, anyway."

"Well, I don't see any I'd want to invite for dinner," Sam muttered as she dismounted and began to rub at her sore buttocks.

Sun Bird was smoldering with resentment as she stared at the white girl. Dog Eyes had told her what he had seen when he had ridden into Wild Spirit's camp last night, how Wild Spirit had been carrying her in his arms. Sun Bird had screamed at him that he lied, but he had laughed and said she only wanted not to believe because she was in love with Wild Spirit, only he did not return her love.

Painfully, Sun Bird knew Dog Eyes had spoken the truth about what he had witnessed, and now she hated the soldier's woman with a vengeance. She bit out the warning, "You are going to work, and if you do not work, you will not eat."

Making her tone as pleasant as possible, Sam informed her, "I don't mind helping your people. Just tell me what you want me to do."

Sam was led to where other women were chopping and tearing apart huge animal carcasses. She swallowed hard against rolls of nausea.

"Buffalo," said Sun Bird. "Fresh kill this morning. We start the tanning, then we help with the cooking."

Some of the other women had already begun stretching the fresh skin out on the ground, hairy side down, and pegging it in place. Sam was handed a flesher, which was an adzelike blade lashed to an elk-horn handle, and told to start removing the meat and fat from the skin. "Dear Lord," she whispered, then took a deep breath and began.

The women moved on to stretch yet another skin, and she was left alone to do as she'd been told. Three hours later, her fingers sore and blistered, knees raw from being on the ground, Sam got stiffly to her feet, alternately rubbing her aching back and sore bottom.

Sun Bird appeared at her side carrying a bucket. "Knead this in to start to make it soft."

Sam stared at the bloody, foul-smelling concoction, swallowed hard, and asked, "What is that?"

"Brains. Liver. Fat. All from the buffalo. You must rub it good into the skin. It will soak till tomorrow, then you will work it in even deeper."

By the time Sam finished the first application of the tanning fluid, she was not only exhausted but sick to her stomach. "Now we eat," Sun Bird told her, leading her to where the other women had gathered for a noonday meal.

The men of the tribe were out for more hunting. A tripod was positioned over a fire, and chunks of buffalo meat had been skewered to roast above the flames. On another tripod, Sam noticed a kind of stew being cooked in some sort of pouch. Sun Bird grudgingly responded to her questions, explaining that the pouch was actually the stomach of a buffalo. Hot, fist-size stones had been dropped into the water to make it boil, then wild peas and root vegetables had been added.

Despite feeling sick, Sam made herself eat and was surprised to find the food did not taste bad at all.

Looking about, she marveled to see that none of the animal's edible parts were wasted. Even bones were broken and the marrow boiled to make fat. The entrails, cleaned and shaped into sausage cases, were stuffed with strips of meat seasoned with wild onions and sage. Buffalo meat had also been cut into thin slices and hung to dry, and Sam saw one of the women making what Sun Bird told her was pemmican. The dried strips of meat were pulverized with a stone maul, then mixed with ground and dried berries and fat. It was then stored in what Sun Bird called parfleches, where it kept for months.

Sam was given two more skins to scrape and begin tanning, and by the time the sun went down, she was too exhausted even to think about eating again. Sun Bird gave her a thin blanket and told her she could sleep in her own family's teepee.

Sam could tell by the way the women looked at her as they talked among themselves while preparing the evening meal that she was the topic of conversation. No doubt they were amused by how she had retched as she worked the skins, her eyes watering. They could see her hands were blistered and her knees bruised and swollen from kneeling all day on the ground. They probably thought she would eventually break down and cry for mercy, but she'd not give them the satisfaction.

Sam was also determined that should she ever encounter Wild Spirit again, he would quickly discover that what had happened between them that night would never happen again. Maybe she had been weak, but no more. And no matter what he, or his people, demanded of her, she would find a way somehow to endure and survive.

But while Sam could control her conscious resolve, she soon realized betrayal in her dreams, as later, when she slept, the wonder of the desires he had ignited came flooding back to tease and torment.

"What the hell do you mean by barging into my office?" Jarman Ballard leaped to his feet as Cade walked in unannounced. "If you've got a problem, take it to General Schofield in St. Louis. I don't want any dealings with you."

Cade crossed the room and sat down. Leaning back in the chair, he tipped his hat up, folded his arms across his chest, and insolently propped his boots on the edge of Ballard's desk. "Well, you're going to deal with me, whether you like it or not."

Jarman swept him with a gaze of contempt. "I don't work with Indian agents. And look at you. You're as scruffy as the savages you represent—hair down to your shoulders, dressed in buckskin. All you need is a feather war bonnet."

With a crooked smile, Cade retorted, "Well, I just might need to put one on if you keep bullying the Indian scouts like I hear you've been doing. So we can talk, or I can go to the general. It's your call, Ballard."

Jarman was seething. He knew Schofield wouldn't like the way he was treating the scouts, but the only way he'd hear about it would be through somebody like Ramsey. The few soldiers who knew about it wouldn't say anything. "Stay out of this," he warned. "It doesn't concern you."

"Everything that concerns Indians concerns me."

"And how did you find out?" Jarman asked suspiciously. "Did one of them run crying to you? I know my men haven't discussed fort business with outsiders."

"Don't worry about how I found out. Just know that I'm here to tell you it's got to stop."

"And if it doesn't?"

"I may go to Schofield, or . . ." Cade's eyes narrowed. "I stop it myself."

Jarman pointed a finger. "You say one word, and I'll drum up a reason to have you removed as an agent, Ramsey. So help me."

Cade chuckled. "If you had that kind of power, I'd never have been made one, and we both know it. So hear me, damn you. Leave the Indian scouts alone."

"You *do* know about my fiancée being abducted by a wild band of Indians, don't you?"

"I heard," Cade admitted tonelessly. "But that doesn't give you the right to bully the scouts. And if they knew anything, they wouldn't tell you."

"All those bastards know what's going on. They may have different names and belong to different tribes, but they're all alike."

Cade could not resist goading him. "Now I wonder why Indians would want to take your fiancée, Ballard. Could it be some kind of revenge? Say for a little Indian girl who was raped by white soldiers under your command? And didn't you get them transferred out of the territory real quick, so they wouldn't be punished, because you didn't think she was worth it?"

Jarman fired back, "You're damn right I did, and I'd do it again. I'm not about to see good men prosecuted over one night of drunken revelry involving Indian scum. But if those savages think they can take revenge, they'll find out they've made a big mistake. And I consider them cowards using a defenseless woman to try to do it."

Cade suppressed a laugh to think of Celeste de Manca in that light and went on to make his point. "Cowardly is avoiding an issue, Ballard, like you did when you got those soldiers out of here, and if anyone is to blame for what happened to your fiancée, it's you. So let's get something straight." He stood, bracing his hands on the desk as he leaned over to warn Ballard, "You will leave the scouts alone. I'm not going to have you taking out your frustration on them. When the Indians are done with your woman, you'll get her back, but while they've got her, think about how she's suffering the same way that young girl suffered. And maybe next time you'll do your job and see that justice is done."

Jarman shrank back in the face of Ramsey's threatening stance. Still, he wasn't too concerned: after all, Ramsey had sense enough to know he would be in big trouble if he hit his superior officer. "You always sympathize with those red-skinned devils. You always take their side."

"Not when they're wrong."

Jarman yelped incredulously, "And you don't think what they're doing now is wrong?"

"I didn't come here to debate with you, Ballard. Just leave the Indian scouts alone."

"Well, just what would you have me do? Sit here and wait for those bastards to get tired of raping her? Wait for them to torture her to death? And when I get her body back, what then? Would you approve of my going after them then? Or would you stand at the gallows and plead for mercy?"

"If they kill her, and you catch those responsible, I'd gladly put the nooses around their necks myself, but if all they want is revenge, there's a good chance she'll be released unharmed when they figure they've got it."

Ballard snorted. "That's a long shot, but not inconceivable. Maybe she's so homely and ugly that even savages won't have her, and they figure true retribution would be giving her back to me."

Cade blinked. "What the hell are you talking about? Don't you know what your own fiancée looks like?"

With a brittle laugh, Jarman admitted, "Hell, I've never even met her. The marriage was prearranged between our maternal grandfathers. I just hope they don't steal her dowry," he went on. "Since her reticule was missing from the train, that means they took it with them."

It became clear to Cade then why Ballard was getting married. But thinking how pleasantly surprised Ballard would be to discover his bride was anything but ugly inspired in Cade a strange feeling of resentment. He chided himself. After all, the motive was to bring a measure of appeasement for the injustice to Little Fawn, not get personally involved with Ballard's woman, by damn. Suddenly he felt the need to get out of there.

"Just leave the scouts alone," he warned one last time. At the door, he turned and added gruffly, "And I hope your fiancée turns up all right."

Jarman yelled after him, "You better hope she does, or you can tell all those red-skinned savages I'll see them in hell."

Cade kept on going, and those he passed on his way out of the building stepped aside. Eyes dark as thunder, lips tight-set and grim, shoulders hunched and hands clenched at his sides, he was not a man to be reckoned with.

What he had just learned from Ballard continued to needle him, because now he knew the betrothed couple were not in love, never had been, and probably never would be. But he also knew he could not let it make any difference to him. He had a job to do, and he would do it.

And to hell with how he was starting to feel inside.

# 13

*Cade decided to remain* at the fort for a few days.

Knowing he was still around, Ballard would doubtless ease up on his heavy-handed interrogations of the Indians. The woman was another reason he delayed going back, wanting time for her resentment of him to build. Not only would she be indignant over how he'd disappeared abruptly, but she would also be plenty mad over being sent to work with the Indian woman. She would blame him, hate him, and maybe then she would just give up trying to communicate. It was best they regard each other with hostility anyway, and he had already resolved not to lose control of himself again. But he did not dare tarry at the fort for long. There was always the chance a hunter or a trapper might spot a white woman among the Indians and alert the army. He needed to return her to the cave and keep her there.

Then he received an invitation to the party being given for the new district judge. He wanted to meet the new official he would soon be working with, but he also knew his presence would gall Ballard, and that by itself was enough of an inducement to attend.

After a bath and shave, and a trim to even up his long hair, Cade dressed in new buckskin breeches and a fringed jacket. With boots spit-polished, he figured he presented himself as a very civilized agent of the federal government.

The party was being held at the commanding officer's residence, which the ladies of the post had been given permission to use for such functions in Schofield's absence. Ballard was standing in the receiving line in the entrance foyer, resplendent in full dress uniform—navy coat with brass buttons, light blue pants with red stripe, wide sash and saber, shining black boots.

Cade was amused at the sight of him. Ballard was pretty; it was an uncomplimentary way to describe a man, but with his golden, curly hair and fair, baby smooth complexion, there was no other, more appropriate word.

Stiffly Ballard introduced Cade to Judge Newton Quigby. "A new Indian agent," he said nonchalantly, as though the position were of no importance, then turned abruptly to the next guest in line.

Cade made it a habit to size up a man instantly. He was good at it and seldom wrong in his first impression. In this instance, Judge Quigby's eyes gave him away—small and mean, like those of a rattle-snake. And his smile was cold, the corners of his mouth quirked ever so slightly in restrained arrogance.

Bluntly Judge Quigby informed him, "Frankly, Mr. Ramsey, I've always found it odd that a man would want to make a profession of ministering to savages."

"You've got it all wrong, Judge," Cade responded coolly but pleasantly. "It's a profession of protecting Indians *from* savages—like the white man."

Unaccustomed to being challenged, the judge had a hard time con-cealing his outrage but managed to respond lightly, "So, you're one of those. An Indian lover."

"I love mankind, Judge. Most of it, anyway. I just try to keep peo-ple from hurting each other, while you have to judge them after they do. I'd say we've both got interesting but responsible jobs."

"Interesting?" Quigby scoffed. "What's interesting about sending a man to the gallows?"

"You speak as though that's the only solution."

"It is. Once a man is dead, he can't cause anyone else to *be* dead, can he? He can't rob another stagecoach or bank. He's no problem anymore. He's out of the way. Which is as it should be. That's *my* job, Mr. Ramsey."

It was Cade's turn to suppress outrage. He didn't like this man at all. "You sound more like an executioner than a judge."

"I am *both*." The judge's eyes darkened. Then, wanting to end the conversation, he focused his attention on Miriam, who was standing beside him. "This is my daughter, Mrs. Miriam Appleby. Widowed," he added for the benefit of any unmarried man who might be listening. Then he turned to the next guest in line.

Cade clasped Miriam's fingertips politely, noticed she seemed embarrassed, and wondered whether it was because of her father's sadistic attitude toward what he considered justice or the way he had emphasized her marital status. He'd heard some of the bachelor officers laughing over the way the judge was pushing his daughter at them and could now understand why a little persuasion might be necessary to find a husband for her. She was about as appealing as a fence post. Skinny, shapeless, lackluster eyes, dull brown hair pulled back in a knot. Her skin was pale, cold to the touch. The gown she was wearing didn't help, either. A dull green color, it was drab, without style or adornment.

"It's nice to meet you," she murmured perfunctorily, dismissing him as her father had.

Cade took the glass of punch a woman offered to him. Glancing about the parlor, he chided himself for thinking about Celeste and how her wedding reception would probably be held here. Wanting to get his mind off her, he walked over and joined a group of officers standing to the side.

One greeted him jovially. "Well, we see you met prune-face. When's the wedding?"

The others laughed and began to recount tales of how the determined judge had cornered each and every one and unabashedly invited them to court his daughter.

"Suddenly we all became engaged to girls back east."

"We were even making up wedding dates. He really makes no bones about wanting to get her married off."

"Makes you wonder how he ever succeeded in the first place."

"Maybe Ballard will turn to her in his sorrow over losing his lady to the Indians."

Cade seized the chance to broach the subject by asking, "How's he taking it? He seems more mad to me than stricken by grief."

The officers exchanged uncomfortable glances, and one ventured, "Yeah, that's about the way it is."

Cade nodded, managing to conceal his pleasure. Things were going exactly the way he wanted. Now all he had to do was get through the next weeks, and the plan would be considered a success.

Sam wiped the perspiration from her brow with the back of her hand, then grimaced to remember her hands were covered in soot. Now her face would be just as black.

It was steaming hot. Ominous clouds were rolling in, and the air was thick and still. A terrible day to have a fire going, but she had three skins to smoke. Smoking would make them resistant to water, Sun Bird had told her. And the last three days had been spent getting them ready for the final step. Each hide had to be pulled back and forth over a taut rawhide rope and several times through a hole in a buffalo shoulder-blade bone. All this was to work the tanning fluid into every cell and fiber of the skin.

Sam had learned it took about six days to complete the tanning and would be glad to see this part end. The hide would, she'd been told, be cut up and stitched into any number of articles, then decorated with ornaments such as porcupine quills and beads. She wondered if there was any part of the buffalo that wasn't put to some purpose. While everything from robes to breechclouts and moccasins was made from the hide, tools like hoes were fashioned from bones, and the horns were carved into utensils, such as spoons and cups, and weapons, too—arrowheads and knives. The rough side of the tongue was used for a hairbrush. The tail became a brush to swat flies. Even soap was made from fat and string from sinew. The stomach became a cooking pot, like the one from which she'd gotten her first taste of buffalo stew. Water buckets were also made from the paunch. Nothing was wasted, not even the dung, which was dried and used for fuel.

At first Sam had been mad and resentful over being treated like a slave. Then, to her amazement, she became fascinated with what she was doing. The work was hard but interesting. When the women saw she was not above helping, they became friendly. Sun Bird, also putting animosity aside, translated, and suddenly there were good and happy times, despite the grueling tasks. She began to join Sun Bird's family around the fire for their evening meal and did not wince or gag at any of the foul-smelling concoctions made of animal innards. It was food; she needed it to survive. So she ignored the smell and taste and didn't think about what she was eating.

At night, when all was quiet and the camp slept, Sam would lie awake for long hours, thinking about her plight. Gradually she came to be proud of herself for the way she was adapting to the life she was forced to endure. But then she'd never really turned up her nose at existence in the catacombs. It had been necessary to survive, so she had done it without question. The same was true of her current situation. She would survive, and in that fact she privately gloried.

Her mind also wandered to Wild Spirit to ponder what had become of him, why he'd disappeared so mysteriously after being her constant guard for so many days. She told herself she should not miss him, should not feel a strange hunger because of his absence. He was the enemy and should evoke fear, not feelings she did not understand.

Breaking the oppressive stillness now, a sudden gust of wind caught the smoke and sent it blasting into Sam's face. Coughing, gasping, she backed away, covering her nose and mouth with her grimy hands. Sun Bird came over to both tease and scold.

"You have black war paint on your face, and you are not keeping good attention to what you are doing. Smoke the hide, not burn it."

"It's my throat that's burning, not the hide." She doubled over with yet another spasm of coughing, then returned to her task. Sun Bird watched with reluctant admiration for a few seconds before turning away.

The clouds became darker, joining hands like great, black giants to cover the sky. Sam cast a wary eye upward, wondering how long it would be before the heavens opened to unleash a torrent of rain upon them.

Sun Bird returned. "Secure the ropes and pegs as tight as you can. The men can't help you. They're out tying the horses to keep them from running away. The wind is going to be bad, and we must seek shelter."

Sam did the best she could, unable to keep from wincing with pain as she worked the ropes with sore and blistered hands. Gales were coming now, with occasional sheets of rain in promise of pending deluge. Fingers of lightning lit up the sky, and thunder shook the ground beneath them.

Sam was hammering at the pegs with a rock when one of the women shouted something she could not understand as she ran by. Sam was about to flee with her, but just then the rope sprang loose from the peg, sending the hide that had been stretched across it soaring into the wind. Fearing it would blow away, never to be found again, Sam took off after it.

She was running straight into the storm, and each time she tried to grab the skittering hide, thunder became booming laughter as the wind flung it out of her reach. Not about to give up, Sam kept on going, oblivious of being abandoned by the others as they ran for shelter. Never having witnessed a summer storm on the plains, she had no idea of the fury nature could wreak.

Intent on her quest, she did not hear the horse galloping toward her until it was right on top of her and a strong arm was reaching down to grab her about her waist and scoop her up. With a cry of surprise and a gasp of wonder, she found herself held tightly against Wild Spirit's broad, bare chest. His long black hair whipping in the wind, he continued to hold her while he gave his horse his head in an attempt to outrun the storm.

Sam threw her arms about his neck and held on for dear life as they raced across the plains. With her head pressed against his shoulder, all resolve flew away with the winds as she reveled in the powerful feel of his flesh. The sheer masculine smell of him invoked a funny little rush, and when he glanced down at her with heated eyes, Sam felt embarrassed to think he could sense what she was feeling.

What was happening to her? Dear God, she was being held in the arms of an untamed being, riding at breakneck speed ahead of what was becoming a violent and dangerous storm, and she was actually enjoying the moment. Had she completely lost her mind in the wake of being forced to live and work among uncultured people? She was supposed to have been married by now, a genteel, obedient wife with no thoughts save pleasing her husband and looking forward to eventual motherhood. Yet she was thrilling to the experience of her plight and wondered crazily whether she really wanted it ever to end.

The Indian women, despite occasional snickers of ridicule, made her somehow feel as though she were part of a family. Sam had thought she'd had that with Celeste, until the marquis exposed his real reasons for taking her in. But all that seemed so long ago now, and she began to feel strangely born to this place, this time.

They reached the cave just as the downpour came. He lowered her to the ground, and she ran inside, picking her way through the brambled passageway. Everything was as before—the buffalo skins spread out on the ground, a water pouch, a few cooking utensils, soap and rags used for bathing and drying; most important, her bag was still in its hiding place. The thought had not occurred to her, till now, that when the time came for her release she'd need to retrieve it. But would the Indians allow her to take it? Odd that they hadn't looked inside, for surely if they knew about the money, they would take it.

Cade entered the cave just in time to see her making sure her bag had not been stolen and felt a twinge of pity. Little did she know that without it Jarman Ballard didn't give a damn what happened to her.

Sam whirled about to see him watching her and, for the first time, was relieved he could not understand a word she said. It was nice to be able to voice her frustrations out loud, something she'd not dare do otherwise. She dropped to the skin to sit cross-legged, elbows propped on her knees, chin resting on her hands as she stared up at him.

"I'd love to know what you're thinking," she murmured, more to herself than to him. "The last time I saw you, you'd just set me on fire with a kiss I never knew could be so wonderful, but then you went away. Oh, dear Lord, what are you doing to me? What are these feelings you ignite in me that I can't control?"

Cade also sat down, maintaining his practiced stony expression. Despite the resolve he'd hammered into himself during his absence, he was still stricken with an awareness of how much he wanted her. Strange that he should feel that way under the present circumstances. Her face was streaked with soot from the tanning fires, her hair was matted and dirty, and the plain deer-hide dress she was wearing was filthy.

Sam noticed the way he was staring at her. "You're thinking how I look, aren't you? Well, you can't know how badly I've wanted a bath, but they've kept me working day and night on the hides. It wasn't so terrible, though." She ran her fingers through her hair self-consciously. "Actually, I enjoyed it after a while. It was interesting. Why, who would have thought that a huge creature like a hairy buffalo could turn into a soft coat, or blanket? Even a pair of shoes."

She talked on, and Cade leaned back and closed his eyes as though not listening. The truth was, however, he was mesmerized by her voice. Melodic. Caressing. The touch of accent he found so intriguing. And as he listened, he thought of how nice it had been to hold her against him as they rode, how he'd ached to kiss her until both of them were breathless. Suddenly it was all he could do to keep from opening his eyes as he struggled to pretend he was not actually listening to her bold words.

"I'm not sure what it is you make me want. I only know I want it. I should hate you, but I don't. And I used to be scared of you, but now the only thing I'm scared of is what I'm feeling inside. I missed you when you left me. I thought of you day and night, dreamed about you, and . . . Oh, what's the use?"

He caught his breath, held it, all the while his heart pounding as a part of him screamed silently for her to stop, another part willing her to continue pouring out her very soul. But she said nothing more, and a silent storm raged within them as nature unleashed its fury on the world outside.

At last it was over.

Sam got to her feet. He opened his eyes. She picked up the soap. "Though it doesn't do any good to tell you, I'm going to take a bath. Maybe when you see what I'm doing, you'll give me some privacy. Thank goodness I'd washed my one dress right before I had to go work with the women," she said to herself, turning to leave. "At least I have a change of clothes."

He had to pretend, of course, that he didn't know what she was saying as he followed her outside. Then, when she walked toward the clump of sage that provided seclusion to the water, he hung back.

"Good, you understood me," she muttered, continuing on. At the little pool that had been created by a fingering off from the river's cove, Sam stripped out of her soiled clothing and plunged in. Overhead, the sky was still gray, but the winds had died down to a gentle breeze and the air was cool and fresh. The water was deep enough to swim in, and Sam was tempted to indulge herself. But she decided that if she took too long, he would come to see whether she had tried to escape again. Lathering with the soap, she began to scrub her skin and hair.

Cade waited far beyond the shrubs, picking aimlessly at a blade of saw grass as he sat in a squatting position. The heat within him was rising with each beat of his heart. He envisioned what she would look like naked, her breasts wet and slick from her bath, body lithe, supple, as she bent to the water to rinse her skin. Her hair, that strange and lovely silver color, would be wet and cascading down her back.

His teeth were clamped together so tightly that his jaw ached as he fought to keep from tearing through those bushes and taking her right there on the river bank. But his job was to keep the braves from doing the same thing, damn it, and the way it was turning out, she needed somebody to protect her from him.

But what difference did it make, he realized with a jolt, whether she was actually raped or not? Jarman Ballard was going to believe she was and didn't give a damn anyway. All he wanted was her dowry, which he would get. But then what? Lovely and desirable as she was, he would feast on her body, but he would never love her. Cade doubted the bastard was capable of loving any woman. So what was the harm if he offered her tenderness now? He would not force her to do anything she didn't want, but he felt driven to find out exactly what she *did* want.

He straightened, took a deep breath, and was about to start forward, but just then she emerged from behind the sagebrush. She had wrapped a soft doeskin about her and, with a self-conscious glance his way, quickened her pace in the direction of the cave.

Cade watched her but had managed in that brief instant to get hold of himself, and he made no move to touch her.

Sam, however, feeling deliciously wicked and ever believing he did not understand her language, could not resist bold confession. As she passed, eyes averted, she whispered, "You don't know how much I'd like to feel your arms around me."

"And you do not know how much I want to hold you."

For a moment she thought it was a trick of her mind. Then, when she dared look back at him, she saw she had not been imagining anything. He was smiling, a warm kind of smile, and his eyes were devouring her.

"You . . . you heard me," she stammered. "You've heard me all along. You speak English. Oh, dear God." She started backing away from him, clutching the doeskin about her.

He reached for her, and Sam melted at his touch. Her covering fell away, and she was naked before him. "I . . . it's wrong," she whispered. "We can't . . ."

And then his mouth covered hers, silencing her feeble protests. He lifted her in his arms, and this time there was no interruption as he carried her inside the cave to lay her down. His hungry gaze feasted on her body to see she was every bit as lovely as he'd imagined. Breasts firm, pointed, nipples already taut with anticipation. Tiny waist and firm belly, sculptured thighs and, between them, a mat of silver hair that was damp and enticing. He felt as though he were bursting through his breechclout and yanked it away with one swift movement. Their eyes were locked together, hypnotized with lust. Almost harshly, he commanded, "Tell me to stop."

Sam shook her head ever so slightly, not to the wonder blossoming between them, but to any doubts she had within that it was truly what she wanted. And he sensed that and lay down beside her to gather her into his arms.

His lips claimed hers, his tongue entering her mouth to swirl deliciously against her own. Sam's breath caught in her throat as she dizzily snuggled closer against him, reveling in the unfamiliar delight of how his hand cupped her breast and began to squeeze, ever so gently. A sigh of delight escaped her as his thumb and forefinger closed on her nipple in a sensation that was almost painful in its pleasure. Every doubt, every guilt, fled her mind as she gave over to her body all will and want. Her hands went to his shoulders; she wanted to meld their bodies into one being.

His mouth began to move recklessly, almost roughly, across her face, lips nibbling as he moved downward to suckle against her throat. His hands upon her breasts grew bolder, rougher. Sam arched toward him, head thrown back in offering. His knee easily parted her thighs, spreading her legs as he trailed a hand to her belly; then he danced his fingertips downward to twine in the damp curls.

Cade had always prided himself in making sure he pleasured a woman, that his own satisfaction was not taken selfishly. But this time he was having difficulty restraining himself, because never had he been so crazed with desire. He wanted only to throw her on her back and grab her legs and spread them wide and up and plunge right in and take himself to release in seconds, but he'd be damned if he would treat her no better than merchandise he'd bought and paid for.

Sam felt like sobbing with her own want, still confused and baffled by the gnawing hunger within but knowing he who held her possessed the ability to satiate. Yet when his lips fastened on her breast and began to suckle, sending fingers of fire soaring to her belly, she could not hold back the gasps of delight, nor the fervent pleas to take her then and there.

Cade continued his sweet torture, wanting her to be completely at his mercy. His seeking fingers found their target, and he began to knead the tender zenith of her womanflesh. He felt her hands move boldly downward and around to clutch his buttocks, digging into his flesh and pulling him forward in gentle, thrusting movements. *God, how he wanted her.*

With a ragged gasp, he raised his head to stare down at her in the muted light and demand the confirmation, "You've never been with a man."

"No, no, only now," she whispered savagely. "Only you."

Suddenly he rolled to his back, at the same time flipping her to straddle him. "It won't hurt you as much this way."

With his hands clasping her buttocks, he impaled her gently. She gave a little whimper of pain at his first thrust, then gave her hair a reckless toss and threw back her head to gasp with pleasure as he began to undulate his hips, pushing himself in and out of her body. She caught the rhythm and began to move with him, and he no longer had to guide her, could instead shift his caressing hands to her breasts, to cup and squeeze in unison, at the same time inflicting delicious torture by pinching her nipples in the way that drove her mad with want and wonder.

He felt himself approaching climax, and only by mustering his last shred of restraint could he hold back to take her to her own. She screamed out loud in wonder, then threw her head forward, her hair whipping into his face as she bucked against him in uncontrolled frenzy. Then he took himself to glory untold.

Afterward, as they lay together in awed silence, they knew that nothing in their lives would ever be the same again.

# 14

*Sam had fallen asleep in* his arms, but she awoke the following morning to instant fury—at herself for being so weak; at him to think how he had deceived her.

She pulled from him and immediately began dressing. Then, seeing he was awake and watching, she lashed out, "Why didn't you let me know you spoke my language? Why did you let me prattle on all these weeks?"

He spoke carefully, guarding his disguise. "I don't understand everything."

"You understood enough that you let me make a fool of myself."

"I understood that I wanted you." He grinned, reaching for her. "And that you wanted me."

She leaped back, feeling terribly self-conscious to think how only a few hours ago she had given herself to him completely, moaning and writhing with ecstasy. Countering chagrin with ire, she told him, "I was insane. What I've had to endure these past weeks is enough to drive anybody crazy. I can't be held accountable for anything I said or did. Now I demand you tell me when I'll be freed."

"It has not been decided."

"But why can't you at least tell me the reason I was taken in the first place? If it's money, my fiancé will pay."

"No ransom." Cade turned away from her beseeching gaze, lest she see his pity. Jarman Ballard wouldn't give a buckeye to get her back but would move heaven and earth to get his hands on the dowry she carried in her bag.

Sam threw up her hands. "I'm treated no better than a slave, and I don't think you intend to ever let me go. What you've really wanted all along was for me to give in to you, as I did last night, and—"

"And you wanted it, too."

Sam began to pace about, arms folded as she kneaded her elbows nervously. "It shouldn't have happened. I'm the biggest sort of fool. First I chatter on to you, pouring out my soul, thinking you didn't know a word I was saying, and then I throw myself at you like a . . . a . . ." She would not say the word. Just thinking about it was bad enough.

"It's never wrong when both want it."

"Easy for you to say." She grimaced. "Now I'm soiled, ruined. My fiancé probably won't have me."

Cade wished he could tell her she could go to Ballard swollen with another man's child, and he'd still marry her if that's what it would take to get her money. But he couldn't say that. Still, he felt regret to know it had not turned out as planned. She was supposed to remain a virgin as an added affront to Ballard, who would believe the Indians felt his woman was not good enough to sleep with. With a stab of guilt, he offered, "Women know how to trick men into believing they are pure."

Sam looked at him as though he were out of his mind. "Do you honestly think he would ever believe I survived all this time without being ravished? Someone I met on the train told me about all the awful things that Indians do to white women."

"You can say the Indians didn't think Captain Ballard's woman was good enough."

It dawned on her then—why she hadn't been mistreated. Because whether she wanted to admit it or not, she knew Wild Spirit would not have made love to her if she hadn't let him know she was willing. No. Lust was not the motive for her abduction. It had to be some sort of revenge against Jarman.

"That's it, isn't it? You knew who I was, when I would arrive, but it wasn't me you wanted to hurt, it was Captain Ballard. But why? What has he done to you or your people?"

"It's better that you don't know."

"I think after last night you owe me an explanation."

"You wanted it, too. I feel no guilt."

"All right," she conceded. "I admit I let you—"

"You did not *let* me. You said you wanted me." Damn it, he was not going to let her get away with making him out to be some lust-crazed animal. Besides, he was mad enough at himself for being so weak without having her accuse him of seduction.

"Yes, I did, but I never would have said so aloud if I'd known you could understand what I was saying. Don't you see that? I'm not that sort of woman, and in case you didn't notice"—she paused, suddenly self-conscious—"I've never *been* with a man before."

He grinned. "I noticed." Then he dared add, "You have much to learn."

"Oh, to hell with you. It shouldn't have happened, and it won't again unless you force me, and I swear"—she stared him straight in the eye—"I'll fight you tooth and nail."

He continued to smile, which he could tell infuriated her. "I say to you again, cat eyes. I do not force you or any other woman. But you enjoyed it. You will come to me again."

"Like hell I will. And don't call me names," she warned with finger pointed.

"A nice name, because your eyes remind me of a cat. Fierce and ready to kill one moment. Warm and ready to love the next." Cade was having a hard time keeping a straight face. Well, he knew her now for the hot-blooded, passion-starved woman she was. All he had to do was pull her into his arms and touch and caress in all the right places, and she would be his for the taking. But he didn't want her that way. He wanted her to come to him freely, of her own volition, as she had done last night.

Sam moved as far away from him as she could get in the tiny cave. "You may call me by my name—Mademoiselle de Manca. And who are you, anyway? You're not a real Indian, are you?"

"I am called a half-breed," he lied glibly. "My mother was taken by Indians in a raid on a wagon train a long time ago. She fell in love with the great chief of the Mescalero, and I am his son." There, he decided with satisfaction, that should really throw Ballard off the scent when he tried to figure out what an Apache from a tribe known to inhabit the area between the Rio Grande and the Pecos River and south into Mexico was doing so far from home. He would at first think Celeste was confused and didn't know what she was talking about, but Cade intended to make sure he told her enough about the Apaches so she'd be quite knowledgeable by the time she was freed.

"Half-breed," Sam echoed, then asked, "Why did you choose to stay? After you were grown, I mean. Why didn't you go back to living among white people?"

He frowned, as though her question touched a sensitive spot. "Half-breeds are looked upon with contempt by the white man. They are not welcome in his world. The Indians accept me as one of them, because I am the son of a great chief." Let Ballard try and figure that one out, he gloated, proud of the story he'd concocted.

Sam was feeling terribly uncomfortable, because she was lying there naked, except for a fold of the buffalo skin thrown over her legs and hips. "I don't care what you are. Or who you are. And you can live in filth and squalor if you wish. I just want to go back to civilization," she cried.

He was becoming annoyed at her condescending attitude. "You don't know what you're talking about, and you were far from clean when I saved you from the storm."

"That wasn't my fault. They made me work like that, scraping flesh, smoking skins. I couldn't help it. Oh, damn you, damn them." Sam started to pick her way through the brambles, heading outside. "I liked it better when you didn't talk. Then I didn't have to listen to your idiotic jabbering."

He made no move to stop her, knowing it was best she get off to herself and sort out her thoughts. Best, too, that she stay angry with herself and with him, for it would make the remaining time together easier for both of them.

Outside, Sam drank in the morning air, for the storm had left everything fresh and sweet-smelling. She thought about the hard work of the past week or so and decided she'd rather be with the women than here, around Wild Spirit. She knew every time she looked at him she was going to think of what had happened last night. Oh, how could she have been so weak? Half Indian, half white, he was her captor and he did not belong anywhere, and she did not belong in his arms. No matter how much she'd enjoyed it.

Cade left her alone for a while; then, because he was hungry, he emerged from the cave and began making a fire. He had brought some coffee and a side of bacon from town. Since she thought of him as a half-breed, it was understandable he would be familiar with the food and drink of the white man. He could see her down at the water's edge as she washed out her buckskin dress. She pretended not to notice him, but he knew the smell of the sizzling bacon would be irresistible.

He was right. At last she hung the dress on a shrub to dry and walked over, not too proud or angry to refuse the food he held out to her. She ate silently but ravenously and could not get enough of the coffee. Finally, grudgingly, she remarked, "Maybe you should leave more often if it means bringing back decent food."

"You don't look as though you are bones yet, cat eyes. I'd say you're much heavier than when I saw you last."

And it was so. She had filled out a little, and it was becoming, but he wasn't about to say so. "I said not to call me that," she snapped irritably. "And who wouldn't get fat from eating all that greasy food you people gorge yourselves on?"

"Only in the summer. Winter can be quite lean." He pointed to the utensils. "You can wash them."

"You go to hell." She stalked away, muttering that she was not his slave, and she'd be damned if she'd be treated like one any longer. He could clean up his own mess, and his women could scrape their own skins. She had tried cooperating with them, made no trouble, but where had it got her? Here she was, back again, being guarded by a man she tried to hate but who could set her blood to boiling with just one caressing look. Well, let him think her haughty. She didn't care. All she wanted was to get away from him before she made an even bigger fool of herself.

Cade caught up with her just as she started back into the cave and spun her about, yanking her tight against him. "Don't walk away from me like that. I gave you work to do, and you will do it."

Her head was back as she lifted her face to meet his fiery, threatening gaze with insolence and rebuke. "Like I said, half-breed, go to hell."

He gave her a shake. "Do not provoke me."

"And what will you do? Torture me because I refuse to be your slave?"

"There are ways to persuade you." He pulled her close to claim her mouth in a deep, stirring kiss, then just as abruptly released her and walked away.

Dizzily, Sam stared after him, thinking that he could have beaten her into obedience. Yet all he'd done was kiss her deeply, passionately, reminding her of how easily her own body could betray her.

Watching as he picked up the utensils and started toward the river, she asked herself what harm there was in taking pleasure where she found it. She'd had her share of misery in the past and was not particularly looking forward to the uncertain future as the wife of a man she somehow knew she'd never love. So what was wrong with enjoying the present? Besides, she reasoned, it was clearly to her advantage to keep peace with Wild Spirit for the duration of her captivity.

He knelt by the water, and she felt a warm rush to recall how good it had felt to wrap her arms around his broad, naked back and the ultimate splendor she had known as he had possessed her completely. At last she knew the joy to be had with a man.

Jarman was either going to believe her or not when she told him she had not been raped by the Indians. Even if nothing had happened, and she had ultimately gone to him as a virgin and sworn she'd not been touched, he was going to think what he wished. The harm, if there was any, had been done. There could be no turning back. And for whatever time she was to be held, Sam vowed to push back any thoughts of guilt as to whether it was right or wrong.

She went to the water's edge and knelt beside him, reaching for the utensils. "I'm sorry," she murmured. "You've treated me well. I should be grateful. I know things could have been worse."

In that crystallized moment, Cade knew he never should have gotten involved in the scheme. He was feeling something for her that he shouldn't, damn it, because nothing could ever come of it except heartache and misery. He knew he needed to make arrangements to send her back where she belonged, but a selfish part of him stubbornly refused. And if all he was to ever have of her was here and now, then, by thunder, he would savor every second.

He stood, drawing her with him. He did not touch her but devoured her with his eyes as he once more avowed, "I won't force you to do anything against your will."

"But I *will* it." Her smile was shy, though her eyes shone with brazen resolve. Sliding her arms up and about his neck, she pulled him forward. "What difference will it make tomorrow, Wild Spirit? All that ever really matters in this life is here and now."

Cade could more easily have changed the course of the great river beyond than deny the surging desire within. Holding her hand in his, he drew her once more into the hiding place, where they could drink of the wonders of their passion.

\* \* \*

As time went on, Sam's feelings for Wild Spirit grew deeper, and she sensed he was also being drawn to her. Yet he spoke no words of endearment, so she told herself her emotions were sired by physical needs, a reaching out from the loneliness and desperation of her plight.

But while nights were spent in the splendor of their desires, days became an adventure, as Cade delighted in introducing her to the world in which she temporarily resided. He took her for long walks, naming plants and birds and animals they encountered. He taught her to catch fish with a spear and make a snare for small game. He also ventured to show her how to shoot a bow and arrow and a gun, by then confident she would not turn a weapon against him. He also taught her to ride a horse astraddle and bareback, and they rode like the wind, laughing and reveling in each other's company.

As they grew closer, Sam began to wonder what Wild Spirit's reaction would be if she confessed to him her true identity and the entire scheme. Would he declare her his woman and refuse to let her go? And if he did, what then? Would she, could she, be happy in his world? But then, when she got to thinking that way, she was ultimately struck by the folly of such an idea. He had, after all, given her no reason to suspect he gave any thought beyond the moment at hand, and she was foolish to let herself care for him so deeply. Best, also, to keep her secret, and when the time came to return to civilization, she would do her best not to look back.

One day Sun Bird came to speak to Wild Spirit in their language. Sam couldn't tell what was going on but knew Sun Bird was upset, and when she turned toward Sam, her eyes flashed with anger.

"Is she mad because I'm not helping the women?" Sam wanted to know after she left.

Cade hedged. Actually Sun Bird was raising hell with him for not releasing Celeste. She and many others felt it was time, but he refused to discuss it.

When he did not answer, Sam pressed on, "Why haven't you taken me back to where they're working?"

"You might be seen there. It is safer here."

He turned away, in that disconcerting way he did sometimes that made Sam feel as if she were suddenly in the company of a stranger. With heavy heart she stared after him, chiding herself for wanting to hear the words, longing to hear him say he wanted to keep her all to himself, and that was the reason they remained in seclusion. But he kept on going, and she did not follow after him, sensing it was one of those times when he desired to be alone.

But what Sam did not know was that Cade was having a difficult time with his own emotions. He was caring too much, and his heart was not listening to the arguments of his head. He knew he loved her. He knew he wanted to be with her forever and always.

He also knew it could never be.

## London

Celeste looked at herself in the cracked mirror over the sink and, at the sight of her swollen face, started to cry again. "I look awful, just awful."

Jacques's face was screwed in a mask of disgust as he hurried to put on his shoes. Though he hated his job washing dishes and mopping floors at the pub, he was anxious to escape her whining and complaining.

"Look at this place." Celeste gestured wildly, tearfully. "It's all I can do to turn around. We eat and sleep and live in the same room. The furniture is falling to pieces. It's still summer, but already it's cold and damp and drafty. What's going to happen when the baby is born? It will stay sick. And we don't even have room for a crib. We've got to find another place before it's born, Jacques."

Tightly, tensely, he reminded her, "It's all we can afford on my paltry wages, and you know it."

"But you won't even look for larger quarters. You sleep all day, until it's time to go to work. You promised you would go with me to look for something better."

"It's hopeless."

"You're always making promises you can't keep, like when you said your aunt and uncle would let us live with them, that they'd help us, but they kicked us out after only a few weeks."

"That was their promise, not mine. I couldn't help it if they went back on their word. And maybe," he dared to add with an accusing glare, "your nagging me all the time had something to do with their saying we'd have to leave. That and the way you did nothing but lie in bed all day wanting to be pampered, wanting my aunt to wait on you hand and foot like Francine. You're not living at the château with your father spoiling you any longer, Celeste. You are my wife, and you can accept the life I can provide. You're also not the first woman to ever have a baby, and I'm frankly getting sick of your moaning about it."

He got up to leave, but Celeste snatched up a mug from the table and sent it smashing against the door just above his head. He whirled around and shouted, "Have you lost your mind, woman? Shall I have you sent to an asylum?"

"If I keep living like bourgeoisie, that's where I'll need to be for sure, but I think I'd as soon be dead." Covering her face with her hands, she began to cry even harder.

With a disgusted sigh, Jacques went to put his arms around her and hold her against him as she wept. It had not been easy the past months, for either of them, but at times like this he wished to God they'd never met. "Things will be better when the baby comes," he offered feebly. Anything to get her calmed down so he could be on his way.

Suddenly Celeste drew away from him. She lifted the hem of her dirty dress and wiped her eyes, her nose. Running away as she had, when their plans went awry at the last minute, she'd had no time to get the bag she'd packed, which meant no extra clothes. Jacques's meager savings had disappeared rapidly, so she hadn't been able to buy new.

"No," she told him finally, swallowing back the desperation and hysteria. "Things will not be better when the baby comes. They will only get worse."

"All right, all right." He held up his hands in defeat, backing toward the door, actually looking forward to the tubs of greasy, dirty dishes awaiting. "I promise to try and find a better job, a better place to live. Just stop crying and nagging at me all the time, all right?"

"I'm going home."

With wide eyes, he stammered, "You . . . you can't be serious."

"I am. I've thought about it and decided it's the only thing to do. Besides, I don't like London. I want my baby to be born in Paris."

He was flabbergasted and cried, "But what about Sam? Your father will find out about the deception. He will write to that Ballard fellow and tell him about it."

With a confident shake of her head, Celeste said that was the least of her worries. "I've thought about that, too. Now that we're married, Papa will accept it, because he has no choice. And he'll be thrilled to find out he's going to be a grandfather. He'll also be happy Sam has a secure future. No doubt she and Jarman are married by now and probably madly in love with each other. Papa will agree to go along with the ruse—and why not? Jarman will never return to France, and neither will Sam. He'll never know the truth, and Papa will have no reason to tell him."

Jacques did not share her optimism. "I don't know, Celeste. It's taking a big chance. He might be so mad he'll turn you away."

"Don't be ridiculous. I'm his daughter. This is his grandchild I'm carrying. He'll have to take us in."

Wrapping her arms around herself, she began to dance about the room—as much as the tiny space would allow. "Oh, Jacques, Jacques, it's going to be wonderful. I just know it. We'll move into my quarters, take over that whole wing of the château. Everything will be as it was before, only this time I'll have you and the baby."

Watching her in brooding silence, Jacques could only pray she was not making a terrible mistake.

**15**

*With each passing day, Sam* felt more and more at peace with the world around her. She thought perhaps it was her early years in the rolling hills of Virginia that made her feel so at home on the plains, for truly she did not miss the crowded city life. There were, however, times she longed for some of the comforts of civilization, but by and large, nature became a friend.

Although Wild Spirit was reluctant to talk about himself, he was willing to answer her questions about the territory and told her how Kansas had played an active part in the Civil War. When it ended, land was opened to freed slaves and settlers moving westward. Railroads were being built and cattle driven from Texas to Abilene for transporting east.

He told her, too, about how the Indians in the territory had been peaceful until the white man came. They farmed and hunted and minded their own business, but then the government began to move other tribes off eastern land and to settle them on reservations in Kansas. Wars broke out between the tribes, and with homesteaders constantly pushing in to crowd out the Indians, there had been much bloodshed.

"To have lived with them your whole life, you certainly seem well educated," Sam marveled. "Your English is good, and you have knowledge of what goes on around you."

Cade realized he might be talking too much and countered stiffly, "My mother taught me the language. I go into settlements sometimes and listen to the white man talk, and I hear things."

They were sitting on a tiny hillock, and Sam was enthralled by the field of sunflowers beyond. Tall and regal, they swayed in the wind like thousands of tiny yellow soldiers, marching to a silent drum. In the distance, a great herd of buffalo could be seen grazing lazily on the plain.

"It's all so beautiful." With a sigh of contentment, she lay back to gaze up at the radiant sky. "Never have I seen such a glorious shade of blue, except when I look into your eyes."

He also leaned back, turning on his side to gaze down at her. As he began to trail a fingertip down her cheek, she caught it and pressed it to her lips. "When I'm this happy," she confessed, "I feel guilty."

"But you're anxious to leave."

She turned her face to the sky once more. "I'm not sure. It's peaceful here. The more I know you, the more I enjoy being with you. But a part of me tells me it's wrong. I know my"—she paused; as always, the word seemed forced, unnatural—"fiancé must be terribly worried. He might even think I am dead by now."

Cade doubted that was the case but didn't say so. If it had been any other man's fiancée, it would be safe to assume such a thing, but Ballard had figured out it was all an act of revenge and that his torment was to be wondering about her fate, the condition she would be in when eventually returned.

"Then you do not miss your home." He broached a different subject, not wanting to think about Ballard and how she would eventually become his wife.

Sam framed her answer carefully. It would be so easy to just tell him the truth, then and there, and explain how she really didn't have a home of her own. With his background, he would probably enjoy hearing of her escapades in the streets of Paris, how she'd survived living in the catacombs by pretending to be a boy. Somehow she knew he would laugh and lament with her, and doing so would bring them even closer. But she dared not risk the truth. Instead she created and embellished a make-believe life as the rich and pampered daughter of a marquis, describing the wonders of the European city, the opulence of the château, and the glitter and splendor of formal balls and socials.

Everything Cade was hearing reaffirmed what he already knew— that all they had together was all they ever would have. Never could she live in his world, and he knew nothing of hers. She belonged to another man. That's the way it was, the way it had to be, and he was a fool to wish it could be otherwise.

He drank in the sight of her as she chewed absently on a blade of grass. Memories had carried her away like the wisps of clouds dancing across the sky above. Hair fanned about her lovely face, skin tanned to a golden bronze, a new ripeness to her body caused by hearty living, she was truly a wondrous sight to behold, and he could hold back no longer.

They were away from the cave, the camp, secluded and alone. They had made love in fields before, and both had come to love the wild abandon of yielding to their passion amid raw nature. He reached for her. She did not hold back.

"I want you," he whispered huskily as he lowered his mouth to hers. His hands moved possessively up and down her body, touching, caressing each curve, lingering at her breasts, then finally cupping her chin to hold her, devour her. When they were breathless, he drew back to lock his heated gaze with hers as he reached to slide up the skirt of her buckskin dress. She took over then, sitting up to pull the garment over her head and cast it aside while he quickly removed his clothing as well. When she started to lie back down, he maneuvered her on top of him.

She spread her hands on his chest, marveling as always at the taut hardness of his muscles. Touching the scar, she asked suddenly, "Where did you get that? It had to be a terrible wound."

He had decided not to tell her he had fought in the war. If she were to describe a blue-eyed half-breed with a six-inch scar on his chest from fighting for the North, it might raise a few eyebrows, especially Ballard's. "War with another tribe," he said brusquely, then proceeded to get her mind on other things.

Hands clasped at her waist, he lifted her up. Her hair tossed wildly across his face, and she cried out with the wonder of it all as he made her his. "Ride me like the wind," he commanded tersely. "I want to feel your hips against me. I want to feel your wild mane in my face."

Sam felt as though she were going to die from the sheer joy of it all. She braced upon her knees to push herself upward, lifting almost to the end of his shaft, then sliding down as their bodies met. He continued to torture her with one hand while he clung with his other to her buttocks to hold her in place against her own frenzied, bucking rhythm.

Sam felt the explosion coming from deep within. She began to ride harder, faster, like a stallion approaching a great and mighty hurdle. Cade felt it, too, and suddenly swung up and over, so he was above her.

They came together. Sam threw her head back once more, arching her body and letting the scream erupt from the very depths of her enraptured soul. Cade's teeth ground together in his own pleasure, every nerve in his body raw and shrieking with silent joy.

As he held her tenderly in the sweet glow of the afterfires, he knew he had never experienced such complete and ultimate satisfaction. And, sadly, he was also aware that once she left him, he would never experience it again.

When the sun began to sink in the west, and the plains were bathed in glorious tones of gold and bronze and pink, they returned to the camp.

Cade had caught fish earlier that morning and left them on a line in the stream. Sam, long ago having accepted her duties to help, retrieved them to clean and make ready to cook while he built a fire.

She was returning with the cleaned fish when she saw him off at a distance talking with an Indian. They came sometimes, the braves, as he called them, but always he would speak with them so far away that she could not see their faces. She supposed that was to keep her from being able to give a detailed description of her captors. Wild Spirit also continued to camouflage his face with the garish streaks of war paint.

He had not finished gathering the wood for the fire, so Sam began to complete the task, careful to move in the opposite direction, away from them, so as not to annoy.

Cade watched her, grateful she obeyed orders most of the time. Despite their closeness, he was well aware of her spirit, as well as her temper when riled.

"You are not listening to me, my brother."

He turned his attention to Bold Eagle once more. "I've heard everything you've said."

"Hearing and listening are two different things."

Cade did not miss the sarcasm. He also knew Bold Eagle was upset about something and had a good idea of what it was. But he asked anyway, "What's on your mind? You didn't come here just to tell me Ballard has stopped sending out patrols. We both knew he'd do that after a while, though I have to admit I'm surprised he kept it up as long as he did."

Solemnly Bold Eagle made the declaration, "It is time to take her back."

"Not yet," Cade said, maybe too quickly, he realized. He stole another glance in her direction. "She's settled down. She's no problem. And I've still got a little while before I report to my post, so we might as well keep her to needle Ballard a while longer."

"Now." Bold Eagle's voice had an edge.

Cade's eyes narrowed. "I decide when."

"Decisions are often unwise when made with the heart and not the head."

"And what is that supposed to mean?"

"Two weeks ago, I told you nothing else was to be gained by keeping her any longer. Captain Ballard has suffered all he is going to. I see him almost every day, if only from a distance, and I see how he goes about his duties, continues his life. He will not feel any more anguish than he already has, no matter how long his woman is kept from him. Perhaps he has even decided she is dead by now. It makes no difference. But she must be taken back, for her good, as well as yours.

"You see," he went on, eyes accusing, "there is talk among our people that you keep the woman now because you have come to want her for yourself."

Cade was not about to admit to anything and scoffed, "You've been listening to Sun Bird. She got mad when I took Celeste away from helping her and the women, but it was risky to leave her there, and you know it."

Bold Eagle shook his head. "I know you, my brother, better than you know yourself. When your heart held love for my sister, I could see that love in your eyes. I see the same look there now, but it is for the white woman. You can lie to me, but you cannot lie to your heart. Give her up now, for it will only be worse to do so later. You know such a love can never be."

Cade knew it was pointless to argue. Bold Eagle could see right through him. "I'm afraid you're right. Even if she wanted to stay, it could never be."

"No, and even if you told her the truth about who you are, what you are, the reasons she was taken in the first place, and she understood and hated Ballard for the evildoer he is, you could never take her for your wife. You have taken on a big responsibility to accept the position of agent. You will honor your father's memory by walking in his footsteps to stand against the white man's injustice not only to our people but all Indians as well. If you took Ballard's woman with you, he would make your job all the more difficult. He would also know our tribe was responsible and take revenge upon us.

"No," he went on to affirm solemnly, eyes shadowed and grim, "you must let her go. Tonight. I have already made the arrangements."

Cade listened with heavy heart as Bold Eagle described the plan. She would be taken during the night and left within walking distance of the fort, where she could see her way at first light.

"You can take her yourself, if you wish."

Cade shook his head, unable to bear the thought of having to say good-bye to her.

"Then leave whenever you wish, and I will take over after you have gone. She will not see my face in the dark. I will tie her so she will not try to run away, and gag her to keep her from screaming out as we ride."

Cade understood the necessity of restraining her in such a way but nonetheless reminded his friend, "Don't hurt her. Be as gentle as you can. And remember she's going to be scared."

"You don't want to tell her anything?"

Again, he declined. Then, not wanting to talk any longer, and wondering how in the hell he was going to be able to get through the next hours, Cade left Bold Eagle and returned to Sam.

She knew right away something was wrong. He did not speak while they cooked and ate, and finally she could stand it no longer. "What has happened? What did that man say that seems to worry you so?"

"Do not concern yourself with the business of my people," he said, making his voice sharp. If she got mad, she would stop asking questions.

Sam stared at him. After the wonderful afternoon they had shared, it bewildered her to see him suddenly so cold. Had she said too much about life in Paris? she wondered frantically. Was he thinking she considered him far beneath her, that their lovemaking actually meant nothing beyond a very enjoyable diversion to her being held captive?

No. She could not let him think that. No matter what the future held, she wanted him to know she cared for him, and cared deeply.

She waited until after they had cleaned up from the meal, not attempting further conversation. Let him brood for the time being, she thought happily, she would soon make it right, with words, and with actions as well. Their lovemaking this night would be so tender, so meaningful, he would know beyond doubt that he had a special place in her heart and always would.

A soft summer breeze had become a harsh, brisk wind. A storm was brewing. Thunder rolled in the distance, and forks of lightning split the sky. He had gone to sit beside the stream, and Sam went to him and urged him to come inside the cave with her.

"Later," he said shortly, almost angrily. "I want to be alone."

"But I want to be with you," she said stubbornly, "and if you don't come with me, I'm going to sit right here beside you, and we'll both probably drown in the storm."

He swore under his breath but got to his feet. Then, grabbing her roughly by her wrist, he led her to shelter. She was not surprised when he made his bed away from her, but her mind was made up not to tolerate his rebuke.

"I know what's wrong with you," she said, stretching out beside him. His back was to her, but she slid her arms about him to hold him tight. "It's what I said this afternoon, about my life in Paris. My"—she nearly choked to speak the lie—"*father*, his wealth. But what you have to know is that none of that matters."

Cade tensed, fighting within himself. His heart wanted to hear the admission she was about to make—the confession that she loved him. But his brain was screaming at him to stop her now, before it was too late to turn back, because if she said the words, he would say them right back to her, and then it would be too late. There would be no turning back, and he could not let it happen. As Bold Eagle had warned, he had an obligation to his people, and there would be hell to pay if he took Ballard's woman and Ballard knew, beyond doubt, the Kansa were responsible. Some of them could even die. He could not, would not, risk it.

Sam went on to admit, "But none of that matters now. Not since I've come to know you, Wild Spirit, and your world. As crazy as it sounds, I want to be a part of it all, a part of you—"

He rolled over then, so quickly that she was startled. Instinctively she pulled back, but he grabbed her and held her so close she could feel his ragged breath and see the frenzy in his eyes. "What is wrong with you?" she cried, frightened and not knowing why. "Does it make you angry for me to admit I care for you? Don't you care at all for me?"

Mustering every shred of self-control he possessed, Cade forced himself to say, "It does not matter what we feel for each other, because this is all we will ever have."

And he took her almost roughly, and Sam did not resist. Afterward she snuggled close to him and told herself that no matter what had happened to upset him so, tomorrow things would be better. They would go the sunflower field and lie side by side once more, and they would be drawn together. He would be tender again, and this time she would pour out her heart to him. And she would find a way, somehow, to share her own awareness of herself and how she would rather live with him in his world than exist without him in hers.

Sam did not fall asleep at once, instead reveling to hear his even breathing and know he was near. In his slumber, his arm about her tightened and he held her close. Finally she drifted away with a smile on her face and in her heart. He had to love her, too. She could feel it, sense it. And while a strange twist of fate had brought her to this time and place, everything would be all right. Love would make it so.

When Sam awoke some time later, she was not alarmed at first to realize that Wild Spirit was no longer beside her. Personal reasons might have taken him outside, or perhaps he had heard strange noises. Sometimes he did get up to walk about, to make sure the camp was secure. But as moments passed and he did not return, apprehension began to creep over her. She did not want to go look for him. Thoughts of prowling around alone in the night were not appealing, but her uneasiness was mounting.

Just as she was about to go outside and call in hopes he was within hearing distance, there was a faint sound from the brambled trail, and she felt relief—but only for an instant. She sat up, nerves taut to know that Wild Spirit would not be making his way through the barrier so clumsily. He knew the way, knew exactly where to step so that not a twig would snap nor dry leaf rustle. Whoever was coming toward her did not know his way as well.

She tried not to think that Wild Spirit might have been attacked, perhaps killed, and now the enemy was coming after her. She could not panic. She had to defend herself and then go search for him. He could be wounded, bleeding.

Remembering she was naked, she found her buckskin dress in the darkness and hurriedly pulled it on. Then, groping about for any kind of weapon, she felt her bag right beside her. She hadn't checked on it in weeks, confident it was safe where she'd hidden it. But who had found it and placed it next to her—and why?

But there was no time to ponder. The monster was upon her. She had time to scream only once before a rag was stuffed in her mouth. Then, despite how she fought, her wrists were bound and she was hoisted over someone's broad shoulder.

Outside, she was positioned astraddle a horse. The night was pitch-dark. Sam strained to see and detected only one Indian. He made no sound as he mounted another horse, pulling hers behind him.

They rode slowly, and Sam was frantic with a million emotions. Where was Wild Spirit? Who had found her bag, and why had it been taken with her, looped about her wrists? Something told her she would not be coming back to the camp, but if she were being taken to work with the Indian women, why in this manner, trussed and gagged, and in the dead of night?

As time passed, Sam realized they were not going to the camp, because they were covering a lot of distance. At last they stopped and she was taken from the horse. The faint light of dawn was beginning to creep from the horizon, and she was able to see the hulking shadow of a building of some sort in the distance. Her bag was placed at her feet, her hands untied, the gag yanked from her mouth.

She whipped about in fury to demand, "Where have you brought me? What—"

But he was already on his way, disappearing into the dregs of night.

# 16

Jarman *had always hated* the waking blare of a bugle, but this particular morning it annoyed him more than usual. He had not meant to drink so much the night before, but each sip of whiskey seemed to ease the frustration a little bit more.

It also had not been his intention to wake up with a whore, especially a wildcat like Martita. She knew ways to keep him going all night, which is about what happened, because he had not gotten back to his quarters until nearly four in the morning. Now his head was throbbing and the roll of his stomach warned he might be spending a lot of time this day leaning over a basin.

He covered his head with the pillow to shut out the brassy sound. Just a few more weeks and he would never have to listen to it again, thank heavens. He was getting out of the service, even though the damned Indians had ruined all his plans and he now had no idea what he was going to do after his discharge. Celeste would probably never be seen again, and he felt no more than a twinge of remorse that he'd cared only about the lost dowry. Sooner or later he knew he would have to get around to writing to the marquis and let him know what had happened. He also intended to express his surprise that Celeste had been sent alone, without a chaperone, although it seemed unimportant now.

Realizing the infernal horn blowing had stopped, Jarman took his head out from under the pillow and snuggled back down. There was no one of higher rank at the fort to chastise him if he was late reporting to his office, and he figured if he could sleep a while longer, he would feel better.

He had just dozed off when a loud pounding on his door made him sit up and yell, "What the hell is it?"

A voice ringing with excitement called, "Captain Ballard, you need to get to the blockhouse quick."

Jarman bounded out of bed to cross the floor in quick, angry strides. "This had better be important," he warned, yanking the door open.

Private Stanley Moulton saw the captain's bloodshot eyes and knew he'd been drinking again. Everybody on the post knew of his weakness with the bottle, but who could blame him after what he'd been going through the past weeks? "You'd better just come see for yourself."

"I don't feel well, Moulton. Whatever it is, I'm sure another officer can handle it. Now get out of here and let me sleep." He started to close the door, but Moulton stuck out his foot to stop him.

"Sir, please come with me."

"I'm warning you—"

Moulton had not wanted to be the one to tell him but knew he had no choice. "It's a woman, sir. She asked for you." He paused and swallowed, then related the shocking news. "She claims she's your fiancée."

Left alone in the lingering darkness, Sam had sunk wearily to the ground in a kind of daze, feeling the need to sort out her thoughts before continuing. She was free now, but her joy was overshadowed by the painful awareness of how Wild Spirit had left her without a word. Obviously she had meant nothing to him and she supposed she should feel shame and embarrassment, to have given herself with such wild abandon. But how could she when the memories were so good, so warm? Hate him, yes, for not caring enough to even say good-bye. But regret? No, she was not sorry to have experienced such wonder. She would survive. That was how it was. That was how *she* was.

Life had dealt her some hard knocks in the past, and she had taken them on and come out with head held high. So there was no need to feel guilty merely because she had discovered what it meant to be a woman and love a man. But she would allow herself rage, in hopes it would ease the anguish of knowing she would never see him again.

Finally, when the last vestiges of night were clawed away by the creeping fingers of dawn, Sam took her bag and with a ragged sigh and heavy heart began the last leg of her long and arduous journey.

Private Moulton had been reporting for duty when he saw what appeared to be an Indian woman coming down the road. Noting the color of her hair, he had paused to stare curiously. Indian women did not have hair like that. Old ones had gray, of course, but not gleaming silver, and that was not an old woman walking toward him. She was young, and—He froze.

*She was also white.*

Quickening his pace, Moulton had yelled to Private Fletcher, the guard on duty, to come quickly.

Sam was weary from lack of sleep, and it had been a longer walk from where she had been released than she'd first thought. Grateful to see the man in a blue uniform, she breathlessly, wearily, asked, "Is this Fort Leavenworth?"

Private Moulton felt a chill from head to toe. It could only be the woman the Indians had taken off the train. "Ma'am," he asked softly, "who are you?"

Sam accepted the seal of her fate by introducing herself in the identity she was to assume for the rest of her life. "My name is Celeste de Manca, and I want to see my fiancé, Captain Ballard."

Moulton had caught her as she toppled forward, then lifted her in his arms to take her inside the blockhouse and placed her on a bench. He had hovered over her anxiously while Fletcher went to find the post doctor, then he had rushed to find Captain Ballard.

When Dr. Potts arrived, he had brought Sam to consciousness with a quick sniff of ammonia. "Your name," he demanded, wanting confirmation that the soldier had heard her right, and she had repeated it.

Word was spreading fast, for Fletcher had told everyone he had passed. As Sam slowly regained her wits, she became aware that the tiny room was filling up with soldiers, staring curiously as they whispered among themselves. She knew she must look a sight and felt terribly uncomfortable and wished they would go away. She heard someone shouting, demanding to be let through, then saw another man in uniform push his way forward. Blond curls reminded her of Celeste, but the true jolt came when she heard the doctor cry, "It's her, Captain Ballard. Praise God Almighty, it's really her."

Jarman stared down at her in wonder, suddenly at a loss for words. Finally he asked nervously, "Are you all right?"

"Yes. I'm fine," she replied thinly. "I was treated well."

Jarman was overwhelmed. He had come to believe she would never be found—alive. Not knowing what to do next, he turned to Dr. Potts. "You will examine her, won't you? To make sure she's all right?"

"Of course. I'll take her to the hospital."

Sam was quick to protest, "No. I don't need to go there, really. If there's a room for me somewhere, a place I could get a bath, change clothes—"

"Clothes, yes," Jarman said quickly, remembering her luggage, which had been taken off the train and stored. "I'll have something sent over, but you must allow the doctor to make sure you aren't hurt."

Sam was scrutinizing the man she was going to marry. He was nice looking in a delicate sort of way. He was not too tall, slenderly built, and exuded authority. Maybe even outright bossiness, she thought as his eyes clouded with his annoyance when she continued to resist. "I told you. I was not mistreated. And I don't want to go to the hospital. I just need to rest."

"You're going," he snapped. "And later, when you've rested, we'll talk. Dr. Potts will take good care of you." He started to turn away, wanting only in that moment to escape from everyone and think about what all this meant; then he decided he should make some gesture of caring. After all, she was his intended bride. He bent and bestowed a perfunctory kiss on her cheek, whispered how grateful he was to have her safe and sound.

"Take this with you," Dr. Potts said, handing him Sam's bag, which was lying next to the bench. "You'll want to put it with the rest of her things."

Sam had no choice but to allow herself to be whisked away, but once at the hospital she refused to allow Dr. Potts to touch her. "I demand my privacy," she stated firmly.

He could do nothing but yield to her wishes, admitting she certainly seemed fit. However, he insisted she remain at the hospital until Captain Ballard came for her, reminding her that he personally did not know what to do with her.

It did not take Sam long to realize that she was an object of curiosity as well as suspicion from all those with whom she came in contact. The nurse who brought the clothes Jarman had sent from her trunk was coolly reserved. She asked no questions and did not offer to help with anything, returning after Sam bathed and changed.

Sam had laid the buckskin dress on the back of a chair, and the nurse picked it up as though it were alive and might bite. "I'll have this burned right away," she said with distaste.

"No." Sam was surprised by the sharpness of her own voice but nonetheless rushed to protest, "No. Just leave it alone. I'll wash it when I have a chance. It's a beautiful dress when it's clean. The bead work is exquisite."

"It . . . It's a *squaw* dress," the nurse stammered, eyes wide with scorn. "Certainly you wouldn't want to ever wear it again, Miss de Manca."

"Probably not, but I'd like to keep it all the same."

"But a squaw dress . . ."

Sam drew a sharp breath. Lord, the last thing she wanted was a confrontation, but already she was fed up with people treating her as if she were a bug of some sort, too hideous to be touched. She wasn't sure what kind of reception she had expected but certainly not loathing and fear. And even though she knew it might make matters worse, she felt the need to relate something Wild Spirit had told her during the long, intimate talks she'd enjoyed so much.

Drawing a deep breath, she said, "Nurse, I think you should know that the term *squaw* is not an Indian word at all. The Indians consider it insulting, because it's a word the white man made up. They resent it, and so do I, and I would appreciate it if you would just put my dress down now."

"As you wish." The nurse turned on her heel and rushed out, anxious to tell everyone how Miss de Manca refused to get rid of her Indian costume and was even defending Indian women.

Jarman had gone to the storage room. After opening Celeste's trunk, he took out a gown, unabashedly selected proper undergarments, then rolled everything up to send to her at the hospital. He had set down her smaller bag but decided to take it with him and picked it up again. He had felt no particular eagerness to look inside, having no hopes whatsoever that the Indians had not taken her dowry, but he was suddenly curious as to what personal belongings they had allowed her to keep. He was surprised she'd had anything at all with her.

He waited until he was in his office, with the door locked and orders left not to be disturbed. Then he opened the bag and, seeing the money inside, was struck with joy. They hadn't taken it after all. Later he would take time to figure out why, but all he was interested in for the moment was finding out how much there was.

With shaking fingers, he counted. Then counted again. Fury became a choking lump in his throat. The amount was paltry, and he had sense enough to know the Indians would not have taken just part of it. They would have taken it all. So that meant they hadn't touched it, and the marquis, damn him, had neglected to send an acceptable amount.

Jarman's head was swimming in a sea of rage. Never had he been so mad. To think how he had been through hell and back these weeks, only to find out Celeste had been sent to him with a dowry that was an insult. This was the last straw.

He let other thoughts creep in, also, unnerving realities he hadn't wanted to dwell on, such as how she had been defiled by savages and stripped of her innocence. He would, of course, stand by her and fulfill his obligation to marry her. It was the noble thing to do. But, in the same regard, her father would have to compensate him for being so honorable.

Jarman reached for paper and pen. He was going to write to the marquis and tell him everything that had happened. He would also inform him that if he did not provide a generous dowry, his despoiled daughter would be returned to France.

When that was done, he felt much better about everything, confident that as soon as the marquis received the letter, more money would be on the way.

He was also pleased with his first impression of Celeste. When she was cleaned up she would be quite pretty, and he told himself he would have to put the past behind them and forget she was not the innocent virgin he'd looked forward to having on his wedding night. He'd try not to think about how she'd been deflowered by the red-skinned bastards, and the money sure to come would make it easier still.

He waited until midafternoon before going to the hospital, wanting to give her ample time to get cleaned up and rest a bit. As he stepped out of his office, the guard on duty was waiting to give him dozens of messages, all inquiring as to the condition of his fiancée. Several officers wanted to know if he would order a patrol to go out, and Jarman was quite anxious to do just that, but first Celeste had a lot of questions to answer.

When he arrived, Dr. Potts was waiting to draw him aside and confirm that Celeste was in excellent condition. "It's extraordinary, actually. She appears even to have gained a little weight. She was complaining about how tightly her gown fits and said she'd like to wash that Indian dress she was wearing when she arrived so she'll have something to wear till she can get new clothes."

Jarman exploded. "She'll do nothing of the kind. I never want to see her in Indian rags again. Now, were you able to get any information from her as to the tribe responsible?"

"She doesn't want to talk about it."

"Well, she's going to. I intend to see those bastards hanged for what they did."

"Apparently, they didn't do anything except hold her captive."

Jarman snorted. "What are you trying to say? Surely you don't expect me to believe they kept her all this time and didn't touch her."

"She looked me straight in the eye and told me they didn't. I've learned to know people pretty well, Captain, and miraculous though it might be, I think she's telling the truth."

"Well, I don't. Obviously she would rather lie than face reality, but I hope she doesn't expect me to be so naive."

He started by him, but Dr. Potts, with a grim expression, reached out to clamp a firm hand on his shoulder. "Let me tell you something, son. Either way, she's been through an ordeal most folks don't live to tell about, and you ought to be on your knees giving thanks to your Maker for sending her back to you, instead of getting all huffy over the way she's chosen to cope with it. If she wants to pretend it didn't happen, let her. Forget the past, because that's your future wife in there."

Jarman felt like screaming to the doctor not to remind him of that unpleasant fact; instead he brushed by the older man and headed into the room, only to freeze in his tracks.

The woman sitting on a chair by the window could not be the same one he'd met only a few hours before. Her hair was clean and shiny and hung full and lush around her tanned face. She had fascinating green eyes, fringed with dusty lashes, and, dear Lord, he breathed, she was beautiful. He ran his fingers through his hair nervously as he thought how it would have been an awkward meeting even under the best of circumstances.

"You . . . you look wonderful," he said finally.

She murmured sounds of gratitude, equally unnerved by the situation, then reaffirmed, "Actually, I was treated quite well."

"You're lucky to be alive, but tell me, why were you traveling alone?"

She explained about Francine, and he seemed angry. Not wanting any more tension than there already was, and noting that he was holding her purse, she changed the subject by nodding to it. "As you can see if you've looked inside, they didn't even steal my dowry."

"I did," he admitted. Then, daring to hope he was wrong about the marquis's stinginess, he asked, "Are you sure they didn't take part of it?"

"Oh, no. I had it with me the whole time." She saw his expression and asked worriedly, "Is anything wrong?"

He was not about to divulge his rancor. "No. I'm just so relieved you're safe." He laid the purse aside, then kneeled before her and took her hands in his. "But we have to talk about this, Celeste, even though you don't want to. There are things I have to know if I'm to find those responsible and see that they're punished."

She tore her gaze from his to stare out the window at the blue-and-gold day beyond. "There's no need. They didn't hurt me, and I just want to forget it."

He pressed on. "Now I know it had to have been a terrible ordeal, and it's only natural you want to put it all out of your mind, but first you've got to tell me everything you remember. Start with describing the area where you were taken."

Irritably, she explained, "I was blindfolded when they took me and also when they released me. I have no idea where we were. And all Indians look alike to me," she lied.

"They were Kansa. They had to have been. They had scalp locks, didn't they? The other passengers on the train said they had scalp locks. You know what I mean, don't you? Weren't their heads shaved except for a clump of hair sticking out in one place?"

"Some of them had long hair."

"They did?" he asked incredulously.

*Only one*, her heart reminded her, but she wasn't about to tell him that. "Yes. And their faces were covered with streaks of paint. All colors. I couldn't tell what any of them actually looked like, and it's just as well, because I don't want to talk about it."

He dropped her hands and stood to glower down at her. "Well, you're going to whether you like it or not, because I intend for those red-skinned devils to hang."

She returned his glare without flinching. "And I told you. I just want to forget it. It's over."

"They have to pay for what they did."

"They detained me for a few weeks, that's all. Nothing is to be gained by hunting them down and killing them. Please, Jarman, can't you let me forget it?"

He exploded, "Woman, you can't forget it. And neither can I. What they did to you—"

"They didn't do anything to me. They did not force themselves on me. *I was not raped.*" She colored slightly to have to say it but nonetheless wanted to make that fact clear once and for all. He did not have to know she had given herself willingly to one man. That would be her secret forever, and she would make it up to him in a hundred different ways if he would only give her the chance. But she was beginning to dislike him immensely. Couldn't he respect her wishes, for heaven's sake?

Jarman fought for self-control. It would do no good to scream out at her, call her a liar. Obviously this was the way her mind was choosing to cope, as Dr. Potts had said. She was blocking everything out, pretending the nightmare had not happened. "Very well," he said finally. "We won't talk about that part of it. But did you hear any names spoken?"

"Nothing. I remember nothing."

"But surely—"

"No." She waved her hands in protest. "Can't we talk of other things? Like our wedding," she suggested. The sooner they were married, the sooner she could adapt to her new life and move ever further from the past and what might have been.

Suddenly feeling awkward, for he had no intention of marrying her until the rest of the dowry arrived, Jarman hedged, "I'm not going to rush you, my dear, not after what you've been through. One of the officers' wives, Mrs. Larkins, told me she would be glad to have you stay with her and her family and offered to help with the wedding. I'll need to go see her and let her know you've arrived, though I imagine she's already heard by now. We'll see if we can get you moved over there right away and settled in."

"I'd rather not stay with strangers. Isn't there a hotel?"

"Don't be ridiculous. You need to be around people. I'll see to it right away." After pressing cool lips to her forehead, he hurried out before she could protest further.

Jarman had steeled himself for the inevitable encounters with his fellow officers. As he made his way to the Larkins house, several stopped him to inquire about Celeste. He told them of her miraculous condition, emphasizing she could not tell him anything that would lead him to those responsible, so it seemed there was nothing to do but try to forget. With no clues, he could not track the villains down. But he could tell by their expressions that they would not soon forget, and the sooner he mustered out of the army and left the fort, the better. He was not going to like being reminded constantly that people knew his wife had slept with Indians, goddamn it.

Mrs. Larkins had heard the news and was waiting to withdraw her invitation amid a cloak of sympathy as she explained, "There's no telling what that poor girl has been through, Captain. She's bound to have nightmares and wake up screaming, and I'm sure you understand I just can't have my children around anything like that."

"Of course, of course," he agreed politely, all the while suspecting her real reason. He was annoyed but not surprised. Lots of people would feel the same way toward anyone who'd been with Indians. Maybe Celeste sensed that, and it was her reason for wanting to be alone. He decided that was not a bad idea and remembered there was a boardinghouse in the city of Leavenworth, run by the widow of a preacher. Perhaps she might be persuaded to take Celeste in for a time.

He thanked Mrs. Larkins and started to leave, but as though struck by a spur of conscience over reneging, she offered suddenly, "When Miss de Manca is up to it, I think the officers' wives will want to have a little social to welcome her to the post."

Jarman told her that would be real nice and knew he would take her up on it. After all, it was the proper thing to do. People were just going to have to accept her. And so was he—but *only*, he reminded himself firmly and furiously, if her father ultimately sent a proper dowry. Otherwise he would send her back to France.

Cade had scrubbed the last of the war paint from his face and torso. After folding away the deerskin pants and breechclout, he stuffed them in a saddle bag. It was time to return to the life of a white man.

It would take him several days to reach his station near Council

Grove, but he was in no hurry. He wanted, needed, the time alone on the trail to brood over what he had to force himself eventually to put out of his mind. Leaving her without a word had been difficult, probably the hardest thing he'd ever done in his whole life. But that was the way it had to be. It was agony to think how everything had gotten turned around. And now he had to suffer the consequences of his own weakness. He had never meant to sleep with her and damn well never intended to fall in love.

Foolishly, he had done both.

**17**

*Sam and Maude Cammon* became instant friends.

Maude had been lonely since her husband had died ministering to the wounded in the war. That was why she had opened the boarding-house, but she soon discovered that single officers were no company. When they weren't at the post, they were courting young women in town. She only saw them at mealtimes, when they couldn't wolf their food down fast enough. So Maude took instantly to Sam, treating her like the daughter she'd never had.

She gave Sam the room next to hers, on the first floor near the kitchen and away from the officers. Maude might have been married to a preacher for thirty-seven years, but she could tell when a man lusted for a woman and hadn't missed the way the boarders had reacted at first sight of the silver-haired beauty.

Instead of being horrified that Sam had been held captive by Indians all those weeks, Maude was fascinated and wanted to hear all the details. So Sam told her about the tanning and cooking and child-rearing methods but carefully refrained from mentioning Wild Spirit.

There was a porch across the front of the house, shaded by colorful morning glory vines. Sam and Maude would sit in the cozy white swing for hours, watching passersby as Sam talked and Maude listened.

At first, Sam did not mind that Jarman did not come to call very often. Every third day or so, he would stop by after dinner to make sure she was all right, explaining how busy things were at the fort and complaining about being tired. He did not stay long, and that was fine with her. After all, they were strangers in a very unorthodox situation, and getting to know each other was a gradual and awkward process. Meanwhile, she was quite comfortable where she was, but Maude soon became annoyed over the way he was behaving.

"I should think he'd want to be with you all the time," she said, "you being engaged and all. And when's the wedding to be, anyway? It's time to start making plans."

Nothing had been said, and since Sam was not eager to marry him anyway, she was not prodding him to set a date.

"Do you care for him at all?" Maude bluntly asked one evening when Jarman left after a short visit.

"No. I don't." Sam saw no reason to lie and reminded Maude that her marriage had been prearranged; then she added with little enthusiasm, "But maybe one day I'll learn to love him. He seems like a gentleman." She could think of nothing else to say about him, was not about to admit she found him at times insufferable.

Maude slapped her knee and scoffed, "Hogwash. Being a gentleman doesn't necessarily earn a man love. A finer gentleman never lived than my Nate. He was good as gold. A man of God through and through. Ours was also a marriage agreed to by our families, and, like you, I told myself I'd learn to love him. But I never did. I cried when he died, of course, and I miss him, because he was my friend, but I never loved him the way I'd always hoped to.

"Maybe that's why we never had children," she went on to say thoughtfully, more to herself than Sam. "That was a side to marriage I avoided whenever I could. Lord knows it was my duty, but I couldn't stand to have him touch me that way. I think he must have known, because after a time he left me alone."

Sam had thought about that part of it but could feel no thrill of anticipation. Why, just looking at Wild Spirit had sent tingles up and down her spine, and when he had touched her, she had experienced a warm glow. Jarman had lightly touched his lips to hers a few times, but she had felt nothing.

"I think he's waiting to see if you're going to have a baby."

Sam's mouth fell open.

"A baby," Maude repeated. "I think Captain Ballard is waiting to set a wedding date till he finds out whether or not what happened to you made a baby."

When Sam recovered from shock over such a thought, she said tersely, "I told you, as I told Dr. Potts, I was not raped." And that was so. "Besides, I had my monthly last week."

"Then you best find a discreet way of letting Captain Ballard know that, or else he's going to stall till you'd be big enough to show, if you were in the family way."

"I can't do that, Maude. I can't talk to him about such things. He's going to have to figure that out for himself."

Maude shrugged. "Well, then, I guess you're going to be living with me for a while yet, but don't worry. That suits me fine.

"And don't forget the little social the wives are having for you next week," she went on. "Maybe after that, he'll decide it's time to go on and set the date. He's getting out of the army soon, anyway, isn't he?"

"Next month."

"Then it's time the two of you got on with it, dearie. Now let's decide what you're going to wear to that party. It has to be something special to make folks sit up and take notice. You're such a pretty thing anyway, and when we get you all fixed up, Captain Ballard will see how the men ogle, and he'll want to wrap you up for himself as quick as he can."

Sam doubted that, and she was not in the least enthused over the social anyway. The thought of being the center of attention made her cringe, but she also knew Maude was a wizard with a needle and thread and was dying to make her a new gown. Celeste's things were too small in the bosom for Sam anyway, and since she had gained a little weight, all of Celeste's gowns had had to be let out.

Maude decided she would design the gown herself but would not let Sam see it until the night of the party. Taking her measurements, she explained, "If you see it ahead of time, you might not like it and refuse to wear it. And it's going to be gorgeous. Just wait."

Sam teased, "You aren't going to make me look like a temptress, are you?"

But Maude, smiling mysteriously, refused to divulge anything about the creation she planned.

As it turned out, the gown was stunning.

"I don't believe it." Sam turned round and round before the mirror. The dress was fashioned of black taffeta and shimmered and glistened as the light caught the folds that billowed to the floor. Tiny stars had been embroidered and sprinkled about the skirt, and they almost seemed to actually twinkle. Sam felt as though she were floating on the night.

"With your silver hair, it's breathtaking," Maude said proudly, "and I knew the bodice would become you."

"*Become* me?" Sam echoed as she looked down at the generous display of cleavage. "You mean *expose* me, don't you?"

"If I'd had a figure like yours, dear, I'd never have lasted as a preacher's wife, because I'd have worn a gown just like this one every chance I got. I can see me now"—she giggled—"the good ladies chasing me out of town with a broom, with Nate right behind them cheering them on. He never even saw me naked. He'd have died to see my bosom poked out."

"Maude, sometimes I think you didn't even like your husband."

"Yes, I did. I told you he was my friend. Lots of wives can't say that about their husbands. But he was also stiff and cold, and sometimes when I think about all the years I wasted, my whole life, really, having to hold myself inside, keeping the real me a secret because of what I was supposed to be, well, it makes me mad. And I guess that's why I enjoyed making this dress so much." She leaned forward to confide mischievously, "The fact is, the material in this dress came from the one I wore to Nate's funeral. I couldn't find any bombazine at the time, so I had to use taffeta. I never knew one day I'd turn it into a party gown."

Hearing that, Sam burst into laughter, and Maude joined her, and the two clung together in near hysteria. Finally they calmed, and Maude styled Sam's hair in a sophisticated sweep, using a curling iron to make provocative tresses twine about her shoulders.

At last she was ready. Maude's final touch was to loan Sam her most prized possession—earbobs fashioned of pearls in the shape of teardrops. "Beautiful," Maude breathed in wonder, standing back to take in the full effect. "Absolutely beautiful."

When Jarman arrived, Maude was waiting to see his reaction but was stunned when he took one look at Sam and cried, "Dear God. Where did you get that gown? You'll have to wear a shawl. With your . . ." His words trailed away. He shook his head. "It won't do without a shawl." Personally he was dazzled and felt a warm stirring, but he certainly wasn't going to take her to meet the officers' wives in such a provocative dress.

Sam was amazed to discover that he was such a prig and was about to say so, but Maude, trying to head off the fight she sensed was brewing, ran and fetched a plain black shawl. Before Sam could give in to the temptation to tell him what she thought, Maude flashed him a glare of resentment and draped the shawl around her shoulders. "Don't worry," she comforted Sam. "You're beautiful, and don't let nobody make you think different."

Jarman ignored Maude as he swept Sam out of the house. He was beginning to feel that Mrs. Cammon was not quite the kind of influence he wanted for Celeste anyway and decided to start looking into other arrangements. Actually, he hoped the money arrived from France soon, because seeing her look so appealing made him want to take her into his bed. Perhaps marriage would not be so bad after all. Finding a woman for pleasuring had never been a problem, but the convenience of having one right next to him every night would be nice.

Sam was still miffed over his reaction. She hadn't thought the gown all that risqué. Once they were in the carriage and on their way, she said coldly, "I wish you hadn't been so critical. Mrs. Cammon worked very hard on this gown."

"Why did you ask her to make it like that?" he retorted.

"It was her design, and I see nothing wrong with it. I'd have designed it the same way myself."

"Sometimes I forget you're not cognizant of our ways. American women are more conservative than the French."

Sam jerked the shawl about her tighter. "I disagree. I saw plenty of women on the ship wearing bodices cut this low, but maybe you should just take me back to Mrs. Cammon's if you're so embarrassed."

"Just keep your shawl on. I suppose it doesn't matter. You're such an oddity, people will stare, anyway."

She looked at him sharply. "What do you mean?"

"Well, you did live with Indians, even if it wasn't your fault, and you have to remember people are repulsed by that. So you shouldn't do anything to draw attention to yourself."

"And that's the most asinine thing I've ever heard of. If people look down on me because of an experience I couldn't help, then they're the ones to be ashamed. Not me."

"Oh, really, Celeste." He sighed and moved away from her. "I'll be glad when it's time to leave this place. At least in a new town, people won't know about you."

"Yes, they will," she fired back. His condescending attitude was really getting her dander up. "I'll probably sprout feathers. Or maybe I'll start tanning hides and making my own clothes out of buffalo hide and deerskins. Maybe I'll just turn into an Indian, and then you'll all be happy."

"Will you please calm down? I'm starting to think some of those savages' ways rubbed off on you, because I can't imagine a lady of your background and breeding behaving in such a manner."

She threw up her hands. "Oh, what's the use? Sometimes I wish I'd stayed in Paris."

"Don't think I haven't wished the same."

They rode the rest of the way in angry silence, but when they reached the fort, Jarman attempted to smooth things over for the sake of the evening ahead. "Why don't we try to have a nice time and not argue?" he coaxed. Later, he vowed silently, fiercely, he was going to set her straight about a few things.

Sam had cooled enough to remember her vow to be good to him. "All right. I'm sorry. Maybe the dress is a bit risqué. I'll keep the shawl pulled tight."

"Good. We've both just been under a strain lately. Everything will be fine." Once the dowry gets here, he thought grimly. Otherwise I won't be able to get rid of you fast enough, you little bitch. . . . And if he did wind up marrying her, she would be quick to learn her place, or he'd take a strap to her curvy little bottom.

The commanding officer's quarters, where the gala was being held, was aglow with lights. The wide front porch was filled with officers resplendent in dress blues, polished scabbards at their sides, white gloved hands holding tiny crystal punch cups. Their wives swished about in pastel gowns, darting glances about to scrutinize what the others were wearing. But all eyes turned to Sam as Jarman helped her down from the carriage. Her hair glistened like quicksilver, and the silver stars seemed to be dancing against a night sky as the folds of her gown swirled about her.

Just then a sudden gust of wind caught the shawl, tearing it from her shoulders. For an instant she was displayed in all her glory, but Jarman moved swiftly to retrieve the covering and drape it about her once more.

Inside, introductions were made, pleasantries exchanged, but Sam was uncomfortable. Clinging to Jarman's arm, she found herself wishing she had not come. No one made any friendly overtures, and she started wondering whether she would ever feel a part of their world.

Jarman was right: it would be better when they went where no one knew anything about her.

Jarman asked her to dance, but she declined. "They'll only gape at me all the more if I'm out there in the middle of the floor."

"Relax. Smile at them."

"Why?" She was suddenly irate. "They aren't smiling at me. They're *staring* at me, and *rudely*, I might add. So why should I humble myself to them? I wasn't with the Indians by choice." *Not at first, anyway*, a little voice inside reminded her.

"You could act like you're ashamed of it."

"Have I acted as though I'm proud?" she fired back.

He shook his head and moved away and this time she did not follow him. Instead she went over to where several of the wives had gathered, deciding to make a genuine effort to be included. "Hello," she greeted them pleasantly. "I just wanted to say how appreciative I am that you've given this lovely party for me. I've been wanting to meet the ladies of the post."

Politely but stiffly, they acknowledged her. Then, returning to their conversation, they ignored her, but Sam continued to stand there, stubbornly determined to be a part of the group. Ida Mae Brackett was fretting about how her infant son cried all the time.

"Day and night. John can't get any sleep, and he's threatening to get a room at Mrs. Cammon's and stay there till Johnny gets over it."

Someone offered, "Maybe it's your milk."

"I thought of that, so I found a wet nurse, and that hasn't helped. He's fed and burped and dried and rocked and sung to, and still all he does is cry. It's driving me crazy. That's why I was so eager to get out tonight, to get away from it for a while, though I hated leaving someone else to have to hear it."

Eager to join in, Sam asked Ida Mae, "Have you thought about just ignoring him?"

Several of the women gasped, and Ida Mae looked at her incredulously. "What did you say?"

Sam plunged on, determined to help in hopes they would accept her. "Ignore him. As you said, he's fed and burped and dry, so his needs have been met. You've cuddled and rocked him, but he won't stop crying, so it's time to just ignore him. Once he finds out his crying is useless, he'll stop."

"Why, I've never heard of such a thing." Ida Mae exchanged glances with the other women.

"The Indians do it. They have to, you see. They can't allow a baby to cry. It's considered antisocial, and a crying baby might also give away a camp position to enemy raiders. So what they do when a baby cries persistently is take him out alone in his cradleboard and hang him on a bush till he cries himself out. When he stops, the mother brings him back around everyone else. After a few times, he realizes the crying is getting him nowhere, and he stops."

Ida Mae's face had seemed to grow redder with each word Sam spoke, and when Sam had finished, it took a few moments amid her choking, rasping breathing before she was finally able to voice her fury. "My child is not an Indian, and I don't intend to treat him like one. Hang a baby on a bush, indeed. Pity any children you and Captain Ballard might have." With noses in the air, the women stalked away.

Sam stared after them and realized with a sinking feeling that she should have kept her mouth shut. She was only trying to be friendly, wanting to join their circle, but they were not fascinated by Indian culture the way Maude was. They didn't want to hear anything about it.

Sam just wished she could find a hole to crawl into. Absolutely, this would be her last social at Leavenworth. Until Jarman was ready to leave, she was not going out of Mrs. Cammon's house, because everything she said or did these days seemed to be wrong.

She looked about in search of Jarman. The best thing to do was tell him she had a sudden headache and wanted to leave right away, but, looking about, she saw that Ida Mae had gotten to him first. Sam could not hear what was being said between them but knew by his instant flash of annoyance that it was not good. She braced herself as he immediately headed in her direction.

"Celeste, how could you?" he whispered harshly, furiously. "How could you tell Mrs. Brackett to go hang her son on a bush? How dare you even mention Indians? These people consider them no better than animals. Haven't you realized that by now? Dear God, I can't take you around civilized people, can I? You've become uncivilized yourself. And I seem to recall you didn't want to talk about any of it anyway, so why here? Why now?"

Hotly, she defended herself. "You only wanted to hear bad things. You didn't want to hear about their culture, things I learned."

"No, I didn't, and let's get out of here before you do something else to embarrass me."

Sam allowed him to take her arm and lead her toward the door. He offered polite good-byes to those they passed, murmuring that she was feeling ill. Sam would not even look at them, suddenly hating them all, hating Jarman, and, most of all, hating the misery of her life. Maybe she was even beginning to hate Wild Spirit, too, because if he had loved her, as she loved him, he could have spared her all this.

Suddenly the thought of living with Indians was quite appealing.

The Marquis Antoine Vallois Bruis de Manca had no warning and was totally unprepared for the shock of his life. Celeste had let herself into the house and made her way past startled servants to his study, then opened the door and walked right in. For an instant he could only stare in surprise, but slowly, comprehension dawned.

"*You*. What are you doing here?" Shakily, he got to his feet; then, remembering the interpreter's notes lying on his desk, notes he had just been laughing over, anger quickly washed away surprise. "How dare he send you back?" he roared. "Who does he think he is, rejecting my daughter over money? This is about honor, a family marriage pact, not a dowry, and . . ."

He trailed off, eyes growing wide as he noticed her swollen belly. "He . . . he even sent you back with child," he sputtered. He sank back onto his chair, only to bounce up again to cry, "But you haven't been gone long enough to be so far along, and—"

"Papa, you must listen to me." Celeste hurried around the desk to fling herself against him, wrapping her arms about him as she endeavored to confess. "I didn't go to America. I couldn't. I love someone else. I married someone else. I'm carrying his child, and—"

"Who?" He grabbed her shoulders, holding her away from him and giving her a violent shake that sent her head bobbing to and fro. "What is this all about? If you're here, if you never left, then . . ."

He released her and glanced down at the notes. Jarman's letter had arrived several days earlier, and Antoine had only received the translation this morning. The arrogant toad was refusing to marry Celeste until he received a larger dowry and threatened to send her back to France if he didn't get it. There was something about her being abducted by Indians. The wedding had not taken place yet, and since she was now defiled, Jarman felt he should have additional compensation to go through with it.

*But Celeste was here,* his brain screamed, and suddenly it was all coming together amid a descending veil of strangling rage.

"Samara." He choked out the name, releasing Celeste with a shove that sent her stumbling backward. She grabbed the back of a chair to keep from falling as he advanced upon her. "You sent her in your place, didn't you? She disappeared the day you did. I spent a fortune trying to find her. I even thought she might have stowed away on the boat, but the authorities assured me that did not happen, that you and only one companion arrived safely in Le Havre and continued on. Now I see how I was fooled. *You never left.*"

He raised his hand to strike her, but Jacques, who had been waiting outside the door for her to break the news, lunged inside. He had never shared Celeste's optimism that her father would be softened to hear that he was going to be a grandfather and was ready to defend her at the first sign of trouble.

"Don't you dare hit her!" Jacques slammed his hands against the marquis's chest and sent him reeling back to fall right onto his chair. "She's my wife, damn you, and you won't touch her, you hear?"

Things were not going at all the way Celeste had prayed they would. In desperation, she pushed by Jacques to fall at her father's knees and plead, "Papa, you must forgive me, but I love Jacques. We're married, and I am going to have his baby, and we need your help. We have nowhere to go. We have no money. Please let us come home. It doesn't matter about Jarman. He thinks Sam is me, and they're happily married, and he'll never know the difference.

"Think about it," she rushed on as he stared at her in stony silence. "It worked out for the best. Sam has a home, someone to take care of her, and you're going to have me with you, and your grandchild. It's a blessing, Papa." Her lips were trembling, and tears streamed down her face.

"Get out."

"Papa . . ."

Antoine pointed to the door, chest heaving, face livid. If they both didn't get out then and there, he was afraid of what he might do. Never had he desired a woman as he had Samara. Young, fresh, innocent. He could have taught her to please him in every way and enjoyed her for years to come. Not only had Celeste ruined that dream, but she had also shamed him by marrying out of her class. He looked at Jacques in contempt and spat the denouncement, "The gardener's son. You are the wife of a dirt servant. Are you really so stupid as to think I would acknowledge a grandchild sired by him? Get out of this house. Get out of my life. I have no daughter," he said with the finality of the slamming of a coffin lid.

Celeste wrapped her arms about his legs and held tight. "No, Papa. Please don't send me away. I need you, and my baby needs you."

Antoine met Jacques's defiant glare with his own. "Take her and go. And tell your father and mother I want them off the grounds by sundown."

"Oh, Papa, you can't do this—"

"Enough groveling." Jacques grabbed her and had to lift her in his arms to get her out of the room. "He's not worth it. He is scum, Celeste. I do not want my child ever to know him."

Alone once more, Antoine poured a drink from the bottle on his desk and leaned back, anger subsiding. He was going to make all of them pay for the way they had disobeyed and deceived him. He was confident that when Jarman Ballard discovered he was betrothed to an imposter, Samara would find herself kicked out in the cold with nowhere to go. She would know better than to return to France, and she could starve for all he cared. The same with Celeste. He never wanted to see her again.

He had his money and position.

And he had his women.

' He needed nothing else.

That night, after Jacques had moved Celeste and his parents into the home of relatives on the outskirts of Paris, he returned to the château. After sneaking inside, he made his way to the marquis's study. Once, while working in the flower bed just outside the window, he had peeked inside to see the marquis move a painting, exposing a hidden cache in the wall.

In only a few seconds, Jacques had enough money to take care of Celeste, and his parents, for a long time to come. He also helped himself to precious jewelry he figured belonged to Celeste anyway. And by the time the marquis discovered anything was missing, they would be far, far away, never to be found.

Italy, Jacques had decided happily, would be a nice place to raise a family.

# 18

*In the weeks following,* Jarman continued to be angry over the incident at the party but was secretly glad to have a reason for postponing the marriage. Until he heard from the marquis, he did not intend to commit himself any further.

At first he made up his mind not to take Celeste to another party, not that there had been any given lately. It seemed that since everyone knew it would be impossible to exclude them from the guest list, social activities on the post had come to a standstill. Yet when Lieutenant Larkins's wife yielded and sent an invitation to a dinner party, Jarman accepted, himself anxious to mingle again.

When he called for Sam, he was pleased to find her appropriately dressed for the occasion and told her so.

Sam, despite her previous resolve not to socialize, tried to summon enthusiasm. After all, it seemed to mean so much to Jarman that they attend the dinner, and she was trying her best to get along. She whirled around in the brandy-colored gown Maude had altered to fit. "I've lost a little weight, so she didn't have to remake it completely."

"It certainly looks better than the other one." He sniffed with distaste. "I never did understand why you would choose black to wear to a party, anyway. Black is for mourning, and I'm still surprised you were able to gain any weight. I hear those people eat dogs." He grimaced.

"I never saw them do that," Sam defended coolly. "And in France, the women wear black gowns whenever they wish. I even saw a few on the crossing," she added testily.

"You aren't in France."

"You don't have to remind me."

Defiant gazes locked and held, and Jarman thought how once they were married she would quickly learn that he expected an obedient wife, one who would not talk back. Irritably he advised her, "I do hope you will remember to watch what you say tonight. Perhaps it would just be best if you listen to the other ladies and not intrude in their conversation."

"In other words, just nod my head like a simpleton and keep a stupid smile on my face."

"If that's what it takes to keep you from upsetting them, yes."

Sam was finding it harder and harder to hold her temper. It was not her nature to be subservient. And she was also starting to wonder whether she could keep her promise to Celeste. After all, by now Celeste was married, far along in her pregnancy, and living in England. What difference would it make if the marquis found out the truth? Besides, she had managed to survive everything life had thrown at her, anyway; why did she have to relegate herself to a miserable, loveless marriage for the sake of security in a strange land? She could do just fine on her own.

"That's not what Maude says," Sam informed him testily. "Maude says those toady women at that party didn't have any reason to be upset. She also said they are the ones who should be ashamed for giving me a party and then snubbing me.

"And besides," she rushed on, forgetting her vow to be as agreeable as possible, "you would think they would want to hear about the cultures of other people. Personally, I was fascinated by some of the things I learned about the Indian women—their weaving skills, their bead work and pottery. Some of their handiwork was exquisite."

Jarman was getting madder by the minute. All he had wanted was a wife with a dowry to set him up in the casino business in Abilene. Never had he dreamed things could get so out of hand. "Please," he said wearily, "just keep your mouth shut about Indians. And I hope, for God's sake, that when we move to Abilene no one will find out about what happened to you."

"But I have nothing to be ashamed of." Not even loving Wild Spirit, she thought, wondering if she would ever be able to put him out of her mind.

It was times like this when Jarman found himself hoping the marquis did not comply to his demand for a larger dowry so he would have an excuse to send his daughter back to France. "You have *much* to be ashamed of."

Earlier, Maude had brought them tea, and Sam slammed her cup down so hard that it clattered against the saucer. "How dare you say such a thing to me?"

Jarman had reached the limit of his tolerance. "I have every right to censure you. And if you are to be my wife, you will learn to obey me and my wishes. Now enough of this conversation. In your belligerent mood, the party would no doubt be as disastrous as the last one. It's best I go alone. I'll convey your regrets."

"Well, that suits me fine." Sam got to her feet in a rustle of petticoats. "Heaven forbid I should embarrass you, so maybe after we're married I should stay home while you go to socials without me."

Jarman also stood, contempt flashing in his cold eyes as he slapped his white gloves against his open palm. "With your attitude, Celeste, there may not be a marriage. Think about that."

Sam was too riled to tread softly. "Why? Do you really think it makes any difference to me now, Jarman? This marriage was never my idea." That was certainly the truth, she thought wryly. "And quite frankly, I am sick of the way you and everyone else have been treating me. As if I'm a leper. If it weren't for Maude and her compassion, I couldn't have stood it."

"All you had to do was keep quiet and let people forget, but no, you had to stir things up every chance you got, as though you were proud of having lived like a squaw. You didn't even want to part with your squaw dress, for God's sake. The nurse at the hospital made sure that story got spread all over the post, and that didn't help the situation."

Sam was not about to tolerate his condemnation. "Someone gave me that dress. I admired the handiwork and wanted to keep it. As for me not letting people forget, you thought I should get down on my knees and ask them to forgive me for something I didn't do and beg them to accept me. But I will never do that, Jarman, because how many times do I have to tell you I've nothing to be ashamed of?"

"I think," he said tightly, "that if you do not change your ways, I shall be forced to decline to marry you."

Sam lifted her chin imperiously. "Fine. I will take my dowry and leave."

"*Your dowry.*" He sneered. "That paltry sum your father sent with you was an insult."

"What did you expect?" Sam knew nothing about dowries, how much money was considered proper.

"Don't concern yourself." He moved toward the door with an arrogant smile. "It will be adequate to buy your return passage to France."

"I'm not going back to France."

"You have no choice. You can't stay here."

"I can, and I will." Sam clenched her fists to keep from grabbing something and throwing it at him as he strode arrogantly out into the hallway.

He took his hat from the rack where Maude had put it. "I think it would be best if I didn't call on you for a while. You need to assess your situation. I'm sure when you have calmed down, you will realize how foolishly you are behaving. Perhaps I should have Dr. Potts stop by and give you something for your nerves. You could be having some sort of delayed reaction to your ordeal." Curtly, he opened the front door and walked out.

Sam felt like running after him to scream that she didn't give a damn if he never came back. But instead of railing, she suddenly realized that the idea of walking away from all the misery filled her with an exciting rush.

*She could do it.* She could go to Abilene and find Belle, and Belle would help her get a job as a professional gambler in one of the saloons there.

"Goodness, child, are you still here?"

Maude appeared in the doorway. She was wearing a heavy woolen shawl, preparing to go out in the chilly autumn evening. "And where's Captain Ballard? Did I hear shouting again? If you two don't stop arguing, I'll have no need to finish your wedding dress."

Sam did not want to talk about it. Not right then, because even though Maude had expressed her doubts from time to time about the marriage, Sam knew the older woman would not approve of what she was about to do. "I just decided I didn't feel like going out tonight. I think I'll go to bed and read."

"You can't do that."

Sam had started by her but paused to ask, "And why not?"

"Don't you remember I told you I'm going to be out till midnight? Miss Flora Gooding is sick, and the ladies in the church are taking turns sitting up with her. My turn is from now till midnight. I agreed to this time thinking you would be out with Captain Ballard."

"But what difference does that make?"

"Not any to me, dear, but you should know by now how folks are. It wouldn't be proper for you to stay here unchaperoned with all my men boarders. I suppose there's nothing for you to do but go with me."

Sam declined emphatically. She was not about to tag along with Maude like a child who could not be left alone. There had to be a way around such dictates. "I'll just stay in my room, and no one need know I'm even here."

Maude could tell her mind was made up, and there was no time to argue, anyway. "Oh, all right. But make sure no one knows you're in the house alone."

She hurried on out, and Sam went to her room and changed into a simple muslin dress. It was too early to go to bed, and she was not sleepy, anyway. Why should she be? She never did anything to get tired. Oh, she tried to help Maude with the cooking and cleaning, but there really wasn't that much to do. One day was like another, and she was beginning to be extremely bored with her life.

But no more. She was going to Abilene. All she had to do was figure out how to get there. She could go by train but had no money for a ticket and knew Jarman would never return any of the dowry. Asking Maude for a loan was out of the question. Despite her spunk and spirit, there were many things Maude did not approve of, and gambling was at the top of the list. If she ever suspected Sam wanted to embark on a career as a professional dealer, she would probably faint.

The sound of footsteps and men talking brought Sam sharply from her brooding. She opened her door and tiptoed quietly down the back hallway to see what was going on. She recognized a few of the officers' voices and wondered why they were returning to the house so early in the evening and also why they were heading downstairs, to the basement. Then she recognized Lieutenant Hamby when he grumbled, "I wish Dunnigan would hurry up with those cards. We can only play till midnight."

Sam felt a rush. *They were going to play poker.* Like a mischievous elf, she gave them time to get settled and start dealing, then went downstairs.

"Miss de Manca." Lieutenant Thorne Hallaby leaped to his feet at the sight of her, his chair falling backward with a loud clatter.

The others also sprang up, exchanging alarmed glances. Captain Brace Finton was the first to gather his wits and apologize, "We're sorry. We thought you were going out, too. We know we shouldn't be here, but we figured there was no harm with you ladies out for the evening. We'll be out of here in no time."

Hallaby was already gathering the cards, and the others were withdrawing their ante. Another of the officers spoke up to plead, "And we'd appreciate it if you wouldn't say anything. We won't try it again, we promise. It's just that we like to play a little poker now and then, and we don't think it's a good idea for the townspeople to see us gambling. We keep it quiet, because if Miss Maude found out, she'd never let us stay here."

Finton added, "That's right, and the officers' quarters at the post are full, due to so many companies coming in for wintering. There's no telling where we'd have to go to find a decent place to live."

Sam laced her fingers. "Relax, gentlemen. Maybe we can compromise."

Finton's brows went up. "I'm afraid we don't understand."

Feeling happy for the first time since the wonderful days and nights with Wild Spirit, Sam said saucily, "Just deal me in, and my lips are sealed."

By the time they heard the case clock upstairs chiming twelve times, Sam had won more than enough to pay for a train ticket to Abilene. The men were astonished. If she had cheated, they could not swear to it. She was good. She knew what she was doing.

Grudgingly, Dunnigan congratulated her but asked for a chance to win their money back. "As soon as we find another place where we can get together, we'll let you know."

"And don't worry about Ballard finding out," Finton chimed in. "Our lips are sealed, too."

"But only if you agree to play again." Dunnigan was not smiling. He did not like losing, especially to a woman, even one as pretty as she was, and couldn't help thinking how Ballard was a fool not to rush her to the altar. What difference did it make if she'd been had by Indians? She was still fine looking.

Sam made no commitment. Neither did she give the impression she was declining. There was no need for anyone to know of her plans.

She made it to her room with only moments to spare before hearing Maude come in. Too excited to sleep, she lay awake till nearly dawn just thinking about the future and hoping she had made the right decision. Jarman would write to the marquis and tell him what had happened, but she could not let herself dwell on that. After all, Celeste had sworn she would never see her father again, and if he got upset to think his daughter had run away, so what? He deserved to suffer for all his meanness.

So be it. Sam's mind was made up. She would, of course, sit Maude down and tell her she had decided it was best she go away. Then she would listen to all her arguments, and no doubt they would cry together and promise to stay in touch forever.

The rest of Sam's life was beginning, and she would have been completely happy to be aware of that fact except for the sadness of knowing that with each step to the future, she was leaving the only man she could ever love in the past.

But no, a painful jolt in her heart reminded her, *she* had not left *him*, and despite how she had tried to hate him, Sam knew had it been left up to her, she would still be in his arms.

Jarman did not really want to go to the party alone but felt obligated since he had accepted the invitation. After he'd made excuses for Celeste's absence, he sipped wine and wished for something stronger. Mrs. Larkins, however, did not approve of strong spirits and never offered them.

It was a dull evening, and he was anxious for it to end so he could slip into town and try to drink away his misery. Not hearing from the marquis was getting on his nerves, but he was not concerned about Celeste's little temper fit. She had no choice but to marry him, and she knew it, as she knew he would send her back to Paris if he chose to do so. All Jarman really worried about was getting his hands on the money necessary to start him on his way to a fortune. He hated army life, but at least it had been a steady income, and he had been raised in poverty. Now it appeared he was going to miss his chance to get rich, all because the marquis had swindled him.

"Why, my goodness, Captain Ballard, I do believe you look mad enough to just snap that wine stem right in half."

He had drifted out to the front porch during the social time before dinner and realized Ida Mae Brackett had followed to stand beside him.

"Is your fiancée ill?" she asked with mock concern.

"Not exactly, but she isn't feeling well."

Ida Mae could not resist leaping on the subject that still rankled. "Well, my baby is still crying all the time. Maybe I'll eventually be forced to take her advice and hang him on a bush somewhere."

He sighed and attempted to assuage the woman. "Mrs. Brackett, I told you I am truly sorry about that. I just don't know what got into Celeste. And she really feels terrible about it," he added.

Ida Mae was still indignant to have someone dare suggest she treat her baby like an Indian. "If you ask me, I don't think she realizes how folks around here feel about those savages."

Jarman tossed down the last of his wine, shifting uncomfortably from one foot to the other. He did not want to be rude and just walk off and leave her standing there, but he was fast becoming annoyed.

"Now you take that sweet Miriam Appleby. Remember her? We ladies had a social for her and her father, Judge Quigby, when they passed through here. Why, I'm sure if she'd been the one taken by the Indians instead of your fiancée, she'd have died from the shame. So nice and proper she was. A man would be proud to have a wife like that. A ready-made family, too. I met her son, and he's a dear child."

Jarman was grateful to hear the announcement that dinner was being served so he wouldn't have to listen to any more, but Mrs. Brackett had brought to mind the judge again. He began to think how he could have married Miriam Appleby for the same reason he'd planned to marry Celeste—money. Oh, the judge was not rich by any means, but Jarman was confident he could come up with financial backing if he wanted to. And if a man agreed to take his homely widowed daughter off his hands, Jarman suspected the judge would be most cooperative.

As soon as he could politely excuse himself after eating, Jarman headed for town to find Martita and a bottle of whiskey. He knew the combination of the two would make him forget his troubles, if only for a little while.

Some time during the night, he returned to his quarters. Weary, as always, from Martita's wild passion, head spinning from drink, Jarman stumbled across the room to fall across his bed and immediately passed out.

He did not see the letter from France that had been slipped under his door.

\* \* \*

Maude cried as she hugged Sam good-bye. Sam had hired a wagon and driver to take her to Kansas City. She would take the noon train from there to Abilene.

"Are you sure this is what you want to do?" Maude fretted. "I certainly understand your reasons. As I told you while you were packing, I've kept it inside me, because I didn't want to come right out and tell you how I dreaded seeing you marry that man. You deserve someone more compassionate and understanding. And he's so stuffy and conceited. But to take off by yourself this way, oh, child, I'm going to be worried sick till I hear you're all right. And what if you can't find your friend?"

"She'll be there. Now don't you worry about me. I'll be fine. And it has to be this way, Maude. Jarman will send me back to France if I refuse to marry him," she reminded the older woman.

Maude dabbed at her eyes with her handkerchief as she sympathized fiercely, "Your uncle is a wicked, wicked man to try to seduce his own niece. No wonder you didn't mind coming all this way to marry a stranger, and I don't blame you for refusing to go back there."

Sam felt a twinge of guilt over the story she'd hastily made up to keep from going into details about the situation with the marquis. She was afraid the truth would lead to exposing her as an imposter, so it was best to lie about having a lecherous uncle. Giving Maude one last hug, she urged, "Remember. You're not to tell Jarman where I've gone, no matter what."

"You have my solemn promise."

Sam hurried down the steps to the waiting carriage, wondering dismally if she would ever find her true destiny.

# 19

*When Jarman had read* the letter written by the marquis's interpreter, he was struck insane by his rage.

To discover he had been the victim of such a hoax was more than he could bear. No matter that there was no real emotional disappointment, because he had never loved her, of course. The delirious fury was sired by the realization of how he had almost been duped into marrying an impostor, a demimonde at that, according to the marquis, a woman of questionable repute.

But at least he had the last laugh on the damned Indians. If not for the abduction, Jarman knew he would probably have married the woman he'd thought was Celeste as soon as she stepped off the train and complained to the marquis about the dowry later. It was thinking about what the Indians had done to her that had made him move slowly, and now, thank God, he was relieved he had.

He had started smashing things, throwing furniture about the room as he screamed and cursed Samara Labonte and the marquis and his insignificant dowry. He would stop momentarily to catch his breath, but then humiliation would flood him and the anger would explode all over again.

The other officers had already left the building to report for duty, so there was no one around to hear the commotion. It was only when a chair sailed through a window in a hail of broken glass that soldiers on the parade ground hastily broke formation to investigate. The officer of the day was summoned, but by the time he arrived, Jarman had calmed down.

Lieutenant Bowman took one look at the shambles of the room and ordered everyone out. Then, with the door closed, he attempted reason. "Sir, I don't know what's happened to upset you so, but believe me, all of us sympathize with what you've been going through." He paused a moment, hesitant to criticize a higher-ranking officer; but under the circumstances he decided he really had no choice. "But I think I should tell you there's been a lot of talk about how much you're drinking lately, and I'm afraid after this, I'm going to have to make a report to General Schofield in St. Louis."

Jarman's laugh was almost maniacal as he waved his arms at the destruction he'd caused. "Do you think I give a damn, Lieutenant? I'm mustering out of here in two weeks, and I don't care what you do."

Shoving him out of the way, Jarman bolted from the room. He went to the stables, saddled his horse, and rode like thunder straight to the boardinghouse. He only hoped he could keep from strangling the silver-haired bitch when he saw her. And who the hell was she, anyway? All the marquis had said was that Celeste had persuaded her to take her place to keep him from finding out she was eloping. He had only found out about it himself shortly after receiving Jarman's letter complaining about the dowry. Magnanimously, the marquis had said he could keep it. As if he would return it, Jarman thought with clenched teeth, such as it was.

Maude was sweeping the porch steps when Jarman reined his horse to an abrupt stop amid a cloud of dust. "Do you have to ride in here like a hooligan?" she yelled. "I'm not doing this for you to make me do it all over again."

"Where's Celes—" He paused as he felt a surge of fresh anger and bit back the impulse to call the bitch by her real name. But there was no need to let people know how he'd been duped, making him look the fool. *"Celeste,"* he completed firmly. "Where is she?"

"Gone." Maude turned her back and continued sweeping.

He quickly dismounted. Her voice and demeanor warned him that something was amiss. "What do you mean, she's gone? Didn't she say where she was going, when she'll be back?"

"She's not coming back." Maude raised the broom in warning when he moved to block her path. She never had liked him. He was cocky, conceited, and too pretty to be a man, anyway. "Now get out of my way."

He caught the broom handle and held tight. "What are you talking about? She can't leave. She has nowhere to go."

"The Lord provides. Now you let go of my broom and get off my property."

"Not till you tell me where she's gone."

"I'm not telling you anything, except that I don't blame her. You ought to be ashamed of yourself, the way you've treated that poor girl. She couldn't help what happened to her, and I'll tell you something else, Captain Ballard. Those Indians treated her better than she's been treated by most white folks since she arrived in this country. Maybe she went to live with them," she added with an airy sniff and a lift of her chin.

With a quick snatch, he tore the broom from her grip to send it flying across the yard. "To hell with her," he cried.

He mounted his horse, reined about, and dug in his spurs to thunder away in another whirl of dust for Maude to complain about.

Jarman knew Samara Labonte must have suspected she was about to be exposed for the impostor she was and had decided to run away. A wise decision, too, since he was not sure what he would have done had he found her.

As he headed back to the fort, an idea suddenly struck him, and he dared think that maybe his dream was not lost to him after all. Maybe Judge Quigby would be willing to be a silent partner. With his contribution, and the dowry, which Jarman had put away for safekeeping and had no intention of returning, he could have his casino after all. And even if the judge did push his daughter at him, sooner or later he would give up.

Fired with enthusiasm, Jarman determined not to brood over how Samara Labonte had tricked him. But God help her if their paths ever crossed again, he thought with a heated rush, because he was not one to forget treachery, and he would take vengeance for his wounded pride.

\* \* \*

Sam knew she had to be careful with her money and bought the cheapest ticket available on the Kansas Pacific Railway. That relegated her to what was known as the immigrant car, which had been designed as a special inducement to attract those recently arrived from Europe. It was plain, with hard seats and bunks with straw-filled bags for mattresses. There was a toilet and a coal-burning potbellied stove for heat, if needed.

Far too engrossed in her latest dilemma, she did not mind the lack of luxury. If she did not find Belle, and quickly, she would soon be in a desperate financial situation.

She had dressed in gray worsted for the two-day trip, having learned from experience how to deal with cinders, smoke, baking sun, and the dust of the prairie. But, carrying on board a change of clothing in her bag, she was able to step off the train in Abilene elegant in a red plaid traveling suit with matching bonnet.

At first sight, Sam could feel the excitement of the town. All around were crowds of businessmen, arriving from the East to make deals or heading back to celebrate success in having made several good ones. Coming from the adjacent stockyard were the sounds of constant bawling and steers' horns clacking together as they waited their turn to be weighed and sent up the ramps and loaded onto the trains. The air was rich with a loamy smell, dust so thick and heavy it tickled her nose.

A conductor inquired about her transportation as her trunks were being unloaded. Sam had to admit she wasn't sure exactly where she was going. He gave her an odd look but directed a porter to put her luggage in temporary storage. She decided to walk rather than hire a carriage, especially since it appeared that the heart of town was only three blocks away. It was also midafternoon, and if she wanted to locate Belle before dark, it meant stopping in every place where there was gambling. Keeping a carriage and driver waiting would be expensive.

Making her way down the plank walk past the jerry-built false-front buildings of unpainted pine, she noted a furniture store, a jewelry store, and the office of the newspaper, the *Abilene Chronicle.* There were signs offering the services of blacksmiths, tinsmiths, and saddlers, as well as dry-goods and clothing merchants, grocers, doctors, lawyers, bankers, and dentists. Finally she spotted the kind of sign she was looking for, the one that identified the first saloon.

Pushing against cut-off swinging doors, she stepped inside, pausing to let her eyes adjust to the scant light. She could make out a bar that ran the length of one wall, with mirrored shelves behind it that held glasses of all sizes. A few men leaned against it. Others sat around nearby tables. All turned to stare at Sam.

"You want something, lady?" the bartender asked with a frown. To the bartender, she did not look like a whore, which meant she was either one of those church ladies come to preach about the evils of whiskey and gambling or a wife looking for a wandering husband. Either way he wanted to get rid of her fast.

Ignoring the whispers and snickers, Sam walked to the counter. "I'm looking for a lady gambler. Her name is—"

"Try the part of town called the Devil's Addition," he said, hooking his thumb. "Farther down the street. Boss here don't want no women gamblers."

"Nah." Someone nearby guffawed. "We got other uses for women around here. Do *you* need a job, girlie?"

Sam silenced him with an icy glare, pausing to sweep the entire roomful of men with contempt. She had no patience with their ribald humor.

In the next block, she entered a saloon called the Alamo, which was quite elegant. The doors were glass instead of wood, and there were paintings of Renaissance-like nudes on the walls. Mirrors made everything seem larger, reflecting rows of rum, brandy, and whisky bottles and pyramids of glass tumblers. It was definitely a better-class establishment than the one she'd just left. Also gleaming in the mirrors was the gold lying on the green baize of the gambling tables, and Sam took her time walking through, amazed to see that the Kansas plains drovers and cowboys appeared to be playing for stakes in the thousands.

Approaching a man playing a tinny-sounding piano, she asked about Belle but was told, "Keep on moving along the street. If she's in Abilene, you'll find her. You might have to go into the Devil's Addition, though, so you'd best hurry. That's not a good place for a lady to be after dark, unless you're a calico queen." He winked and kept on playing.

Sam was unfamiliar with that term but had an idea what it meant, so she did not ask. She did, however, want to know about the Devil's Addition. "You're the second person who's told me I might find her there. Where is it?"

"Nothing but whores there. A little gambling. But mostly whores. The morally indignant citizenry of Abilene drove them out of this section, because they're harder to control than longhorns in a loose cow pen. One strode right down Main Street last week wearing nothing but a pair of six-shooters, and just yesterday two of 'em were seen skinny-dipping in the Smoky Hill River with their customers."

Sam was quick to tell him, "I'll have you know my friend is not a whore. She's a—"

But there was no time to say more, for suddenly the world seemed ripped apart as gunshots rang out. Before Sam knew what was happening, the piano player had grabbed her about the waist, thrown her to the floor, and fallen on top of her, as everyone else in the saloon also dove for cover.

Outside, two drovers were riding their wiry little cow ponies along the plank walk, firing into the air as they "yipped" and whooped to let off steam after a hard summer riding herd on twenty-five hundred or so longhorns.

As they rode on down the street, the sound faded, and the piano player crawled off Sam. He got to his feet and helped her to hers as he explained, "They're harmless and just celebrating, but sometimes folks get caught in the way of a stray bullet, so never take any chances. A little boy got killed a few weeks ago when he had the misfortune of being out in the street at the wrong time.

"My name's Hank, by the way," he added, and held out his hand.

Sam shook it, then asked, "Do all of them celebrate by shooting like that? If a child was killed, why doesn't the law—"

"Oh, there's no law to speak of. The judges travel around a lot, and there's no marshal, anyhow. The farmers and a few businessmen put pressure on, but nobody seriously tries to keep law and order. The latest to try is Jake Whaley, but he spends all his time at that store of his on the edge of town. But it's like I heard somebody say back in the spring, once cattle season starts, hell is in session. Murder, robbery, gunfights, fistfights, lust. It's all here, lady, which makes me ask"—he regarded her with narrowed eyes—"*why* are *you?*"

"I told you. I'm looking for my friend. She's here somewhere, working as a card dealer."

He scratched his head thoughtfully, then grinned and snapped his fingers. "Seems like I do remember something about a lady gambler coming to town a while back and hooking up with a fellow by the name of Lyman Guthrie. He's got a place in the Devil's Addition. If she's still in these parts, that's where you'll find her. Just go outside, turn right, and keep walking. You can't miss it. It's called the Lucky Steer."

Sam was already on her way. On both sides of the street, everything a cowboy fresh off the trail could want was offered. A bath and a haircut was fifty cents, and a glass of Kansas sheep dip—hard liquor —could be had for a quarter. Casinos seemed to be everywhere, along with an abundance of painted women. They lounged outside the saloons in their bright feather-trimmed gowns or boldly sat in the upstairs windows wearing flimsy, provocative robes.

At the very end of the street, Sam spotted the Lucky Steer and was heading in that direction when a calico queen leaned out a window to yell, "You're wasting your time. Lyman don't allow no whores to work in his place. They got to work for Louretta. She rents out the upstairs. You'll have to talk to her if you want a job around here. We don't need nobody else."

Sam supposed it made no difference that she was nicely dressed. Any woman walking the streets of the Devil's Addition was obviously assumed to be a prostitute. "I'm not looking for that kind of work," she called back. "But would you happen to know if Mr. Guthrie still has a lady card dealer?"

"He sure does."

Sam broke into a run then, bursting through the doors of the Lucky Steer with heart pounding so hard, she feared it would leap right out of her chest. And before she even had a chance to glance about, someone screamed, "Celeste, my God, I don't believe it!"

The next thing Sam knew, Belle Cooley was pouncing to hug the breath out of her. "I still don't believe it," Belle cried, finally standing back to drink in the sight of her. "What happened? Why, I thought you'd be married and out to here by now." She giggled and patted Sam's flat stomach.

Sam had still not had a chance to speak, and just then a tall, thin man walked over to flick a curious glance at her. "So, who are you?"

Belle answered for her. "This here is Mademoiselle Celeste de Manca, from Paris, France, and if what I'm thinking is so, she just might be the new dealer you've been wanting. Am I right?" She gave Sam another squeeze. "Are you here to look for a job because things didn't work out for you to get married?"

Sam was happy to confirm, "That's right," then added quickly, "except for one little detail."

Belle cocked her head to one side. "And what's that?"

"The name is Sam. I'm not Celeste de Manca."

"What on earth are you talking about?"

Enjoying the moment, Sam smiled. "It's a bottle of wine story,

Belle, which means it may take the whole bottle to tell you about it. Think you can find one in this place?"

When Cade had reported to Council Grove, he was told he had been chosen to work out of the office as an undercover investigator for several reasons. He could speak the language of most of the tribes in the area, and with his bronzed skin and black hair, which he still wore hanging to his shoulders, he could pass for an Indian—from a distance. Up close, blue eyes would arouse suspicion, but he did not intend to get in that position until he was ready to make his move.

In the span of only a few weeks, he had arrested several white men who were illegally selling whiskey and guns to the Indians. He had also busted up a ring of traders who had been kidnapping young Indian girls and smuggling them down to Mexico to be sold into slavery.

Cade liked his work. Not only did he feel he was doing some good, but it also kept him from thinking about Celeste de Manca. Pining, was more like it, he admitted privately. She had crawled under his skin to become a part of him, and no matter how hard he tried to lose himself with other women, he could not get her out of his mind—or his heart.

Bold Eagle had been discharged from the army only a short time after Celeste got to the fort, so all he could tell Cade was that the last he knew, she had not married Ballard. But that had been a couple of months ago. Cade figured the ceremony had taken place by now. It was time to get on with his own life, by damn.

He was camped outside the town of McPherson, waiting for Bold Eagle to report back on what had happened in court that morning. Cade had turned over his latest prisoner to another agent for prosecution, not wanting to be seen in the law arenas any more than necessary in hopes of keeping his true identity a secret.

But one look at Bold Eagle's face when he arrived told Cade his dire predictions had come true. The judge had let another lawbreaker go free.

"He does not care about the Indians," Bold Eagle said stonily. "He will hang a man in the blink of an eye if he uses a gun in a crime. It is said he has become insane with his hatred of guns. But if a man commits a crime against the Indian, the judge treats it as though it is unimportant and lets him go with a lecture."

Cade felt a hot flood of anger. "Well, what damn good does it do for me to risk my neck to catch the bastards if all he's going to do is let them go?"

Bold Eagle gave a sad shake of his head. "I do not know what you can do, my brother. This man is a judge. His word is law."

Cade had been idly whittling at a branch with his knife but suddenly sent the blade slashing into the ground with a vengeance. "Well, maybe it's high time he got reminded of his obligation to enforce all laws, not just the ones that get his dander up."

"And how do you plan to do that?"

"I have to make a run into Indian territory to track down those bastards that stole some supplies headed for the Osage reservation last week. When I get back, I'm going to pay him a visit.

"Whether he likes it or not," Cade vowed darkly, "Judge Quigby is going to hear me out."

# 20

Belle listened, fascinated, while Sam told her about the scheme for her to pose as Celeste, as well as her abduction by the Indians. And when she was done, Belle slapped her on the back and praised, "If ever a woman was able to cope with the wild and woolly West, it's you, Sam Labonte, and I'm proud to be your friend."

Lyman Guthrie was only too glad to hire Sam to work in his casino but admitted, "It ain't a fancy place, but there's money to be made down the road as things grow. Belle has helped a good bit, because some men come in here just to try to beat a woman at cards. But she's good, and she never gets caught cheating."

Sam glanced at Belle and saw her slight smile and covert wink. Just because she had not been caught did not mean she wasn't doing it.

Lyman went on to brag about how he had won the money in a poker game to start his own place. "Otherwise, I'd never have been able to. You see, I was working in Texas, just tending bar, but then I heard how Abilene was growing and knew there was money to be made. So I came out here to find out, got lucky, and here I am," he concluded proudly.

Later, Belle confided to Sam how she feared that one day Lyman would lose the Lucky Steer because of his weakness for gambling. "He just can't leave the cards alone. I'm all the time having to get him out of messes. He'll run up a big debt to somebody, and then I have to step in and win it all back for him. One of these days I'm not going to be around to come to his rescue, and he'll go under."

"But you aren't planning to move on, are you? I just got here."

"Things are pretty dead come November, I'm told. From then till spring, with no herds coming in, there's nothing going on. I figure I'll head to Texas then, and who knows? By that time I might even have enough saved up to get my own place. You can come with me."

Without understanding all her reasons, Sam declined. "Maybe I'm just tired of traveling and want to put down roots somewhere. Abilene seems like a nice town. I think I'd just like to stay here."

It was midmorning, and the saloon was empty. Business did not really get started before noon. Sam and Belle were sitting at a table, shuffling cards aimlessly. For a time, Belle did not react to Sam saying she wanted to settle in Abilene, but finally she put her cards aside and said bluntly, "Maybe you're just wanting to hang around these parts hoping the Indians will drag you off again."

Sam looked at her as though she'd suddenly lost her mind. "That's ridiculous. How can you say such a thing?"

"Maybe"—the corners of Belle's mouth turned up in a teasing smile—"you're hoping one of them would have blue eyes."

Sam was becoming agitated. She had told Belle about Wild Spirit but not, of course, that they had been lovers. So why was her friend trying to goad her? "I think you're being absurd." Her hands began to shake, and she dropped a few cards, which went sailing to the floor.

Belle laughed softly and gave her arm a squeeze. "Oh, Sam, I've been around. I know all the signs. There was something in your voice, your eyes, when you talked about him. I sensed you cared. And I've also got an idea you aren't telling everything that went on between the two of you, either."

Sam briskly gathered the cards. "You're imagining things. He was a brute, a savage, as people around here seem to be so fond of calling Indians. I never want to see him again." Oh, why couldn't she stop trembling? "My goodness, Belle, you're as suspicious as Jarman. *I was not raped.*"

"I didn't say I thought you were."

Sam eyed her suspiciously. "Then what are you getting at?"

"Oh, nothing, really." Belle gave an exaggerated shrug. "It's just that I find it hard to believe you were in the company of a man as handsome as you described, for weeks at a time, under the most intimate of circumstances, and didn't sleep with him. I think you *did*, and I also think you fell in love with him, whether you'll admit it or not. Maybe you aren't even admitting it to yourself.

"And like I said," she added with a knowing smirk, "I've been around, dearie. I know the signs."

"Well, you're wrong, and now I wish I'd never told you about him. I'm not interested in any man, and the only thing I want is to make money so I can take care of myself, then I won't ever need one."

Belle giggled. "Well, I'll go along with that, but believe me, it's nice to have a man around when you want some loving."

Sam was grateful a few cowboys wandered in just then, ready and eager for an early morning game. She was having a hard enough time running from the velvet memories of moon-mad nights with strong arms holding her as fevered kisses made her soar to the very stars twinkling above. Dear Lord, she did not need to be reminded of the joy of it all, to be tormented with the realization of how she longed to experience the wonder again.

In the next weeks, Sam fulfilled Belle's prophecy that she was skilled and proficient in her trade. In addition, she became adept at faro, perhaps the most popular casino card game of all. Lyman put in a table, which required three people to handle the game—a dealer, a lookout, and a casekeeper to sit with an abacus-like device to show which cards had been played. So others were hired, and eventually Sam could return to what she liked best—poker.

Business grew, and Lyman was jubilant. He abandoned his sloppy dress and took to wearing dapper outfits—frock coats and ruffled shirts and silk string ties. He began to smoke long, expensive cigars and stocked the bar not only with beer, the most popular drink in town, but also with imported French brandy for the really big spenders. In addition, he generously outfitted Belle and Sam in expensive, fancy gowns.

But despite his ever-growing fortune, Lyman still did not allow prostitutes to work his establishment. "Soiled doves lead to trouble," he declared adamantly. "I've got enough to worry about keeping peace with all the drinking and gambling going on. I don't need some cowpoke getting mad and maybe busting up the place over finding out his favorite whore has been taken for the evening by somebody else. They want a woman, they can go up to Louretta's place."

Sam and Belle were glad Lyman took that attitude, wanting the men who came into the Lucky Steer to have nothing on their minds except gambling and drinking. Other saloons were filled with fiddle and piano players and song-and-dance men, and waitresses flirted about with trays of brimming beer mugs while offering to sell pleasures of the flesh. Lyman, however, provided only gambling, and the high-stakes players came in droves, eager for the more subdued atmosphere that prevailed in which to contemplate their strategy at the gaming tables.

Occasionally, Belle would appear interested in a man for reasons other than taking his money. The two of them might disappear for a night. Sam, however, was all business. She was making good money and daring to think that one day she might be able to own her own place. The idea was not impossible, and she wanted to plan for the future since she had come to agree with Belle over the prospects of Lyman's continued success. He did drink too much and took risks gambling, and sooner or later he was going to go too far and lose everything.

Sam spent little time in her room above the Lucky Steer. Louretta did not like her and Belle staying there, but Lyman insisted, and it was cheap and convenient. But for the time being, Sam mostly took one day at a time, staying busy, sleeping little—and trying, without success, to forget those caressing blue eyes and moon-mad nights.

Cade left the barbershop, his hair freshly washed and trimmed, face clean-shaven. He had visited the bathhouse earlier and donned clean trousers and shirt and fresh-shined boots. He looked nothing like the feral scavenger of the plains he passed for when doing his undercover work. Instead, he was presenting himself as what he actually was—an Indian agent, working for the federal government, because he was on his way to see Judge Newton Quigby and demand that he start meting out justice to all who came before him, not just the cases that incensed him personally. Cade knew Quigby had a house on the outskirts of Abilene but, of course, wasn't in town much. When he was, hearings were held in one of the saloons for lack of a courthouse; but no court was in session for the moment, and Cade had heard Quigby could be found at home that day.

The house was not hard to find. A plain white clapboard, it was the only one near a small church and cemetery. Cade made a habit of keeping his ears open, especially in bars, and before cleaning himself up, he'd stopped in at a few places to catch up on the local gossip. He had heard a few men snickering about how the judge would never give up until he found a husband for his homely daughter.

One man told a story that Cade knew could only have been made up as a cruel joke. "Last week the judge offered a condemned man a reprieve just as the hangman was about to slip the noose around his neck. He told him he'd give him a pardon if he'd marry his daughter. They say that man turned white as a sheet at the thought and grabbed that noose himself and pulled it tight around his own neck and then leaped right off that scaffold."

His companions had exploded with laughter, but Cade had been struck with compassion for the plain and shy young woman he remembered meeting back at Fort Leavenworth. Someone else spoke up to say something about how it was being said Miss Miriam was tetched. "They say she was having séances in her house, trying to bring her husband back from the dead, and now she's gone plumb loco since. . . ." But Cade had not wanted to hear any more and moved on.

At the Quigby house, he found others waiting to see the judge, so he headed back to town, figuring to return first thing in the morning. He stopped in a few more saloons before going to the Devil's Addition. He hadn't had a woman lately and didn't particularly want one now. After Celeste, they meant nothing, but he was lonely. And a few drinks and a wild-spirited whore could satisfy him for a little while, anyway. Still, nothing could take the place of the tender wonder he had experienced when he had held her in his arms, and once more he cursed himself for not being able to get her out of his mind—or his heart.

He had been to visit Louretta a few times and found her accommodating, so that was where he went.

Pausing in front of the Lucky Steer, he was impressed to see how it had grown. An addition had been built onto the back, and the place looked crowded. He was about to go in and have a look around, but Louretta had already spotted him from her window and came running down the steps to throw her arms around him, crying, "Don't you dare waste time gambling in there. I've missed you, and I'm going to keep you with me all night long, and the first tumble is on the house."

Returning her hug with not quite the same enthusiasm, he peered over her head as someone brushed by, opening the swinging doors into the saloon. He could see that Guthrie had obviously spared no expense to offer good playing conditions, for oil-burning chandeliers cast a bright and cheery light over the crowded tables. In the brief moment a view was afforded, Cade scanned the room, and suddenly his heart slammed into his chest.

*Silver hair.* At the far side, he could see the shimmering silhouette of long silver hair trailing down a woman's back. He had seen that lustrous color only once before.

At the strange look on his face, Louretta asked, "What's wrong? You look like you saw a ghost."

The doors had swung closed. Cade blinked, shook his head to clear it. Surely it had been his imagination, but something urged him to make sure. "I thought I saw a woman inside with strange-colored hair —like silver."

"You did. That's Guthrie's new dealer. She's good, too. She's really brought in the business. She's a wizard with the cards, but so far, nobody has caught her cheating."

It couldn't be, Cade told himself. Celeste de Manca was married by now. She was Mrs. Jarman Ballard, and she couldn't possibly be here, in what preachers called the Sodom of the plains, dealing cards. Still, after seeing that gleam of moon-colored hair, he felt pressed to ask, "Do you know her name?"

"Sam. But you're wasting your time. She takes men in card games. Not in bed." She squeezed his bottom boldly. "So forget her and come on with me, and I'll remind you what it's like to be a man."


Jarman was uncomfortable. And not just because of the prickly horsehair sofa he was sitting on and the nearly unpalatable meal he had just eaten. The fact was that he felt like a fly caught in a spider's web and wished he were anywhere but in the parlor of Judge Quigby's house with Quigby's daughter.

She was spooky. That was the only way Jarman could describe Miriam. She was wearing a black shroudlike garment, and her hair hung limp and stringy down her back. When it fell into her face, she made no attempt to push it back, which was just as well, since it partially hid her woeful expression.

Judge Quigby had been delighted to see Jarman, ushering him right into his study, forgetting all the others waiting to see him. He had reacted with astonishment and sympathy when Jarman had confided the way he had been deceived by Samara Labonte, then shared his own tragedy, how his grandson had been caught in crossfire on the rowdy streets of Abilene and killed.

Jarman could see how grief had aged the man, and he also shuddered to witness his rage as he had expounded on how he intended to do everything in his power to rid Kansas of gunslingers. He had bragged about the number of men he'd sent to the gallows, vowing that if a crime was committed with a gun in his bailiwick, the criminal would pay with his life. Jarman was not sure that sounded entirely fair but was not about to argue the point.

He had got straight to the point of his business. Since they were alone, with no one to overhear and question the ethics of a judge becoming an investor in a gambling establishment, Jarman had come right out and asked for his help.

For the first time, there was a light in Quigby's eyes. He had contained his enthusiasm, however, shaking his head and murmuring uncertainly, "I don't know, Ballard. I just don't know. It wouldn't look right."

"No one would find out. I've got a little money. All you have to do is add your part to that. I'll be doing all the work, and you just sit back and enjoy your share of the profits."

"I'll have to think about it."

Jarman had pressed on. "Well, don't take too long. I've got to get started. There's money to be made, and I don't like sitting back and watching others make it."

Quigby had lit a cigar, then leaned back in his leather chair. Jarman had not spoken, wanting to give him time to consider the offer. Finally Quigby had said, "I'd like to. I really would. And I've got the money, but the fact is, I may need it for Miriam. She's not well, you see."

Jarman had experienced a sinking feeling. "I'm sorry to hear that."

"She needs constant care. Since losing Tommy, she's not been herself. She does strange things, and I can't be around to look after her, not the way a judge has to travel, so it looks like I may have to hire help. It may even be necessary for me to send her back east to one of those private hospitals, and that would take all my savings." He shook his head. "It's a shame. I'd love to join you, but I've got to think of my daughter. She's all I got left."

The old man was shrewd. Jarman had got his message loud and clear: if he would marry Miriam, Quigby would put up the money needed for the casino. But Jarman wasn't sure he could do it. He wanted to think about it, and Quigby figured on that but still insisted he stay for supper.

Miriam had not said a word as she had served tasteless boiled chicken, mushy potatoes, and a watery bean soup. Afterward Quigby had said he had some papers to read over and had pointedly left them alone in the parlor. And now Jarman felt trapped. The evening was still young, and no matter how rude it seemed, he knew he'd soon have to get out of there. Still, he made an effort to be polite and offered his sympathies once more.

"I'm really sorry about Tommy, Miriam. It was a tragic thing."

She nodded for so long, he wondered if her head was going to fall off. Finally she spoke in a whispery voice that sounded as if it were coming from a grave. "He's in a better place. He'll tell me that when I'm able to get through to him."

Jarman leaned forward, not sure he'd heard right and hoping he hadn't.

She saw his skepticism and seemed to come alive as she explained eagerly, "The dead can communicate with the living, if you only believe, Mr. Ballard. I have friends who are also trying to reach their loved ones who have crossed to the other side. You should come to one of our home circles sometimes. Perhaps there's someone you'd like to try to speak to."

Jarman could not take any more. Swiftly getting to his feet, he made the excuse, "I just remembered I have another appointment." He edged toward the door. "Would you say good night to your father for me and tell him I'll be in touch?

"And thank you for a nice dinner," he added as he rushed out.

He stood outside a moment. Wiping his hand across his brow, he felt a cold sweat. Good Lord, the woman *was* crazy, and he was going to have to think long and hard about the judge's proposition. Maybe there was another way. He was pretty good with cards and knew lots of tricks. Maybe he could get some rich cattleman in a game and take all his money. Then he would have what he needed and could forget about Quigby. Jarman knew there was just no way he could tie himself down to a wife like that.

For the next few hours, he wandered up and down the streets of Abilene. Seeing the hordes of gamblers, gold flashing, liquor being poured, and money being spent, he could feel his mouth watering to be a part of it all.

When he overheard someone remark that the Lucky Steer was so crowded that no one could get to the tables, Jarman headed in that direction, curious to learn the reason. He found it difficult to see anything, because people were packed in so tightly. The bar was lined with those waiting their turns to play at the tables, and he spoke to a few and asked why didn't they just go elsewhere to gamble.

"The scenery is nicer," the man next to him said with a snicker and a nudge of his elbow. "I figure if it ain't my night to win, I'd rather lose to a pretty face than the ugly codgers dealing at other places."

Jarman lifted his glass to down the last of his whiskey, at the same time turning to follow the man's gaze. Suddenly he choked, doubling over to gasp for breath as the man pounded his back and asked anxiously, "Are you gonna be all right, mister?"

Jarman did not answer. He was having trouble breathing and not entirely because the liquor had gone down the wrong way; when he dared take another look, he knew there could be no doubt.

It was Celeste.

No, he corrected quickly, furiously. It was Samara Labonte. And suddenly he realized it was not the liquor choking him anymore.

It was rage.

# 21

*It was nearly three in the* morning, and Sam was exhausted as she climbed the stairs on the outside of the building. Below, gamblers still packed into the Lucky Steer, and ordinarily she'd have stayed till dawn. But how could she smile and charm a player into raising the stakes when she was in such a dreary mood?

Belle was gone. She hadn't revealed her plans until the very last minute, when she was all packed and ready to leave town with a wealthy cattle baron from Texas. He had promised to buy her a casino of her very own, and maybe later on they might even get married—*if,* she'd confided with a wicked grin, he could figure out what to do with the wife he already had. She had wanted Sam to go with her, but Sam repeated her need for security and her desire to stay where she was. Belle had teased her again about the blue-eyed Indian who had stolen her heart, and Sam had continued to protest vehemently that he had done nothing of the kind. Finally, after hugs and kisses and tears, Belle and her lover had left on the midnight train, and Sam found herself alone.

She let herself into her room and locked the door behind her. The windows looked out onto the bustling street below, and she pulled down the shades before striking a match to the bedside lantern. The room was sparsely furnished, with only an iron-postered bed, a rickety table and two chairs, and a dilapidated armoire that looked as though it might collapse any second. The walls had never been painted, and it was a drab, dismal place, but Sam really didn't care. After all, she was there only to sleep and bathe and change clothes. Most of her time was spent downstairs.

From beneath the bed Sam took out the box where she kept her money until she could get it to the bank. She placed her latest bundle inside, for Lyman had paid her when she quit for the night. She extinguished the lantern. Eyes burning, every muscle in her body aching, she undressed, put on her nightgown, and was asleep as soon as her head hit the pillow.

She did not hear the lock on the door being picked, nor did she hear the hinges squeak when it opened and someone crept into the room. It was only when hot, moist lips pressed against her ear that she awakened with a jolt of terror to hear the vicious whisper, *"Bitch."* At the same instant, cold steel touched her cheek along with the command, "Scream and you're dead."

With fear-widened eyes, and in the light filtering from the street below, Sam recognized Jarman. "You," she whispered fearfully.

"Mademoiselle Celeste de Manca," he taunted. "You conniving little whore. I know who you really are. Did you really think I wouldn't take revenge for your making a fool of me?"

Sam could smell the whiskey on his breath and knew he was drunk beyond reason; but she had to try to make him see she'd never meant him any harm. "I would have done everything I could to make you a good wife, Jarman. You have to believe that. But you wouldn't give me a chance."

"Shut up. You lied to me, damn you, and you'll pay. I know all about your little scheme to pretend to be Celeste, and now the marquis knows she was in on it, too. You knew I'd eventually find out. That's why you ran away when I didn't marry like you'd figured on. But you've managed to make some money, haven't you? I've heard all about you, and I figure some of that money is mine to make up for what you and Celeste cheated me out of. Now where is it?" He pressed the gun into her face harder.

Sam did not hesitate. All she wanted was to get him out of there before he hurt her. "It's under the bed. Take it and go. I won't say a word to anybody. I swear it."

He laughed scornfully. "You swear? Is that what you said? That you swear? As if your word means anything."

Clambering off the bed, he kept the gun pointed while he reached for the box. He pushed off the lid with one hand and grinned at the contents. "Good. Real good. Not enough, but it'll keep me from having to marry the lunatic."

Sam did not know what he was talking about and didn't care. She only wanted him out of there, because as drunk and angry as he was, he was capable of anything.

He saw the terror on her face, then dropped his gaze to her bosom, fascinated by the way it rose and fell in rhythm with her deep, frenzied breathing. The sheet had fallen away, and through her gown he thought he could see her delectable nipples; he wet his lips and blinked against the drunken fog that clouded his vision. Desire struck like a kick to his loins. He could stand no more.

Pushing the box aside, he leaped on top of her and began to tear at her gown with one hand, his other still holding the gun—but it was to the side of her head, no longer aimed right at her face. "Never thought I'd be second to an Indian, but at least he won't have something I didn't—"

Gun or no gun, Sam started swinging, at the same time yelling at the top of her lungs. He was attempting to straddle her, but she swiftly brought up her knees to slam against his buttocks, propelling him forward. With her arm thrown out, she deflected the gun just as he accidentally pulled the trigger. The explosion so close to her ear deafened her momentarily, but she was still able to turn her head and sink her teeth into his wrist. With a yelp of pain, he dropped the weapon.

In the room next door, Cade had fallen asleep after pretending to be too drunk to make love to Louretta. The truth was, despite feeling an urge for sex, he could not get Celeste out of his mind. She was the only one he desired and, yes, damn it, loved, and it was going to take time, and a hell of a lot of it, to be able to share passion with another woman.

But at the sound of the first scream, he was wide-awake, and by the time the gun went off on the other side of the wall, he had his pants on and was out the door.

Louretta also came alive, to sit up and cry dazedly, "What the hell?" She realized Cade was gone at the same instant she heard the sound of wood splintering.

In the scant light coming from outside, Cade could see the man and woman struggling on the bed. In two quick strides he was upon them to slam the butt of his gun across the man's head. With a grunt, the man collapsed.

"Are you hit?" Cade asked the woman.

"No. It missed me," Sam replied shakily, drawing back against the end of the bed as she pulled the sheet up to her chin. She could hear footsteps running and saw people starting to gather in the doorway.

Louretta, clutching the robe she'd pulled on, pushed her way into the room to yelp, "My God, Sam, what's going on in here?" She rushed to strike a match to the lantern. "And since when did you start your own business? You owe me, you know. This is my place. Lyman may own the building, but he rents the whole upstairs to me. I only let you have a room as a favor to him, and you can't whore around unless I get my cut, damn it.

"Are you hurt?" she finally thought to ask.

Cade's back was to Sam as he stared at the man on the floor. Suspicion began to creep over him ever so slowly when he saw the tousled golden curls. Could it actually be Ballard? Here, in Abilene?

Cade rolled him over, then drew back in surprise. It was him. At the same instant, a needling sensation began to prickle up and down his spine, as the woman on the bed assured Louretta she had not been injured. He heard the familiar touch of a French accent, and it all came rushing back in a maddening whirlwind—the glimpse of silver hair, and now, with Ballard here, could it mean . . . ?

Slowly, Cade turned. Sam, still shaken, glanced at him only vaguely, but then her gaze fell on his bare chest. Suddenly, memories swirled like mist from a swamp as her eyes locked on the scar. In that spellbound moment she had no doubt, and her whisper was barely audible.

"Wild Spirit."

Cade rocked on his heels, brain spinning as he tried to frame a response.

"It's you."

He shook his head. "Lady, I don't know what you're talking about." He needed time, damn it, to figure out what it all meant.

Louretta, eyes glittering, was taking it all in.

"It *is* you," Sam persisted, sitting up. Rage began to push aside astonishment.

Just then a shout rang out and a barrel-chested man was pushing his way through the crowd. Jake Whaley pushed into the room. He looked from the unconscious man on the floor to the bullet hole in the wall behind the bed and said, "Well, I guess we'll be having us another hanging before long. Judge Quigby loves to stretch the neck of anybody slinging a gun around. Well, what happened?" he asked of no one in particular.

Sam's eyes were still locked with Cade's, and she knew beyond doubt it was he. How could she not recognize his blue eyes? They had gazed heatedly at her too many times to forget. Haltingly she attempted to explain, "He broke into my room to rob me, then he . . ." She fell silent, not wanting to divulge that Jarman had tried to rape her. She drew a ragged breath and concluded, "We struggled. The gun went off. I don't think he meant to shoot me. Now please. Just get him out of here."

"Sounds cut and dried to me." Jake motioned to some of the onlookers. "Lock him up."

Louretta, meanwhile, was tingling with curiosity. She was also mad and, as soon as the room cleared, started firing questions. "You two know each other, don't you? Just what's going on? You been humpin' behind my back and not giving me my cut?"

Sam was not sure how much longer she could contain herself and did not want a scene in front of Louretta. With a trembling finger, she pointed to the door. "Get out. Both of you." Later, when she had got hold of herself, she would find him and learn the truth, but for the moment she wanted to be alone.

Louretta stubbornly refused. "I'm not going anywhere till I get some answers here."

"Then *we're* leaving," Cade announced suddenly. He grabbed a blanket and wrapped it around Sam so fast that she did not have time to react. Then he lifted her up and tucked her under his arm like a sack of potatoes and walked out.

Sam did start protesting then, and Louretta was right behind them. "Where do you think you're going with her?"

"Some place where we can talk. This doesn't concern you." He gave Sam a shake and warned, "You keep screaming, damn it, and the whole town is going to come running. Now shut up, and we'll get this settled between us."

Sam did quiet down, because she didn't want another scene like the one in her room, but inside a storm was raging. They would settle it, and she would find out once and for all who he was and why he thought he could play with others' lives.

The few people on the streets at that hour paid little attention to the man walking along purposefully carrying a woman wrapped in a blanket. After all, it was Abilene; anything could happen. Teeth ground together so tightly her jaws ached, Sam raged, "Where are you taking me?"

He laughed and warned her, "If you start cursing me again like you did before, so help me I'll dump your haughty little butt in the nearest horse trough."

"You wouldn't dare." But she knew he would and held her tongue.

He decided the livery stable would be the nearest and most private place to talk. He wasn't about to walk into a hotel and ask for a room with his only baggage a wriggling, sputtering, red-faced woman in her nightgown.

The air was pungent with the smell of hay and horses. A small lantern, hanging from a post, cast enough light for him to see. Repositioning her on his shoulder, he carried her up to the hayloft and unceremoniously dropped her onto the thickly piled straw. "Now we talk."

Sam was so mad that she could scarcely find her voice. "Just . . . just who the hell are you?" she sputtered.

Cade drank in the sight of her and felt a tremor to think of all the nights he had dreamed of holding her in his arms. It was all he could do to keep from gathering her close, then and there, but those blazing cat's eyes made him hold back.

She bit out the angry plea, "Will you please stop staring at me like that? First you made a fool of me by pretending you couldn't speak English, and then you lied and said you were a half-breed. I want the truth."

He knew he had no choice and supposed it no longer mattered, anyway. "Cade Ramsey," he introduced himself, then went on to tell her everything, finishing with an apology for any distress she had suffered as a result of the Indians' revenge on Ballard.

"In that instance, you did me a favor," she admitted, overwhelmed by all she'd just heard.

"So now it's your turn. I want to know what you're doing in Abilene using a fake name and working in a casino."

"Not that it's any of your business, but Sam *is* my real name. It's short for Samara." She proceeded to reveal Celeste's scheme and her reasons for going along with it.

Cade truly admired her spunk, as well as her determination to escape the marquis. "It was a good plan, and it might've worked, even if you hadn't been abducted by the Indians, *if*," he emphasized, "the dowry had been enough to satisfy Ballard. Because that's the only reason he wanted to marry Celeste in the first place. I found that out right away. So if the marquis hadn't been so stingy, Ballard wouldn't have written to him complaining, still wouldn't know the truth about who you are, and the two of you would be married by now."

Sam could not help laughing. "Then it seems I owe the old rake my gratitude for unknowingly saving me from such a fate."

"So what got Ballard so riled tonight? Why did he come after you?"

She was quick to explain, "Oh, I don't think he knew I was here. You see, I left on my own, because I made up my mind I couldn't go through with it, no matter what I'd promised Celeste. He was threatening not to marry me, anyway, but he obviously didn't find out I wasn't Celeste till after I'd gone. I guess he saw me in the casino and went a little crazy and followed me up to my room.

"You know the rest of the story. I suppose it was a good thing you were next door with Louretta," she finished, unable to keep the bitterness from her tone and chiding herself for it. But the fact was, she could not help the emotions surging within her, for despite all resolve, she knew she still cared for him, deeply.

There was not much light coming from below, but Cade could see her face and the anger and pain in her eyes. He whispered, "You were hurt by all this. I'm sorry."

Boldly, she admitted, "I was hurt that you could leave me as you did. I was fool enough to think you cared. But it doesn't matter, anymore," she lied, "because I've come to realize I was vulnerable, that what we had was only something to pass the time, and—"

He kissed her, taking her by surprise, shocking her to silence as he cupped her face in his hands and told her, smiling all the while, "You always did talk too much, cat eyes. And don't you know I died a thousand deaths when I had to let you go? There was no way I could have kept you with me. To do so meant telling you the truth then, and I wasn't sure you'd go along with it. Besides, I'm an Indian agent for the federal government. Ballard would have found out I had a woman, and when he learned who she was, he'd have used all the troops he could muster to come after me, as well as the Kansa. They would have suffered terribly, and I would also have lost my job, maybe even been sent to prison. So I had to send you back, don't you see?

"But it's not important now," he rushed on, raining kisses over her face. "You didn't marry him, and he's not in the army anymore, and he can't prove anything anyway."

She continued to stare at him, frozen, as she tried to absorb all that he was saying. Finally she found her voice to ask tremulously, "And if I forgive you for what happened to me, the way you left without even a good-bye, what happens to us?"

"This," he said huskily as he reached for her. They kissed sitting up, face to face. With one hand he dug into her thick hair to hold her against him, and with his other he drew the blanket down, exposing her nightgown, which he quickly tore away. Cupping her breasts, he held her for long moments.

Sam's hands fastened on his waist momentarily, then began to trail down his thighs. He opened his legs to encircle and pull her against him, and she went eagerly, drowning in his kiss, wanting to stay there forever and always, bodies locked together. Finally he drew her down to the floor, then swiftly maneuvered himself out of his trousers. Then they were both naked but oblivious to the strands of hay prickling against their flesh. His lips, hot and eager, nibbled at her throat as she arched against him.

"I've dreamed of this," he whispered fiercely. "I couldn't get you out of my blood."

There was no right or wrong of it. There was no yesterday or tomorrow, only the glory of the moment and the rapture of being held so close that their hearts seemed to beat as one.

"I never stopped thinking of you," Sam proclaimed, her mouth seeking his to seal the affirmation of her love. She felt his hardness against her as he coaxed her legs apart, and then he was inside her, and she felt as though she were drowning in a sea of liquid sensation. Her body commanded she not hold back, and she rocked against him in the ancient rhythm not to be denied. They came together in a sweep of fire that stunned in its intensity. He muffled her scream of joy with bruising lips, and she drank of his sweetness, nails digging into the rock-hard flesh of his back.

For long moments neither spoke, and then the language of passion began once more. He began to move against her, and once more they sailed to the stars on wings of rapture. When at last they were spent, they slept in each other's arms. There would be time later for dreaming and planning and just reveling in the wonder of requited love. But for the remainder of night, they wanted only to cling together and lock out the world as each mused the magic of all that had transpired on yet another star-mad night.

* * *

The jail was crude, no more than a squat wooden building without windows, but Jarman supposed it was better than some frontier lock-ups he'd heard about. One sheriff, he had been told, confined his prisoners merely by spreading a cowhide on top of them and then pegging it to the ground. Still, he was miserable, especially having to share with the two sour-smelling drunks who alternately retched and passed out.

Light filtered through cracks in the walls, so Jarman knew it was day. His head throbbed, but the pain was nothing to the fire in his gut over the anger at being told it was Cade Ramsey who had struck him. One of the men who'd brought him to the jail knew him. Jarman vowed he would take care of Ramsey one day, but meanwhile he was stewing over why Quigby hadn't shown up. The one who seemed to be in charge—Jake Whaley, he'd said his name was—had promised, after Jarman finally managed to convince him the two were friends, that he'd get word to the judge, but where in the hell was he?

Footsteps sent him rushing to peer through the slit in the door, and at the sight of Quigby and Whaley, he called out frantically, "Get me out. I can't breathe with these sots in here."

The door was unlocked and opened, and Jarman rushed out. Quigby nodded curtly to Jake Whaley and snapped out the command, "Leave us."

When they were alone, he swept Jarman with a look of contempt. "You sure got yourself in a mess of trouble, boy. I don't take kindly to anybody who uses a gun. You know that. I'm told that shot went right through the wall, and if anybody had been in the street when it came down, they'd be as dead as my grandson."

Jarman shuddered fearfully to see the look on the judge's face and rushed to defend himself. "It was an accident. I swear. I was only trying to scare her. I wasn't going to shoot her, but she hit my hand, and the gun went off. That was Samara Labonte, Judge, the one I told you about who tried to trick me into marrying her."

"I don't care about that. You had no right to break into her room at gunpoint. I can send you to the gallows for what you did." He had shoved his face into Jarman's, and Jarman could feel the heat of his wrath.

"I told you I didn't mean her any harm. You've got to believe me." Then, thinking Quigby might really be mad enough to sentence him to death, Jarman sank in terror to his knees in a plea for his life.

Quigby's expression relaxed, and he suppressed a smile to think how things sometimes had a way of working out. "Get up," he ordered. Shakily, Jarman obeyed. Quigby turned away. "Let's go to the house. Miriam will have breakfast ready soon. You need a bath, a change of clothes first. I'll send somebody to wherever you're staying to fetch your things."

Eagerly, washed with the joy of reprieve, Jarman fell in step beside him.

"She likes to get an early start on her day," Quigby said as they walked along in the morning stillness. Few people were stirring about yet. "You see, she just can't wait to get with the rest of those crazy women in her home circle, as she calls it. They've lost loved ones to violence, too, and they think all they have to do is believe and keep trying, and sooner or later the spirits of the dead will speak to them. I suppose there's no harm. Whatever gets a person through their grief, I always say. Me, I stay busy, trying to bring law and order to this godless land. But I do worry about her when I'm gone.

"She needs a husband to look after her," he added pointedly with a glance at Jarman.

Jarman swallowed hard. He knew what was coming, for he suspected the ultimate price of his reprieve.

With an exaggerated sigh, Quigby continued, "Oh, I know there's folks who'll say it's too soon, because she's still in mourning, but I figure it's none of their business. After all, if I have the wisdom to decide whether a man lives or dies, who would dare question my judgment as to my own daughter's welfare?"

Doggedly, Jarman walked beside him, nodding now and then but not trusting himself to speak. What could he say, anyway? Quigby was laying it all on the line. He had been pardoned on the stipulation that he marry Miriam.

She was standing on the porch, watching expressionlessly as they approached. Dark circles ringed pale eyes set in a face bleached by grief and hopelessness. She turned and went back inside without a word of greeting.

Jarman felt his knees go weak at the thought of the dismal future ahead.

As though fearing he would break and run despite everything, Quigby placed a firm, steering hand on his shoulder as they climbed the steps and in a token gesture of compassion said pleasantly, "We won't make a fuss over the wedding. Simple. Quiet. Then you can set about getting that casino open and running to make us rich. Everything is going to be fine, my boy. Just fine."

And Jarman knew that although he had been spared from the gallows, there was still a noose around his neck.

**22**

*Dawn came with sobering* clarity, for despite wondrous passion, Cade and Sam knew they were actually strangers. After all, they had met under a guise. So as sunlight crept into the stable to chase away the night, they sought to know each other in every way.

Cade detailed his bond with the Kansa so Sam would understand why he'd been involved in the plan to torment Jarman Ballard through his fiancée. He also explained how his dealings with Ballard during the war caused his personal contempt for the man.

Sam related everything in her past, about her family, her life in the catacombs. She was lying with her head on his shoulder, her fingers trailing up and down his flat, hard belly, as he held her tight against him.

He listened quietly, then said, "I think it would be a good idea for us to get out of town for a while. Ballard is going to get mad all over again when he finds out it was me who busted into your room. Seeing us together would only make it worse. He needs time to calm down and realize it's best he just move on, and we need time to get to know each other.

"Besides"—he kissed the top of her head—"I didn't want to let you go before, Sam . . . ." He paused to savor the name fondly, for although it did not yet seem natural to call her anything but Celeste, he was amused to think how "Sam" seemed to suit her more. "I feel even stronger against it now. So what do you say? Would you like to run away with me for a few weeks?"

Sam was not about to be coquettish or coy. "I'd like nothing better."

"Then you get ready, while I pay a visit to the district judge, which is why I'm here. But don't pack anything fancy. I've got to keep working, so we'll be visiting Indian reservations, camping out. Maybe I can even talk you into moving back to Leavenworth and getting away from this place for good."

Sam was taken aback to realize he apparently did not approve of what she was doing and was quick to let him know, "I don't want to live anywhere else. I like it here. I'm also making good money."

"There are other ways to make money than dealing cards in a saloon filled with drunks and whores."

"The whores work upstairs. As you well know," she could not resist adding.

He winked. "That's where I found you."

"I wasn't working, and you know it."

He grinned lazily. "The fact is, Sam Labonte, you'd make a real fine whore if you wanted to be one. I could recommend you to all my friends, except for the fact I'd kill any man who touched you." He began kissing her, but not in a hurried, lustful way. It was slow and tender, and he held her for long, spellbound moments, then drew back to proclaim breathlessly, "I care for you, Sam, more than I ever meant to care about any woman, but I can't make any promises."

Their gazes met, held, in the pink-and-gold light of the new day upon them. Cade cursed himself. Damn it, he loved her. And he wanted her. Not just now, but for always. But he wasn't the kind to tie himself down to a wife, a family. *Was he?* Things were happening too fast. He needed time to understand not only himself, but her as well. He had seen too many men make fools of themselves over a woman, and he did not intend to do the same. Until he could be sure of her feelings for him, he vowed to keep a tight rein on his heart.

Sam searched his face, bewildered as to the motive behind his proclamation. Did he think she *wanted* promises? He now knew she had been willing to marry a complete stranger. Maybe he thought she was desperate for a husband. Well, she would show him.

"I'm not asking for anything, Cade. Why do you think I'm so happy with my work? I can support myself. I don't need a man."

"Except at certain times," he teased, eager to end the tension now that they seemed to have an understanding. "But unfortunately, this isn't one of them, because we've got to get out of here before the stable hands show up."

She agreed but refused to leave as she had arrived, with a blanket wrapped around her; so Cade hurried to her room and brought back some clothes. When she was dressed, he walked her to the Lucky Steer and promised he would soon be back to get her.

Sam went upstairs to gather a few things before looking for Lyman to tell him she would be going away for a while. She was determined not to worry about anything except enjoying being with Cade again.

Preoccupied, she did not notice Jarman Ballard standing just across the street, did not see how his face was twisted with fury that rocked him to his very soul.

And at that particular instant, Jarman did not know whom he hated more—Samara as she skipped merrily up the steps or Cade Ramsey as he walked so confidently down the street. Because now it was all starting to come together, the whole rotten scheme, and he cursed himself for not suspecting Ramsey's involvement sooner. He'd heard talk in the past about how Ramsey was a blood brother to the Kansa, and suddenly it made sense that he would have been part of it. And now he knew they were lovers. They had met while Samara was held captive, and Jarman would not be at all surprised if they had been sneaking off together while she was living in Leavenworth, the little slut.

Now it was *his* turn for revenge. It didn't make a damn that he had never loved Celeste, had only wanted her dowry. If not for what the Kansa and Cade Ramsey had done, he would have married Samara upon her arrival, paltry dowry or not. She was beautiful. He would have been proud to have her for a wife. And maybe he wouldn't have had enough money to open his own casino, but at least he'd not now be condemned to wed someone who seemed more dead than alive.

Damn them. Damn them to hell, because if it was the last thing he ever did, he would make them pay for sending *him* there.


Judge Quigby glared at Cade. Who did this man think he was to criticize or question his judgments?

Cade knew the judge was sorely vexed but pressed on. "I lay my life on the line to catch lawbreakers and send them in, but you let them go, Judge. I want to know why. If the crimes had been inflicted on whites, you'd have sent some to prison, others to the gallows. But when you let them go because the crimes were committed against the red man, that's not justice."

"I resent your censure, and I recall when we met at Fort Leavenworth, you regarded me as an executioner."

"And you held me in contempt and called me an Indian lover, but I don't care about your opinion of me. I care about justice, which you aren't meting out, and that's why you were sent here in the first place. And I would also like to point out," he added tightly, "that your failure to fulfill the obligations of your appointed position is making my job extremely difficult."

Quigby was struggling for composure. He did not want to give Ramsey the satisfaction of making him lose his temper. "Frankly, I have little respect for Indian agents. Most of you are ineffective or just plain dishonest. Like that Cheyenne agent who amassed a small fortune of over twenty-five thousand dollars in less than two years by selling goods that rightfully belonged to the Indians. And just this year it was learned that another agent had disappeared from his post, along with thousands of dollars meant to pay bills for the Indians. In my opinion, you're all a sorry lot, and I put no stock in your word, and I'm not passing judgment on a man based on anything you say.

"And perhaps I should remind you," he concluded with a smirk, "I can have you removed from your post."

"That door swings both ways, Judge. I also have means to register displeasure with your conduct."

Quigby sat up straight. "You dare threaten to file a complaint against me? I think you'd best get out of here right now."

Cade did not move. "Formally complaining is the last thing I want to do. That's why I came here, to see if we can come to a better understanding of the problem, and I want your assurance you will enforce the law, regardless of the victim."

"I would not have been appointed to my position if I were not deemed qualified to pass judgment."

"And I wouldn't have been appointed to mine if I weren't expected to bring in criminals to receive that judgment."

"If the sentences I pass out do not meet with your approval, that's too damn bad, Ramsey."

Cade knew he had wasted time hoping he could reason with the judge. Obviously Quigby's mind was set, and there was nothing he could do to change it. Filing a complaint would probably do no good and would only make matters worse. And he did not believe for one minute it had anything to do with Quigby's opinion of agents as a whole. Though he would not admit it, Cade knew Quigby just didn't like him. So it was better to let it go and in the future turn his prisoners over to an agent in another district where the case would be heard before a different judge, even if it made him look as though he weren't doing his job. But what difference did it make if the criminals he brought in were set free?

He stood. "I see we aren't getting anywhere."

"I'm not forgetting this, Ramsey."

Cade bit his tongue to keep from firing back that neither would he. He had tried and failed and would now take a different route to try to obtain justice. He thought about inquiring as to what was going to be done about Ballard but decided not to. He did not want to think about anything for the time being except Sam. He hurried to meet her.

They stayed away for nearly two weeks, and during that time Sam and Cade grew close as they experienced the wonders of their love and the joys of just getting to know each other. She adored him for his compassion with the Indians, especially the children, as he took the time to encourage them in their studies. She also admired how he dealt with the older people, listening to their complaints and always promising to do everything he could to try to remedy the problems.

They visited several reservations, and Sam had been particularly delighted to return to the Kansa. At first they had not understood why she was with Wild Spirit, but Cade had quickly explained Celeste was really Sam and that she now knew everything and they were friends. It was all confusing, but they had secretly grown to like the white woman who had met a challenge with bravery and courage, and they were glad to see her again.

When she saw Bold Eagle, Sam chided him good-naturedly for the way she had been treated when taken off the train.

With good humor, he scolded her for her tongue-lashing. "Some white man words, I prefer not to know," he said with a mock frown.

They apologized to each other for any affront, and by the time she and Cade left, Sam knew she'd made a good friend in Bold Eagle.

"If you ever need me, you need only to send me a telegram," he told her.

"But to where?" she wanted to know.

He explained, "My people have ears to the white man's wires all the time. We know the sounds the words make as they sing through the air, and your message will find me. Ask Wild Spirit. He will tell you he can find me whenever he needs to."

All too soon, Cade received word he had to return to Indian territory. Goods meant for a reservation had once again been stolen by outlaws. He would track them down, but this time he would see to it the culprits were not tried in Judge Quigby's bailiwick.

On their last night together, they slipped quietly into Abilene, and Cade rented a room in one of the smaller hotels. Sam sneaked up the back stairs to meet him. After all, she was recognizable to many people and did not want gossip, especially when she had left word she had gone to Leavenworth to visit an old friend. So it would not do for her to be seen in a hotel with a man.

After a night of passion that seemed insatiable, they clung together in an afterglow dulled by the realization that they would soon have to part. Finally he told her, "I hate to leave you, Sam. Especially here. It's dangerous. I told you about Judge Quigby's little grandson getting killed by a stray bullet."

She had heard, and her heart went out to Miriam Appleby. She had seen her once but kept her distance for fear the poor woman would recognize her and try to persuade her to conduct a séance.

"Is there anywhere else you'd like to go?" he persisted. "I'll take you there."

"No. I make good money here, Cade."

"And is money so important?"

"It is when you don't have any. Being poor can put a person in a situation that makes her weak, vulnerable. I know, because I've been there, and I don't intend to ever let it happen again."

He was silent for a moment, then reminded her gently, "I told you I couldn't make any promises, Sam, but you know I care. You know I'm hoping someday we'll both want to settle down. Till then, I'd like to know you're somewhere safe, that I don't have to worry about you so much."

Sam was clutching every shred of pride she could muster to keep from asking him who the hell he thought he was to expect her to sit back and wait for him to decide whether or not he wanted to settle down to marriage. Besides, Belle had taught her to hide her emotions, lest she tip her hand to another player and give him the edge. That rule could also be applied to life; she wasn't about to let Cade know how much she cared, for to do so would grant him the upper hand. And this was a high-stakes game, because Sam knew she stood to lose her heart.

Cade mistook her silence for concern over finances rather than reluctance to give up her job, and he offered, perhaps sounding too magnanimous, "I can help you financially, if need be."

It was the wrong thing to say.

"You think I want to be your *fille de joie?*" she cried, hurt and indignant.

"What are you talking about?"

She bolted from the bed and began jerking on her clothes. "*Fille de joie* in France. *Puta* in Mexico. 'Soiled doves,' 'calico queens' here. Different names in different places, but it's all the same. Whore. Prostitute. I'll be damned if I'll be kept by a man, Cade Ramsey. And who are you to offer, anyway?" She glared at him as she struggled with her camisole. "You told me you make a hundred and twenty-five dollars a month. I can make that much on a slow night." That was actually stretching it a bit, but he didn't need to know it, she thought.

"By cheating at cards?" he fired back.

"I will have you know I never cheat an honest player. It's only when I suspect somebody is trying to cheat me that I set out to take him for everything he's got. And I don't feel a moment's guilt over it, either, by God."

Cade well knew his temper, just as he knew his breaking point and when to walk away from an argument. They were both getting too riled up and would wind up saying things they would regret later. He got out of bed and started getting dressed himself. Finally, with double holster buckled on, he reached for his hat and headed for the door. "I guess you can find your way out," he said tightly.

"I can also find my way back to the Lucky Steer. At least there I don't have to apologize for what I am."

He had opened the door, was about to step outside, but he turned. The cat's eyes he adored flashed with peppery glints of red amid the golden green depths. Her shimmering silver hair hung loose and wild about her face, and her cheeks were flushed—but not with passion, for he knew she was furious to the core.

"We needed time together, but now I think just the opposite. Take care of yourself, Sam." And he left her.

Fighting tears, Sam went out the back way. No matter that she loved him with every beat of her heart; she would not give up her independence to any man. And all she wanted right then was to get back to where she could be herself.

Most of the casinos stayed open until the last gamblers finally gave up trying to win back all they'd lost earlier in the evening and staggered into what was left of the night. All establishments, however, closed before dawn to give workers a chance to clean up before another day began.

Sam saw them busily sweeping butts out and down through the cracks in the boardwalk. As she passed open doors, she could hear the sound of glasses being washed, chairs and tables being shoved back into place. A few of the workers glanced at her, but with only mild interest. She was wearing a simple muslin gown and boots and looked like an ordinary woman bent on morning errands.

In the Devil's Addition, Sam reached the end of the street and the Lucky Steer. She was about to go upstairs when she noticed Jimmy Tucker, Lyman's cleaning boy, sitting outside with his chin propped glumly in his hands. She hurried over to chide him gently, "What are you doing? You know Mr. Guthrie will have your head on a platter if he catches you loafing."

"Naw, he won't. He ran me out, and now I got nothing to do. None of the other saloons needs any help. It's my momma who's gonna have my head when I go home with no money to give her."

Sam was bewildered. "Why would he run you out?"

Jimmy threw up his hands. "I don't know, Miss Sam. I walked in ready to start work. He was sittin' at a table with his head down, and when he saw me, he just started cursing and told me to get out. You'll have to ask him."

Sam was already on her way to do just that. Lyman looked up. He had not moved.

"Well, you're back," he said dully. "But you're too late. It's all over." He lowered his head to his arms again.

Sam marched right over. She could see that not only was he drunk, but also he had been crying. Hoping she was wrong, she accused, "You've been gambling, haven't you? How much did you lose this time?"

There was a bottle on the table, and he reached to take a long swallow before admitting, "Too much. Can't pay it back. Gonna lose this place, I am. And maybe it's just as well. I'm not cut out for this life. I think I'll head on to Texas. Hell, I can always get me a job tending bar. That's what I should've kept on doing. Should've known

I'm no good around cards. Got the fever, my wife told me 'fore she finally upped and left me. She was right, too. She—"

"Be quiet and let me think." Belle had got him out of trouble like this before. Sam was confident she could do the same. "How much did you lose? I'll have to find a way to win it back."

He took another swallow from the bottle, hiccuped, and offered her a shameful smile. "You'll do it, too, won't you, Sam? 'Cause you're my friend. Just like Belle. But this time, I swear it won't happen again. 'Cause this time, I'm going to let you take the place over. Yessir, the Lucky Steer will be all yours. Just give me enough for a stake to get me back to Texas, and you can have it."

Sam felt a surge of interest. If she owned the Lucky Steer, she could make it the best saloon and casino in all of Abilene. Why, she could even move it out of the Devil's Addition and locate somewhere close to the swanky Alamo. "I might just take you up on that, Lyman. If I don't buy you out, some tinhorn gambler is going to come along and steal it from under you, anyway. Now are you going to tell me what I'm up against this time, and who I'm dealing with?"

"Ten thousand."

Sam gasped. "What on earth possessed you to get involved in stakes that high?"

Lyman's voice shook with contempt as he described the man who had goaded him to keep raising his bets. "He kept saying I couldn't win on my own, that the only reason the Lucky Steer was even able to stay in business was on account of a woman. I was bound to show him different, only I didn't. . . ." His voice faded on a sob of defeat.

Sam felt the waving heat of challenge. "Well, we wouldn't want to prove him wrong, would we? And we'll just have to show him the Lucky Steer will also *stay* in business because of a woman. Now who is this pompous scalawag who thinks he can't be beat?"

Lyman's red-rimmed eyes mirrored the very desolation of his soul. "Ballard, his name is. The one who broke into your room, the son of a bitch. He married Judge Quigby's daughter while you were gone. Said he wanted to give his bride a casino for a wedding present."

Sam felt pity for Miriam Appleby. She had no idea why she would marry Jarman, but that was Miriam's business, because all Sam cared about was getting revenge against Jarman for trying to use Lyman to hurt her. And how sweet that revenge was going to be, she thought wickedly, deliciously, when served out of a deck of cards.

"Don't worry," she assured Lyman. "I promise the bride is going to be disappointed, but not half as much as the *groom.*"

## 23

Sam was not about to go to the Quigby house to contact Jarman and suspected he probably wasn't spending much time with his new bride anyway. Knowing him as she did, and recalling how anxious the judge had been to get his daughter married, she was sure the union had not been one of love. No doubt the judge had come up with the kind of dowry Jarman was after.

She knew a lot of the local men congregated for beer and gossip at Jake Whaley's dry goods store on the outskirts of town. If Jarman was not there, they might be able to tell her where to find him.

"Ain't seen him," Jake told her brusquely. He was sitting on a flour barrel, picking his teeth with a knife. She did not miss the smug gleam in his eye or the way he exchanged amused glances with the other men.

"Well, then, maybe you'll tell me what happened after you arrested him for attacking me that night."

Jake was quick to remind her, "I ain't no marshal or sheriff. I don't try to enforce the law, and I don't arrest folks. All I do is haul 'em off to jail till a judge decides what to do with 'em."

"But surely you know whether or not he received a sentence." She didn't think Jarman had, otherwise he would not have been in the card game with Lyman, but she wanted to hear it from Jake.

Suddenly one of the men burst out laughing. "Havin' to marry a loony. That was his sentence."

Everyone roared except Sam, who thought the remark callous and cruel. But it caused her to think that maybe a dowry was not what motivated Jarman to marry the judge's daughter after all. Maybe it was the only way he could escape jail. Still, she pressed, "He had a gun, and he fired it. Someone could have been killed. Surely he wasn't let off scot free."

Jake told her how, after a night in jail to calm him down, the judge had let him go. "And after all"—he snickered—"who can blame a man for going a little crazy when he finds his fiancée in bed with another man?"

"That's absurd. I am not Jarman Ballard's fiancée, and besides—"

"Oh, we know that now." One of the men chuckled. "He said he wasn't about to marry no soiled dove."

Someone else chimed in, "And we done told you he's the judge's son-in-law now, so he don't have nothing to worry about."

" 'Ceptin' bein' married to a loony," repeated the man who'd initiated the joke.

Amid a roar of hee-haws and giggles, Sam whirled to face him, glaring. "You are disgusting. As for you . . ." She turned to the first man who had interrupted. "I am not a soiled dove, as you call it, and not that it's any of your business, but I was alone in my room when Jarman Ballard broke in. Someone heard me screaming and came to help."

"Don't make no never mind to me. I just know what I heard."

"To hell with you." She stunned him with her words, then turned back to Jake. "Is there somewhere Jarman goes during the day?"

The laughter had died down in the wake of her fury. Jake glanced at the wall clock. "This time of day, I suppose he'll be having dinner at the Drovers' Cottage. Now that he's got a judge for a father-in-law, he mingles with the hoity-toities," he added with a sneer.

Sam got out of there fast, lest she really unleash a tongue-lashing. The lazy old fools, spending all their time loafing with their beer while they spread lies about people.

The Drovers' Cottage was the grandest place in town. Three stories high, it stood out from the other buildings in Abilene, brightly painted yellow with green trim and Venetian blinds. A broad veranda offered a place where drovers could relax while making deals or merely watching the trains arrive and depart. Inside, the food was said to be as good as any of the poshest restaurants back east.

Sam had changed from the simple dress she'd been wearing that morning to a nice day dress of blue cashmere with a double-breasted jacket to match. Heads turned as she entered the restaurant. A waiter rushed to meet her, for it was not a place women frequented or were particularly welcome.

Before he could even begin his tactful dismissal, Sam had spotted Jarman sitting with two well-dressed cattlemen and requested, "Would you please inform Mr. Ballard that Mademoiselle Labonte awaits the pleasure of his company on the veranda."

With a sigh of relief that she had not demanded to be seated, the waiter hurried away, only too happy to oblige.

Sam did not have to wait long. Positioning herself at the far end of the porch, away from everyone else, she hardly had time to sit down on one of the rocking chairs before Jarman arrived, red-faced and indignant.

"What can you possibly want with me, you little strumpet? How dare you summon me as though I were your lackey?"

She looked up at him with aplomb, even managing a tiny smile. "You know you broke into my room that night because you were drunk and angry. And also because you wanted to steal my money, which you didn't succeed in doing, thank heavens. So how dare you spread lies about me, saying I was still your fiancée, and that you caught me with another man?"

"I'll say anything I damn well please. In case you haven't heard, my father-in-law happens to be a very important man, and that gives me certain privileges. Besides, I had a right to be upset. That was a wicked thing you did. And you owed me, for all the misery you put me through."

"You're crazy. Anyway, you should be ashamed of yourself for wanting to marry Celeste for money. And you kept her dowry. I think you're a liar and a thief."

"And you are a deceiver and a whore."

Sam had primed herself for the confrontation, vowing not to lose her temper no matter what. Her goal was to attack his pride and goad him into accepting her challenge to a game of poker. To let him get her dander up would defeat her purpose. Still, she could not resist taunting, "You brag about your father-in-law, but could your marriage have anything to do with your not receiving a sentence for your crime?"

"I committed no crime. The judge said what I did was understandable." Leaning back against the porch railing, he folded his arms across his chest. "But that's not why you came here. By chance, would you be wanting a job once I take over the Lucky Steer? Sorry. When I told Louretta she could bring her girls downstairs, she said she wouldn't agree to it unless I got rid of you. Seems she's more than a little angry over your stealing Ramsey from her bed."

When Sam did not respond, he pressed on, enjoying himself. "Maybe I'll have pity on you. Maybe"—he lowered his gaze to her bosom—"you could persuade me to let you stay on despite Louretta."

"I would rather die than work for you, Jarman."

"Fine." His taunting smile faded. "I don't want you around, anyway, and if you've nothing more to say, I would like to get back to my friends."

She made her move. "Actually, I came here to challenge you to a game of poker. I want to try to win back what Lyman lost."

He threw his head back to laugh raucously. "Don't be ridiculous. I'd never play poker with a woman."

Some of the men at a distance heard and glanced about curiously. Jarman realized then how it must look, the way they appeared to be conversing so intimately. "Get out of here. I'm a married man now, and I plan to be a leader in this town. I don't need gossip and can't afford to be seen in public talking to someone like you." He started to walk away but stopped short at her next words.

"If you don't, I will see that everyone in town hears about it. Your refusing to gamble with a woman will make you look like what you are—a coward. And I doubt that will be good for your business *or* your reputation."

He turned to glare coldly at her. God, he hated her and now wished he had tied and gagged her that night and taken her brutally to put her in her place. Then she wouldn't be sitting there arrogantly provoking him. But no. He'd been a fool, attacking when he was drunk, stumbling, making mistakes. He'd let her scream, and Ramsey, the son of a bitch, had ruined everything.

Jarman was also cursing himself for being weak enough to let the judge bully him into marriage. Damn it, he should have just hightailed it out of town, but no, he'd been stupid and dared think it might not be so bad. It was only after he'd found out the judge really didn't have much money that he had realized he'd made a fatal mistake. That was when he'd hit on the idea to manipulate Guthrie into high-stakes poker after hearing that Samara wasn't around. So now the fastest-growing casino in Abilene was going to be his, and when he really started making money, he'd find a way, by crackers, to get out of the mess he was in.

Sam saw how his jaw twitched and how he'd developed a sudden tick in his left eye. She had him, and she knew it. "Well, what will it be?" she asked almost sweetly. "Do you have the guts to accept a challenge?"

In the short time he had been in Abilene, Jarman had heard how she was considered one of the best dealers around. Nobody ever caught her cheating, but she won big and had to be a sharp. And she was right. To refuse to play her, especially to deny her a chance to win back her boss's losses, would be a black mark against him. What was he worried about, anyway? he mused. He knew all the tricks. He even kept his fingers sandpapered till the blood all but oozed through the skin so he could read the cards he had marked.

Finally he returned to stand over her, placing a hand on each side of the chair so that when he leaned down to whisper his ultimatum, there was no chance of being overheard. "I will play you on one condition."

Solemnly she shook her head. "No conditions. I play to win back what you took from Lyman, and that's it."

"Do you think I'm crazy? Why should I go into a game with you when you don't even have a stake? If I win, what do I get? I doubt you've got that kind of money."

Sam was well aware her savings were no more than a drop in the bucket against what Lyman was already in debt for. Bravado fading, she promised, "I'll find backers. If I should lose, you'll get your money."

"No." He ran his tongue across his lower lip as he devoured her with hungry eyes. "There may be certain advantages to being married to Quigby's daughter, but satisfaction in bed is not one of them. So if you lose, you don't pay me with money. You pay with your body. Any time I want. As long as I want. You give your solemn word, and if you don't keep it, I swear I will find a way to kill you, and I will see you die slowly.

"So now it's my turn to ask"—he paused to smirk—"do *you* have the guts to accept a challenge?"

Sam stood up to face his mocking expression with one of her own.

"*I'm* the one who made the challenge, Jarman, and *you*"—she poked him in his chest and winked—"just accepted it."

She hurried back to her room. They had agreed to play that very night, and she was going to spend the next hours practicing with the cards.

She was annoyed when Louretta pounded on her door a short while later. "I'm too busy to talk now," she said irritably.

"Well, that's too bad." Louretta stood in the doorway, fisted hands on her hips and a scowl on her heavily painted face. "I think it's time we talked. I don't know as I rightly appreciate your taking off with my best customer, and—"

"Cade is not in town often enough to be your best customer," Sam told her tightly, not wanting a fight. Besides, her heart was heavy over the way they had parted, and she didn't want to think about him, much less discuss him with a woman he had bedded.

She started to close the door, but Louretta was quick to push her foot in to stop her as she ordered angrily, "Find another room. I want you out of here."

Sam knew the only way she was going to get rid of Louretta when she was obviously spoiling for a fight was to give her something to stew about, so she proceeded to do so. "After tonight, you will be the one who will need to find another place. Go talk to Lyman, and he'll explain everything." Giving Louretta a gentle shove backward, Sam closed the door in her astonished face, then locked it.

Louretta stood there a moment, biting back her rage. Haughty little bitch. Who did she think she was? Louretta knew she'd never meant anything to Cade Ramsey except a tumble in the sack once in a while, but he meant much more to her. Not only was he the only man she ever enjoyed, but he was also good company when they weren't having sex, and he never made her feel as if she were only a whore. So she hadn't liked it one little bit when he'd rushed to defend Sam that night. And his taking off with her the next day had really burned.

Hearing Sam was back, Louretta had made up her mind to run her off, but she had seen Cade first. Only he hadn't hung around long. She had opened her door, just a crack, to see him slip an envelope under Sam's door. She had stepped out in the hall in hope of conversation, but he'd only tipped his hat and asked how she was in a way that told her he was just being polite and had kept on going.

After he was gone, Louretta, curious, had gotten the spare key and let herself into Sam's room long enough to snatch up the envelope. She had intended to burn it, but maybe it was worth something. After all, her new best customer, Jarman Ballard, had told her she should let him know anything that went on concerning Sam or Cade Ramsey. Now, after Sam had been so snotty, Louretta couldn't wait to give him the letter.

There was a back room at the Lucky Steer that Lyman always reserved for the high-stakes players. It filled hours ahead of time as word spread of the challenge game between Sam and Jarman. No one but the two of them, however, knew about the secret stakes. They were aware only that Sam was going to try to win back what Lyman had lost so he could keep his saloon.

Lyman's hands were shaking as he served beer and whiskey, along with pickled eggs and smoked pigs' feet. "Just win it back for me, Sam," he told her nervously when she arrived just before the appointed hour of eight o'clock. "Win it back, give me enough to get me started in Texas, and the place is yours."

Sam nodded absently. She did not feel like talking, wanting all her energy, her concentration, to be on the task at hand. She had dressed carefully, wearing a bright blue satin gown with plenty of ruffles—especially around the cuffs of her sleeves, for that was where she had hidden the cold deck, should she need it. What she was hoping for, however, was that Jarman would not be as good a player as he boasted. After all, Lyman admitted to drinking too much during their game. Careless mistakes, and not Jarman's prowess, might have been his undoing.

Jarman swept into the saloon, dandily dressed and grinning from ear to ear. It was his night, he told everyone with whom he stopped to chat. He could feel it in his bones.

In the back room, he went straight to where Sam was already seated and boldly leaned over to whisper in her ear, "I've taken the liberty of renting a room for us at the Alamo for the night. I thought you'd agree it best we go there instead of upstairs. I also asked for champagne. It will be the wedding night we never had, my dear." He kissed her cheek and drew back quickly, lest she slap him, which was exactly what she'd had in mind.

Pointing to the chair opposite, she informed him in a voice as cold as ice, "I want this over with quickly, Jarman. I don't want to be in your company any longer than necessary."

He winked. "We're going to be real close, Samara. Just wait and see."

Sam had dared hope that Jarman might be one of those gamblers who got nervous with a lot of people watching, but he seemed very calm, very self-assured. Then her heart fell all the way to her buttoned kid shoes when she noted how he seemed to have mastered what was known as the faro shuffle. She watched as he divided the deck into two stacks of twenty-six cards each, interweaving them precisely. There was nothing she could call him on, however. No doubt he had somehow managed to get hold of the cards Lyman had produced for play, expertly marking them to suit. He would have used a special template and pins to prick the face of the card, raising bumps only he would be able to detect.

Sam was not going to make a scene. Her time would come, she hoped.

They took turns dealing, and Sam tried to find the marks to prove him a cheat, but without success. She knew he was aware of her suspicion, for his eyes were glittering. The winning hands, as well as the deal, tossed back and forth.

He was toying with her like a cat before the kill. He had let her know he had control. Even when she insisted on a new deck of cards from Lyman, in no time at all it appeared that Jarman had somehow managed to scratch or nick the important cards with his fingernail. He knew what he was doing. He was good. She had to give the devil his due.

Sam was losing. Despite all her talent and skill, she was falling deeper and deeper in debt. She had hoped to beat him fair and square and let him know she'd used no trick or treachery, but no matter how hard she tried, luck was not with her that night. She had taken all of her money out of the bank and brought it with her, and when it was gone he infuriated her by announcing to the onlookers, "From here on, Samara and I have a private agreement as to her ante and her calls. Cash isn't needed."

There were a few nasty snickers as some of those watching guessed his meaning. Sam was bristling. She could not, would not, lose, and not just to keep from seeing Jarman take possession of the Lucky Steer. Suddenly she knew it meant more to her to stay out of bed with him. He'd sworn he would kill her if she reneged, but she knew she would rather die anyway.

Jarman's winning streak was phenomenal. Sam counted that he had twenty-two sets of threes without her winning a single hand. If she had three kings, then he would draw three aces. If she had the three highest cards in the deck, he would manage a small straight to beat it.

"You've lost," he said finally, slapping down four sixes to beat her three queens. "It's over. It's late. I'm ready to go to bed." He winked and gave a mock yawn, then pushed his chair back from the table with a loud scraping against the floor.

Lyman had long ago retreated to a corner to hide in the shadows with his whiskey. Hearing his fate sealed as Jarman declared victory, he gave one long, loud moan and slumped to the floor.

As attention turned first to Jarman as he crowed in triumph, then to Lyman as he passed out, Sam seized the opportunity to slip the cold deck from within the lacy folds at her wrist, replacing it with the old one. "Wait just one minute."

All eyes were on her instantly, and Jarman regarded her warily, expecting a trick. He scanned the table. The cards were as before, in a haphazard stack, ready to be shuffled had he not called the end of the game. What was she up to?

"One more hand. All or nothing."

He crooked a brow in amusement. "What for? You've lost everything, my dear. *Everything*," he emphasized.

Not caring what others listening thought, she told him bluntly, "I know we have a private bargain. I want one more chance to win. My deal."

"Why should I? I've won. And you've nothing more to wager, anyway. Besides, I probably won't get my money's worth out of our private bargain, anyway. So why should I take the risk of one more hand and maybe losing?"

"Because you're a gutless bastard if you don't."

Her words were like a whip, cutting into the tension of the moment. Some of those watching had started to leave but turned back quickly to await Jarman's decision. It might have been a call to duel, because he could not walk away and save face.

"If I catch you cheating—"

"Don't say that if you can't back it up."

Both Sam and Jarman glanced up in surprise to see Jake Whaley standing there, his hand close to his holster, as he told everyone, "If there's one thing I can't stand, it's a sniveling loser whining he's been cheated."

"I haven't lost yet." Jarman made a mental note to see that the judge had Whaley removed from his job, ineffectual though it was. "And I'm sure as hell not sniveling." He nodded to Sam. "Deal, damn it. I'm in a hurry to collect this pot, for sure."

Lyman got shakily to his feet and staggered over to join the crowd to witness the outcome. Sam ignored the way Jarman was looking at her, knowing he was trying to get her riled. She pretended to shuffle, then cut the cards but expertly returned them to their proper position in the deck. Then she dealt him a pat flush—five cards of one suit—a hand that allowed him to stand and not discard in order to get more cards.

Ordinarily, Jarman was able to keep the proverbial poker face, so as not to give away his hand. But this time he couldn't help himself. He began to chuckle and finally said, "What a waste of time." He flipped over his cards.

Everyone gasped out loud and began chattering excitedly among themselves. Lyman felt dizzy and clutched the arm of the man standing next to him. It appeared that Jarman had won the final hand.

"Not so fast." Sam met his gloating expression with one of her own as she lay her cards down one by one, a pair of tens and three sevens. She had a full house, which beat his flush.

With the most charming smile she could muster, she declared, "*Now* the game is over."

# 24

*Jarman stirred and moaned.* His head was throbbing, and his stomach was giving warning lurches that told him to stay right where he was. Opening one eye, he could tell by the light filtering in around the shades that it was nearly day. He had to get up and get out of there before folks started moving about. Besides, it was Sunday, and he was expected to take Miriam to church.

It was a good thing Quigby was out of town for the rest of the week; otherwise, Jarman knew he would be in plenty of trouble for staying out all night. But when he'd lost the poker game, all he had wanted to do was get drunk and he had proceeded to do exactly that, with some help from Louretta. Now he was in her bed, feeling like hell, and it didn't help to know Samara's room was right next door.

She had cheated by being able to replace his marked deck with a cold deck without anybody seeing. But he couldn't prove it. She had won. And now he wished he'd never even thought about owning his own boom-town casino, damn it. To hell with all his plans and dreams, because suddenly the only thing he wanted was his freedom.

Marriage to Miriam was like living with a corpse, because he might as well have been with one on their wedding night. She'd been so stiff and cold, he'd been unable to consummate the act. He had gotten up, dressed, and slipped out of the house to pay Louretta a visit. And he had returned regularly ever since.

Miriam never said a word when he stayed out late at night, oblivious to everything around her anyway because of her obsession with trying to communicate with the dead. Jarman thought she was a lunatic and needed to be put in an asylum, but he knew Quigby would never agree. After all, that was why he had bullied him into marrying her, so she would have someone to take care of her.

Jarman despised Quigby, too, for helping make the situation even more intolerable. He was always ordering him around like a servant, never letting him forget he was in his debt. Had it worked out for him to take over the Lucky Steer, Jarman was confident he'd have eventually made the money necessary to escape his misery. But Samara, damn her, had ruined that, just as she had ruined so many of his other dreams. And somehow, he vowed with teeth gritted against the pain hammering inside his skull, he had to make her pay, and Ramsey, too.

Beside him, Louretta suddenly rolled over on her back and began to snore. Disgusted, he jabbed her with his elbow, and she awoke with a surprised grunt to ask, "You still here? Good. I was afraid that redeye you guzzled cheated me out of a night's work, but if you're ready, so am I."

She made a move to snuggle closer, but he threw up his arm to fend her off. "Don't be ridiculous. I'm half-dead. Now get up and find me some hot coffee so I can try to get myself together and get out of this dump."

Louretta frowned, hurt by his criticism. She had tried to fancy things up. Red lacy curtains hung at the window, and she had bought a flowery bedspread. There were oil lamps with fringed, velvet shades and soft pillows and some pictures on the wall. She had even hung strings of beads at the door that made a cozy, tinkling sound whenever somebody walked by. So it really wasn't so bad, and she suspected there was another reason he was so cranky and sympathized. "It's her, ain't it? Hell, I don't blame you, sweetie. I don't like having her right next door, either, but there's nothing we can do after what happened last night."

"Don't remind me of last night." He burrowed his head under the pillow.

Louretta hated to be the one to tell him but knew he had to know sooner or later. "She's probably going to kick me out once she takes over the place."

Hesitantly, he peered out at her. "What do you mean—when *she* takes over?"

"Lyman told me if she won back what he lost, he'd sell her the place. He wants out. Says he don't have no business owning a casino when he's got gambling fever."

Jarman bounded from the bed, forgetting how sick he felt. "That settles it. That just damn well settles it. I can't stay here," he whispered hoarsely, not wanting the little tart to overhear if she was in her room. There was just no way he could live in the same town with Samara Labonte prissing around as the owner of her very own casino while he was nothing more than husband to a crazy woman and lackey to her father. He had to find a way to get out, or he was going to go insane.

"You'll move me somewhere else then?" Louretta tried to keep her voice down. "Oh, this is wonderful, Jarman. Do you have any place in mind? I don't need anything real big. Five rooms would be nice. I've got three girls working for me now, but I could keep another one busy, and—"

"Not now, Louretta." He pressed his fingertips against his temples. The way his head was hurting, it was hard to think. "Will you just find me some coffee so I can get out of here?"

Louretta threw her clothes on, then dashed down the street to a hotel café, where the owner gave her a pot of coffee and two tin mugs after extracting her promise that she'd bring the utensils back later.

She waited till Jarman had finished his first cup before broaching again the subject of moving. "I can go out today and look around. Maybe we could start this afternoon."

He did not want to alienate her. Neither did he want to waste time talking about something that was not going to happen. He was getting out of Abilene. He did not know when, or by what means, but he was not staying. But until he could get away, he wanted Louretta to keep her bed warm for him. With a caressing smile, he murmured, "Give me some time to think about it. After all, we want to look at all the possibilities, don't we?"

"Of course we do." She was bouncing up and down with delight. He would find a way, she just knew it, and she wouldn't have to eat her heart out whenever Cade came back to see Sam, and . . .

She touched a fingertip to the corner of her mouth thoughtfully as she remembered, "What did that letter say? Is he coming back any time soon? I'd like to be out of here before he does."

Jarman was putting on his hat, moving toward the door, anxious to be on his way. He needed to be alone, to make plans. "What are you talking about? What letter?"

"The letter I gave you last night. The one Cade Ramsey slipped under Sam's door."

It all came flooding back. He had just stumbled upstairs, having gone to the saloon down the street as soon as the game was over to toss down too many drinks to remember. Louretta had been waiting for him in her room. She'd heard what happened and known he would show up sooner or later. Now he recalled that she had given him an envelope and said something about Samara and Ramsey, but he'd been too drunk to pay any mind to what she was saying.

With both hands, he patted his coat, then felt paper crinkling inside the left front pocket. Drawing out the letter, he felt rage flaring along with excitement as he read:

*Dearest Sam,*

*I'm sorry about what happened at the hotel. I was wrong. I've never been good with words, but I'm trying to tell you I love you. That's why I want you where I can look out for you, and if marrying you is the only way I can do that, then this is really a letter of proposal, if you'll have me. Lord knows, I never thought I'd see the day I'd ask a woman to be my wife, but then I never thought I'd meet one like you.*

*I'll be back sometime next Sunday. Whether I like it or not, I've got one more hearing set before Judge Quigby on Monday. I will see you Sunday to find out your answer.*

*Till then,*

*Cade*

Louretta had refilled her mug and moved to stand at the window as she drank. If Jarman didn't want her to start looking for a new place yet, she would spend the day napping. He would probably come back later, anyway. He usually did when he had been too drunk to get his pleasuring the night before.

She heard the wagon coming down the street and watched it go by. The driver was in no hurry, allowing the team of horses to set their own pace. Beside him, the guard sat with head nodding, rifle across his knees. "You can sure set a clock by the Sunday wagon to Juby Fowler's place," she murmured. "Right at dawn, those two hired guns of his, Harold Veazey and Charlie Knight, take the winnings from his saloon to his house, just so's Juby can count his money in private. One of these days somebody is going to hold them up."

Something was dancing around in his mind, something Jarman could not quite grasp, but it was there all the same, an answer to his dilemma. Louretta's comments were coming to him through a kind of cleaving mist. "No, I don't think so," he responded thoughtfully. "I've heard the menfolk talking about Juby, and they say it's not far to his place. Ten miles or so. Saturday night is when the casinos take in the most money, and Juby doesn't trust banks. They say he's got plenty of guards at his ranch. It's like a fortress, and . . ." He trailed off and, at the same time, felt a tingling from head to toe as the idea struck full force. "My God, that's it," he cried softly.

Louretta turned. She had not really been listening to what he was saying, because it sounded as though he were talking to himself. She saw the way he was staring down at the letter in his hands and the way his face had suddenly gone pale. "What on earth does it say, Jarman?" she asked, excited.

He was so lost in thought, she had to ask again, and finally he replied, "Oh, they had a fight at some hotel where they were staying. It's not important. I have to go now." He hurried out before she could say anything else.

The more he thought about it, the more excited Jarman got, because come dawn next Sunday, that wagon was going to be robbed, by thunder. And it would all be so convenient, because he had learned a lot about the citizens of Abilene in the short time he'd been living there and knew the road to Juby's place conveniently went right by the judge's house. It would be a perfect setup.

Quickly Jarman untethered his horse, mounted, and rode hard until he had the wagon in sight. Then he slowed to concentrate on allowing his plan to evolve from dream to reality. He followed all the way to Judge Quigby's house, then dismounted to watch as Harold and Charlie continued on down the road, passing the cemetery and the church to finally disappear around a thick-shrubbed bend.

It would work, he thought excitedly. He was going to have to move quickly to take care of all the details before next Sunday morning, but he could do it. He could do anything, if it meant freedom from Miriam and her father and ultimate retribution against Ramsey. As for Samara, Jarman would take care of her later, in his own way, and next time Ramsey would not be around to come to her rescue.

He went inside and was only mildly annoyed at the lingering odor of candles and incense from the previous night's séance. Miriam might appear docile and withdrawn in her dealings with those who did not share her belief in spiritualism, but she was certainly cunning enough to anticipate that Jarman would stay out all night when her father was out of town. The table and chairs were still in place, and she hadn't picked up cups and plates after serving refreshments.

But this morning Jarman was too keyed up to give a damn what she did. He wanted more coffee and made a pot, then went over everything in his mind once more. When Miriam wandered in sometime later, looking so detached from life as to be walking in her sleep, he was able to inform her pleasantly that he would be taking her to church that morning.

Later, as they sat side by side in the pews, Jarman pretended to listen to every word the preacher spoke. All the while, however, he was studying the church, thinking of every nook and cranny. It was a perfect hiding place. No one would think to look there, and why should they? He would claim he heard gunfire and ran out of the house just in time to see the outlaw make his getaway. Later, when it was all over and Ramsey hung from the end of a rope, sentenced to die by Judge Quigby for using a gun in a crime, he would return to the church and retrieve the loot, and then *he* would be the one to ride away—only he would not be caught, because he would never be suspected.

Then, thinking about it deeper, Jarman came to realize he was going to need help to make it all go smoothly. There would be enough money involved that he could split it and still have plenty to make a new start somewhere else, and he needed somebody who resembled Cade Ramsey so the description would fit.

So late that afternoon he rode into town to find the perfect man for the job—Pike Albritton. He was tall and big and had long black hair. Unlike Ramsey, Pike did not take care of his flowing tresses, which hung dirty and greasy down his back, but Jarman felt that was unimportant. He would be wearing a bandanna on the lower part of his face, and all that mattered was that his hair was similar in length and color. Jarman had heard Pike was a gunslinger who would kill a man for the price of a beer. Judge Quigby had remarked about him once, when he and Jarman were in town and Quigby recognized him.

"First chance I get, I'll send that bastard to the gallows," he had snarled under his breath. "If he knows what's good for him, he'll stay down in Indian territory and out of my bailiwick."

But the gambling and women he enjoyed were in Abilene, and that was where Pike liked to spend his time. So far, he had not been in any trouble, and Jarman figured if everything worked according to plan, it would stay that way.

He got right to the point: "I've got a job for you, if you're interested."

Pike looked at Jarman and frowned. He was sitting in a corner of the Red Bull saloon and did not want to be disturbed, and he explained why. "I'm having a little drink by myself while I make up mind if I want to play poker or *poke her*"—he nodded to a prostitute plying her trade to men at the bar—"and since I don't know you, I ain't interested in nothing you got to say. So move on. You're blocking my view."

Jarman took a deep breath, pulled out a chair, and sat down.

"I guess you don't hear too good. Maybe I need to mash your ears a little to see if that'll help." Pike pounded his fist on the table for emphasis.

Jarman dared to lean closer. No one was around, but he was taking no chances. He held out his hand, but Pike just stared at it insolently as Jarman rushed to introduce himself, adding, "Judge Quigby is my father-in-law."

Pike bellowed, "Now I'm positive we ain't got nothing to talk about. That son of a bitch sent my cousin to the gallows, and I'd like nothing better than to send *him* straight to hell."

"Listen, I know how you feel. I hate him as much as you do. That's one of the reasons I'm making this proposition to you, so I can get away from him. I want out of this place, and if you help me, we can both leave rich men."

Pike waved him away. "I ain't swinging from the end of a rope for no amount of money, and if I use a gun in these parts, that's what'll happen if I go before Quigby, just like my cousin," he added bitterly.

"That won't happen if you do as I say. Now I've got it all figured out." Jarman proceeded to confide his plan.

Pike listened intently, but then, eyes hooded with apprehension, he wanted to know, "How come you're going to call me Cade Ramsey in front of them two on the wagon? How come you want them to think he did it?"

"Because I have a personal score to settle with the son of a bitch, that's how come. But don't you worry about that. You just shoot them when I call you by his name, say that since they know who you are, they've got to die, but don't kill them. Just wound them. I want them alive so Ramsey will get the blame. Afterward we ride off a piece and divide up the money, then go our separate ways." Jarman went on to assure Pike he had selected the perfect spot for the robbery. "It's near the judge's house, so I'll hurry back there, change clothes and horses, then rush back, pretending I heard gunfire, and go for help. The judge won't be back till Sunday evening. By then, I'll have Harold and Charlie all fired up to demand that Ramsey be sentenced as soon as possible."

Pike thought a moment before admitting, "It sounds good, but you haven't told me why you picked me to help you out. Why don't you just do it by yourself? Sounds like an easy take."

Temporarily forgetting how dangerous the man was, Jarman burst out in disgust, "Oh, for heaven's sake, you idiot. What am I going to do? Stand there and call myself Cade Ramsey? The driver and the guard have got to hear his name so they can tell the law, and he'll be blamed. Idiot," he repeated with an impatient sigh.

Pike moved so fast that Jarman never even saw his arm snaking out, knew only that suddenly his big, burly hand was wrapped around his throat and squeezing so hard, he could feel his eyes bulging. "Who are you calling an idiot, you skinny little polecat? I'll crush your neck like a chicken bone, you hear me?"

Jarman could not breathe and began thrashing his arms wildly, not about to strike out at the man for fear it would make matters worse. He tried to speak, to say he was sorry, to plead for mercy, but no sound came except for thin, feeble gurgles.

Pike released him, flinging him away so hard that Jarman fell from the chair, clutching his throat and desperately sucking air into his lungs. "I'll take you up on your offer," Pike said matter-of-factly, pouring himself another drink from the bottle on the table. "But I ain't takin' your guff. So watch your mouth. Now get up here and let me hear it all again. If I decide to get involved, I want to make sure you know what you're talking about."

Lyman put down the quill pen and shoved the paper across the table at Sam. "That's it. The Lucky Steer is all yours."

Sam looked at the document that made the land, and the building, legally hers. It was a poignant moment, for she could not remember ever owning anything in her whole life, except for the clothes on her back. "Are you sure?" She searched his face for any sign of doubt. If he was the least little bit reluctant, then she would refuse to let him go through with it.

"Positive."

"Then at least let me pay you more."

"You paid me exactly what the land cost me and the lumber to throw this place up. I got back what I put into it, so that's fair."

Sam shook her head to argue. "No, it isn't, Lyman. You built it into one of the most successful saloons and casinos in the Devil's Addition, and it doesn't belong here anyway, because you don't run a bawdy house. At least not downstairs, anyway." She relished the thought of evicting Louretta and her covey of soiled doves.

Lyman lifted his glass of rye whiskey in both salute and surrender. "Nothing you say can change my mind. We both know I've got the fever, Sam. If I stay here, I'd lose the place."

She reached to cover his hand with hers. "You can work for me. Tend the bar. I need you."

"Can't do it. I'm heading back to Texas. The truth is, I've been homesick, and I'll do just fine as long as I've got a roof over my head and enough to eat. The way I see it, if I ain't got nothing, I can't lose nothing, so it won't matter whether I got the fever or not. As for you" —he smiled at her fondly—"why, you don't need a man, Sam. You're the sort of woman who can do just fine without one. So stop frettin' about me and get busy turnin' this place into a highfalutin' oasis like the Alamo. You can do it, too."

After he left to catch the afternoon train to Salina, Sam wandered about the empty casino, thinking of how she would rearrange things, trying to get her mind off what Lyman had said about her not needing a man. Because he was wrong. She *did* need a man. But not just any man. She needed, wanted, Cade Ramsey, and if she ever got another chance, she was going to tell him so. And maybe, if he weren't so stubborn and would admit he loved her and wanted to marry her, she would be willing to give up the casino and be his wife. But to just quit her work and wait for him to come to her when he felt like it, why, that was one of the reasons she had made the decision to leave Paris —so she'd never be relegated to the life of a courtesan. If that was all she wanted, then she was no better than a whore like Louretta.

*Louretta.* Sam took a deep breath of resolve and decided to get it over with.

She went upstairs and knocked on her door, and a moment later Louretta appeared to ask defiantly, "So, what do you want?" She was wearing a red satin robe, holding it together over her fleshy breasts. "I work at night, remember? And I don't like getting woke up while it's still day."

"Well, that's what I came to tell you, Louretta. You won't be working here anymore." She held up the paper Lyman had signed. "I now own the Lucky Steer."

Louretta's eyes narrowed. "I knew you'd do this, and it's not because you don't want my girls working downstairs, 'cause you know me and Lyman had an agreement about that. It's because of him. Cade. You can't stand it because you know he came to me. You're jealous."

Sam was not about to admit that might be partly true. She was also not in a mood to argue. "There's no need for this to get nasty. I'll give you a week to clear out and take your girls with you."

"Oh, it won't take me that long to find a place. I can be out of here tomorrow."

"Maybe that would be best." Sam turned away.

"Hey, would you do me a favor, though?"

Sam turned, wary. Louretta had made her voice too sweet, and now she saw her eyes were shining and the corners of her mouth were twitching with the grin she was obviously trying to hold back.

"As soon as I know where I'll be," Louretta cooed, "I'll let you know in hopes you'll be fair enough to pass it along to Cade. He was here yesterday morning. Said something about you two being at a hotel and having a big fight. I'm used to listening when he's mad, and I know how to make him happy again." She winked, then gave a little feathery laugh. "Of course, I didn't know all this was going to happen then, you kicking me out and all, and he'll wonder where I am when he comes back.

"And he *always* comes back," she added goadingly.

Sam struggled for composure, not wanting to let on how Louretta's words had crushed her. Louretta could not be lying. How else would she have known they had been to a hotel, that they'd argued, unless he had been here and told her?

Louretta saw the effect her hastily concocted story had had on Sam and continued with relish. "I'm surprised you didn't see him. You were downstairs with Lyman, and—"

"Just let me know where you'll be," Sam cut her off, biting out each word. "I'll be glad to tell him if I see him."

Sam could not listen to any more. Oh, how could he have held her in his arms all night long, only to go straight to another woman's bed just because they'd had a few words? Was that all she had meant to him? A few hours of pleasure that could be forgotten in a moment of sudden anger? To hell with him.

Rushing into her room, she closed and locked the door behind her, then threw herself across the bed as the tears she had been fighting began to stream from her eyes. She would cry one last time for what was, what could never be, and then, she swore fervently, would banish him from her mind, and her heart, forevermore.

# 25

Sam stood at the window of her room, thinking how she should go downstairs and fire up the stove. Like Lyman, she didn't open the casino on Sundays, but the gray, overcast skies of dawn warned of a chilly day. She might be bored and lonely, but at least she could keep warm.

In just the week since Lyman had left, Sam knew the Lucky Steer was going to be very profitable. Lyman had made some money, true, but his drinking was against him, and customers knew it. They ran up debts for gambling losses, as well as their drinking. They would pay a little along, but most of them didn't worry about it, and neither had Lyman. Sam, however, insisted on cash. The customers still flocked in, but instead of a drawer full of IOUs, she had a box full of money every night.

But what was she going to do if she did get rich? she wondered idly as she stared out at the empty street below. What good was any of it when there was no one to share it with? In a year, maybe two, she might be set for life and she supposed then she could sell out and go —*where?* And do—*what?* None of it mattered, she thought dismally, without Cade. But he was too stubborn to settle down, and she'd be damned if she'd be any man's mistress.

She saw the Fowler wagon pass by, right on time. The Sundays she was up so early she never failed to see it. She had remarked about it to Lyman, and he'd told her about Juby Fowler and how the eccentric old man wanted to count his money in the privacy of his home. Sam just did as Lyman had. She paid Jake Whaley, along with one of his hired guns, to take her gold and cash to the bank late Saturday night. Edgar Miller was very obliging about opening up at that hour to receive the deposits of any of the casino owners who did not want to have large amounts around until Monday.

She watched the wagon until it was out of sight, then decided she could no longer stand being in the tiny room. Since Louretta and her girls had moved out, the upstairs was as quiet as a tomb. Maybe if she went below, someone would stop in for coffee and conversation. She hoped so, just as she hoped for anything that would take her mind off Cade and her aching heart.

Harold Veazey held the reins loosely. He had made the trip to Juby's place so many times, the horses knew the way. All he had to do was sit back and let them set their own pace. Beside him, Charlie Knight was nodding, his head having dropped to his chest. His rifle was at his feet, close by should he need it, but neither man was worried. After all, it was not a long trip, and bandits would be more likely to go after bigger booty, like Edgar Miller's bank on a Saturday night.

They passed Judge Quigby's house, a small white clapboard with a porch across the front. A picket fence surrounded it. Harold knew the judge had wanted something closer to town when he'd first arrived in Abilene, but he'd been lucky even that place was available. And it would not have been had Preacher Larson not moved his wife and children into Salina to live with his ailing mother. The house was actually the parsonage for the church right across the road. So far, Preacher Larson had made it back every week for Sunday preaching, but he no longer wanted to live nearby.

Harold saw everything was quiet at the Quigby place. Probably the judge was glad now that he did live so far out, the way his daughter had gone loco since her boy had got shot. Sad. He shook his head. He'd heard about her and some other crazy women, how they got together and tried to talk to the dead. Best thing that could happen would be for every one of them to be locked up in one of those insane asylums before they hurt somebody.

Harold yawned and stretched as the wagon headed around the bend in the road. He gave the reins a pop to hurry the horses a bit. As soon as the trip was over he could head back home, where his wife would have a big plate of hotcakes waiting. Then he would go back to bed and sleep till noon.

He looked at Charlie, saw he was dead to the world, and thought about waking him up to keep him company, but it was not much farther, maybe another twenty minutes, and—

"What the hell?" Harold cried, and jerked back on the reins, bringing the horses to an abrupt halt. Beside him, Charlie was pitched forward, head snapping to and fro as he came awake with a start. He reacted faster than Harold, who sat frozen, staring at the two men standing in the middle of the road. Bandanas covered the bottoms of their faces, and despite their pointed guns, Charlie instinctively reached for his rifle.

"Don't try it," Pike Albritton yelled, firing off a shot that struck Charlie's wrist.

As bone splintered and blood sprayed, Charlie dropped the rifle and screamed in pain, grabbing his wrist with his other hand. Harold did not move. After he realized it was, indeed, a holdup, he was not about to give his life for Juby's money. "Take it, mister," he called shakily. "Just don't shoot me. It ain't my money nohow."

Jarman was annoyed that Pike had shot so fast. He'd wanted no gunfire until after they'd got the box with the money in it off the wagon. He only hoped there was nobody around to hear. "Wait till I get the box," he said quietly as he dismounted. He hurried over to take it out of the back and set it on the ground.

Harold continued his plea. "Don't hurt me, all right? Just take it and leave us be. Hell, we don't care—" He screamed and fell backward as Pike fired off another round, hitting him in his shoulder.

"You son of a bitch!" Charlie roared, sitting up straight.

Pike fired again, the bullet hitting Charlie right between his eyes.

"You fool!" Jarman shrieked, abandoning the money box as he rushed toward Pike. "You weren't supposed to kill him." Then, despite his frenzied state, he remembered to add: "Ramsey, you've killed him, damn you."

At that, Pike laughed and squeezed the trigger once more; hit for the second time, Harold toppled over and fell to the ground with a thud.

Jarman looked from one body to the other and shook his head wildly as he cried in near hysteria, "You killed them both, you stupid bastard. You killed them both. I didn't want anybody to die. You were supposed to wound them, so they could say—"

"Shut your mouth." Pike pointed the gun at him. "I might just blow you to hell, too."

Jarman's lips moved wordlessly as he found himself looking into the deadly barrel.

"Now let's divide the loot, before I change my mind and take all of it." Pike holstered his gun and dismounted.

Jarman knew better than to argue. He was also experiencing a surge of hope that his plan for Ramsey to be charged with the crime was not ruined after all, because he had noticed that Harold Veazey was still alive—lying on his side with his face toward Jarman, eyes open and taking little gasping breaths. Pike was paying no attention; he was too busy getting the box open and pulling out his part of the loot.

"I took a little extra." Pike grinned as he headed for his horse, his pockets crammed full. "I charge extra for killin'." Back in the saddle, he reined about and tipped his hat. "I'm heading south of the border. Adios, amigo." And he spurred his horse into full gallop and rode away.

Jarman took advantage of Harold's consciousness to mutter loudly, "Damn you, Cade Ramsey. You didn't have to kill 'em."

He knew he had to move fast, but the box was not large, and with Pike having taken his share, it was not very heavy, either. He lifted it to his shoulders easily and, pulling his horse along by the reins, turned to go back up the road to the church.

And that was when his heart slammed into his chest at the sight of Miriam. She was running toward him, clutching her robe about her. He had lowered the bandanna once out of Harold's sight, and Miriam slowed in recognition, finally stopping to wait for him to reach her.

"What are you doing here?" Jarman wanted to hit her, he was so mad. He put the box on the ground. "Get back to the house, damn you."

Miriam had gone pale, for she could look beyond him and see the wagon and two bodies on the ground. She saw the box at Jarman's feet, the way the bandanna hung around his neck. He never wore a bandanna. "I . . . I heard gunshots," she stammered uneasily. "I came to see what was happening."

Jarman was seething. He didn't need this, damn it. Nothing seemed to be going according to plan. "I told you to get back to the house. You've no business being out here."

But Miriam did not obey him, because men were hurt, maybe dying, and Jarman did not seem to care. Her gaze dropped to the box once more. "What's in there? Why are you worrying about it instead of doing something to help those men? They've been shot, haven't they? The shots I heard—"

His hands snaked out to wrap around her throat and squeeze. Her eyes bugged out, and she started making little choking noises, her fingers clawing at him in terrified desperation as he lifted her from the ground so that she was barely standing on her toes. "None of it concerns you. Now go inside and stay there and forget everything you saw or heard. I will tell you what to say when the time comes. Understand?"

She tried to nod, but he was holding her so tight that she could barely move her head. "And if you don't do exactly as I say, I warn you: I will kill your father, and no one will be able to prove I did it. Certainly not you, because everyone thinks you're tetched anyway, and I'll have you locked up with crazy people, and you'll never get out.

"Now get inside." He gave her a rough shove that sent her stumbling backward and struggling to keep from falling.

Miriam ran as fast as she could, all the way to the house, and slammed the door behind her. Her heart was pounding, and it hurt to breathe because her throat was bruised and sore from Jarman's crushing hold. But despite the horror that had her shaking all over, she was struck even more by the chilling reality that he had actually been a part of robbery and murder. Worse, she could not say a word about it, lest he make good his threat.

She waited a moment for her chest to stop heaving, then eased to the window to peer out from behind the curtains. Maybe he had changed his mind and would kill her anyway to make sure she never told. Then she saw he was walking toward the church, carrying the box. *What was he doing?* Something told her to find out, no matter how scared she was.

When he went inside, she hurried to follow and peeked between the doors. He had gone to the pulpit and shoved it aside. He lifted several boards beneath the pulpit. It was obvious they had been loosened earlier. He put the box under the floor, then replaced everything.

By the time Jarman got back to the house, Miriam was sitting at the kitchen table, face lowered to her hands. She wondered what in the world she was going to do.

Jarman sat down next to her and abruptly knocked her hands away. "Now listen to me, damn you. This morning"—he spoke slowly, evenly, so she could understand and grasp every word—"we were awakened by the sound of gunfire. I went to see what was going on and came back a little while later and told you Juby Fowler's wagon had been robbed and the driver and guard were hurt. I said I was taking them into town, which is exactly what I am about to do. Now that is all you need to know, all you need to say, should anybody ask. Do you understand?"

She withered before his deadly eyes, and her whisper was barely audible. "I won't say anything different. I swear to you, Jarman."

He grabbed a handful of her hair and yanked painfully. "Make sure you don't, or *I* swear to *you* I'll do what I said I would."

He released her, and she ran to her room and dove into bed, pulling the covers up over her face. Why, she asked herself miserably, had she ever let her father browbeat her into marrying Jarman? But he had made her feel so guilty, saying he worried about having to leave her, and that she owed it to him to take a husband to ease his mind. Jarman had also been persuasive, talking about how he wanted a family, how good he would be to her, and she had foolishly believed him. The truth was, he could not bear to touch her, and she had overheard a conversation between him and her father and was pained to learn there was some sort of financial agreement between them over her.

She began to cry, but quietly, lest Jarman hear her as he made ready to leave. The way he was acting, there was no telling what he would do if he got annoyed with her again. And her father would be home later in the day, so she had to compose herself; otherwise he might become suspicious and start asking questions. Even if he did pay Jarman to marry her, she knew he'd never stand for her to be mistreated. If only she could get through to the other side, if only she could talk to Thomas or her son, they would have words of comfort. She just knew it.

Stuffing a corner of the pillow in her mouth to muffle the sound of her anguished cries, Miriam thought how Jarman had nothing to worry about. She would tell no one. She did not want her father to die. And she certainly did not want to go to an asylum.

*Because they would never allow her to hold a séance there.*

\* \* \*

Sam heard the commotion and ran to the door in time to see horses galloping down the street at breakneck speed, pulling a wagon with what looked like two bodies in the back. People were running out to follow after it, but she turned back inside. In such a lawless town anything could happen, and she knew she would hear all about it sooner or later, anyway.

She did not have long to wait. It was nearly dark when Mae Calhoun, a calico queen who worked at the saloon across the street, came rushing in, all in a dither. "Did you hear? Juby Fowler's wagon got held up. Happened out past that church on the fork road. Charlie Knight is dead, and Harold Veazey is all shot up. And guess what? That man you beat to win back this place brought 'em in. Somebody says he lives near where it happened."

Sam realized then it had been Jarman at the reins of the wagon but thought no more about it as Mae left to continue spreading the news. She went back to her work, rearranging glasses, checking supplies, doing anything to keep busy and occupy her mind. But nothing was working. All she could think about was Cade and how her love, combined with the pain he had caused, tormented and confused her so deeply.

She was about to finish for the day when a man came in whom she recognized as one she had seen in Jake Whaley's store.

"Jake sent me to get you. He said to tell you that friend of yours he had to lock up wants to see you."

Sam had no idea what he was talking about and said as much, only to be rocked to the core by his next words.

"Cade Ramsey is his name. Jake locked him up for holding up Juby Fowler's wagon and killing Charlie Knight. Then Harold Veazey died, so now he's charged with a double murder."

Sam swayed, felt her knees go weak. "He couldn't have."

"Yes, ma'am, he did it. Right before he died, Harold gave Jake a description that fit Ramsey and said he even heard the other robber call Ramsey by his name. He's asking to see you, and that's why I'm here."

Sam hesitated only long enough to grab her shawl, and then she was out the door and on her way. She was not thinking of her anger at Cade in that moment. She was thinking only of her love.

A crowd had gathered around the squat structure located behind Jake's store. Jake was nowhere around, so Sam approached the man closest to the jail door. "Let me in. He wants to see me."

He frowned, and the others began to mumble among themselves. "Well, I don't know," he hedged. "Jake ain't here, and—"

"And she's not going in there anyway."

Sam whirled about to see Jarman striding toward her and did not miss the way his eyes were glittering with triumph over the situation. "If you're real nice, we might let you have a word with him right before he swings."

Sam swallowed against her fury. "And what business is this of yours, Jarman?"

"Oh, let's just say my father-in-law sort of put me in charge of getting this little hanging party together."

"Hanging?" Sam glanced about wildly but saw no friendly face, no one to help her understand the madness. "He hasn't even had a trial. You can't hang a man without a trial."

Jarman smirked. "Oh, he had a trial all right. As soon as the judge got back in town this evening, he listened to the evidence, how Ramsey was identified by a dying man, and that was enough to send him to the gallows. He'll be executed day after tomorrow at dawn. We've already sent to Junction City for the judge's favorite hangman." He winked. "He knows how to snap the neck just right, so they'll suffer a bit before they go, give them time to ponder their sins."

Sam was not about to let him goad her into hysteria. "I want to see him. Jake said he was asking for me."

"Well, that doesn't mean I'm going to permit it."

"You haven't got anything to do with it, damn you."

Jarman was the one to lose control then, grabbing her and slinging her away from the door as he warned her, "Don't you dare curse me. I'll have you run out of town, you little strumpet. I'm sick of all the grief you cause."

"You aren't doing anything, Ballard, except getting out of my way."

All eyes turned as Jake Whaley appeared to give Jarman a rough shove. Jarman backed away a few steps before threatening, "You'll be sorry for this, Whaley. I'm going to tell my father-in-law, and he'll take care of you. You'll see."

Jake was busy unlocking the door to the jail. "You go do that, Ballard. You go do it right now. 'Cause if you keep pissin' me off like you're doin', I'm gonna hammer your skinny little butt right into the ground with my bare fist." He turned around, but Jarman was already in hasty retreat as laughter rang through the crowd.

Jake turned to Sam. "Go on in. I can't give you but a few minutes."

Sam brushed by him to hurry inside, where Cade was waiting to grab her and hold her tight against him. "Thank God, you're here." He nuzzled her hair with his lips, drinking in the feel of her, the scent of her. "I was afraid they wouldn't let you in."

She did not return his ardor, instead pulling back to look him straight in the eye and ask grimly, "Will you please tell me what this is all about?"

Cade detected something strange in her demeanor, hostility almost, but he brushed it aside as tension. Quickly he told her what he could, about how when he'd been heading into town that afternoon, he had been arrested and charged with murder. "The next thing I knew, I heard I'd been sentenced to hang day after tomorrow. That's all I know, Sam. I sent for you to see if you could find out anything else."

Sam fought to keep her voice even. It still hurt to think how easily he had gone to another woman when he was upset with her, but she could not deny she loved him. And she did not want him to die, would do anything to save him.

"One of the men identified you before he died," she told him.

"Yes, that's what Whaley said, but it doesn't make sense. I was nowhere near the fork road this morning."

"Can you prove that?"

"Unfortunately, no. I camped out last night between here and Council Grove. I didn't see a soul, and nobody saw me, either. Hell, Sam, you know I'd never do anything like that. I'm not a thief, and I'm damn sure not a cold-blooded murderer." He turned away and began to run his fingers through his hair in agitation.

Yes, she thought with heavy heart, she knew beyond doubt he was innocent, but if a miracle didn't happen, and soon, he was going to hang.

Then the idea struck. She moved closer, clutching his shoulders and standing on tiptoes to whisper so no one outside could hear as she divulged her plan. "I'm going to get word to Bold Eagle. He'll know what to do, how to get you out of here. He said if I ever needed him, all I had to do was send a telegram, and he would come to me. Once you're out, we'll find a way to prove your innocence."

"No."

Sam stepped back, shocked at his sudden granitelike expression. "No," he repeated, keeping his voice low. "Bold Eagle would break me out all right, but it might cause the law to go after all the Kansa. They'd be slaughtered. I can't risk that."

"It may be your only chance."

"Then I don't want it." His eyes were on fire, the nerves in his cheeks jumping. "I'm not going to be responsible for the deaths of innocent people. Now just do whatever you can to find out if Jarman Ballard is behind this."

Sam felt a stab of apprehension. "You think that's possible?"

"I don't know, but it all seems a bit too pat. Too cut and dried. It could be he did this to get back at me for busting things up with you that night."

"Or maybe revenge on me for keeping him from taking the casino away from Lyman." She told him about the poker game.

When she had finished, he smiled for the first time and reached to take her in his arms once more. She stiffened but did not pull away, and he felt it but let it go. "I guess I didn't realize how good a card-sharp you are, Sam. Now I'm starting to understand why you enjoy it so much. And if I try hard enough, maybe I can even understand why you aren't willing to give it up. Unless you've changed your mind after reading—"

The door opened, and Jake appeared, holding a lantern up to flood them with light. "You better come on out now, little lady. Somebody said Ballard is on the way here with the judge, so all hell is gonna break loose if they find you still here."

"Do what you can," Cade told her. He stepped back, lest he yield to the calling of his heart and pull her close to kiss her until they were both breathless. And he did not want to do that in front of Jake.

Sam longed to ask him what he had meant about her changing her mind after reading—what? But there was no time as Jake grabbed her elbow and hurried her away from the others. At first she was annoyed, thinking he was merely anxious to get rid of her, but before she could protest, he began talking, fast.

"Now listen careful, girl. I ain't got no business getting involved in this, but maybe I feel bad about being so smart-mouthed to you before. I've gotten to know Ballard better, and I'm sure now he was lying about what happened that night he broke into your room. Now I don't know if you cheated him in that card game like he claims, but I don't care if you did, and neither do other folks. They've learned to hate him real fast since he hit town, and they're glad to see you put him in his place."

Exasperated, she urged, "Will you just tell me what this is all about, Jake?" She was in a hurry to get to the telegraph office and send word to Bold Eagle to come as fast as he could, despite Cade's objections. It was their only hope. Otherwise, God forbid, Cade was going to hang.

"I talked to Harold Veazey before he died."

She glanced at him sharply. "And did he identify Cade?"

"Afraid so. He said there were two of them, and the other one called Cade by name. I asked him what he looked like, the one called Cade, and he gave a description that fit—same size, same color hair, wore it long, too. Things sure point to Ramsey."

"But what about the second man?"

Jake shook his head. "Harold didn't give a good enough description to figure out who it might have been."

Sam's determination to get word to Bold Eagle was only strengthened. "I have to go." She tried to pull from his grasp, but he held tight, and she cried furiously, "Damn it, Jake. What do you want from me?"

"There's just something that bothers me about all this."

"For God's sake, tell me." If he didn't get to the point fast, she was going to give him a sound kick in the shins and take off running for the telegraph office.

"Harold said he saw a woman."

She stiffened. "I thought there were only two robbers, and both of them were men."

He nodded. "That's right. But Harold said after he was shot, the one that was called Ramsey rode off, and he saw the other one talking to a woman. He couldn't tell who it was or hear what they were saying, 'cause he was fading in and out. But he was sure it was a woman, and it don't make sense."

Sam jumped to the conclusion fast, pointing out, "But if it was Miriam Appleby the robber was talking to, it would make a lot of sense."

He nodded grimly. "That's exactly what I was thinking."

Sam grabbed him by the front of his shirt. "Have you talked to her?"

"It wouldn't do no good. She's a loony, Sam. Nobody would believe anything she said. And if Ballard is involved, you can be sure he thought of that."

Sam felt like screaming. "Then what can we do? We can't let Cade hang for a crime he didn't commit."

"We need proof."

"But you just said nobody would believe Miriam even if she could be persuaded to talk."

"If we knew where the money box was hid, if we could come up with that, Jarman couldn't lie his way out. Her knowing where Jarman put it would be proof he did it. Otherwise, how would she know where it was? Loony or not, folks would have to believe her."

Sam felt the smile originating from the depths of her soul, and by the time it reached her lips, she felt a warm, positive glow from head to toe. "She'll talk," she said confidently. "And I know how to make her do it."

She hurried to the telegraph office. Now it was more important than ever that Bold Eagle get there as quickly as possible. After all, it would be hard for her to conduct a séance alone.

# 26

*It was nearly dawn, and Sam* had not slept a wink. She'd tossed and turned, her nerves raw, her brain on fire with worry.

Would Bold Eagle receive the message and arrive in time? The dispatcher had been stunned to read the cryptic message she instructed him to send down the lines all the way to Kansas City: "Bold Eagle. Need you. Sam." If he did not show up, she would have to rely on Jake, and she hadn't yet even approached him with her bizarre plan. She felt sure she could rely on him, but she still needed one other person and could not trust just anyone. And she would not even be optimistic about Jake's loyalty if he and Jarman had not crossed swords.

She had left the shades open, and the room slowly became tinted in the special bluish light that seems to trap the world between darkness and dawn in mystical magic, if only for a few moments.

It was then that he appeared, slipping through the window without a sound. Sam was not frightened to see him standing over her bed, tall and fierce; she knew only relief. "Bold Eagle. You came."

"As fast as I could." He stood with legs apart, deerskin breeches stretched across powerful thighs, fisted hands on his hips. War paint streaked his face, and his head was shining and bald except for the traditional scalp lock. "My people have many ears and many ways to use them. I know about the injustice to Wild Spirit. I will free him. I have already sent a signal to the warriors to rally." His face seemed chiseled with lines of fierce resolve.

Sam had not bothered to undress the night before. She threw back a blanket and sat up. Then, taking his hand, she drew him down to sit beside her. "He doesn't want it that way." She told him of Cade's fears for the Indians, hastening to explain, "But I have a plan to save him, and I need your help."

"Go on." He looked skeptical but was willing to hear her out. She told him about the séance, how he was needed to do certain things to make it seem real. He did not understand, for he had never heard of anything like that, but he said he would cooperate. "But," he added, "if you do not succeed, I will take my brothers and fight for Wild Spirit."

"It has to work. Meanwhile, I don't want anyone to see you in town. I want you to stay here and be ready to start setting things up when I get back."

She gave him his instructions, then left and hurried to Jake Whaley's store. She found him sitting out front on the steps, his face a thundercloud.

"Ballard did what he said he'd do," he grumbled. "He took over my job. Didn't pay much, anyway, but it was something."

Sam was not surprised but was chilled by what he went on to tell her. "The judge put Ballard in charge, and he says nobody is to get anywhere near that jail. Guards are everywhere."

Sam took him at his word. She could not stand knowing Cade was inside the wood building and that she would not be allowed to see him or talk to him.

"Everybody is edgy because the dispatcher told about you sending a telegram to an Indian yesterday evening. Ballard says he knows for a fact Ramsey is friends with the Kansa, and he's got everybody terrified they're going to attempt a jail break. Ballard even tried to get the judge to go ahead and hang him before they get here, but he refused. Says it'll be done the right way, at the time he set."

Sam was not surprised that the dispatcher had reported the oddity of a wire being sent to an Indian, particularly by a white woman. "Jake," she said quietly, bracing herself to confide everything and praying she really could trust him, "the Indian I sent for is here."

He stared, wide-eyed. "Are you gonna try to bust Ramsey out?"

"If it comes down to that. But I've got another plan that just might work—*if* I can have your word not to tell anyone, and you are willing to help."

He did not hesitate. "You can count on me. I don't want to see a man hang for something he didn't do, and if Ballard, the weasel, is behind all this, I'd like nothing better than to help prove it and see him swing instead."

"Good. Now listen. I used to go for buggy rides with Belle Cooley in the mornings before things got busy at the Lucky Steer, and I remember that just about every Monday we would see Miriam Appleby going into your store. Was there a reason she came on that particular day?"

"Yes. On Mondays I get early delivery from the farmers. Ben Townley brings in his eggs and fresh-killed hens. Everett Brubaker comes in with sweet cakes his wife has spent all weekend baking. The ladies in town come by, and Mrs. Appleby, or I should say Mrs. *Ballard,* is one of them.

"As a matter of fact, she should be here in a little while," he added.

Sam shared everything, and he was astonished as well as fascinated. "And you want me to be the voice of her husband?" he asked incredulously.

"You have to. Bold Eagle can't do it. He speaks English, but it's stilted, and I just don't think she'd be fooled."

"What makes you think she'll believe me? She's sure to know her own husband's voice."

"You won't sound guttural like Bold Eagle can't help doing, and I'll rehearse it with you and help you sound like the voice of the man at the séance I went to, as though you're speaking from far, far away."

"Well," he said slowly, thoughtfully, then his whole face seemed to light up with enthusiasm. "Sure. I can do it. Where's this little ghost gathering going to be?"

"My room upstairs over the Lucky Steer."

"And you really think it will work?"

Sam's smile was confident. "If everything goes the way I believe it will, Miriam will lead us straight to where Jarman hid Juby Fowler's money box. It has to be near where the robbery took place. No doubt he's planning to leave town with it as soon as the excitement dies down."

"What if she doesn't know where it is? What if she didn't actually see him hide it?"

Sam did not want to think about that possibility. "We'll just try to get her to tell what she did see and go from there. And if there's nothing to prove Jarman did it, then I'll let Bold Eagle take over."

She hurried back to make sure Bold Eagle was following her instructions, then returned to position herself across the street from Jake's store.

About an hour later, Miriam appeared, head down and shoulders slumped, carrying an empty basket. Sam watched her go inside, then waited another few minutes before following, making sure to appear nonchalant and in no hurry. Jake, busy with a customer at the counter, did not look up but was quite aware of her presence. Miriam was picking over the eggs, selecting the ones she liked. Intent on what she was doing, she did not notice Sam. Sam sympathized to see how much the woman had aged in the past months, her face a mirror of desolation and hopelessness.

Finally, when it appeared Miriam was just not going to look up, Sam took a deep breath and walked over to reach right across her on the pretense of taking a spool of thread from a nearby rack. "Excuse me," she murmured, making sure to bump into her ever so slightly.

Miriam raised lackluster eyes, but only for an instant; then recognition struck. With a splat, the egg she had been holding fell to the floor. "It's you," she gasped. "Oh, dear God. My dear, dear God." Her hand flew to her throat and she backed away, first in fright, for she'd never expected to see Sam again, then in wonder, to realize her prayers had been answered. "You . . . you're alive. Oh, praise the Lord."

Miriam threw herself at Sam then, to embrace her and, at the same time, whisper frantically, "Oh, you don't know how I've prayed for this moment. You must help me. I've lost my boy, too, and I must talk to him, and Thomas, and you can reach them for me. I know you can."

She was sobbing loudly, and people were turning around, including Jake, who was frowning because he well understood the need to keep things quiet. They did not want word getting back to Jarman or Judge Quigby that Miriam had been seen talking to Sam.

Making eye contact with Sam, Jake nodded toward the back room, indicating she should take Miriam there. Sam put an arm about her and ushered her behind the curtains, careful to keep her back turned to the customers in hopes she would not be recognized. Because it was a definite clue to her identity, she had carefully pinned her silver hair beneath her bonnet. She sat Miriam on a chair, then pulled another close to sit opposite. Taking her hands, she coaxed gently, "Now tell me what has you so upset."

How wonderful it would be, Sam thought with a surge of hope, if Miriam would reveal everything now, making the séance unnecessary. But it was not going to be that way. All Miriam would say was that she had to talk to her dead husband.

"I've tried so many times, but there's not a medium anywhere near here. I've formed a home circle with other women who've lost loved ones. We gather and pray and try our best, but without success. But now that you're here"—she squeezed Sam's hands tight, beseeching her with tear-filled eyes—"you can do it. I know you can. I feel it in my heart."

Sam pretended to protest but finally agreed after extracting a vow of secrecy. "No one must know. Not even your home circle, understand?"

"Anything you say," Miriam cried, shaken with emotion.

"Can you sneak out of your house tonight?"

"Oh, yes. That's no problem. There's to be a hanging tomorrow, and I overheard my husband tell my father he's planning on sleeping outside the jail, because there's talk of some trouble. I can leave as soon as my father goes to bed, and he never stays up late. I should be able to get away by nine o'clock at the latest. Just tell me where to go."

Sam gritted her teeth to think of Jarman camping outside the jail to make sure nothing happened to prevent Cade's execution. How she burned inside to prove he was the one who should be headed for the gallows.

Finally, with everything set, Sam sent Miriam happily on her way. There was nothing to do but wait, and the day seemed interminably long. She went over everything carefully with Bold Eagle, how he was supposed to slip into the room and blow out the candle on the table. The window shades would be adjusted to allow scant light from below, enough to illuminate the dancing ghost as he lifted the sheet with a broom handle. He had a tambourine ready to rattle and shake to give the effect of music of the spheres, and after careful rehearsal, he knew exactly where to stoop by the table to reach underneath and lift it quickly with one hand, as well as when to make the knocking sounds with his fist.

Jake practiced his ghostly voice and what he was to say. Sam was pleased but remarked how much better it would be if he could mimic a child. "She might balk at her dead husband telling her to expose her present husband as a murderer, but I think she'd obey her son without question."

Jake assured her he would do the best he could. "I just don't think I would be very convincing as a little boy, Sam. Sorry. I'll try to work on it between now and then, though."

Absently, she told him not to worry about it and went back to staring at the clock and wishing the hands would move faster. She would not let herself think of failure. She would succeed, by God. She would prove Jarman was guilty, and Cade would go free. But then it would be over between them. She would give him back his life, in return for her heart, for never again would she trust him. She would throw herself into her work and not look back, and to hell with the memories. She would find a way, somehow, to forget and go forward with her life. It was the way it had to be.

Finally, nine o'clock came. Bold Eagle was in position down the hall, ready to act as soon as Miriam arrived and took her seat at the table. But Miriam did not come. Not at ten, or eleven, and as the hour moved toward midnight, Bold Eagle slipped in to express his fear that she was not going to come at all. "Your plan has failed. Now it is time for me to act. I must gather my warriors. They wait for my signal, and we must move swiftly to get Wild Spirit out of jail. We will not let him die," he said fiercely, vehemently.

Jake also came in, equally concerned. "Something must have happened. Maybe I should ride out to the judge's place."

"No. Both of you stay here and be ready in case I'm able to bring her back with me." She turned to Bold Eagle. "Please. You've got to give me a little more time." She could see his eyes in the candle's glow and how they were steely with his resolve.

"Just before dawn, the Kansa braves will ride." He was giving her a few more hours.

Jake told her to take his horse and where he'd left him, then she hurried out.

The ride to Judge Quigby's house took less than ten minutes. She could see the glow of light from one of the windows, which meant he had not gone to bed. No doubt Miriam did not dare leave until he did.

A little distance away, she dismounted and went the rest of the way on foot. Stealthily, she crept to the window the light was coming from to peer inside. The room was obviously the judge's study. He was sitting on the sofa, in front of the fireplace, with a man she'd never seen before. They were sipping drinks, and from the sounds of their laughter and sluggish movements as they lifted their glasses, it was obvious they were well into their cups.

Suddenly a bolt of rage struck Sam to hear the judge declare proudly, almost reverently, as he raised his glass in salute to the man sitting beside him, "Best damned hangman in the state of Kansas. Maybe the whole country. Nothing I like better than to see you stretch those bastards' necks. Slow and easy. Make 'em suffer."

So! He was entertaining the executioner, which explained his staying up so late. It was all she could do to keep from smashing the window and telling him just what a heartless brute he was. But she forced herself to be calm and tend to the task at hand, which was finding Miriam and getting her to town.

It was a small house. Sam went from window to window, tapping quietly on each. When she reached the rear corner, she was relieved to hear Miriam's fearful voice call out, "What's that? Who's there?"

Sam leaned closer, speaking as loudly as she dared. "It's me, Miriam. Celeste," she added, since Miriam did not know her true identity. "You have to come with me now. The spirits are moving this night. I can feel them."

Actually, she was experiencing a wave of self-loathing to think how she was duping this poor woman, but surely the end would justify the means.

The moon was nearly full, and when Miriam's face appeared at the window, Sam could see her joy as she opened it. "You came for me? Oh, thank goodness. I've been tearing my hair out, knowing I couldn't walk all the way to town at this hour and didn't dare saddle a horse for fear Papa would hear me."

Sam helped her crawl out, then pulled her along to where she'd left Jake's horse. In minutes they were on their way back. "Normally, I would have just waited till another night," Sam told her calmly as they settled at the table. "But as I said, the spirits seem to be moving tonight, and I didn't think we should miss the opportunity."

"No, no. Begin, please." Miriam wriggled deliciously on her chair, squeezing her eyes shut and clasping Sam's hands. Sam's heart went out to her. So innocent and gullible.

Recalling everything about Madame Felice's performance in Paris, Sam began to chant. After a few moments, right on cue, Bold Eagle blew out the candle. Miriam gave a startled gasp, and Sam whispered in warning, "Do not make a sound. You will frighten them away." She continued, challenging, "Show yourself. Give us a sign, Thomas Appleby."

Miriam jumped again as the ghost began to float around the room. Sam had told her to keep her eyes tightly closed, knowing all the while she wouldn't. She wanted her to see, and hear, which she did as Bold Eagle rapped on the table at the same instant the ghost disappeared. He lifted the table too soon, but Sam knew he was in a hurry. Not only did she have to make Miriam tell where the money box was hidden, if she even knew, but they also had to find it if she did. Jake had said that once they had it in their hands, he would take over and was sure he'd get support from his friends to control the situation and stop the hanging. He was also prepared to send a telegram to the federal marshal in Salina to come as quickly as possible.

Sam held her breath. It was time for Jake to speak for Thomas Appleby. The signal was given when she pretended to cough twice, but nothing happened. She coughed again, but still there was only silence in the room. Finally she broke from the script to beg, "Thomas Appleby, if you are with us, speak to your wife, please. She has a heavy heart. Something weighs on her terribly. You must help her to free her own spirit to bring peace within her soul."

And then she heard him, faint and tentative at first, and Sam fought to keep from quivering with joy to hear how good Jake sounded and how well he had mastered the breathless, high-pitched voice of a young boy. "Mommy. You have to tell them."

At that, Miriam lost control and jerked her hands from Sam's, screaming, "Tommy. Oh, Tommy, is it you? Sweet Jesus, my baby. Speak to me, please."

"Tell them, Mommy. Tell them where the bad man hid the box. Tell them."

"Tommy, Tommy, are you all right? Are you happy? Speak to Mommy, darling, please."

Sam reached to grab Miriam and hold her down on the chair, afraid she was going to start moving about, maybe knock over furniture and make a lot of noise. The casino was open. She'd dared not close it. Too many questions would be asked. She had a new bartender running things, but he would wonder about a commotion over his head and might come to investigate, and that would never do.

"Miriam, please," she pleaded, "Calm down. You've frightened him away, and it's over."

"No. It's not over. Not yet."

Sam hurried to find a match and light the candle, hoping Bold Eagle had made his exit as instructed. He had. There were only the two of them, and Miriam was staring at her, white-faced and shaken.

Sam braced herself, deliberately ignoring Miriam's last statement to ask, "Did your son's message have any meaning for you?"

Miriam began to come out of her stupor, eyes growing wild. "Oh, yes. Tommy remembers me teaching him right from wrong, and he wants *me* to do what's right, to tell what that evil man did. But I can't. He said he'd kill Tommy's grandfather, and you've got to call him back so I can explain why I can't do it." She grabbed Sam's hand and squeezed almost painfully. "Get him back. Now. You have to."

Sam was afraid she was on the brink of hysteria. "I can't do that, Miriam. I'm sorry. Not tonight. The spirits are gone. But what are you talking about? Who is going to kill Tommy's grandfather? And why? Who is the evil man?"

"I can't tell you. He would kill my father. Lock me away. He says I'm crazy. Says everybody thinks so."

Sam knew then Jarman had terrified Miriam with threats of what he would do if she exposed him. "Maybe there's another way. Maybe you can let someone else find out who the evil man is so you won't be blamed."

Miriam stared at Sam in the hope that she might have an answer. After all, if she were powerful enough to reach Tommy, perhaps she had wisdom about many things.

"Did the evil man hide something, Miriam? If he did, and you saw him, you could tell me where it is. I could find it, and then he wouldn't be mad at you. He doesn't know you saw him, does he?"

Miriam shook her head, and Sam's heart leaped to her throat. She was right. *Miriam had seen Jarman hide the money box.*

Trying not to appear too anxious, she continued, "I'm sure it would make Tommy happy for me to find whatever he hid, because then it would prove he was an evil man." Panic was creeping through her to think how long it was all taking. She feared Bold Eagle was going to lose patience and signal his braves to action. Then it would be out of her hands.

Miriam was studying Sam's face thoughtfully as she attempted to cope with the maelstrom within. Finally she drew a deep breath of resolve and said happily, as though the great weight Sam had spoken of had finally been lifted, "Yes, you're right. I will tell you where he hid it, and you can go there, and he'll blame you for telling. But you don't have to be afraid of him. He'd never dare hurt you."

Every nerve within her screaming, Sam managed one more time to maintain composure as she asked, "Where did he hide it, Miriam? Where did the evil man hide it?"

## 27

*Sam was careful not to say* or do anything to make Miriam suspect the séance might have been a hoax. To do so would break her heart. Later, when it was all over, she would pay her a visit and make up a story about why she would conduct no more séances, but first things first. Desperation was gnawing, and Sam knew she had to get Miriam out of there so she could search for the box.

For a long time, Miriam sat with her head in her hands and cried with the wonder of it all. Sam tried to be patient and not fidget as she waited for her to get hold of herself. Finally she could stand it no longer and gently said, "You know I have to do something about what you told me, Miriam. I can't let an innocent man die for something your husband did."

Miriam looked at her in horror. "But I told you what he said he'd do if I told anyone."

"He was only trying to scare you, and he didn't think anyone would believe you, anyway. He didn't know that you saw him hide the money, remember? He didn't think there was any proof, and once he's arrested, he can't hurt you or anybody else."

Miriam thought a moment, then decided Sam was right. "All right. Do what you have to do. That's what my Tommy wanted." She managed a brave smile.

Sam hustled her out and downstairs, where they both mounted Jake's horse. Bold Eagle followed at a safe distance, but Miriam probably would not have noticed had he been right alongside, for she was too lost in her happiness. "He spoke to me," she kept saying over and over. "He really spoke to me. If you're never able to reach him again, I'll have that memory."

And Sam intended to let her believe and keep that memory, if at all possible.

The house was dark. Evidently the judge and the hangman had drunk themselves to sleep. Miriam said she would not have to crawl back in through the window, and, confident Sam would take over and make everything right to stop the execution, she disappeared into the shadows.

At once, Bold Eagle appeared beside Sam. "We must move quickly."

Sam could not have agreed more. Every nerve within her was raw and screaming.

Seeing the outline of the church against the night sky, she hurried to lead the way. "The pulpit will be at the front," she said as she reached the front doors and yanked them open.

After locating the raised platform from which the preacher delivered his sermons, Bold Eagle shoved it aside, then bent to easily yank up the loose boards. Groping within, he gave a soft cry of jubilation to feel the wooden box.

Sam gave his arm a yank. "Let's go. There's no time to waste. We have to find Jake."

She was almost down the steps to the aisle but suddenly froze to remember she hadn't thought of him since he'd spoken as Tommy. "Where is Jake? Why did he leave so fast? I thought he'd be anxious to hear if I was able to get Miriam to talk. We need him to take over like he said he would if we found the box."

Bold Eagle's tone evidenced the end of his patience. He set the box down. "Enough of this. I go to signal my braves."

Sam cried, "No. We've come too far. And there's still time. Nothing was ever said about Jake going with us to look for the box if Miriam did talk, so he might just be downstairs in the saloon having a drink while he waits to see if we found it."

Bold Eagle picked up the box again. "I will go with you, but I warn you, I will not wait much longer to free Wild Spirit."

They had skirted around Jake's store and the crude jail behind it when Sam had taken Miriam home. But when Sam noticed brighter light coming from that direction, she felt uneasy and began to move closer.

"More torches," Bold Eagle observed warily. "That means more people. I sense trouble. I go to get the braves now."

Sam reached to grab his horse's harness and held him back. "No. You have the evidence in that box that Jarman is guilty. You can't go anywhere. Now wait and let me see what is going on here."

She was off her horse and heading for the jail before he could protest, and she prayed he would not make good his threat to signal the Kansa to attack. Then, drawing nearer, she tensed when she realized what was taking place.

There were more people gathered, and the hanging scaffold was framed against the eerie light of the torches they held aloft. A man was being led up the steps from one side, hands tied behind his back, and, dear God, no . . .

She swayed as a wave of dizziness struck. They were getting ready to hang Cade.

A scream erupted from the very pit of her soul, and she began to run toward the macabre scene as fast as her trembling legs would take her. "Stop! You can't do this. He didn't do it. Jarman Ballard did. I have the proof."

Everyone turned around, and Jarman, who had led Cade to the scaffold, looked out over the crowd, face contorting with rage. "Shut her up," he yelled to no one in particular, then snapped to the waiting hangman, "Get on with it. The sooner he's dead, the quicker we can stop worrying about the Indians attacking."

Jake lunged from the crowd to grab her and say in a frenzy, "I tried to stop it. I swear I did. That's why I left your place. I was at the window and heard talk down on the street about how the hanging was set to go earlier, because Indians had been spotted, and they wanted to get it over with to avoid trouble, but by the time I got here, Jarman had already convinced the judge to do it early, and there was nothing I could do."

"But I found it," Sam cried, "right where Miriam said Jarman put it. Oh, God . . ." Her voice trailed away as she turned her face back toward the gallows to see that the hangman had placed a hood over Cade's head and was tightening the noose around his neck. He stepped back and reached for the rope that would open the trap door beneath Cade's feet.

Sam felt herself slipping away as the fingers of merciful oblivion reached out for her, but she fought for consciousness, tearing herself from Jake's hold to try to push her way forward, screaming all the while.

The trap door dropped. At the same instant, a shot rang out. Shouts and gasps went up. The rope exploded just as Cade fell through the opening to disappear from sight.

Jake whipped about to see the Indian who had fired the shot. A wooden box lay on the horse's back, between the Indian's legs. Drawing his gun, Jake yelled out to those he knew he could depend on to back him while he took control. "Get Ballard. He did it. We got proof. And somebody get over to the telegraph office. Break in if you have to, but send to Salina for the federal marshal."

Jarman had reached for the gun inside his coat, but the hangman reacted in time to wrest it away. "Let's just wait and see what this is all about before you get all excited."

The crowd parted for Sam, who hurried to the scaffold to crawl beneath it and yank both the noose and the hood off of Cade. "It's all right," she told him in a breathless rush. "We can prove Jarman did it."

Someone else appeared to cut away the binding about Cade's wrists, and once freed, he paused long enough to gather Sam close and kiss her before demanding, "How did you do all this? And that was Bold Eagle who saved me. You sent for him after I told you not to, didn't you?" He grinned down at her. "Thank God you're a stubborn little filly, Sam."

Judge Quigby, red-faced and livid, was arguing with Jake when Sam and Cade came out from under the scaffold. "I want that Indian to hang with him, do you hear me? And you're going to be next if you don't put your gun away and tell your men to do the same. I'll not have vigilantes taking over my town." He whirled toward the hangman he had been toasting only a short while earlier. "And you give my son-in-law his gun back, or I'll be bringing in somebody to put a rope around *your* neck, damn you."

The hangman looked doubtful, but only for a moment. Like everyone else, his attention suddenly became focused on Bold Eagle, who was riding his horse forward. People scrambled to get out of his way.

He dropped the box at Judge Quigby's feet.

"I found it right where Jarman hid it," Sam said loudly enough for everyone to hear.

For an instant Quigby stared at it, not knowing what to say; then he threw his head back and laughed. "You expect me to believe such a wild story? Of course you found the box—right where Ramsey told you to find it to save his neck," he finished with a scowl, and pushed his face into hers.

Jake spoke before Sam had a chance. "That's not the way it is, Judge."

Quigby whirled on him. "And how would you know?"

"Your daughter told . . ." Jake looked uncertainly at Sam, not knowing whether she wanted him to tell about the séance. She didn't and took over for Jake.

"Miriam told me where to find it. She saw Jarman put it under the pulpit in the church across from your house." Sam saw no reason to tell him the circumstances of the conversation.

Suddenly Jarman let out a roar and, taking the hangman by surprise, snatched the gun from his hand to point it at Sam. But Bold Eagle was ready with his rifle, and Jarman made a perfect target where he stood up on the scaffold. He was dead before he hit the ground.

Jake put his hand on Judge Quigby's shoulder as he stared mutely at Jarman's body. "You might want to get on home, Judge, and get started writing that letter of resignation I think the authorities will want when they hear complaints from everyone about how you've been doing things around here."

Quigby, head down, shoulders slumped, turned and walked away.

It was understood now that Jake was in charge until the marshal arrived, and he decreed the excitement was over and began breaking up the crowd. "It's over folks. Go home."

Cade still had his arm around Sam, and she was starting to feel uncomfortable at his nearness. It was over for them, too, and all she wanted was to return to the sanctity of the Lucky Steer, where she didn't need a man.

Bold Eagle told Cade he had to go and signal the Kansa not to head into town, as they were prepared to do before first light. Sam tried to thank him for all his help, but Bold Eagle reined his horse about to ride away, not giving her a chance.

"He knows you appreciate him," Cade told her huskily, drawing her close as they found themselves alone. "And so do I," he whispered, mouth moving to claim hers once more.

She pulled away. "I've got to get back." She would not look at him.

He held tight, not about to let her go. Something was wrong. He had sensed it when she came to the jail. He'd assumed she was upset over the situation they were in at the time, but that was past. The future awaited, bright and beautiful, unless . . .

He cupped her chin in his hand, forcing her to look at him. "Then the answer was no."

"No to what? You didn't ask me anything. I told you I have to get back to the casino. The bartender will be wanting to leave, and—"

"You were going to say no to what I asked you in that letter I slipped under your door last Sunday, weren't you?" His eyes narrowed, and his hands fell away from her. "It means that much to you, doesn't it? The money. The gambling. I guess I've been a pretty big fool."

Seeing him mad got her riled, and she could no longer hold back her frustration. "No, *I'm* the fool, Cade Ramsey, for thinking you could ever be honest with me about anything. First you make me think you can't talk. Then you make up a big bald-faced lie about being a half-breed, the son of some Apache chief. The next thing I know, you've gone off and left me, and when I forgive you, and think I can trust you, you make me think you care, but then I find out you go running to Louretta when you get the least little bit upset with me, and now you're lying about some letter you say you wrote, and I'm fed up, you—"

With a laugh, he clamped his hand over her mouth. "Just simmer down, Sam. I've heard all the cuss words you're about to spout, and I'm not wanting to hear them again."

She struggled, but he continued to hold his hand against her lips while he maneuvered with his other to pull her arms behind her back.

He could see her cat eyes blazing in the glow of a torch someone had left stuck in a notch of the scaffold post. Lord, if looks could kill, he knew he would be deader than if Bold Eagle had not cut that rope with a bullet. "Did you read my letter?" he asked.

She continued to fight, trying to kick him, but he managed to move in time.

"I'm not going to let you go till we get this settled. I left a note under your door after we had that fight, and I told you I was sorry and asked you to marry me. I told you I'd be back yesterday to hear your answer, and . . ." He fell silent to see that the fires of rage in her eyes had turned to a glow of wonder. He let her go.

"You . . . you put a letter under my door?" she stammered, then quickly asked, "And did you mention we'd had a fight at the hotel?"

"I sure did."

"*Louretta.*"

It was Sam's turn to laugh, but with relief, as she told him what had happened. Cade knew then how Jarman had been able to set him up. Louretta had stolen the letter and passed it along to him, and he had known when Cade would be coming back to town. "He timed it all perfectly, and Louretta was able to make you think I'd been to see her and get you mad at me. A perfect scheme. Only it didn't work, thank goodness.

"By the way"—he grinned as he scooped her up into his arms and held her against him—"what is your answer?"

Sam put her arms around his neck and jutted out her lower lip as if deep in thought. "Well, I'm not sure. I'll have to think about it. Marriage is terribly serious, especially when I'd have to sell the casino."

"Don't be too sure about that." He started walking. "I've decided maybe I'd like having a rich wife." He winked wickedly.

When they reached the front of Jake's store, Sam realized he was turning in the opposite direction from the Lucky Steer. "Where are you going?"

"Someplace where we get along real good." He hugged her even tighter against him. "The hayloft."

Sam felt a warm rush and knew that while she had never been happier than in that moment, it was nothing compared to the joy the future was sure to hold for them.

Just then Jake came running out of the store, waving his arms. "I just want you to know I'm sorry I had to let you down," he told Sam in a rush. "But when I heard talk about the situation getting worse here, I decided I'd better hurry over. There wasn't even time to tell that Indian I was leaving. But what I want to know is, how'd you manage to pull it off without me? Was he able to make her think it was her husband's voice?"

Cade looked from Jake to Sam and asked, "What's he talking about?"

"I'm not sure." Sam was staring at Jake. With a chill creeping over her, she dared ask him, "Are you telling me you didn't speak in a little boy's voice?"

"A little boy's voice?" he echoed, dumbfounded. "Sam, I'm trying to tell you I wasn't even there. Mercy sakes." He ran his fingers through his hair. "That Indian must have done a real good job." He turned and went back inside, shaking his head.

Cade shook her gently. "Are you going to tell me what's going on, Sam?"

Clinging to him, she promised, "Later."

But first, she had to figure it out for herself.